DIRE WOLF MATES

Volume One

C.D. GORRI

Dire Wolf Mates
Volume One
by C.D. Gorri

Includes:
Shake that Sass
Breaking Sass
Pinch of Sass

Edited by BookNookNuts

To my readers,
Thank you so much for your support and encouragement. Without you this journey wouldn't be possible.
Del mare alla stella,
C.D. Gorri

Before you begin sign up for my newsletter here:
SUBSCRIBE HERE

VOLUME ONE

DIRE WOLF MATES

The Dire Wolves are parking their bikes for good on the outskirts of Blue Valley. But can these sexy prehistoric Shifters find their mates and plant roots of their own?

Includes:

Shake that Sass

He's an Alpha looking for a home.
She's an outsider with no one to call

Breaking Sass

What happens when a sassy Dire Wolf, with a penchant for breaking rules, and a Lion, who's in love with the law, clash?

Pinch of Sass

Will this stoic Dire Wolf admit the sassy feline is his fated mate and stake his claim?

SHAKE THAT SASS

BLURB

DIRE WOLF MATES

He's an Alpha looking for a home.
She's an outsider with no one to call her own.

Can they find what they're searching for in each other?

Derrick Rand is an Alpha Dire Wolf, a rare and powerful species of Shifter. When he hears about the seemingly ideal town of Blue Valley, New Jersey, he, and his crew, fill their tanks and mount their bikes for the long cross-country ride. Tired of the nomadic life, Derrick is determined to find a place to call home.

Lucy Corwyn leads a fairly simple lifestyle, moving from town to town and working crappy jobs to make ends meet. Feline Hybrid Shifters aren't exactly high enough on the food chain to claim territory.

After her junker breaks down, Lucy finds herself stranded and without funds. Time is of the essence for this not-so-big Cat. She needs to earn some fast cash to fix her car before some dumb Shifter tries to turn her into a chew toy.

Luckily, she spies a help wanted sign at a biker bar. Walking into Serious Moonlight to inquire about a job is a piece of cake, or so she thinks. Imagine her surprise when the sexy new owner turns out to be her mate… and that's not all.

The gorgeous male is not only a Dire Wolf, he's the Pack Alpha. Larger than life and chock full of testosterone, this monster is used to getting his way, but that doesn't mean Lucy will make it easy on the big guy.

No way. No how.

If the big bad Wolf wants to catch this little she-Cat, he's gonna have to *shake that sass.*

PROLOGUE

DIRE WOLF MATES

The air buzzed with electricity a split second before the loud roar of six—*no, make that seven*—magnificent, suped-up Harley Davidson motorcycles, speeding down the highway like so many bats out of Hell, reached Lucy's hypersensitive ears.

The symphony of engines drowned out all other traffic as Lucy sat criss cross applesauce on a patch of dusty weeds just off the shoulder of the parkway, right next to her old, not-so-reliable, Ford Aspire.

Her knowledge of mechanics was seriously lacking. But even Lucy knew the engineers who'd designed this particular vehicle had fallen short of their aspirations.

And then some.

As if to punctuate her point, the car let off another ghastly noise followed by a progression of thick, black smoke from the tailpipe.

The rust bucket was a constant drain on her limited funds, but Lucy had no choice but to keep fixing the clunker. And now she would have to look for a cheap mechanic at whatever town was located off this exit. South Jersey was chock full of small communities, safe for a week or more, but that was it.

There was no place left for a Shifter like her to hide for the long term. She was too submissive. Too small. And too damn tasty, according to the last Pack of Hyenas she'd run into.

"I sure love the taste of pussy cat in the morning. Gonna get a big ol' chunk of you, kitty freak," the Alpha fem taunted just before the attack.

Lucy was a fool thinking she could let her guard down at that shit-hole motel in Newark. It was not the place for a loner. But Lucy was so tired of running.

She'd managed to escape before the Hyena Shifter Alpha could bleed her too badly. It was nothing her healing abilities couldn't repair. Just a few smooth silver lines across her shoulder and stomach remained. But that incident still haunted Lucy.

The hybrid curse. Unwanted. Unloved. Doomed to walk alone.

Lucy's mixed blood was the source of all her problems. Her hybrid heritage kept her from forming alliances. None of the Big Cat Prides wanted anything to do with her.

She'd been shunned, targeted, and tossed out of more towns than she cared to remember. Feline Shifters were such shits. Snooty fuckers, all of them. But what she wouldn't give for a Pride of her own.

Someplace where she belonged. A home. A family. But those were fairy tales for Lucy.

Shit. Shit. SHIT.

Her cell phone was dead. She had no food. No money. And it was getting late. Of course, her stomach decided to rumble right then.

Totally cliché for a chubby chick. But society's opinions on the perfect female body could go right to hell as far as she was concerned.

Lucy had curves. And yeah, she got them from eating. Food was the one source of comfort she could rely on.

Rrrrrr.

She rubbed her stomach. It had been twelve hours since she'd eaten her last granola bar. Much too long for a Shifter to go without feeding her animal.

She stood for a moment, head back, staring at the darkening sky, and watched the line of Harleys until she couldn't see them anymore.

Dust clouds rose in the air behind each one of those mile-eating machines, and Lucy grinned like mad.

Lucky SOBs.

Damn, she'd love to jump on the back of one of those badass bikes, holding on to the rider and whooping in the air like a wild thing. Of course, in her fantasy, someone else had to drive.

Lucy had never ridden a motorcycle before. She would likely end up in a ditch if she tried.

Clumsy should be my middle name.

Despite being a Cat Shifter, graceful, she was not. Lucy could still see dust clouds shooting up into the air. She stood, staring at them a while longer. Her grin widened in its place.

Those little particles seemed like magic to her. Yeah, she knew they were nothing but grit, sand, and dirt. To Lucy, they were fairy dust.

Silly she-Cat.

A wistful sigh escaped her lips and she wrapped her arms around her body. Standing on the side of the road, broke but not broken, Lucy allowed herself a moment to dream.

Wouldn't it be wonderful if one of those big, sexy bikers was all for me? Some untamed, wild, beast of a man. A magician. Casting a spell with that powerful machine between his legs, carrying me off someplace safe and permanent.

She hugged herself tighter, head back as she made her wish. Lucy blinked slowly when she was done. She shook her head at her overactive imagination.

That's what she got for reading too many romance novels. Her inner beastie stirred, reminding her of her situation. She had an empty stomach, and a broken down vehicle.

Rrrrrr.

Oh well. No use sitting there dreaming stuff and nonsense when she had to keep moving to stay alive. She felt a great sense of loss when she could no longer hear the motors or see the dust clouds in the air.

What was wrong with her? They were just a bunch of strangers, for fuck's sake. Just some guys on motorcycles, passing through life without a care in the world, and that was all they were.

None of them were for her. No one ever was. Didn't Lucy have enough drama in her life?

No men.

That was her one, unbreakable, firm, completely non-negotiable rule. She was not going to fall into that trap. Not after witnessing what her mother had gone through time and again.

Pitiful, just pitiful. Don't waste wishes on men. It ain't worth it.

Those bikers rocketed down the black asphalt wherever the hell they were going on the backs of their powerful, and apparently dependable wheels, without a care in the world. Unlike her.

Shit.

Night was falling and Lucy had to get a move on. She started walking, taking the exit she should have been driving down on foot. Thank goodness her sneakers still had some sole left to them.

She turned her head, looking down the empty road. There had to be some place she could charge her cell phone and call for a tow.

The sounds of engines and horns caught her attention. Too far away to make out yet. But at least now she had a direction.

The moon was almost full, hanging bright and low in the sky. Horns meant traffic, and traffic meant people. Lucy took a long, deep breath, then exhaled. She'd wasted too much time mooning after those motorcycles.

But sometimes dreaming was all a person had. What could a little fantasizing hurt while she made her way to a phone charger and maybe a little something to eat? As her sneakers ate up the miles, she played a game with herself.

What would I do if one of those big barrel-chested men were mine? Easy. I'd wrap my arms so tight around him and just hold on for dear life. My mystery man would keep me safe.

We would share secret smiles, hand holding, and deep kisses. He'd take me for rides, driving like a wild thing, taking tight corners before stopping in some abandoned meadow.

Then he'd reach around, pull me in front of him, and claim my lips with his in a bruising kiss designed to bring me to my knees.

And that's exactly where I'd go next. On my knees, unbuckling his belt, biting my lip in excitement to see what he'd hidden behind his thick denim jeans.

He'd be thick, long, and hard just for me.

Oooh yeah. Lucy could sure get behind a dream guy like that.

Meeee—ooww!

CHAPTER ONE

DIRE WOLF MATES

"Dammit."

Leave it to Lucy to step in a pothole. Ugh. She rolled her ankle too. Walking it off sucked, but it was necessary.

"I was just getting to the good part of my fantasy, too," she mumbled to herself.

Pausing a minute, she hissed and spat out a curse, checking her ankle with her fingers when the wind suddenly turned. The breeze blew right in her face, bringing with it the smell of leather and motor oil.

She closed her eyes and inhaled. Her senses tingled from something unidentifiable lingering in the scent. Before she could get more from the interesting notes hidden within the air, a big flatbed rolled by.

The damned truck leaked pollution and Lucy nearly doubled over, choking. Damn sensitive feline nose of hers.

Achooo.

She growled aloud and hobbled up the driveway of the small gas station convenience store.

"Hello."

"Hi there, Miss."

Lucy's ankle throbbed. She was tired, hungry, and annoyed.

"Do you have an outlet so I can charge my phone?"

The older man nodded at where an outlet sat unused behind a shelf full of mostly expired snack cakes. Plugging in her ancient flip phone, she leaned against the wall and waited for it to charge enough to call a tow service.

The cashier was an older man, a *normal* if her nose could be trusted. He looked her over through narrowed brows, pausing when the sound of her rumbling stomach reached him.

"You can help yourself to one of those packages there. They might be a little stale, but I imagine it's better than nothing," he said, pointing to the snack cakes.

"Sorry, I'm on a budget," she muttered, embarrassment heating her cheeks.

"The company comes and swaps them out every week. They are due tomorrow morning. No one will go looking for one," he added kindly, nodding at her to go ahead.

"Okay. Thank you," she replied softly, grabbing a chocolate frosted cupcake and scarfing it down in two bites.

"Hell. Have two then, child. Must be starving. Go on now."

"I appreciate it," she said, looking in her pockets for loose change.

"Don't you worry about it. Look, my name is John, and I'm a widower, but my Nancy would have hated me leaving a young girl to go hungry in my store."

"That's really kind of you, John. I'm Lucy," Lucy replied, tears welling in her eyes.

"What's the matter, little lady, you okay?"

"Yeah," she mumbled, wiping her face hastily. "I'm sorry. It's been a long time since someone was kind to me."

"Look, don't you worry about the snack cakes. You can get me back some other day. You havin' car trouble or somethin'?" John's eyes were round with sympathy. He was a good soul, showing kindness to a stranger.

"Car trouble. Waiting on my phone to charge so I can call a tow," she told John, deciding to trust the honesty she heard in his voice.

"Well, I can help with that. This is a local place. You might have to haggle a bit, but he's the closest you'll find without having to pay an exorbitant amount for them to bring your car in," he told her, handing her a card.

"Thank you so much. My phone is at fifteen percent already. Do you think I can charge it a little bit more while I wait on the truck?"

"Of course, Lucy."

"Thanks, John." She offered a real smile that time, and the old man gave her a semi-toothless grin.

"Glad to help."

Lucy dialed the local mechanic's roadside assistance number while John went back to whatever he was doing behind the counter. The receptionist told her a driver was on the way, and that was that.

"All sorted?" John asked.

"Yes. Thank you so much."

"You're welcome. Good luck to you," he said, waving goodbye.

The snack cakes stopped the bite of hunger, but she would need more than that. Still, the hike back to her car was manageable at least. There was nothing else she could do about it now, anyway.

Lightning cracked overhead, splitting the sky apart and flashing brightly overhead. Thunder rolled in like an angry Mama Bear scolding her errant cubs, and Lucy shook her head as she quickened her pace.

Lucy knew all about Mama Bears. One had taken her in when she was thirteen and on the run from the fresh hell foster care had placed her. She'd had four cubs of her own, but needed the help.

At the time, Lucy had been willing to do anything for a place to sleep and a warm bed. Taking care of the cubs was easy while Jaylinn worked as a waitress at a greasy spoon down the road from the motel where she lived.

It was the kind of place that took cash every week for rent. But it had been the closest thing to home Lucy had for a long while. She liked it there.

It was the happiest time of Lucy's young life up to that point. It only lasted eight months before authorities caught up with her. Her mother's ex had called in the police, claiming he missed his step-daughter.

Lying sack of garbage that man. He said her mother was beside herself with worry when the foster family had misplaced her.

"Misplaced," she mumbled.

Like she was a sock or glove. Truth was, that asshole just wanted to use Lucy to keep her mother in line. It worked for a while. The sleaze had griped the entire ride back to their dirty, cramped apartment about stupid human authorities.

He'd said they had no idea what they were doing, placing a Shifter cub with normals. It bothered her that he was right about that. Keeping the secret of the supernatural world was tantamount to their survival as a species.

At thirteen she'd been on the cusp of her first change. While Jaylinn might have been able to help her through it, the Mama Bear had no time for Lucy.

She needed another Big Cat, someone more dominant to keep her steady. Preferably her mother. While that did not happen, Lucy did the best she could with her inner animal. Her hybrid Shifted form was a shocker.

"The shit really hit the fan then," she mumbled to herself.

She had a while yet for the truck to arrive, and she saw her car in the near distance where she'd left it–or rather, where it had left her.

She'd been lost in her memories as she walked. They'd rolled across her brain, like a runaway train without stops or any real destination.

An unfortunate side effect of being alone so much was talking to herself. Lucy did that a lot. She'd had time to get used to her animal, but the truth was off putting to a lot of Shifters.

Lucy was an unfortunate and somewhat curious looking combination of her mother, a sleek and petite Bobcat Shifter, and her sperm donor, a big old Mountain Lion Shifter.

She mostly resembled the latter, but smaller by a third of the average Mountain Lion Shifter. She also had the short, cropped tail, and pointed ears of her mother's beastie.

Freaky, as her stepfather had put it after that first change.

"Perfect timing," Lucy muttered as a light spattering of rain started falling.

Minutes ticked by as she hustled to her car, by then more thunder and lightning cracked across the sky, and drops fell in earnest. She fumbled with the rusted door handle.

Locked. Fuck.

Lucy checked her pockets, cursing under her breath. There was a gaping hole in the back right one. It was her favorite and most often used pocket.

Empty. Of course, it was.

"Shit," she growled.

Slamming her hands against the glass to see inside, she bent over and peeked. There they were, sitting on the driver's side like they were innocent in all this.

Stupid keys. Stupid hole in my back pocket. Stupid stupid rain.

Well, at least the tow truck was coming. John had assured her Blue Valley was only six miles or so in size. Small and close knit, that's what he'd said.

"On his way, my ass," Lucy growled and huddled into her soaked hoodie.

Two-hours had passed before the tow truck arrived. The ornery driver cursed the whole time he had to work in the rain. Took him thirty minutes to load her tiny car, and he made her stand outside the whole time.

Finally, inside, Lucy shivered uncontrollably. She was dripping in the seat next to Tony, the chubby, sweaty, and somewhat creepy tow truck driver.

She'd taken off her soaked hoodie, desperate to quell the chill racking her bones, but regretted it now. The white t-shirt she'd had on underneath clung to her skin, giving the greasy jack-off a perfect view of her abundantly large breasts.

Thanks for the tatas, Mom.

The woman hadn't given her anything else by way of genetics, but Lucy usually liked her boobs.

Not right now. But usually.

"Hey, eyes on the road," she growled and snapped her fingers at Tony the Perv.

"Oooh, spunky. I like that in a chick," he said with a leer.

She clenched her teeth against the snarl that rose in her throat. Slashing him across his stupid face would not win her any favors. So, with a great deal of strength she did not know she had in reserve, Lucy ignored the revolting man.

He was definitely icky, but he was a human, a *normal* as Shifters called them. Nothing she couldn't handle. She might be short for a female, but she was still a Shifter, which meant if Tony here got handsy, Lucy would be kicking his ass ten ways to Saturday.

Of course, if he'd been a Shifter, she would not have been so confident. A she-Cat-Mountain Lion hybrid was a bit on the low, *squishable* side of the predatory hierarchy.

Always a quick study, she'd learned early that in order to survive, Lucy had to stay out of towns and cities where the more dominant species tended to congregate.

Without a Pack, Clan, or group of her own, she was at the mercy of whatever bigger, stronger predators ruled the areas she passed through. It was a lonely existence, but it was her life. And she did just fine on her own.

Independence was crucial to Lucy. She'd watched her mom flit from male to male, seeking protection and affection time and again from anyone who would give it to her all through her troubled life.

Her mother had always been kind of desperate and sad, and nothing ever seemed to work out for her. Especially not the last time.

Lucy shuddered. She refused to be like her mother. She could and would protect herself.

What did she need a man for? Not a single thing, that's what.

As far as she was concerned, Lucy did alright. Yes, she missed her mama, even after ten years. But she was still here. No strings or ties. No anchors to slow her down. Nothing to hold her back.

Lucy might never get very far, but wherever she wound up, she would get there on her own.

She watched Tony the Perv turn the AC on, fucker was trying to make her nipples harder beneath the chilled, soaked shirt.

Screw him. She pointed the vent away from her and grabbed her wet hoodie and backpack, clutching both to the front of her body.

"How long?"

"About fifteen minutes," he grumbled.

Curiosity about the place she was currently stranded in had Lucy turning towards the window. It was dark, and she couldn't really see much because of the rain.

But anything that kept her mind off the rank smelling cab of the tow truck, and Tony the Perv, who was currently chewing gum with his mouth open like some dull-witted cow, was alright with Lucy.

It was all she could do not to scratch his face off.

Grrrrr.

"Shit." Lucy knew she'd entered the Garden State a few miles back, but she had hoped she'd landed on the Delaware side of 95.

As they sped past the *Welcome to New Jersey* sign, those hopes were thwarted.

"Blue Valley coming up," Tony grunted.

He was right. The next sign said Blue Valley. More followed, telling how far they were from Barvale, Maverick Point, and Maccon City.

Unfortunately, none of those towns were far enough for her liking. This part of New Jersey was run by Shifters, Big, dominant, furocious Shifters. Bears, Tigers, Wolves, and even Dragons, if the rumors were true.

Oh, I am so fucked.

Everywhere she looked, there were predators. She only hoped Tony the Perv's boss was good at fixing cars. She was barely healed from her recent Hyena attack.

"What's that?"

"Nothing," she replied with a tight smile. "Um, Tony? Would you happen to know of any place I can rent a room? Somewhere quiet, on the outskirts of town, maybe?"

"Sure, I do," grinned Tony.

Lucy felt her stomach drop.

Yep, this was definitely gonna suck.

CHAPTER TWO

DIRE WOLF MATES

"It's been two months, Derrick. Opening night is two days away, and we don't have enough bartenders. I'm telling you this is gonna be a disaster," Sheila shrieked and stomped her foot like a giant diaper baby brat.

His little cousin was always quick with her temper, but it was nothing Derrick could not handle. He raised an eyebrow, and clever little Wolf changed tactics, pouting, and giving him those big goo-goo eyes like she used to when she wanted him to carry her around piggy-back when they were kids.

Fucking hell.

Classic Sheila. Always resorting to what he thought of as overly dramatic tactics whenever she was attempting to wrestle Derrick's attention from whatever he was doing, so he could do what she wanted instead. But not this time.

Derrick was busy AF. Okay, fine. Maybe not busy. But he was trying to settle his inner animal, and that was a hell of a thing for a dominant Dire Wolf. He'd tried everything. Doing the books, stocking the upstairs coolers, checking the kegs, and counting the number of fucking beer glasses he'd ordered for the bar.

Right now, he was outdoors in the giant barn they'd converted into a garage, polishing the body of his custom *Harley Davidson VRSCDX Night Rod Special.* Just because his small Pack of Dire Wolves had given up life on the road, didn't mean they could let things go to shit.

Hell, he still loved riding, but it had been years since his boots had stood in one place long enough to leave a print. Things were changing. The animal inside him was restless, looking for permanence. It was time to settle down.

Six months ago, he'd contacted the Shifter Council with his intentions and sent out feelers for a stable territory, nothing too big, and without any other Shifter presence, so he and his Pack could build a home. Within a few weeks, Derrick was looking at available real estate in Blue Valley, New Jersey. The small east coast town seemed the perfect fit for him and his Pack.

That did not mean Derrick was going to abandon his wheels. A biker at heart, his love of crotch rockets had always been a huge part of him. It was what had him outside right now, cleaning, polishing, and making sure every single bit of his chopper was in top form.

Sheila should know better than to interrupt him when he was taking care of his baby. Was he wrong for being outside when they were about to launch their new business?

Maybe.

But his baby cousin knew exactly what was up when Derrick was busy with his bike, especially considering she felt the same about her own snazzy little Softail Convertible. All his Pack mates shared that same deep love and respect for their mounts. They were also all meticulous when it came to caring for them.

They were a Pack of seven strong, a blip compared to the Macconwood Wolf Pack which held most of North America under Rafe Maccon. That Alpha was good, strong, and he'd recently turned down the role of High Alpha, a position of great power over all standard Wolf Shifters. Derrick had followed their trials and tribulations under the Curse of Natalis, and its demise at the hands of a teenager from New Jersey. That young woman had accepted the role Rafe had refused and was now facing hell trying to organize and control the Werewolves of the world and their newfound powers.

All very interesting, but nothing to do with Derrick and his Pack. They were not standard Wolves. They were something else. Something rare and powerful. Seven was all he needed. Derrick's leather cut, complete with its DWMC patch, flapped in the breeze as he straightened his spine and turned to face the little redheaded menace. He sniffed the air and rolled his head on his neck. Rain was coming.

Patience, he told his beast when his cousin met his stare for a beat too long. She averted her gaze, baring her throat slightly in deference to his inherent dominance.

"Sheila, what is it you're telling me that you think I don't know?"

"We need another bartender, Derrick, or we are gonna bomb on opening night."

"And has no one answered the advertisements you sent?" he asked.

Sheila flipped her red hair and closed and opened her mouth a few times. Sometimes, all it took to stun her into quiet was being reasonable. Fiery little brat.

"I'm just concerned," she muttered, and he could not blame her in the least.

The Pack had pooled its resources to invest in this venture, and it was a huge risk. Not only because of the money, but because they had never tried anything like this before. Dire Wolves were nomadic creatures, if not by nature, then because of circumstance.

His Pack consisted of the toughest, most loyal badasses in the world as far as Derrick was concerned. He would do everything in his power not to let them down. Especially not baby cousin over here.

"It will work out, Sheila."

"Yeah, well, I wish I had your confidence," she replied, biting her lip the same way she had when she was a nervous little kid.

"If you did, you'd be Alpha," he teased, earning him a smile.

He could hardly believe they were now the proud owners of a real life roadhouse, hovering right on the city limits of Blue Valley, New

Jersey. Locals had warned him about the place. Said it got too little traffic to make ends meet, but Derrick was not worried. He had something the previous owners did not.

He was a Shifter, and as such, the supernatural community, though secret from the human world, would come check them out in droves. He hoped to woo them into a steady clientele with his unique food and beverage offerings. The bar itself was a piece of work. It had been abandoned, left to rot, but with a little elbow grease, he and the Pack got it in tiptop shape.

Everything was all neat and polished, ready for business. There were the last minute things that needed fixing, of course, and he would see to it. After he tended to his bike. Customized to fit his bulk and handle his strength by their very own mechanical expert, Cole Mingan, the big beast of a Harley, seemed to call out to the big bad Wolf inside Derrick, begging for a ride.

Cole was good at his job. So good, in fact, that Derrick had decided to give the younger Shifter charge of the twenty classic bikes he'd recently bought and had shipped here to their new permanent address. The idea was to fix them up and put them on display. Sort of a draw for motorcycle fans and would be customers.

Currently, the best looking hogs were lined up on the far side of the roadhouse, which they'd named *Serious Moonlight* after a unanimous vote. The rest of the bikes were inside the garage, waiting to be fixed.

"Sheila," Derrick asked after a minute. "Did you advertise for bartenders and waitstaff in both the town weekly circular and the daily newspaper like I told you to?"

Sheila growled, then heaved an exasperated sigh. She was no dummy, but it didn't hurt to check.

"Course I did, cousin. But we're strangers here, and small towns on the east coast are not as friendly as I thought they would be," she replied heavily.

Sheila's growling grew louder, and when he turned, he saw her staring at the open garage doors, towards the open road. It was a problem he'd been anticipating, the call to roam. But they'd all agreed before coming here, they were committed to trying to grow roots.

Derrick stared at his cousin. Poor thing was trembling from head to toe. Her green eyes were glowing with the force of her Wolf, and fur had already started to sprout along her arms. Another reason they needed a place to settle.

"Be still," he said, using the force of his power to soothe her angsty beastie.

"Alpha?" He heard her frightened plea and understood it.

Derrick's eyes narrowed. Sheila was scared, and her pupils were dilated. He growled deep. The rough sound forcing her eyes downward. That was good. She was not too far gone yet. He used his Alpha voice, never to cow, but only to calm her emotionally heightened animal.

"This is a good place for us. I feel it, Sheila. I wouldn't steer the Pack wrong."

Sheila closed her eyes, nodding her head. She trusted him, and that was a balm to his heart. After standing perfectly still for one long, drawn out breath, she opened her eyes, and he was pleased to see her Wolf had abated.

"Everything alright?" Brock, his Beta, poked his head inside the garage. Derrick met his eyes, then waved the male away. Things were fine now.

Sheila's beast had quieted, and Derrick's felt steady after her helping her through it. That was one of the things he had not expected of being Alpha. Helping his Pack mates calmed his beast, as if he knew his place and reveled in his position.

It was not always easy, and sometimes, he downright hated it. But Derrick was born to lead, like his mama always said. It was a hard road, but he'd been born to it. Leaving life on the road for a place here was difficult for all of them, Sheila more than the rest. He understood her predicament all too well.

As the only female in the Pack, she felt more alone than the rest of them. Their mothers were off, living life in a Pack MC made up of only females. She'd gotten her invite last year but turned them down. Sheila was not ready to give up on the good things yet, and he did not blame her.

Staying put was going to be hard on all of them. Life on the road was not easy, but it was something they knew and understood. This was different. Unchartered territory. Scary and exciting.

Derrick and his Pack had eaten up mile after mile on the backs of their bikes together. They would learn to settle together as well. Pack was family. There was nothing more important than that. But even families had hierarchies, and for Dire Wolf Shifters such as they were, that meant the person who was not only the strongest, but who had the most control was the Alpha, and he was responsible for everyone.

As Alpha, it was Derrick's job to protect his Pack. Even from themselves. Helping them control their giant, prehistoric animals was one of his responsibilities. Many thought an Alpha ruled by simply dominating around those under his care. They couldn't be more wrong. Dominance and subjugation had their place, but it was Derrick's unique ability to control his urges and instincts that made him the undisputed Alpha of their Pack.

"Sorry, cousin. Thank you for helping me, uh, I think I'll call the paper again."

Sheila spoke with her eyes downcast, and her throat exposed. Derrick pulled her into a quick hug, patting her shoulder when she stepped away. Dire Wolf Shifters needed touch to settle their animals, and as Alpha he understood and craved that connection as well. He dismissed her gently, worrying his lower lip as she walked away.

"You do that, cousin. I'll be along shortly," he murmured, knowing full well she heard him.

Dire Wolf hearing was aces, even after years of listening to motorcycle engines. With that, his attention back on his bike once more.

Always take care of your Pack first, then your wheels, his late father's voice echoed in his brain as he put away the degreaser and wax.

He grabbed the few rags he'd been using and tossed them on top of his bundle, stooping to pick it up before returning it to the far side of the garage. The rain had started in earnest now, and he wondered if it would be a flash storm or something wilder and more untamed.

Their new property sat alongside an expanse of woods, and Derrick looked forward to running through the mud and tearing through the trees later on tonight in Wolf form. It was one of the perks of this spot. Edge of town, no close neighbors. There was a shopping center fifteen minutes away, but that was back on the highway. A gas station was another ten down the other way, and the road into town was a good twenty minute drive.

They were close enough to have a steady business, and far enough to not get caught in their fur. It was the main reason he'd felt drawn to the old, abandoned bar. The property came with a couple of acres of forest, as well as two other buildings and a large parking lot.

The huge, barnlike structure had already been converted into a makeshift garage. They'd just made it better. It sat at the opposite end of the bar, through the long, paved parking lot. It was perfect for storing, maintaining, and fixing up motorcycles, and the boys had all gone apeshit for it.

A few hundred yards west of the garage, past an old, wooden privacy fence he intended to have replaced with something sturdier, was an enormous two-story house. The driveway for the house was private, and far enough away from the bar to be comfortable. There was a gate in the fence and a lock, only he and his Pack had the key too. The bar crowd could not access it from the parking lot, and that was enough security for him and Sheila and the guys.

It really was some house. At first, grossly overgrown with weeds, field mice, bird's nest, and a host of cobwebs, but after some TLC it was all sparkly and fine to move in. The twelve-bedroom monster had been abandoned for some time, but someone had loved it at some point.

Derrick could see that in the stained glass windows on the doors, and the hand-painted flowers someone had put in every bedroom. The guys moaned and groaned about it, but no one had painted over them just yet. It was a little worse for wear, in truth, *all* three buildings were, but none had anything wrong with them a little spit and polish couldn't fix.

They'd been working on it for just a couple of weeks and already the place was unrecognizable. The property positively gleamed. There were new locks on the doors and windows they'd installed. Security systems in place. Cable and Wi-Fi already hooked up. Hell, there was nothing they hadn't thought of, and when they couldn't get a crew in well, Derrick and the guys, Sheila too, just dug in themselves. They'd power-washed, scrubbed, scraped, and repainted just about everything, except that flower trim inside the house.

They'd repaired or swapped out most of the outside moldings and trappings, got new TVs, and furniture galore. Sheila, Weylin, and Phoenix were into antiques and had insisted on hitting flea markets and secondhand stores as opposed to ordering everything new, which is what Derrick would have done. Still, he allowed it. It made them happy, and he could see why they preferred older digs. They simply did not make stuff the way they used to, and Dire Wolves required sturdy seats and what not.

Sheila had a real knack for things like that. The older furniture added character and comfort in the house. Lucky for them, the bar had been mostly intact on the inside. They'd had to do a massive cleanup, and the kitchen needed new appliances, but the old wood bars were good.

Thor had sanded and refinished both the front and back bars with Derrick's help until they gleamed and sparkled. Same for the floors and fixtures. They'd ordered glasses, booze, and a few of the newer, more energy compliant fridges and coolers along with the ovens and prep tables for the kitchen.

Serious Moonlight was a bar first, but they would start with the staples. Wings, Burgers, fries, pretzels, and such. Eventually, they would bring in a larger menu for dining in. His Beta, Brock Laurent, was a talented chef, and Derrick had left him in charge of outfitting the kitchen.

This was a risk. A Huge one for a group of nomadic Shifters, but something about Blue Valley called to Derrick. It pulled him in like a magnetic pole. He sighed as he dropped the bucket of cleaning supplies. They were going to open in just a few days and everything was near perfect. Except for a few minor details. Like hiring another bartender. But all in all, Derrick was confident the Pack would make back their investment and then some.

We damn well better.

The Pack had some money, but this endeavor had taken a huge chunk of that. As Alpha, Derrick was responsible for the money, the investment, and the decision to settle in Blue Valley. Was it the right move? He sure as fuck hoped so.

His Pack was not like others. They needed this. Unique and rare even in the paranormal world, they'd traveled long and hard for an opportunity to settle in a place unoccupied by other Shifter groups. Most Shifters didn't want the trouble they brought with them.

Not that it was their fault. Not really, anyway. But that's what happened in supernatural circles, and for the sake of keeping their big secret, it was best their kind stay away from settled areas.

The issue was dominance. Dire Wolves were bigger, stronger, lived longer, and grew more powerful than most other species of Shifter. Derrick was the biggest and baddest of them all. In the past, challenges had come at him from every direction whenever he'd settled in one place for too long. It was his natural dominance combined with the fact he was a rare, and almost extinct species of Shifter.

True, their numbers were few, but they were still kicking and fuck anyone who tried to make it otherwise. Their prehistoric species of beast had died out in the wild thousands of years ago, but their Shifter relatives were still around, though rare and small in number.

The most basic difference between a Wolf Shifter and a Dire Wolf Shifter was size. In their fur, they were more than double the size of the modern Wolf Shifter. That, coupled with their unique ability to tap into elemental magic, made them special as well. His kind practically oozed power and strength.

A fact other Shifters, especially Alphas, had a hard time dealing with. He had no wish to take over other Packs, Prides, or Clans—but did they believe that?

Hell no.

Fuckers always wanted to try to take a piece of him. Not that they got close. Derrick was one hell of a fighter. His body was a testament to that. At almost seven-feet tall and two-hundred-ninety pounds of pure, rock hard muscle, he was, in a word—*efuckingnormous.*

They all were.

Sheila said it was time they got lucky when he'd been sent the listing from the Shifter Council. Derrick didn't know a thing about luck, but he was damn grateful for this shot. His entire Pack—Brock, Cole, Phoenix, Weylin, Thor, and Sheila—were all grateful. So tired of life on the road, they'd broken off from their nomadic parent MC two decades ago and had almost immediately started searching for a place they could land.

The graybeards and old ladies didn't believe any town where Shifters resided, which was every town these days, would ever accept Dire Wolves in their territory. Not without a war, anyway.

It went without saying that Derrick did not want that. War was not good for anyone. He just wanted a small piece of earth to call home for him and his Pack. A place of their own where they could settle down, find mates, maybe even have cubs.

Cubs.

His Dire Wolf growled inside of him. The great black beast's loneliness was a heavy and constant presence in his heart. It was time to change that. Time to find a mate before he succumbed to the wild side of his existence—a condition that often led to death.

Once a Dire Wolf went feral, there were few who could take him out. It was often left to his Pack to do the dirty work. He did not want that for them.

Derrick watched the rain smack against the newly paved lot and breathed deep. It was true, he'd tried this before. Tried settling once or twice, but it had never felt right. He was taking a hell of a chance, but he had to for the sake of survival.

I'm not ready to call it quits. Not yet. This time will be different.

This time. This place. Derrick would make it work.

Mistakes, accidents, a misalignment of fate or whatever other reasons past attempts had failed were not an option now. Past hurts, jealousy, and bitter disappointments abounded in his memory, forever ingrained in his mind. Yes, he made damn sure he remembered them. All of them. Without memory, history repeated itself, and fuck that. Derrick refused to be a sad statistic.

The tattoos covering his massive frame told his story. The story of his Pack. Good times and bad. Every significant event in his life and the lives of his ancestors covered his arms, chest, stomach, and even his legs.

His back, though, that was bare. An empty canvas of skin and muscle. That place was reserved for his future mate, his family. He'd left it alone solely for the bonding ritual that would one day complete his mating to his one and only true mate.

He'd only ever seen it done once, and Derrick had wanted it for himself ever since that day. He wanted someone of his own. Someone to love, to protect, and cherish for all his days.

Gods willing.

CHAPTER THREE

DIRE WOLF MATES

"Fucking hell."

Lucy bit her tongue as she hopped out of the smelly cab of the tow truck. The rain had finally stopped, but her hair was still wet in its messy bun, and her clothes were damp and clinging to her overheated skin.

Her she-Cat was itching to be set free, but Lucy had to get this settled first. Tony the Perv had finally gotten around to dropping her off at the old boarding house he'd mentioned, but only after his boss had quoted her an estimate for her car. Sixteen-hundred bucks to fix that pile of junk.

Mother humping butt licking poop chomping fart flakes. Rrrrrr.

It was highway robbery, dammit, but what was a girl to do? Lucy was no mechanic. She'd only bought the old car because it was all she could find after she'd scoured the used car lot for something affordable.

The faded yellow paint with big daisy stickers all over the bumper, as well as, covering the seats of faded beige interior, had sweetened the deal. She was a sucker for aesthetics. Daisy stickers were fun, and she'd needed fun at the time. It was cute in a retro sort of way.

Of course, she'd had no idea the darn thing was going to be impossible to fix without spending a fortune. The grizzly old mechanic over at *Big Tom's Tow and Go* had given her a song about it, taking three weeks to get the special parts he had to order before it would be ready. Then it would be a waiting game of how long to take apart the engine and put it back together again.

There was no upside, as far as she could tell. But at least she was out of that tow truck. The cab had smelled like a week old tuna sub complete with onions, vinegar, and gods knew what else had been shoved under one of the seats and left to rot.

Gross, she thought to herself as she lifted her bag onto her shoulder. Ripped jeans and wet shirt clinging to her curves, Lucy grunted miserably. She should have changed into something dry after at *Big Tom's.* But with her luck, those guys would have recorded her in the bathroom.

It was a sad day for humanity when that was the first thought a girl on her own had when stranded in a strange town. But she couldn't afford to go apeshit on a couple of normals. The Shifter Council would have her ass. Screw that. Lucy could deal with wearing a wet shirt for a little while longer.

Sigh.

With all the rain, she would've thought the humidity would've lightened up, but nope. It was still humid despite the growing chill in the night air. Her shoulder length hair was piled on top of her head in a messy bun and her sneaker-clad feet squeaked a little once she hit the newly paved parking lot.

Nice. No puddles, she thought absently.

But where the hell was she? She turned in a full circle and took in the bright pink neon sign with the words *Serious Moonlight Roadhouse & Bar.* Underneath was a plastic banner that someone had tied to the pole with the words *opening soon* in bold red block letters.

Didn't look like any boarding house she'd ever stayed in, but what did she know? There was a huge house in the next lot over. Maybe that was it.

"You lookin' for somebody?" A deep voice asked, and Lucy whipped around to see a giant stranger approach from a crouched position behind the pole that held the bright pink sign.

"Fuck a duck, you scared me!"

"Uh, sorry?"

The stranger grunted, rubbing the back of his head, but his apology sounded more like a question to Lucy. It seemed comical that such a masculine person was standing there bathed in pink light, but there it was.

She guessed he'd been working on the electrical box, and her assumptions were confirmed when he bent down and shut and locked the metal door. He had short black hair, wide shoulders, and looked big as fuck. He was wiping his hands on a rag, trying to seem less intimidating she gathered, and appreciated the effort.

"Uh, yeah, I guess, I am looking for s-someone," she replied, stuttering when a sharp breeze dragged his scent to her.

Uh oh.

The man was big, imposing, handsome in his own way, but what really concerned Lucy was the fact he smelled like Wolf. Only, the scent was different from Wolf Shifters she'd encountered before. There was something powerful, wild, and maybe a little untamed about him. Of course, that could have been his biker vest or his deep-set eyes that caused chills to run down her spine.

Shit.

"My name is Cole. Cole Mingan. You here about the job, lady?" he asked and immediately Lucy nodded.

She might not have been looking there for a job, but she did need one. From what she knew about Wolf Shifters in this part of the country, they all answered to Rafe Maccon and that Alpha was a no-nonsense kind of guy. Surely, this guy had enough sense not to attack a lone feline. Hell, he wasn't even growling, and that was all the encouragement she needed.

Desperate times, she thought, recalling the sixteen hundred dollars she needed to accrue to fix her wheels.

"Right," he growled. "Come on, this way." Cole turned to walk through the empty lot to the front door of the roadhouse.

Lucy followed, mind wandering as a result of her mild panic at following a strange predatory Shifter into a dark bar. It was almost midnight, but Shifters tended to be night owls. She wondered if it was politically incorrect to call someone a night owl if they weren't actually owls? Like, did Owl Shifters get pissed when they heard that remark?

"You alright?" Cole asked, his head cocked to the side as he waited for her to catch up.

Lucy straightened her shoulders. In her experience, it was best not to let her fear show, and she really did need a way to make some money. If they were hiring, she should at least try to get the job.

"Yep," she replied and tried to smile, but it came out more of a grimace and Cole frowned at her.

His eyes strayed to her wild hair and wet clothes, and she remembered why she was there in the first place. Lucy needed room and board. She was dead on her feet, but she also needed a job. With any luck, she'd find both right here. But probably not if Cole here thought she was a total wack job for thinking about owls and political correctness in the Shifter world.

Best keep that bit to myself.

Her thoughts could get random sometimes, but that was simply her overactive imagination at work. She followed the giant to the door he held open and walked through it with her shoulders straight and head high.

While the exterior seemed plain and simple, the interior of the place was impeccably clean and edgy. She approved the industrial look, with the ceiling exposed and open barn doors separating sections. Wood gleamed and metal shone, and Lucy could smell the myriad of cleansers they'd used along with fresh paint, stain, polyurethane, and polish to spruce the place up.

Clearly, the guys who'd bought the place had gone through a lot of trouble fixing it up. Cole did not bother showing her around. He simply stomped down the corridor and expected her to follow. Her first whiff of him already told her why.

Dog—*no matter how big or small*—always thought they were better than cats. Of course, this amused Lucy. Silly canines. Everyone knew cats were better.

Meow.

Lucy followed him down the hallway to a closed door that had the word *office* painted in thick black letters. The scent of Wolf was stronger, and dominance heavier the closer she got. Whoever was behind that door was undoubtedly the leader of this small group.

"Hey yo, Derrick! Someone's here about the job," Cole yelled, then turned the knob at the grunted *"send him in"* that came from inside.

"Go on," Cole said and walked away, leaving Lucy to face whoever was behind the large door.

A little nervous, and a lot desperate, she squared her shoulders and inhaled one deep breath. She wanted to get a better read on the room's inhabitant. Wolf, yes, but what kind? There were different subspecies of Shifter she'd studied in her quest to keep herself safe from big predators.

Gray Wolves. Red Wolves. Arctic Wolves. Each one with its own quirks and temperament. Maybe they were not Wolves at all. There were also other canids like Coyotes, Foxes, and Jackals to consider as well.

Shit. She was psyching herself out now. Lucy was almost panicking. The place was just too full of cleaners and fresh paint for her to get anything more than something from the *Canidae* family. More than likely, she was dealing with a bunch of Gray Wolf Shifters. They were the most common and the most growly.

That would be just her luck. A bunch of butt sniffing fur balls who'd think they could boss her around because she was, and had, a pussy.

Sniff.

Her inner she-Cat huffed at her vulgar description, but hey, she wasn't lying. Lucy was a hybrid she-Cat. A small, yet ferocious animal whose inner voice was as haughty as any high-class feline's.

Hmph.

For fuck's sake, she growled softly. Once again, she managed to piss off her beast.

Oh well. Suck it up, buttercup.

Ignoring her she-Cat's attitude problem. It took a moment, but her little beastie got over her feigned insult, and crept forward silently inside her mind. Lucy needed her extra senses to solve the mystery of who and what she was dealing with here.

"I said come in," the deep, gruff voice repeated impatiently.

This was definitely the man in charge. His brisk command was delivered with the practiced ease of someone used to being obeyed. Lucy took a breath and was immediately struck by a myriad of emotions, picking up on his sheer dominance, the scent of his fur, and a spicy male musk that made her inner feline freeze and take notice.

OMG. He brought me to the Alpha.

Lucy exhaled, fiddling with her hair as she battled her rising hysteria. She was mainly a solitary creature and pretty low on the totem pole of the Shifter hierarchy. She rarely got to see the head honcho of even a small Pack. Lucy pushed the door wide, curiosity burning inside of her.

Standing with his back—*his broad, heavily muscled, and totally naked back*—towards her, the room's only inhabitant remained perfectly still. He was even bigger than Cole—maybe six and a half feet or more—at least a foot and a half taller than Lucy.

His hair was longer, brushing his wide shoulders in thick, dark waves. Physically, he was devastating, tall and built, biceps showcasing intricate tribal tattoos. He wore tight jeans and leather biker boots, and nothing else. The stranger practically oozed power and sex appeal. He was a total badass, and Lucy practically swooned, taking him in from the top of his dark head to his large, booted feet.

Holy hell. His arms were bigger than her thighs, and that was saying something. Both bore full sleeves of beautifully detailed tattoos showing a variety of scenes from full moon runs to a flock of birds rising over a stand of trees that ended with a pair of wings flapping high on his neck. She wondered what he would do if she walked on over and traced them with her fingertips, or tongue.

Eeek! Where did that thought even come from? Lucy knew better than that. Alphas did not dig submissive little nobodies like her. But no amount of self-deprecating thoughts could stop her from looking. There was no harm in that, was there?

It took only a moment, but she was reeling from the sheer masculine beauty of the man. She couldn't make out the words inked across his skin, but she wanted too. Wanted to touch, to smell, to kiss. She had a thing for guys with sexy hair, and his was black as pitch, like motor oil, and just as glossy.

An image of those wide shoulders, and that inky dark head bent between her legs had her shivering in the quiet. Shit. She needed to get her mind out of the gutter. Bad enough she was even feeling this way at all, worse because he would know. Freaking Shifter sense of smell would pick up the tiniest change in her body chemistry, including the ones that corresponded with arousal.

Every single survival instinct she'd honed screamed at her to get out of there, to run far away, but she remained rooted to the spot. Like some magnetic force was drawing her to the big, sexy as hell man. Finally, he turned, and she realized he must've spoken.

Oopsie.

Embarrassment caused her face to heat, but she refused to duck her head or shy away. She met his steady gaze despite the almost overwhelming urge to avert her eyes and bare her throat. Between the heaviness of his natural Alpha dominance, and the sudden, persistent throbbing ache between her legs, Lucy could hardly breathe, let alone think straight.

"Uh, sorry, what?" She managed between suddenly dry lips.

His black eyes flashed gold as he cocked his head in a way that reminded her more of an animal than a man. He was positively gorgeous, with chiseled features, kissable lips, thick eyebrows, a day's worth of scruff on his cheeks, and eyes that glowed inhumanly at her. Lucy couldn't take her eyes off of him.

"Who are you?"

"I'm Lucy Corwyn," she whispered back.

A deep rumbling growl came from his throat. His eyes turned completely golden as he swept her entire body with his gaze. She noted the deep, dusky tan that made his skin look like sculpted bronze. Probably from years on the open road. She'd seen his leather cut with the DWMC #55 patch on the back and surmised this was not only a Pack, but a motorcycle club too.

Swallow.

Was there anything sexier than a Shifter on a bike? Warmth spread throughout her limbs and her she-Cat purred deep inside her mind's eye. By the time the stranger opened his perfect lips to respond to her statement, her heart was pounding inside of her chest.

What was he going to say? His name? She bet it was something cool like Michael or Damien. Her imagination as running wild, but a girl had to do something to entertain herself when she lived mostly alone. Lucy liked to spin yarns in her head about strangers she'd see on the road. It helped quell the loneliness.

Pity, he would be just another stranger passing through her life. But that was how things were for Lucy. That's how they had to be, for her safety. So Michael or Damien was probably Bill or Ted. Her imagination was always better than the reality.

He cocked his head to the other side, his body practically vibrating with the force of his growling, and oh my gods, that sound was doing something crazy to her inner cat. It was like he was casting some strange spell on her without any words. She wanted to beg him to speak already. To end the madness churning deep within her. Then he did it. He finally spoke. One word only, but with it, Lucy felt her whole world turn upside down. The husky syllable fell from his mouth like liquid honey.

"Mine."

His voice had gone even deeper, if possible. Lucy bit back her groan. His scent had surrounded her, and it was like nothing she'd ever breathed in before. Her she-Cat hissed and purred, then yowled so loudly, she actually winced.

"Um, what?"

"Mine," he repeated, stalking her slowly across the room.

Lucy backed up against the wall, cursing herself for being dumb enough to get trapped. Her pulse increased and heart raced as his natural, wild musk—*like open road and well-oiled leather, hot and clean and so damn sexy she felt her panties dampen*—filled her nostrils. The cat growled at her to get closer, to rub her body all over the big mountain of a man—*not man, Wolf*—but she held herself still. Barely.

No. No. No. NO!

Yes, her cat insisted.

Lucy's eyes flashed, her animal pushing to be let out. Her inner feline ready to go belly up for Mr. Big and Hunky.

Slut, she hissed at her beast.

Mate, replied the wily she-Cat.

Dammit. She couldn't believe this. The enormous, sexy, tatted out Wolf was her mate.

"Fuck me," she murmured, and was shocked when the man pounced over the desk and pinned her to the wall.

"Anything you want, you just have to ask, baby," he growled into her ear.

Lucy closed her eyes and tried to ignore the throbbing of her sex as it instinctively prepared for his invasion.

No. Hard no.

She pushed against his impressive pecs and shook her head firmly.

"Whoa there, big guy. Back up a step," she murmured and pushed again, but it was like trying to move a mountain.

"You smell so good," he growled and nipped her earlobe, sending another wave of moisture dripping down her panties.

Lucy moaned. She needed to get away from him before she did something really stupid. A cold shower would work. Yes. She needed a cold shower to get her head on straight.

"Hey," she growled. "No means no, buster, now back up!" Eyes narrowed, she gave him what she hoped was her *I mean business* face.

The stranger backed up a half step but kept his frying-pan-sized hands firmly on her waist. Lucy exhaled and tried counting to three. She knew what guys like him were like. Big, macho, bossy, and sexy as hell. They were monsters in the bedroom, wrecking a woman for life by getting her addicted to him. Then he would leave. They always left.

Sexy he might be, but he was a Wolf and an Alpha, and she was just *her*. No matter how much her inner kitty begged, Lucy knew better. Acting on this would be a huge mistake. She needed to work to make money to fix her ride, then she was out of here. Surviving was her gig, not shacking up with a bored Wolf.

"Your skin is so smooth," he murmured in that deep, growly voice, drawing circles with his fingertips on her waist.

When had he hiked her damp t-shirt up? Dammit. She wanted to grab his hands, but if she let go of his chest, she knew he would be right back to smushing her against the wall.

Yes, please.

Her she-Cat was so down for that. Lucy shook her head.

No. Big fat double no.

"I said, back the fuck up," she growled.

This time, he allowed the full force of his smile to spread across his ridiculously handsome face. His grin widened, and he took another, larger step back.

Come back.

Shut it, kitty.

"I am here for a job, not to be manhandled by some oversexed puppy," she snapped.

"Puppy?" The cocky male snorted.

"You're right. Puppies have better manners. You can't just push women into walls with your big, muscular body, you know," she told him, halfway to panic city.

"My apologies, mate. You just caught me off guard," he replied, arching one perfect eyebrow, grin still in place.

"Fuck this fucking day," she mumbled, then began to pace.

Her brain was going a mile a minute. She needed to try to get her thoughts under control, but first a little ranting was in order—in her own head, of course.

What in the ever lovin' hell just happened? I just came in here for a damn job. Stupid freaking car! Always breaking down. Now this? Really? He called me mate. Mate. For fuck's sake. He is my mate. My animal thinks so, yeah, but she is a horn ball. Besides, he can't be mine. Is he a Cat like me? Nope. He's a freaking Wolf. A huge, hairy, bossy, thinks he's all that, Wolf. FML!

"Um, darlin'? You wanna take it down a notch? And I'm not that hairy," he said, slightly annoyed.

Well, damn. So much for an inner rant. She'd said all of that out loud.

Double oopsie.

Lucy straightened her spine and turned to look at the tall, gorgeous Alpha Wolf.

"Look, Fido, there's been a mistake—"

"Oh, I don't think so, darlin'."

Cocky. So fucking cocky.

Lucy had always had a secret thing for bad boys, and this guy was the motherfuckin' head honcho of bad boys. But was he really her mate? She knew all the Shifter myths of fated mates and true love and finding yourself in one other person created solely for you by the universe itself.

But she'd never really believed in them. It certainly never happened for her mother. Hope was a terrible thing for someone like Lucy, but right then, it was brewing inside of her like the beginnings of a storm.

If he was the storm, would Lucy be the calm? She wondered, really wondered, and for a minute, hell, she wanted to find out. Was she brave enough to stick around? Curiosity was a particular downfall for her kind, but one thing was certain, she would not be bossed around by this guy no matter what the Fates decided he was to her.

"No mistake here, darlin'. You're mine," he said, that sexy growl was back, and she shivered in response/

"Well, I don't think so. And my name isn't darlin'," she muttered.

"Alright darlin', how about baby instead?"

"It's Lucy, My name is Lucy. And you are?" she asked.

"Lucy. I like that. My name is Derrick, Derrick Rand," he replied, and reached out to shake her hand.

Fuck. His name was sexy. Not Bill or Ted, then. Dammit.

Lucy did not stand a chance in hell of surviving this.

"Oh, no you don't. No touching," she yipped, pulling back her hand at the last second.

She knew better. As worked up as they both were, if sexy Derrick here got his hands on her, it would be seconds before they started going at it like rutting beasts. As a feline Shifter, Lucy had to worry about going into her heat cycle only a few times every few years. But when presented with a viable male, one who claimed she was his, her cycle could start at any moment. Chances were, this meeting would have her coming into her heat in a matter of days.

Shiiiiit.

"Fine, darlin'. No touching *yet*," he murmured.

"Ever. Unless I say so," she countered.

And that will be never. She amended inside her head. She did not want to touch him. That would only start the mating fever even sooner. She'd been getting away with every three or four years since puberty, but she knew the stories. Once a female she-Cat Shifter found her mate, her ovaries basically exploded.

"Whatever you say, mate."

She could tell he was a cocky bastard from the arrogant tilt of his head to the way his knowing gaze seemed to undress her right there.

Yes, please. Too many clothes.

Down, girl!

Lucy was not ready for this. She turned to him with her eyes narrowed and hands on her hips and said the only thing she could think of.

"This isn't going to work. I don't want a mate."

CHAPTER FOUR

DIRE WOLF MATES

Derrick sat behind his desk and finished inputting the newest invoices, using the software system Phoenix had developed to help them run *Serious Moonlight* smoothly. Once he clicked pay on this last invoice, that would be it. All of their suppliers would have a zero dollar balance on their accounts. He clicked the button with a move of his wireless mouse and sighed.

Satisfaction thrummed through his veins, and yet Derrick's Dire Wolf growled inside of him. For some reason, his animal was on edge. He stood up and walked around to the huge shelf he'd claimed as his.

It was part of the original office, but like so many of the things they'd found here, had been left to rot. After stripping and sanding it down, he replaced two of the shelves, refinished the whole thing after salvaging it from the same mildew and mold that had sunk into various parts of the building.

A lot of the original furniture had been repurposed by him and his crew. Thank the gods they were all strong and good with their hands. But that's what happened when you lived your entire lives on the road. They'd picked up this and that along the way.

Of course, he'd started investing their money a few decades back and managed to increase their accounts. He'd used that money, plus a big chunk of his own funds, to buy this place. Looking at them, people probably figured they had little more than a pot to piss in, but the opposite couldn't be any truer.

The Pack accounts were healthy and fat. Added up, they made a nice, round eight figure number spread out across the globe. Personally, Derrick's account was of a similar status. But he was a man of few needs, and material things were never that important.

Money never mattered much to him. It was a means to an end, not the end. Not for him. He'd lived too long to not know what was truly important in this world.

Derrick may look a little over thirty, but he was triple that age. His Shifter abilities included living a much longer life than humans. Sometimes, they outlived other Shifters as well. It was a Dire Wolf thing.

His own mother was over three-hundred-years old. Still alive and kicking, leading her own Pack of twelve widowed she-Wolves who preferred to live honoring the memory of their mates by riding their bikes cross country the way they had when they'd been together.

It was sad and beautiful. Tragedy plagued those destined to live after their loved ones passed into the next adventure. Derrick had worried about leaving his mother when he'd decided to branch out on his own with a few Wolves, but she'd slapped him on the side of the head affectionately and told him to stop cramping her style. She was a good mother and had assured him she'd be just fine. After all, she'd taught him how to ride. He still blushed at the memory, but he'd only been a kid and she was so strong and wise. His mama sure had taught him a thing or two on the back of his first Harley, and he was damn proud of her.

His Wolf paced and grumbled inside him, feeling unsettled and anxious. Fuck. This was something the bar was supposed to calm in him. Derrick wiped sweat from his brow. Suddenly, he was hot in the tiny office. He ripped off his black t-shirt and leaned on the shelf, allowing the air from the vent to cool his overheated body.

The Wolf was getting aggressive, pushing, and snapping at his skin, demanding to be released. He knew settling in one place was going to be a challenge for his Pack, but he'd forgotten his own animal might not take to it right away. It would take some time, he supposed. And that was something he had plenty of.

Fuck. He felt really *really* hot now.

It was like his blood was boiling. Not in anger, though. More like anticipation. A knock sounded on the door, and he listened to one of his own speak. Someone was there for the job they'd been advertising.

Finally, he thought, relieved. Sheila had been bitchin' about getting more help and here was a guy applying for the job. It was a little late, but who was he to judge.

"Send him in," he grunted, not bothering to turn around.

His Wolf would tell him if he was in danger from a threat. Derrick closed his eyes and listened to the footsteps of the stranger. They were lighter than he would have guessed. Much lighter than a Shifter male, even a regular human male.

He sniffed the air, sorting through the harsh chemical cleaners and paint that still hung in the air from their massive remodeling of their bar.

A female?

After his initial shock, he breathed again. His Dire Wolf had gone silent, the hunter inside him weighing the threat of the newcomer. His heart rate increased as the beast found something else in that new fragrance. Something intoxicating and terrifying in the female's scent. It was heady and dangerous, and very, very tempting.

Derrick sucked in a deep breath and held it in. Her scent was light and woody, fresh as spring flowers and just as uplifting. Like that moment you step off your bike after a seventy-two hour straight run, taking in the life bursting all around from the sunrise to the insects, the birds, and even the weeds on the side of the road. The scent invaded his senses, and he took a moment to savor it as his pulse sped up inside of him, thundering like a herd of wild stallions. That crazy, beautiful, wild scent seemed to wrap around his limbs, shooting straight for his cock. The damn thing grew thick and hard in his already tight jeans. He ached and throbbed, his Wolf growled and scratched, urging him closer to the source of that amazing smell.

Fuck.

Need pulsed through him, making thought almost impossible. He breathed again. The woman was calling to him, and he hadn't even seen her yet. He tried to steady himself before turning around. His Wolf was riding him hard, but Derrick did not want to scare her. He should take a minute, try to assess the situation.

Sniff sniff.

Feline Shifter. Sexy little kitten. Mine.

It didn't matter that she wasn't a Wolf. All he cared about was how fucking fantastic she smelled. Derrick growled deep and low in his throat. The sound reverberated through his chest. The near thousand pound animal inside of him urged the man to turn around and take a look. He asked her who she was, and waited, but she didn't respond. He needed a name to go with that scent.

Derrick turned, eyes flashing with his beast. "I said, who are you?"

Eyes the color of wild spear thistles met his, and he knew. Right then and there. This woman, *sniff,* this she-Cat was his. His one true and fated mate.

After that, it was a matter of self-control. He'd finally managed to get his hands on her, couldn't seem to stop himself, he had to breathe her in up close. Once he'd recognized her as a Shifter, he figured it was all going to be fine, eventually. Surely, she would rejoice. The same way his heart did at the thought of finding his one true and fated mate.

She had a momentary panic, and he waited patiently for her to get through it. Discovering your mate could be shocking. And she was so fucking cute, pacing and shaking her pretty little head as she ranted. But imagine his utter and complete shock when she'd turned around and refused him.

"I don't want a mate."

Derrick recoiled inside as if she'd slapped him, but he didn't allow her to see it. Nope. Yes, it sucked. She wasn't as overjoyed as he was, but he didn't let that get him down. This sassy little feline was all his. She just didn't realize it yet.

"Lucy, we can talk about the mate thing later. Why did you come here?" he asked, openly curious.

"I need a job so I can pay for the repairs to my car and a place to stay for a little while until it is fixed. Then I'm leaving," she said, not quite meeting his eyes.

His Wolf snarled at the thought of her leaving but reined in the animal. He wanted her to choose him, but he would not get that by bullying her. If his life had taught him anything, it was that in order to play the long game, you had to be patient.

Derrick could be patient. Even if he wanted to tear her clothes off, make her come until she was screaming his name, and begging him to mark her with his bite, he would hold off. Wooing the sexy little feline was going to be fun, he mused, determined to make her so crazy about him, she would never want to stray from his side.

"So, you need a job and a place to stay. How come you came here?"

"Tony the Perv said this place was a boarding house," she explained.

"Who the fuck is Tony the Perv, and where can I find him?" Derrick asked. He couldn't help the growl that entered his throat.

Why would she call someone a perv unless he was acting pervy? That was just totally fucking unacceptable. He knew by the way his Wolf snarled that his eyes were full on gold with his beast, but he couldn't help it.

The sound of his pretty little mate snapping her fingers in front of him brought his head up. Her violet eyes were glittering as she did. Damn, she was hot when she was pissed. Derrick growled deep in his throat and a wicked hint of a smile grew on his face.

"Hey, knock it off, Fido. Quit the grumbling, he didn't touch me. Besides, I mean, *hello*, I'm a Shifter. I can handle myself."

"But you call him the Perv?"

"He was just a creepy little human. He didn't do anything to me. Anyway, I'm fine," she said.

That she was reassuring him without realizing it made his insides warm and his beast rumble in satisfaction. She was taking care of him, sweet, sexy, thoughtful mate. And she was right. She was a Shifter and a badass. As long as she was happy, so was he.

Damn, that was fast, but that was the way it happened. Derrick felt as if he'd been struck by lightning. His entire body was wound up and tense, but he couldn't let her see that. He wanted her calm and relaxed, ready to accept his claim. He just had to work on the *when* part.

"Alright," he said. "I will let it go."

It wouldn't always be the case. He was bound to be pigheaded and overprotective, not to mention possessive as fuck, especially once he claimed her, but he could see that she was perfectly fine. Good for Tony. The Perv would never know how close he came to being mauled by a pissed off Dire Wolf. Still, his beast wanted him to sever the man's head from his body.

Bashing heads and taking names was kind of an old, favorite pastime. His other half could be a bit bloodthirsty. Just another Dire Wolf thing.

The prehistoric animal had some very black and white notions of what was acceptable and how to deal with what was not. Mostly, what that meant was something or someone was bleeding at the end of the day.

Derrick had yet to be on the receiving end of such dealings, but he'd dished out his fair share of bruises and broken bones. Of course, he tried to limit his maiming to the really bad fuckers. Which is the category he'd put anyone in who tried to fuck with his mate.

Mine. Grrr.

Did he mention he was a possessive asshole? Well, yeah. It would only get worse the longer he went without claiming her. Mating fever could take him if he didn't get a handle on this now.

"Lucy, I understand you came in here looking for a job, but you know what we are to each other. I know you can feel the pull," he began.

"And I know what you'd like to *think* we are, but I am telling you, the Fates made a mistake. I'm not looking for a mate," she told him firmly, shaking her head and looking him dead in the eye.

Dammit, if he didn't find it hot as hell, he'd wonder if she was challenging him. Derrick was not used to anyone showing so much indifference to his dominance. She had spirit and spunk, and fuck, he was intrigued.

He narrowed his eyes, but she held his gaze. Derrick was an Alpha. Not many people could hold his stare. Okay, no one had ever held his gaze for more than a few seconds, but there she was, staring him down, and his Wolf was preening like a lovesick fool.

"Lucy," he said, testing the weight of her name on his tongue, and finding he liked it very much.

"I know my name. What's yours again?" she inquired with that certain haughty air only felines had.

Fuck it, he shrugged, finding he kind of liked it. Haughty looked sexy as hell on her.

"Derrick Rand," he replied immediately, unable to resist trying to please her.

Goddammit.

He was acting like a lovesick puppy already. The notion should've pissed him off, but he couldn't help grinning.

"Well then, Mr. Rand—"

"It's Derrick, darlin'," he drawled.

"Fine. Derrick darlin'," she teased, rolling her pretty purple eyes. "Do I get the job?"

"Yes," he said automatically.

"And the room?"

"Yep, that too," he smiled.

He did not relish the idea of his mate working in the bar, but it was the only way. He wasn't so pigheaded he couldn't figure that much out. Derrick had to keep her there with him, otherwise how could he claim her? And claim her he would.

"Come on."

"Where?" she asked, not completely trusting him.

Good girl, being careful with a stranger. But Lucy was safer with him than anyone else on the planet. The sassy little feline didn't know it yet, but she was. His dire Wolf had already claimed her in his mind.

"Grand tour," he growled and held the door open, staring at her ass as she sashayed in front of him.

Sexy little kitten.

Derrick walked her through the bar, out the door, and to the Pack house. It was dark and cool outside, middle of the night and all, but he was sweating bullets. He frowned as he looked around.

"It still needs work, but we are on it," he told her, wanting her to like the place.

"It's fine. The house is huge," she replied as Sheila came bounding over.

"Hi, I'm Sheila Rand. And please tell me my cousin hired you," Sheila screeched, stopping just short of plowing down his tiny mate.

He couldn't help his warning growl. Sheila yelped, and his mate's cute little head popped up. She glared at him, treating him to eyes that blazed purple fire.

"Really? Down, Fido," snapped Lucy in his direction before she turned to smile at his cousin.

"Hi, my name is Lucy, and I'll be working here for a couple of weeks till my car is fixed. By the way, your cousin has some serious issues with personal boundaries."

"Does he now, Miss Kitty?"

Sheila lifted both her eyebrows and whistled long and low. Derrick was not amused.

"What happened to your car?" Sheila asked, ignoring his warning growl.

"Broke down. It's a hopeless old junker, but it's mine. Car repair shop says it's going to be sixteen hundred dollars to fix, but the tow truck driver said you all ran a boarding house?" she asked, biting her lower lip, and making his dick go even harder.

Shit. She really shouldn't do that. If his mate wanted nibbles, Derrick was her man.

"We don't run a—*er*, yes, I mean, we do," Sheila said, wincing.

"Knock it off," she snapped again, and he cut off the growl he did not even know he was making.

"See what I mean?" she asked Sheila.

"Boundary issues?" his cousin replied with a teasing lilt to her voice.

Shit.

"Yep, loads of them. Anyway, to answer your question, *yes*, I got the job, and now I'd like to go to my room—"

"Cole," bellowed Derrick, turning his head to the door where the Wolf came running.

"Call the local tow company and have them bring Lucy's car here. When it arrives, fix it."

"Hey! That is my car, and it stays where it is," Lucy snarled at him, and fuck if he didn't find that hot too.

"*Ohmygods*," Sheila yelled, and jumped up and down excitedly. "Please tell me you are for real!"

"Uh, yeah, I am real. I mean, I am standing right here," Lucy replied, head cocked to the side, staring at his cousin like she was daft. A sentiment he echoed at the moment.

"Derrick, I can't believe you found your mate already!"

"Who said anything about a mate?" Lucy asked, her voice getting all high and squeaky.

"Yes, Lucy is my mate," he stated aloud, and fuck, it felt good to own that.

"Damn cousin, you lucky SOB. But why do you always have to show everyone else up?"

"Ugh. Not you too," Lucy argued. "Look, I am no one's mate! I'm just gonna work here and get my car fixed."

"Cousin, she's awesome. Congratulations," Sheila said, jumping up and down and clapping like she used to when she was a kid and something excited her.

"Alright, Sheila, yes, you guessed it. Lucy is mine, but we haven't discussed any of the logistics yet," Derrick told his cousin.

"Oh, I see," Sheila said, still clapping.

"Hello? I am right here. And no, Sheila, for the record, I am not *his*, I am not anybody's. Look, I am tired, and wet from the rain, so how about you show me to my room, please?"

His sweet-tempered mate ignored him as she sashayed across the lot and through the narrow path to the gate and pushed the door open. Derrick growled softly in his throat. He nodded at Sheila, who seemed to understand his orders without words, as she usually did.

Out of all of his Wolves, she was the most intuitive. His sweet Lucy turned around one final time and gave him the stink eye. Fuck, her eyes were so pretty. A blue so deep, they were indigo. Purple eyes, blonde hair, sexy as fuck curves covering her petite frame.

Damn, she looked good. He'd never expected a sassy little kitten was his future, but now that he'd met her, Derrick couldn't imagine it any other way. This was definitely going to be an interesting mating. Derrick's Wolf howled in his mind's eye, the huge beast clamoring to be closer to her.

Mine. Mate.

Soon, he told his animal, *soon.*

CHAPTER FIVE

Lucy inhaled the fresh evening air outside her new job at *Serious Moonlight*, grateful to finally be outside.

Yes, the night before, she'd slept like the dead. Her inner feline had felt safe and secure for the first time in a long while. What that said about her circumstances, she did not want to look too deeply into.

The room she'd slept in was just fine. Clean and spacious. Okay, she'd been given the best damn room in the house, a fact that made her wary. It took her all of a minute once she'd stepped inside to recognize it was *his* room.

Fury had filled her, and she'd wanted to hunt him down and castrate the heavy handed bastard, but her inner kitty would have none of that. The dumb feline thought it was sexy and romantic. The big bad Wolf wanted her—*a cat*—in his Den, surrounded by his scent, where he could protect and watch over her.

Prrrr.

She'd readied herself to be strong against the wooing she'd felt coming, but to her surprise, he'd stayed away. Confusing man. He'd insisted they were mates, set her up in his bedroom, with his things, but that was it. With a hurriedly whispered goodnight, Derrick had left her alone in his space. He didn't even ask her to come in.

Not that she needed him inside to know what he was doing. His heady musk covered every damn surface, driving her she-Cat wild with need. Screw him and his restraint. She was feeling unfulfilled and angsty after her restless night.

Fine. She was horny. Really fucking horny.

Lucy had thought he would have tried knocking on her door in the wee hours of the morning, playing on her weakness for him, but nope. He'd given her the space she'd asked for.

Stupid overbearing, Alpha.

She replayed the events of the night before in her mind, trying to find fault with him, but couldn't.

"This is your room, isn't it? No, I can't stay here—"

"Look, if putting me out of my room bothers you so much, I could stay," he'd murmured and stalked her until she'd backed against the wall. "I want to stay, Lucy, but I think you need some space to wrap your head around this thing between us."

"There is nothing between us," she'd argued.

"So, you don't need space, then?" he'd teased, cocky bastard that he was.

Lucy had wanted his hands on her, and as if he could read her mind, he'd smoothed one long-fingered hand down her arm, skimming over the skin, conjuring goosebumps across her flesh, but barely touching her at all.

That whisper-light touch had almost been her undoing. She'd wanted to press against him. Something of a feat for a woman who prided herself on control. Truth was, she had little real sexual experience. Her mother had flocked from man to man and Lucy refused to get caught up in that cycle of use and abuse.

Still, her she-Cat urged her to rub her skin all over his mountain of a body and mark him with her scent. She resisted. Barely.

"You wish," had been her reply before stomping out to the delicious sound of his laughter.

Of course, she'd left his room with yet another pair of wet panties on the pretense of using the bathroom. Thank goodness they had a washer and dryer in the house. She had one backpack that held her clothes, and laundry day was every day for Lucy. But her meager eight pairs of panties were going to be threadbare if this kept up.

If this kept up, she was gonna buy stock in *Victoria's Secret,* for fuck's sake. She'd managed to avoid him for two days. Only saw him at mealtimes, which was uncomfortable, but doable since she was often hungry enough to focus solely on her food.

The blond Beta of the Pack was a real chef. His Texas chili with juicy, thick chunks of beef, and homemade jalapeno cornbread, were outstanding. She'd expected Derrick to make a stink of her, refusing his invitations to join her for walks and evening runs in the woods behind the house, but he didn't. Took her refusals in stride and never stopped watching her.

Was he waiting for her to cave? Maybe. Lord knew she wanted to. Hell, her she-Cat wanted her to. But each time he asked, she turned him down flat. Lucy couldn't explain it.

Her body said *go get him girl,* but her mind said *be cautious.* She could not believe he had anything other than a quick roll in the sack in mind, and the thought terrified her. If ever a man was made who could wreck her body and heart, it was Derrick Rand. Maybe he was counting on wearing her down, but she was no easy mark. No matter how worked up he made her, or how desperate for his touch she became, Lucy needed to keep strong.

I will not end up like Mom. No fucking way.

Being afraid sucked, but there it was. Lucy was no match for a big, strong Alpha. She was a scaredy cat. No pun intended.

She'd do anything and everything to avoid the inevitable heartbreak fucking around with Derrick Rand would bring. She did not know how to separate love and sex. Had tried it once in her teens. She'd given her virginity to her high school boyfriend, but idiot that she was, she'd fallen for the guy. They grew apart and went their separate ways, and fuck, it had hurt.

Lucy was in no rush to experience that pain again. Only this time, she knew it would be a hundred times worse. She was not a kid anymore, and her loyal heart would be well and truly damaged if she gave it to him. She could not afford it. Staying away from Derrick was her only option.

Good thing work kept her busy. Tonight was opening night, and Lucy had spent the afternoon cleaning and making sure the bars and kitchen were fully stocked along with the rest of the Pack. She'd been introduced to them all over the last forty-eight hours and was amazed at their very existence.

Dire Wolf Shifters. Who knew?

At least she was not the only female, even if Sheila wasn't exactly warm and friendly. At least, the female wasn't a bitch either.

Another dog joke, she mused. They'd been trading cat and dog jokes almost nonstop with Sheila calling her Mr. Whiskers, and Lucy leaving an old tennis ball she found in the parking lot by Sheila's door. No matter how far the female tossed it, Lucy always found it and brought it back.

Snort.

The men were pretty distant with her, but that probably had more to do with Derrick introducing her as his mate than for any personal reasons. Lucy gritted her teeth just thinking about his unwarranted proclamations.

"You aren't going to bully me into accepting your claim, Derrick," she'd told him, but the big, sexy male just grinned.

"I'm no bully, darlin'. I'm an Alpha willing to do anything to keep you happy, safe, and secure. You'll see. I won't stop until you do," he told her, and that had been the first time he kissed her.

A quick press of his lips against hers. She'd been so shocked Lucy hadn't moved a muscle. No response, no rebuttal, she just stood there stone still. The touch was gentler than she'd expected, and brief. Too brief.

Want. Need. More.

Dammit. He wasn't going to seduce her. Not for a quickie and certainly not into accepting his claim either, for fuck's sake. Lucy was her own person. Once upon a time, she'd once dreamed of having a mate to love, who loved her. Someone to build a home with, complete with white picket fence, cubs—the whole nine yards. But that was a child's dream.

Lucy was a woman now. After her mother's last lover had cleaned out her bank account, even the coffee can that held a few random twenty-dollar bills, the female had simply wasted away. She'd died on a Wednesday, leaving Lucy with a week left till graduation, and nothing but the clothes on her back.

Lucy had stayed to get her high school diploma, then she'd taken off. Her mother was buried in a pauper's grave, and it shamed Lucy still to know she could not have given her any better. She'd had to skip out on the landlord, not having the money to pay the rent.

All alone to fend for herself in the big, bad world at just eighteen. It took her a year to save the two hundred bucks and mail it to that old man, but she did. She had her pride, after all.

Her father had never really been in the picture. She didn't know how to contact him and wasn't sure if she would have, even if she did know. Some Shifters just didn't stick around. She'd had years to get over her abandonment issues, but repressed feelings had a nasty way of resurfacing now and again. Pushing back the hurt, Lucy took a deep breath and went over what she knew.

Derrick Rand was the Dire Wolf Alpha, head of their MC, and he'd announced to all and sundry that she, Lucy Corwyn, hybrid feline Shifter, belonged to him. His mate.

Crap.

What did she know about how Wolves mated anyway? And really, what the hell was a Dire Wolf? Some kind of mutant gene had led this subspecies of Shifter to maintain their prehistoric animal, long since extinct in the natural world. She was curious, but she wouldn't ask questions. She didn't want to get involved. No matter how much her she-Cat yowled and hissed at her. Lucy was simply not going to budge on this.

I don't want a mate.

She kept on repeating the mantra inside her brain, telling herself she believed it. But if that were true, she had to ask herself why she couldn't stand to be in the same room with Derrick for more than ten minutes at a time.

True, he was an Alpha, and power seemed to ooze from his pores when he walked into a room. But Lucy was not frightened of him, nor did she feel compelled to obey him. On the contrary, his inner strength, that special Alpha magic he had, turned her on like nothing else ever had.

She loved his inky hair and the way it fell to his chin and brushed his shoulders in dark waves. Her fingers itched to brush the constant shadow that seemed to always cover his chiseled features, making him even more outrageously gorgeous than seemed fair. He hadn't kissed her again, but the curve of his smile and the heat in his eyes made her want to climb him like a mountain and slam her mouth to his.

Rrrr.

Going to his room after cleaning the bar to shower and dress did nothing to cool the fire in her blood. Lucy felt her heat coming on, and it worried her something fierce. If her animal had her way, she'd be wearing Derrick's claiming mark already. She tugged on her uniform, grinning at the shirt Sheila had dropped off earlier that evening, as promised.

Lucy had laughed out loud when she'd seen it. Clearly, Sheila was trying to get her laid. Her so-called uniform was nothing but a pair of tight, high-waisted cutoffs that showed a little too much of her ass cheeks. Two Wolf paws were painted on each back pocket in hot pink. That alone would undoubtedly draw eyes to the bottom half of the ensemble.

As if that was not bad enough, she'd paired it with a skin-tight, black tank top that left the tops of Lucy's creamy rounded breasts bare. Across the front of the shirt was the *Serious Moonlight* logo, written in a brash, hot pink scrawl with a glowing white, full moon above it. The moon sat right on her left nipple, and made Lucy laugh even harder.

On her feet she wore a pair of black leather, mid-calf harness boots that she'd picked up at a second-hand store during her travels. They'd been barely used and too good a deal to pass up. Glad now that she'd grabbed them, even though they cost more than she'd ever spent on shoes before.

Living on the road meant little opportunity to make money, but she'd always managed. Her she-Cat was agile and hearty, enabling her to do physically demanding jobs when need be. Though she was short, and a fair bit curvier than most Shifter females, Lucy was happy with her body.

This outfit left more of it than usual on display, but she was comfortable with herself, and it would be easy to work in. Thank goodness she'd shaved. If her shirts were any shorter, her *hooha* would be hanging out.

Snort.

Bad enough her skin was pasty and pale, white as milk. She'd have liked having a tan to at least give the appearance of slimmer thighs, but it was what it was. Most customers would probably not be looking past her cleavage, which was pretty impressive if she said so herself.

Big boobs, big ass, thick legs, hell yes, Lucy was the real deal when it came to being curvy. She liked her body and did not mind flaunting it. So, take that, assholes of the world who thought all women were supposed to fit into the same size pair of pants!

Truth was, she'd never stuck around a man long enough to find out if her body was a problem. If Derrick had anything to say about the way her rounded body filled out the stupidly skimpy uniform, then he could go to hell. She pulled up short, realizing with a gasp that she was nervous about him seeing her like this.

When the hell had it ever mattered to her what a man thought about her looks? Eyes narrowed, she decided to grab her wobbling self-confidence by the horns. She was not gonna stand outside and worry about anything as ridiculous as whether her mate—no, not her mate, her boss—liked it or not. He picked the damn thing out, after all.

"Dammit," Lucy muttered to herself as she pulled open the heavy double doors and sauntered into the bar with the wind blowing back her thick, blonde hair.

She'd taken time to blow out her long locks to a glossy sheen. Yeah, the rumors were true, Cat Shifters were really into their fur. Lucy was proud of her golden locks and her plus-sized shape. She'd taken extra care tonight with her makeup, too. She'd put on liquid eyeliner and mascara, some glittery shadow on her eyelids, and a smear of gloss over her already pink lips.

The place fell quiet the second Lucy walked in. It was half an hour till opening, so it was just the guys and Sheila, but still. Lucy looked up to see several pairs of glowing eyes staring at her, beneath them, mouths were hanging open.

"Wowza! I wasn't sure you'd wear it," exclaimed Sheila, before running over to grab Lucy in a girl hug.

The redheaded beauty wore a similar outfit, only her legs were tan and about a mile long, and her high, perky breasts seemed to stand up and salute. Sheila held Lucy's arms wide, eyeing her body in a mock-leer that had Lucy giggling.

"You look great, girl. My goodness, you are gonna get so many tips!"

"Oh, please, look at you. You're like runway model gorgeous," Lucy replied sincerely.

"Damn, ladies," said a Wolf with red hair two shades darker than Sheila's. His name was Weylin, and he'd been quiet but friendly to Lucy over the past two days. "We're used to this one here, but Lucy, you look good enough to eat!"

Similar comments and a long wolf whistle sounded just before a menacing snarl came from the back of the room. Everyone shut up and Weylin backed away, hands raised in surrender. His glowing eyes were averted, and he bared his throat in deference to his super pissed off looking Alpha.

"It was a compliment, man. No disrespect intended," Weylin ground out, throat still bared.

She'd seen Derrick staring at her with his eyes glowing gold, that angry rumble still coming from his throat. Instinctively, she stepped forward, shoulders back, head high. So much for being nervous about him seeing her this way. Her inner kitty lent her some much needed cool, and she approached him with the slinky gait of her kind. Sex and confidence dripping with each step as she got closer to him.

He liked what he saw. She could tell by the wicked gleam in his eyes and the bulge in his tight jeans. Fuck, she really liked the way he wore his jeans, perfectly molded to his muscular thighs and calves. Lucy bit her lip, watching as he tracked the movement, but she didn't slow down.

Derrick tensed, as if waiting for her to stop, but Lucy had other plans. She walked right past him, not stopping until she reached her post at the bar in the back room. Of course, she could not help but shiver when she passed him by, noting the heat that seemed to radiate off his skin.

"Back to work," Derrick told the rest of the males, who seemed stuck where they'd been standing.

Lucy had to work hard not to grin stupidly. Truth was, she enjoyed rattling the big, bad Alpha. It made her feel powerful, knowing he couldn't stop staring at her with all the intensity of a hunter stalking his prey.

"What are you wearing?" Derrick's voice asked from just beside her ear, and she realized he'd snuck up on her while she'd been checking the coolers.

"My uniform. Sheila gave it to me," she replied.

"Fuck. We don't have a uniform, Lucy. If we did, it would have more material," he muttered, and ran a hand through his hair. "Go throw something else on."

"What?"

"I said you don't have to wear that."

"No, you said I should 'go throw something else on'. What I want to know is why me? Sheila's been in here for hours, and no one said a word about her outfit. But suddenly, I show up, wearing the same thing, and it's a problem?" Lucy's voice was growing louder by the second, but she couldn't help it.

"Lucy—" Derrick growled, but she did not let him finish. Not this time. Lucy was pissed.

"Is there something wrong with my body? Too many rolls and jiggles for you, Mr. Muscles? Is that it?"

"What? Fuck! Lucy, of course not—"

"Is there something showing I should be ashamed of? Or would you prefer I wear a tent to cover my fat?" Lucy demanded, angry and shaken that he had been so serious in his command.

"Dammit, Lucy! Fuck, no. That's not what I said or meant. Here, come here," he growled and took her hand, tugging her down the hall.

She was so angry she went without hardly a fight. Her heart was pounding so hard it was liable to explode from all the hurt and rage. She hardly had time to think about what she was going to say, let alone how to react to the way he quickly pushed her up against the wall the second he closed the door inside his office.

Derrick was vibrating with his own emotions, his ever present growl filling the space and turning her on so much, she wanted to die from embarrassment. Damn him for making her want him, even when he was clearly ashamed of her.

His hard, muscular body pinned hers in place. She felt the thick ridge of his cock pressing against her soft belly, and she couldn't stop the whimper that escaped her lips. His face was so close she could smell the peppermint he'd sucked on after they all had dinner an hour ago.

"Feel this?" Derrick growled and ground his lower body against her belly.

Oh yeah.

She felt that.

Holy. Fucking. Giganticock.

"I'm harder than I've ever fucking been, Lucy. My dick is aching like a fucking virgin in a strip club, for fuck's sake, and it's all because of you," he growled, chest heaving as he tried to regain control.

"What—*why* did you say that then?" she asked, voice so low she hardly recognized it.

"You look fucking beautiful, Lucy, and I'm losing my mind with wanting you. My Wolf is going wild with the need to claim you, and I am trying, Lucy, I swear to fuck I am. But the longer I wait, the more possessive I get," he grunted.

"I can't help it. I'm trying, but I'm bound to fuck up a thousand times a day."

"So, you don't think, uh, I look bad in this get up—"

"Fuck, no. Never. You are the sexiest female I have ever seen. I fucking love your curves, Lucy. You were made to fill my hands, and I got big hands, darlin'," he said, and she could hear the truth in his deep, growly voice.

He was so damn hot, so masculine and forceful, and he was being real with her. She could hold herself back when he was being bossy or cocky, but when he was being honest, fuck, he made her eyes cross with need. His tone was rough but held an edge of pleading to it that made her want to swoon at his feet. It was enough to make all her pink bits throb with desire.

"Look at me, Lucy," he told her, his long fingers catching her chin when her eyes would have dropped.

Forced to meet his midnight gaze, Lucy trembled in his arms. Derrick blinked again, his eyes glowing with the gold of his Wolf. For the first time, she took stock of the beast peeking out at her, and what she saw was stunning. His Wolf was a wild and untamed beast. A prehistoric monster full of dominance and power. The animal wanted her, wanted to sink his teeth in and claim her, and the only thing holding him back was Derrick's human side.

The sheer force of his will was what kept her from being claimed already. He was waging an internal war with his animal, and all for her. Nothing had ever touched her so deeply as knowing what this man was doing for her. Shit. She was being selfish. Fate was not something easily denied, and his animal was clearly stronger than any she had ever encountered. If nothing else, that told her loudly and clearly what kind of man he was.

Good. Strong. Honest. True. Caring. Loyal. Trustworthy.

Derrick's whole body seemed to tremble against hers, and she automatically reached out to cradle him. He was vulnerable with her, in that moment, and maybe that was when she first started to fall for him. Like really fall for him. Big, sexy man, letting her see his soft side.

The raw need on his face plain, and fuck, she felt it too. Lucy swallowed hard. Was she hurting him as well as herself by neglecting his claim and their growing bond? Maybe she was wrong to deny what she already knew to be truth. Derrick Rand was hers every bit as much as she was his.

"Lucy," he whispered her name and pressed his forehead to hers, holding her as if she were something precious to him.

"No one ever really stuck with me before," she said, feeling the need to explain a bit of herself to this beautiful, strong man. "I didn't grow up with an abundance of love and security. My Dad walked out when I was a kid. Mom died after a string of boyfriends left her broken and bruised. If this is real, Derrick, I'll need a little time to get used to it, to get used to you being here," she whispered, hating her past.

"It's real. I know you need time and I'm trying to give it to you."

"I know you are," she whispered, petting his chest and shoulders, loving the rumble of pleasure that rattled through him at her touch.

She was not lying. This would take some getting used to. If Derrick really was her fated mate, she'd have to accept him and his claim. She would have to open herself up to hurt. That part was scary, but worth it, right?

Yessssss.

Her she-Cat hissed in righteous joy as she acknowledged the truth, even if only to herself. Derrick's nostrils flared, and he groaned, closing his eyes as he unconsciously flexed his hips against her. Was it wrong that she found it sexy that he was struggling with control?

She couldn't help it. Having his body pressed up against hers was doing things to her she'd never felt before. Desire pulsed in her blood, catching like wildfire in her veins. She could hardly breathe, definitely couldn't talk anymore.

Her lips parted as she tried to suck in air. A whimper escaped her, or was that a sigh? Fuck if she knew. Her body was on fire. Lucy moved slightly, nuzzling his nose with hers, their breath mingling.

"Just a kiss," she murmured, and he nodded, dipping his head, and pressing his mouth so softly against hers it barely registered at first.

She pushed her tongue into his mouth, needing more, and he gave it. Damn, did he give it. The man was a god at kissing. His teeth nipped, tongue stroked, and lips brushed against hers until she could no longer think clearly.

Derrick grunted and lifted her up. Lucy whimpered, wrapping her legs around him like some crazy, clingy octopus. Her heated core rubbed over his bulging jeans, stroking her needy clit just right.

It wasn't enough, though, not nearly. Lucy could have cried, she wanted him so much. The scent of her desire grew thick and heavy, and Derrick flared his nostrils. His chest vibrated with a slow, deep growl that seemed to shoot waves of lust straight to her sex.

"You got me so damn crazy, woman," he growled, kissing her deeper as he pulled her tighter against him.

He felt so good between her thighs. She moaned and allowed him to move her just so. Every brush and stroke had her Cat closer to the edge. The man was so damn strong, holding her with no effort at all. Every pant and groan made it harder for her to think. She'd almost forgotten why they were in his office to begin with.

"Do you know why I wanted you to get changed now?"

"No," she murmured, chasing his mouth for more kisses, but beast that he was, he denied her.

Fucker.

"It's cause I'm a possessive asshole, darlin'. These curves," he growled, cupping her ass with one hand, and reaching for her tit with the other, "are mine. The idea of dozens of eyes on you has my Wolf tearing at my insides. I'm greedy and I don't share, but you have nothing to hide or be ashamed of, woman." He paused a beat and she let his words sink in.

Holy. Fuck.

He was breaking down walls with words. Destroying her armor and making a mess of her well-laid plans.

"Look at you. Fucking goddess. I want to rip those shorts off your body and bury my cock so deep inside you, you won't know where you stop, and I start. I don't want another fucking person to see you and be tempted to touch, cause I don't know if I can stop my Wolf from going after someone tonight," he continued.

"Derrick—"

"No, kitten, let me finish so you understand what kind of man I really am. I am protective of what is mine, and bite mark or not, you're mine. It's just a matter of time—"

"Cocky bastard," she butted in, but she was grinning.

"Yes, I am. And you, you are perfect. Every fucking inch of you is a thing of beauty. Now, I spoke too quick before, and I am sorry. A real man doesn't tell his woman how to dress. He lifts her up and compliments her. Tells her how good she looks and how she makes him feel. Well, Lucy, you look better than anything I have ever seen, and you make me crazy with wanting you," he confessed.

She was caught in the golden stare of his Wolf, and she wondered who was in control at that moment. Since he was still holding her, and she was not bent over his desk being claimed by his rutting beast, she figured the man was still in charge.

What Lucy could not figure out was whether or not that fact made her happy? Derrick's control was immeasurable at this point. But did she want the big brute to keep it or to claim her already? Her she-Cat had already decided. The Bobcat-Mountain Lion Hybrid inside her knew what she wanted.

Mine. Mine. Mine.

"I make you crazy?" she asked.

"Fuck yeah, you do. Every delectable inch of you has me wanting to be inside you so damn bad I can't think of anything else. Far as I am concerned, we're mates, kitten. My Dire Wolf is jealous as hell, but I'm keeping him at bay. The fact you won't let me claim you is making him feral. I almost attacked Weylin back there just for commenting about how you look in those *fuck me shorts* you got on and he's been part of my Pack for five decades."

"You guys are old as fuck," she stated, and he barked out a laugh.

"Maybe, but I've never seen anything that compares to you, darlin'."

She swallowed at his confession. Loved the power she felt having brought his animal so close to the surface, but at the same time her she-Cat longed to soothe him, insisted she tend to her mate.

Lucy ran her hands across his perfectly sculpted shoulders in the soft, black button-down he wore over a plain white t-shirt. He was so damn big. Big enough to make her feel positively small, even though she knew better. She totally loved it.

"You're playing with fire, kitten. Keep petting me and I'm gonna take what you're offering. I can't help it. Want you so bad," he said, eyes closed in an almost painful expression.

Lucy cupped his cheeks in her hands, offering him what they both wanted, and Derrick did not hesitate. He opened bright gold eyes and pinned her with his stare before dipping down to capture her lips in a soul-searing kiss. All Lucy could do was hold on and let it happen. His lips were soft yet firm, demanding but tender, and so damn hot she could have come just from having his mouth on hers.

Her she-Cat yowled inside her mind's eye. The little beastie was happier than a pig in the mud because she finally had her mate in her grasp. Lucy purred and lapped at his lips, sighing when he opened for her and tangled his expert tongue with hers.

He was all spice and heat. His flavor unique. A mouth-watering, smoky combination of forest and peppery fire. She couldn't get enough of him.

Lucy growled and nipped his lip, delighted by the way he tightened his hold on her ass and face. His claws extended, and she felt them pierce through her tiny jean shorts, but he didn't break the skin there.

Not yet.

The hint of pain made her she-Cat hiss and growl in pleasurable anticipation. The feline wanted her mate to mark her, to claim her, here and now, but Lucy was not ready for that. Not yet. Her stomach clenched and pussy throbbed.

Dammit. Her heat was coming, and fast. But not tonight. It was close, the mating fever almost had her, but not quite yet. She had some time left, time to get to know him. Things were moving at light speed, but that was the way for Shifters. She knew that even if she did not understand it.

Lucy had a decision to make. One that would change her life forever. Derrick's gruff voice interrupted her thoughts as his lips left hers and skimmed her jawline and neck. It felt good, so good, when he nibbled her there.

Just like that.

"Will you wear something of mine? Something to carry my scent. My shirt? My watch? Fuck," he growled, moving back to her mouth and shaking her from her sweet, lust-filled thoughts.

"Will it help?"

"I think so. I can't promise I won't go after the next fucking person who sees you like this tonight without you wearing my mark," he told her, and she heard the truth in his words.

His voice dripped sex and power, a heady combination Lucy found irresistible. She knew he was talking about hurting someone for looking at her, and were she a regular old human, that might have made her nervous. But Lucy was a Shifter. She found his possessive attitude as sexy as she did exasperating.

Shifters were notoriously territorial. She might not have accepted his claim verbally, but they both knew it was a matter of time. She bit her lip and looked at his glowing gold eyes.

"You want me?"

"You know I do," he replied.

"You really want me?"

"Fuck, yes, woman," his voice sounded rough, full of his Dire Wolf.

"Then you're gonna have to prove it, Fido," she said, licking her lips as she slid down his body till her boots hit the floor.

"How?"

"You might be the Alpha, but if I'm your mate, that means I'm one, too. Your Alpha fem. Is that right?"

"Yes. Mine," he grunted.

"Then you're going to have to trust me. Let me live my life, Derrick Rand, Dire Wolf Alpha. Back off and believe me when I say that I can take care of myself."

"It's not an easy ask—"

"I know. That's why it will prove you're the kind of man I can be mated to," she said. "I want a partner, not an owner. I want a man who appreciates me and makes the effort to understand me."

"I'm the only man for you, Lucy Corwyn," he clarified.

"Good. Now, you just have to prove it," she told him and winked before walking out of his office.

If this thing had any chance of working, then Lucy needed him to know she would not be bossed around. She had to be his equal. Sure, it was tempting as hell to just bend over and let him claim her, but she'd witnessed firsthand what happened when sex was used to manipulate a person. Lucy would not fall prey to her own desires.

She wanted Derrick more than she wanted air, but Lucy wanted this to last. She had one shot at making a life with him as his mate, and she was going to fight damn hard to make sure they made it.

She demanded respect. Needed independence. Craved companionship. Wanted to be wanted. And then there was love. She'd never believed in it before, but something about Derrick Rand had Lucy hoping for that one particular miracle.

Mates were supposed to be for life, and Lucy was not about to settle for anything less, regardless of what life had taught her.

Meow.

At least her she-Cat agreed.

CHAPTER SIX

DIRE WOLF MATES

Derrick frowned hard at the sixth fucker who walked up to the back bar, eyeing Lucy like a hungry hyena coveting a lion's kill across the wide expanse of wood before placing an order.

Motherfuckers.

Why the heck had he ever promised to let her take care of herself tonight? She had nothing to prove to him. He knew her she-Cat was fierce and bold. But she was his, dammit. He wanted—*no, he needed*—to protect her. Wanted to provide for her. To keep her safe and secure.

It was ingrained in his DNA, for fuck's sake. He watched as she smiled at the *soon to be dead* asshole, waving a crisp fifty-dollar bill at her while ordering his drink. The dickface tipped it towards her, almost brushing the filthy bill across her ample cleavage, but she snatched it before it made contact, and turned her back on him while hastily stuffing the bill in the tip jar by the cash register.

Good mate. Strong as hell woman. Badass Shifter.

Derrick grinned as he watched her return with the man's drink in hand, and Lucy's brilliant white teeth flashed between her plump pink lips. Immediately, Derrick's thoughts went south. He imagined that mouth wrapped around his cock, how hot and wet she would feel sucking on him. Fuck, he went cross-eyed at the image. He had to adjust his cock in its tight confines. Ordering himself to stop picturing all the things he was going to do to her incredibly fuckable body the second she said yes.

Please be soon.

The strap of her tank top fell off her shoulder as she bent to grab a beer from the cooler for another customer. What the hell was Sheila thinking with those outfits? Obviously, the stack of bills tossed inside the tip jar was what.

Grrrr.

When he'd first seen her in that tiny excuse for a uniform, he almost lost his fucking mind. He knew she was beautiful, had thought so from the second he'd laid eyes on her. She was so petite compared to him and curvy as fuck. Pure sex appeal packed into five-feet, six-inches of purple-eyed passion.

He'd never seen eyes like that on anyone, and Derrick had been around the block more than a few times. Lucy Corwyn was a fucking bombshell with her rounded ass and full breasts, tiny, indented waist, and long, smooth legs.

Her straight glossy hair was thick and dark only at the roots like fresh ground coffee beans, then lightening to gold and platinum at the ends. Her eyes fucking amazing and her mouth, hell, if he thought about that now he'd spend the rest of the night doubled over. Then there was her scent.

Holy. Fuck.

She smelled like heaven to Derrick, light and woody like that perfect moment in a quiet forest just before the sun broke out over the canopy. Sweeter than cherry pie, warmer than a shot of whiskey, his sweet, sassy mate smelled like home to Derrick, and for a Dire Wolf just learning to put down roots, that really meant something.

His beast wanted to roll around in her scent until it covered him. He wanted to stamp himself all over, make sure everyone knew she was taken. She was the perfect culmination of everything he'd ever fantasized about in a female. Strong, sassy, funny, tough as nails, with skin soft as satin, and eyes that floored him.

Her kisses started fires in his blood, and when he'd pressed his body to hers, Derrick was delighted to discover they were a perfect fit. Of course they were. He was dying to really find out, though. Could not wait until they were together, really together.

With anyone else, sex was a formality, a physical need, an urge. With her, it was so much more. Attraction, yes, but it was more than her perfect tits and round ass that called to him. It was her soul, her heart, and that quick witted mind he wanted.

Life was not always kind, and his sweet Lucy had been hurt before. Derrick was going to cherish her, covet her, tend to her every need. He was going to earn her trust and thank the gods every day for delivering her into his arms. She made him want to control his beast. Made him want to be a better man.

For her. Always her. Only her.

Every cell in his body was attuned to her already, and he hadn't even claimed her yet. Licking his lips, he tasted her on the air and frowned as another fucker raised his hand to get her attention. The man's eyes were too greedy, his leer too familiar.

Shit.

Derrick could not afford to blow their opening night by losing his temper. Even Shifters drew the line when it came to fighting in public places. He was blowing hot and cold, his mood changing from wanting to claim his heart-stopping mate, to wanting to murder every single asshole in the bar who even dared to breathe the same air as her.

Grrr.

Fucking fuckety fuck. That skimpy uniform left way too much of her on display. That was it. Derrick was going to kill his cousin for giving Lucy that damn thing. *Fine*—maybe not kill—but he was damn well going to eat every box of whatever fruity cereal his cousin was most likely hoarding in their kitchen. Little she-Wolf thought no one knew they were there because she always double-wrapped them in freezer bags and aluminum foil, but Derrick was a motherfucking Alpha. His sense of scent was superb.

Not only would he snag a bowl for himself, but Derrick was going to tell Cole where they were, too. The younger Wolf loved cereal. Another customer leaned over to whisper into Lucy's ear, and Derrick almost went berserk. His eyes were glued to his mate's perfect face, while every fucking dickhead in the place was staring at her body.

Fucking Sheila.

The she-Wolf definitely did this shit on purpose. He really needed to calm down. The animal was riding him hard, claws popping out every few seconds, and it was all he could do to hold on to his skin while standing there.

Focus on the bar, he told himself.

But his Wolf would not allow him to stray far from Lucy's station. Doomed to failure, he tried looking around to see how the others were progressing. The animal was keen on protecting his territory and his people.

The crowd was good. The local Shifters had sent a fair amount of their kind to see them get started, and as promised, he gave a ten percent discount to all Shifters tonight. The Shifter Council had sent him the names of some local Shifter-run businesses, and they'd responded with generally welcoming replies. Some even promised to send some customers his way. Normally, he'd be looking forward to chatting with a few of their customers, but he was too distracted. The need to mark his mate was overshadowing reason, testing his control to the limit.

He could hardly fathom how she had kept him at bay for two whole days. He'd been worried when she claimed she did not want a mate at all. So fucking glad she'd changed her tune to *prove you want me by trusting me*. Not that that shit was any easier. As if trusting her was the problem—ha! It was the rest of these fuckers Derrick didn't trust.

He turned his head and inhaled a good, deep breath, filtering the different scents to try to get a read on who, *and what,* were occupying his bar. He noted a few Bears from the nearby Barvale Clan, a few Macconwood Pack Wolves, including the men and women in the band he'd hired for the night, and a couple of Tigers from the Maverick Pride.

Sniff.

Mostly, the crowd was comprised of Wolf Shifters. Regular Gray Wolves, not Dire, but those existed in abundance in New Jersey, so that was to be expected. There were also the odd Fox, some Coyotes, a Stallion or two, and was that a Hedgehog? The local Vampire Clan was asked to give the Shifters their space, but Derrick had promised them a *ladies' drink free night* for the following week.

As he took in the crowded room, pride filled him. They'd done a good job with renovations. Every inch of the place gleamed with polish and new paint. The industrial style roadhouse looked both modern and classic, with the newly refinished beams now on display after they'd ripped out the godawful popcorn painted ceilings. Derrick was quite fond of the huge wooden beams and the large iron screws, nuts, and bolts that were now visible.

Coupled with the old barn doors they'd found and repurposed to act as partitions between sections, the gleaming refinished oak floors, and the new paint job, the place looked incredible. The sturdy old bars had been on the verge of destruction in the dusty old relic of a roadhouse before they'd saved them from the mildew and rot that had started to infect them both.

Thor had taken a particular liking to the one in front and insisted they find a way to keep a lot of the original furnishings. Derrick had wondered at the time if it would be worth the huge amount of work, but he was glad he'd went with his Enforcer's suggestion.

They just didn't make bars like that anymore. The original craftsmanship was something to truly wonder at. Plus, they were large and built for use, which was exactly what a bunch of Shifters needed. No dainty glass-topped tables for *Serious Moonlight*. This was Shifter country, even if the normals had no idea. Built to withstand a bunch of rowdy Shifters out to let their hair, *er*, fur, down.

They'd all agreed that the atmosphere should invoke fun, promote social interaction, and give off a generally good vibe. Of course, they expected fights to occur now and then, but it would not be the focus of their establishment. This was their home now.

They installed standing tables only around the dance floor, where a raised stage, featuring the band, had been redone with expert lighting and sound equipment courtesy of their resident tech geek, Phoenix. You could sit and eat, but the dining area closed at ten. After that, there were a couple of dozen stools surrounding the main bar if you wanted to sit and have a drink. Another two dozen were at the back bar.

Where Lucy was stationed.

His mind flitted back to his sexy little unclaimed mate. *Don't go there yet,* he warned himself, and took another wide sweep of the room. Every surface was either gleaming wood, metal, or had a fresh coat of matted cream or black paint. Plain, simple, and neat.

Of course, their logo was another story. Almost garish, truth be told. The bright neon pink sign Sheila had designed and ordered, without asking anyone's opinions, had taken a huge chunk out of the Pack's accounts, and was, of course, non-returnable. Brock and Weylin liked it just fine, thought it added some fun to the otherwise severe appearance out front.

Derrick supposed they'd never get a lot of women inside if the only thing greeting them was the two dozen gleaming Harleys they'd put on display outside. Thor, their acting bouncer, stood at the door, able to keep an eye on the bikes and the crowd easily. Should anything happen, Derrick had absolute faith that he'd notify the rest of them immediately.

His eyes continued sifting through the crowd. Lots of talking, smiles, and drinking, which was good. Drinking meant money, and that meant success. Derrick used a bit of his Alpha powers to locate his Pack mates and the Wolf inside him breathed easier, knowing his people had this.

He watched Sheila work for a little bit. His baby cousin was one hardheaded woman. She'd had a miniature neon *Serious Moonlight* sign made up for behind the main bar, and it was glowing in the otherwise dark atmosphere, washing everything in pink and making everything more appealing somehow. He smirked at her know how.

Combined with the t-shirts and tank tops carrying the logo that she'd insisted the bartenders and cooks wear, Sheila was becoming something of a marketing genius. They were even selling modified t-shirts to customers, and he saw at least three big Bear Shifters wearing them already.

The front bar was crowded with people, normals and Shifters alike, Every single one of them clamoring for drinks, food, or just some attention from his Pack. Sheila worked with a steady hand and a ready smile with Weylin at her side.

Derrick nodded at them, then his gaze traveled, landing on Thor's tattooed, bald head, standing high above the rest. His bulk combined with his almost black eyes, bronzed skin, and close-cropped beard made for one scary as fuck bouncer. Perfect fit for a New Jersey roadhouse. His real title was Enforcer, and Derrick couldn't have chosen a better man for the task either way.

Next, he found Phoenix and Cole on opposite ends of the place. The two were working the crowd, dressed in their best jeans and button downs. They'd insisted they would look more like managers without the pink logo t-shirts. Derrick had agreed, much to their undying happiness and Sheila's annoyance. But they were doing a bang-up job, ushering folks with drinks to empty standing tables and helping other customers to empty spots on the dance floor. Cole was taking food orders back to Brock, his Beta, and head chef. The scent of barbecued wings, ribs, and burgers tinted the air with delicious, savory spices.

"Just enough of an aroma to tempt them to order." Brock explained when installing the expensive and truly excellent ventilation system.

All his people were working together to make this a success, and Derrick was so fucking proud right now. The future looked good as hell from where he was standing. It was what they'd been doing, what they'd done best, for all those years on the road together.

He knew a few of them were unsure about this place, wary of settling down in Blue Valley, but Derrick felt it in his bones. This was it for them. This was home. And that feeling had only grown stronger the moment he'd met Lucy.

Two days had passed, but she was already fitting in with his Pack. She'd joined them for meals and engaged in playful banter with the gang. He'd been nervous about that, worried she might feel uncomfortable being a hybrid she-Cat amongst Wolves. He had yet to see her beastie, and he had to admit, he was dying to do just that.

His gaze flicked over to where she was working, tending bar, and he noticed her laughing at something a customer was saying. She looked good enough to eat with her purple eyes flashing and pink lips tilted up in a welcoming grin. Lucy tossed her head back as she laughed, and her thick, glossy waves made her look like an angel. Unfortunately, he also noticed her customers' eyes flick to the large amount of cleavage on display and his Wolf tensed.

Grrrr.

Eyes narrowed, he walked over. There were more men than women, but that was usually the way with places like this. Roadhouses were notorious for fighting and carousing. Sure, he wanted their place to be known for other things. Like having the best, coldest beer on tap, the highest quality whiskey on hand, and the most delicious, freshest food cooked on site by a professional chef, with live music every night of the week.

However, if that smooth-talking fucker with a death wish didn't stop flirting with his mate, Derrick was going to put *Serious Moonlight* on the map as the first roadhouse in New Jersey to host a vicious murder in view of an entire fucking barroom full of people within three hours of them opening the door.

Mine.

CHAPTER SEVEN

DIRE WOLF MATES

Lucy snuck a peek at Derrick from across the room. He'd been watching her all night. A fact she found as disconcerting as it was sexy. His quietly persuasive, alarmingly powerful aura was unlike any other Shifter's she'd ever met. She knew all too well that males, especially Alpha males, could be a possessive bunch of assholes—to the point of suffocating the happiness right out of a relationship.

Cat Shifters were loners by nature, even if for her, it was more a circumstance kind of thing. Still, she found herself wanting more from life now that she'd met Derrick Rand. Even his name was sexy. Bonus points to him for not letting her down on that front. Could this work?

She'd been mulling it over for two days now, and in Shifter years that was like a month at least, right? The man was an Alpha seemingly loyal and fierce, and even better, he wanted her.

He. Wanted. Her.

No one had ever wanted her as their own before. Not as a friend. Not as family. And certainly not as a mate. She'd been skirting the actual claiming, but even without his bite, she felt the weight of his promise to make her his. His golden eyes followed her, and Lucy's heart sped up so much she thought he must be able to see it pounding through her skimpy little tank top. The bastard grinned, nostrils flaring as if he could smell her need from all the way over there.

Cocky much?

Hell yes, he was and surprise, surprise, Lucy liked it. In fact, she liked just about everything she'd learned about the huge, tattooed male. It was difficult for her, trusting strangers, especially men. Allowing herself to feel safe long enough to create bonds was something she did not think would happen easily for Lucy. And yet, it was happening now. She felt her chest tighten and squeeze when she thought of this Pack and this place.

Typically, she'd be planning her escape right about now. But Lucy did not want to go. Maybe she was warming up to the idea that Derrick was her mate, even if he was still basically a stranger.

We could remedy that tonight.

Her inner beast pushed the thought into her head, and dammit all, she was actually considering it. She could seduce him. It would be easy. He would let her. Yes, he'd already made sure she knew he meant business. But what did she really know about him besides the fact that he was a Dire Wolf Shifter and a biker.

Was he really willing to settle down or would he take off and leave her first chance he got? Her animal was tickled with the idea of having a mate and cubs—furry little traitor purred with delight every time she saw him or felt him near. But her human side was still uncertain.

What did fear ever get you?

Lucy bit her lip. It was too fast, but she knew that's how it happened sometimes. For the lucky ones, anyway. But when had she ever been lucky? No. Screw that. Lucy stomped down those negative thoughts and focused on pouring beer and whiskey. Reading the label on the bottle in her hand, she smirked.

Of course, a Shifter bar would have *Bite* on hand. The handcrafted artisanal whiskey was distilled by Mason Lane, a Wolf Shifter over in Maccon City. Lucy had heard all about him from some Wolves over in the seaside town a few summers back. She'd been passing through, as usual.

Always looking in from the outside.

Morbid thoughts were not welcome tonight, so she pushed it aside and made the next drink. Lucy approved of the label. *Bite* was some damn fine whiskey. It came in several flavors and had fun little names to go with. Now she poured a second shot of *Winter Bite* into a glass for her customer. The guy was with a friend, a relative probably, and they were both sinfully good looking, but Lucy found she only had eyes for one Wolf.

One very large, pretty pissed off Wolf, who was heading her way, looking like he was about to break something or someone in two. She turned her head to the two good-looking strangers and winced. Someone was about to have a new asshole torn in his backside.

"Thank you so much, babe. I think maybe you should gimme your number so we can talk, hang out, what do you say?" the guy asked.

Lucy sniffed. Oh fuck, this was not good. The man was Wolf, and he was leaning over the bar. Too close now, but he was a smart fucker, cocking his head as he read her tank top aloud.

"Serious Moonlight? Catchy name."

"Yeah, it is. Um, stay on that side of the bar, please," she responded noncommittally.

"Oh yeah? That an insurance thing?" he asked, winking at his buddy while he tapped the bar for her to pour another round.

"Uh, yes? I mean, probably," she muttered, following Derrick's angry stride.

Fuck. Fuck. Fuck.

"You're new to town, right? Come on, babe, gimme your number," he said, giving her a wide grin that must have melted hearts wherever he went. The dog.

"Yeah, I came into town a little while ago, but no on the number. Sorry, pal."

"Can't date your customers, huh? You know, this is a nice place and all, but I know another bar you can work where that sort of thing is allowed. Want me to make a call, I will, babe."

"No, thank you. I'm fine."

"You sure, cause I think you're missing out—"

"Everything alright here, Lucy?" a deep, familiar voice asked.

"Fine, Derrick, thank you," she replied, eyebrows raised.

She could see his control wavering and had to applaud his attempts to follow her request to allow her to handle things herself. The stranger took one look at Derrick's bright gold gaze and dropped his shot on the table like it was hot. She could not blame him. Dominance rolled off him in waves, even the humans who did not know Shifters existed seemed to want to move away from him. Fight or flight instinct was a real thing, and anyone with half a brain felt the urge to run from Derrick Rand.

"Enjoying yourself?" he growled the question at the Wolf.

The stranger narrowed his eyes at Lucy, then tried to meet Derrick's stare, but dropped his gaze after three seconds.

"Uh, yeah. You are?"

"Derrick Rand. I run things here."

"Oh. Nice. We heard you all were settling down," the Wolf said, looking uncomfortable as he tracked Derrick's golden gaze to Lucy, then back again. His buddy idled up to him, a blank expression on his face.

"Hi, I'm Jordan. This is Zeke."

"Nice to meet you, I'm Derrick. This is Lucy."

The silky, deep, possessive notes in Derrick's reply had hit a cord straight in her heart. The *my* before her name was implied, and she couldn't help the quick twerk of her lips upwards at the thought. The way his golden eyes washed over her had her heart beating double time before he turned and settled his stare on the now grinning stranger.

"Looks great in here," the Wolf named Jordan said. "I work at The Thirst Dog over in Maccon City. My boss wanted to wish you all good luck, but he's home with the wife and kids tonight. Family game night."

"Tell him thanks. Have a beer on me?"

"Sure, bro," Jordan grinned.

Derrick asked Lucy for three beers, and she grabbed some cold long necks of a good, old fashioned American lager, no crafty IPA shit.

"Cheers," Zeke mumbled, lifting his beer to his lips.

He gave Lucy one sad look, like she was this missed opportunity, but she just shrugged. Her heart belonged to someone else, and it was about damn time she faced it. The three Wolves remained at her station while she served other customers, and she couldn't help the thrill of knowing Derrick remained close to her because he wanted her. It was quite a feeling, being wanted. Lucy liked it.

A pretty and sophisticated looking woman sauntered up to the trio, placing a possessive hand on Jordan's shoulder. With a knowing smile, she turned that pretty face to Derrick, and fuck, Lucy was not prepared for the size of the green-eyed monster that roared to life.

"You must be Derrick Rand," the woman said, offering him her hand.

She was a very pretty woman. But Lucy's jealousy was totally unnecessary. Her name was Isa, and she smelled like magic. She was also Jordan's very claimed and very happy mate.

Nice.

"I have to tell you, this place is freaking awesome," Isa said.

"The Thirsty Dog is pretty exceptional too, but it has a different vibe. As does Bar None in Barvale. Between the three of us, I think we'll be giving folks like us some diversity when it comes to hanging out and letting loose. Besides, a little healthy competition is good, don't you agree?" Jordan grinned at the question.

"I can see that, but how would we track how we're doing?" Derrick asked.

"Well, Wade Kettle, he's the owner of Bar None, and Mike run a monthly poker game. Sometimes trusted staff joins in, like me, and we talk shit and talk cross promoting each other's places. It's a lot of testosterone and horse foolery, but it clears the air and settles the animal, if you know what I mean," he murmured.

"I do, thank you. I would be happy to join."

"Awesome, I will tell Mike."

"Thank you for a wonderful time," Isa said, waving to Lucy who nodded at the stunning female.

"Yeah, man, good luck with the new place and, uh, other things," Zeke muttered, looking miserable.

The Wolf was not smiling as much as he was earlier, but he still dropped a fifty on the bar, and gave Lucy a wave that he cut short once Derrick growled softly in his throat.

Beast of a Wolf. But so totally hot.

The three Macconwood Wolves stood to leave, and Lucy lost track of Derrick for a moment. The bar was busy, flooded with new customers, and she had work to do. She moved about, flipping bottles and catching them before pouring out drinks for the thirsty crowd. Shifter reflexes were awesome for this kind of thing. That and she wasn't tired standing on her feet for nearly nine hours straight. Her antics with the bottles earned her a few more twenties in the tip jar. But she frowned at the growing pile.

Weird. She should be thrilled. Lucy needed the money to fix her car, but the idea was to leave once she paid for the repairs. Suddenly, that didn't strike her as a good thing.

Stay. Stay. Stay, her she-Cat begged.

"*Cocktail* fan?" Derrick asked.

Somehow, the giant man had managed to sneak up behind her after she'd finished pouring a couple of shots of *Cinnamon Bite* for a group of young Shifter females. Lucy half-smiled and handed the shots over to the trio, who did not bother to leave a tip.

Bitches.

"Hey there, handsome. Wanna do a round?" one of them asked Derrick.

Lucy was going to rip this female's head off if she didn't back the fuck up off her man. Derrick replied noncommittally, but that was not enough to sate her angry she-Cat. The young she-Wolves were all thin and good looking, eyeing Derrick like he was a chocolate buffet, for fuck's sake.

A snarl escaped her lips, and she felt her claws extend before she could stop them. Derrick placed both big hands on her hips and pulled her back into him. The feel of his hard, muscular body at her back calmed her inner beastie. She leaned back into him, loving the way his scent enveloped her. Her inner animal purred happily.

Good mate, offering us comfort and reassurance.

Lucy did not disagree.

"Um, yeah," she replied to his earlier question. "I watched three Tom Cruise movies on a constant rotation when I was a cub. All we had was this TV/VCR combo and only the VCR part worked. Mom got us the movies at a flea market," she replied, offering him some insight into her life.

If he really wanted her, he should know what he was getting. Lucy was not fancy. She was not educated past high school, and she had little experience at much except running. She was a hard worker, though, and she was honest.

Shame was not something she felt very often, and her past had never been in her control. She shrugged off him, uncomfortable with the way she missed his touch almost instantly.

"You sure about this?"

Lucy turned her back on him, determined to keep him from seeing the way he affected her.

"Lucy, I have never been more certain of anything in my life," he drawled in that deliciously low growl of his—*the one that seemed to always conjure moisture between her legs.*

Fuuuck.

Wet panties again. Just for that she turned around, pressed her body into him as she reached for a bottle of something behind him. Her breasts were smushed against his hard torso, and Derrick stiffened—*everywhere.*

For the first time, the Alpha looked unsure about what to do next.

With a hint of a smile on her face, Lucy slowly raised herself high on her tiptoes, her nose brushed along the side of his neck, and she did something that shocked the shit out of her. She opened her mouth and bit down slightly, teasing him before turning quickly to pour a shot.

She didn't have a customer waiting. This one was just for her. And as she tossed it back, he grabbed her hips, slamming her back against him. Fuck, she loved this. Loved the feel of his big, strong body, his giant, hard as steel cock pulsing against her ass.

Somehow, he'd moved them over to the side where no one could see them, and she thanked the gods for it. Derrick's mouth was on her neck now, and she was purring, actually purring out loud at the feelings he was creating inside her body. They shot through her like lightning strikes. He was sucking on her neck in earnest now, a steady growl reverberating from his chest straight through her back. He was so much bigger than her, but somehow, they fit as he ground his cock against her ass.

Suck, lick, kiss, bite, bite, bite.

He was making her dizzy with his attentions, and Lucy loved every second of it. She wanted him so damn badly. Wanted his kiss, his cock, his bite. All of it. All of him.

Her she-Cat demanded she get her ass in gear. Pushing back against him, rubbing herself on the massive hardness she felt right alongside of her cloth-covered cheeks, Lucy told him without words she was ready.

Derrick growled with his mouth over her neck. He held her there before dropping the skin, kissing it gently and holding her close while he tried to gain control of his breathing. He stilled her movements with arms like steel bands, wrapping them tightly around her waist.

"You're driving me crazy, woman," he grunted and dipped his head, catching her earlobe with his teeth. He tugged on the sensitive skin, and she moaned helplessly.

"Fuck, kitten, if you don't stop those noises, I'll have you right fucking here in front of the whole damn world. I'll claim you now,

Lucy, and an audience won't even slow me down," he growled, sounding tortured, and she stilled.

Shit.

He really was holding on by a thread, and as much as she wanted him, Lucy was not into fucking in front of crowds. Her whole body tensed with a need she had never felt for the big, warm, sexy Wolf. Heat seemed to exude from him like a furnace, wrapping around her and keeping her warm. The deep, powerful rumbling coming from his chest vibrated through her body, and she could almost imagine how good it would feel if he did that with his head between her legs.

"Be good," he grunted, and bit her earlobe again. She could hear the teasing note in his voice and breathed easier, knowing the real danger had passed.

"That was the most erotic thing I've ever felt, Derrick," she whispered.

"Keep on teasing me, kitten. It's gonna make things so much better when I finally claim you," he growled, and she heard the promise in his voice clear as day.

He bit her again, harder this time, but not enough to break her skin. Her animal loved the nip, and her body reacted to it as well, swelling with need, growing wetter by the second. She groaned as his tongue laved the spot he'd bitten, soothing the delicious hurt.

Lucy looked in the mirror behind the bar at the picture they made, hiding, and making out in the far corner. He was behind her, holding her like she was something precious, eyes glowing gold and chest rumbling with his beast. Tattooed arms held her, and fuck, was he sexy. His whole body was a work of art. The intricately detailed design of his tats uniquely beautiful. She wanted to trace each one with her hands and tongue.

Lucky Lucy. The Fates had given her a king, and in that moment, she wanted desperately to be his queen. She wanted to learn everything about him, memorize every inch of his body, stamp herself on his heart. She wanted to make him a part of her, become part of him.

Lucy froze, this level of intensity scared her. She'd never been this needy, this desperate for someone. Even so, that enormous wall she'd built around her heart so long ago seemed to crumble and crack a little bit more with every second she spent with Derrick Rand.

At this rate, she'd be bending over for him by the time they closed the bar. Then she would be at his mercy. He would have power over her no man had ever had, and Lucy was terrified. She wanted to move away from him, but couldn't go. Her last chance to save herself from the agony that had destroyed her mother was slipping away, and she was scared to death.

"I won't hurt you, Lucy. Let me satisfy you, darlin', we both know I am the only one who can. Tonight, let me claim you tonight," he begged.

Lucy closed her eyes, wanting to give in with everything she had. But what happened after? When he grew tired of her, and realized she was no match for a powerful Dire Wolf like him? The thought chilled her, and Lucy found the strength to push off him. His arms dropped, and he expelled a harsh breath. She was hurting them both and hated herself for it.

"No."

"Lucy—"

"No," she repeated, and nodded at a sour looking man who appeared to be waiting for a drink.

"Can I help you?"

"You one of them, aren't you? For years I been tellin' folks to watch the woods. We got animals here. People-animals. Like you," the nasty man spat in her direction.

He stunk of booze, fear, anger, and hatred. The combination hit her in the face like a slap, and Lucy flinched.

"Sir, I think you've had enough—"

"Ain't taking no backtalk from a stinkin' animal," he slurred. He was about forty with a heavy paunch and a week's worth of stubble. "Can't lie to me, girly. I worked as a guard for a top secret research facility until they canned me a month ago for taking some pictures home with me. Had to prove it to my wife, see," he mumbled, and Lucy backed up another step.

Secret research? Animals? Fuck, this did not sound good.

"Okay, mister, I think you better leave now," Lucy stated firmly.

"Yeah, you are one o' them, ain't you? I saw you letting that big freak over there grope you by the wall. You think I couldn't tell? Freaks, all o' you. Fucking animal whore—"

Lucy backed up at the man's violent outburst, but what really had her in shock was Derrick. He'd somehow vaulted over the bar and had the human by the collar of his shirt and off the ground. With one shake of his head Thor ambled over and took hold of the man.

"You think you can just come in town and take over with your sluts? Freaking animals! All of you!"

The man's yell was cut off by Derrick's threatening growl. A few customers had stopped drinking, watching the scene with glowing eyes and she exhaled as they made a wall around them. Keeping the Shifter secret was an important part of their world, but somehow this human had stumbled on them. Lucy did not know who needed to be called in, but if the government had research facilities involving Shifters, the Council should be told.

"What should I do with him, boss?" asked Thor.

The Dire Wolf was even bigger than Derrick, angrier, more menacing somehow. He was the biggest man Lucy had ever seen. Even so, there was no doubt about who was in charge. Derrick was the Alpha. He glared angrily at the drunk, then leaned over and whispered something into Thor's ear. The male nodded and took the drunk outside to be dealt with.

The crowd around them resumed their revelry, and the band played on. Most of the customers didn't seem to notice anything wrong. Folks were still drinking, snacking on wings and pretzels, and those on the dance floor kept on moving.

Good, she'd hate a fight to ruin their opening night. This Pack had worked so hard and deserved to succeed. Lucy watched Derrick's back as he stood guard in front of the bar. She noted a few other men sneaking off, leaving almost immediately after that jerk had been thrown out, and she knew her mate had taken care of it.

Good Alpha. Good mate.

She wondered briefly what would happen to him, but trusted Derrick implicitly to keep her, his Pack, and their secret safe. Lucy could not afford to spend loads of time on it. She had work to do. People were thirsty and the crowd only got bigger, but nothing she couldn't handle alone. Not that she had the chance to find out, since Derrick wouldn't leave.

He stayed and worked right alongside her. A fact that surprised and pleased her, though she would never admit it. Every second together, the sexy Alpha was chipping away at her armor.

Chip, chip, chip.

"I can handle this," she whispered, knowing full well he could hear her even with the music.

"I know you can, kitten." Derrick winked. Lucy's irritation rose over his manhandling, but, if she were being honest, it kind of tickled her pink bits too.

Sexy, caring, protective man.

For the next couple of hours, they worked side by side, taking orders, cleaning glasses, opening bottles. He was no slacker. She'd give him that. He kept the ice coolers full and did all the heavy lifting. He restocked the beer, carried another case of whiskey, and unloaded the dishwasher before she could ask.

Lucy's inner animal huffed a breath and rolled over where she rested in that metaphysical plane until Lucy needed her. It was clear then that her animal was done with her. Until her human half accepted the fact that this Wolf was her mate, her animal would be discordant.

Dammit. Was it getting hot in here?

She felt her temperature spike and her stomach tighten. Dizziness threatened to make her wobble, but before she could fall, she felt something firm and strong wrap around her arm. A second later, something cold and hard was pushed into her hand.

"Sit. Drink," came the crisp order, and Lucy's eyes narrowed.

She was not going to obey him like one of his damn Pack. He could take that glass of, *wait*, what was it? She opened her eyes against the headache that was beginning to form and looked down. Her rant stopped immediately. Lucy's heart squeezed, and she found herself fighting back a gasp.

Oh, no, he didn't. Yep, he did.

He'd poured her a tall glass of iced sweet tea with a curl of apple hanging from the rim. It was beautiful. It was perfect. It was her favorite drink. All the wind left her sails, and she sunk down on the stool he pushed underneath her.

"Take a break, kitten. The crowd's thinning out. I'll handle last call."

Well, damn, she thought, and brought the glass to her lips.

The cool liquid slid down her throat and quieted the fire that was starting in her blood. This was the first sign of her heat. It was coming on sooner than she'd thought. The question was, would she be strong enough to take what came with it?

Would Lucy be strong enough to let the Alpha of the Dire Wolf Pack claim her?

Yessssss, her she-Cat hissed.

Eeeep!

CHAPTER EIGHT

DIRE WOLF MATES

Derrick frowned as he listened to his mate pacing around in the bedroom upstairs. A week had passed since the bar had opened, and as usual, they closed at three o'clock. Instead of staying to clean with the rest of the Pack, he'd left Brock in charge, and hauled Lucy on home.

Home.

The word sounded right, but his animal was not feeling it yet. It could be a real home at long last, if only the sassy little feline would accept his claim already.

Fuck.

He was losing his mind. Yes, she had only known him for a couple of weeks, but his beast knew the second he'd seen her, she was his. It was driving his Wolf insane, being so close, and shoved in the corner. Her refusal to acknowledge they were fated to be together was breaking him.

Patience. Be patient. Be worthy of her.

It was difficult, but he had no choice. He needed her. Doubts assailed him whenever he got this bad, and even now he wondered if he could be wrong. Maybe Lucy didn't feel the pull, the bond, not like he did.

No.

That couldn't be true. His Dire Wolf snarled. He was impatient, but he was completely sure Lucy Corwyn was his one and only. Sassy, pigheaded, smart, funny, beautiful, infuriating, perfect, gorgeous, sexy ass woman. Fuck, he loved her.

Feeling it, and admitting it, were two different things, but right then, he had no choice. He loved her, exasperating little tidbit that she was. They had a working garage and a top class mechanic right there, but did she listen? No. She'd insisted on keeping her car at that damn human pervert's garage instead of letting him bring it here. Kept right on ignoring him about everything and anything until he thought he would lose his damn mind.

Furniture moved, and she whimpered softly, but he still heard her. Fuck. She was not going to make it through tonight. He felt it. His animal had been attuned to her every molecule, and it was just getting worse. He'd made some calls, found out about feline Shifters, and knew the hell that was coming for his sweet Lucy.

Feline Shifters experienced a different kind of heat cycle than others. More intense, designed to propagate the species. Sometimes, the pain was so intense, it caused females to accept males they would never look at otherwise. The thought made Derrick furious. He would kill anyone who touched a hair on his mate's head without her consent. Himself included.

I am fucked. So fucked.

The scent of her incoming heat cycle had grown each minute they spent together. As a male Dire Wolf, the closest he would ever come to that was the *mating fever*. It was a compulsion, a biological imperative that would soon take over rational thought and any semblance of reason. Mating fever threatened to consume him, but he was fighting it.

Things were so intense between him and Lucy right now, the rest of the Pack had taken to going out for long rides on their bikes after their shifts, trying to give them space. The rides were hard on them, the open road calling, but every day, they came back. His Pack was trying to settle, but instead of being there for them, he was caught up in his own battle of wills.

His Changes were out of control. Man to beast and back again. He could not go a few hours without shifting into his massive black Dire Wolf, something unheard of for most Shifters. But trying to control his animal, like his emotions, was like trying to keep a tidal wave from hitting the shore.

Please, Lucy, he begged inside his mind's eye.

He saw more than she knew. Understood her reticence was partly because of a childhood she could not control. Trust issues were bound to be a problem, but he could only hope by being steadfast she'd see he was in it for the long haul. She was not getting rid of Derrick. No way, no how.

Stopping his Wolf from taking what the beast already saw as his was hard fucking work. But Derrick was not kidding when he said he would never harm a hair on her head. He would never trick or force her into accepting him. That was not the way he wanted to claim her. No, he wanted her to come to him, ready and willing. Not forced by some side effect of their supernature, she could not even begin to manage.

In his hand, he held something he'd had to search long and hard for. An elixir, a potion, of sorts, he'd learned about from Thor and his contacts with the Guardians of Chaos. That elite group of Shifter warriors had a calling all their own, but among them was a Witch and scientist who'd developed an agent that could theoretically stop or stifle a female Shifter's heat cycle.

Derrick was uncertain about it, but he trusted Thor. He knew what he had to do, and as he listened to her moving upstairs, her discomfort loud though she tried to be quiet. No more stalling, his Wolf snarled and chomped inside his mind's eye. The huge, prehistoric Wolf's instinct was to be everything his mate needed, and that meant claiming her before her heat began.

No. We will give her the choice.

Derrick heard the stories. If he denied her during her heat, she would suffer immeasurable pain, and there was no way he could do that. Already his feelings echoed with love and complete devotion for his Lucy. Crazy or not, it was just the way he was built. And every inch of him, heart included, was built for her.

His hands clenched tightly at his sides, Derrick was aware of her every move as he stalked her to the bedroom he'd originally claimed as his own. He hoped they could make it theirs together, but he could wait. For her, he would wait forever.

He never expected to be this caught up in her, but it was out of his realm of control. Not something an Alpha could admit easily. The sound of one of the other bedroom doors opening broke his concentration, and he turned to find his cousin waiting, staring at the floor.

"I came to apologize for the uniform and other things this week, you know," Sheila said, and he could tell from her scent she meant it. "I didn't mean nothing by it, Derrick, just thought maybe you needed a little prodding."

"Thank you, Sheila. Unnecessary though. But I don't need any prodding. I know what I want, and I will get there. You don't need to help me, cousin."

"Alright, I guess, I'm just kind of hopeful now that you've found the one. I mean, she's really your mate, right?"

Big green eyes met his for a flash before she averted them in reverence to his position and dominance.

"Yes," he said, and fierce pride filled him with the admission. "She's my mate."

"Then what are you waiting for?"

Derrick thought carefully before speaking, his eyes riveted to the door that kept Lucy separated from him for the moment.

"She needs time, Sheila. I'm going to do everything I can to give it to her."

"Why don't you go for a run? I can keep watch," Sheila offered.

"That's not a bad idea. Might help me expel some of this energy.

Will you give this to her? It's supposed to help with her heat," he murmured, handing the vial to Sheila.

It was probably best if he did not see her right now. Once whiff of her delicious scent, and his animal might wrest control from him. Derrick refused to do that to her. He wanted her so badly, but only when she was ready. Not one second before.

"I will," Sheila said, taking it from him. "You know, you are going to make a wonderful mate."

Outside the Pack house, Derrick growled. He felt on edge and angsty, knowing his mate was inside and about to imbibe a potion to stop something he wanted to revel in. That made him a selfish prick, but he could not help it. He wanted to see her through her heat cycle. To be there to sate her every need and desire. To put a cub inside her belly.

Fuck. He got hard just picturing her swollen with his young. A little feline that looked just like her would be his choice. Derrick had only seen her Shifted once, and the female had knocked his socks off. She had soft, gold fur and gorgeous violet eyes. So sleek and majestic, powerful though petite. He fucking loved her animal, wished she could run with him tonight.

Tucking away his human skin, Derrick shifted into his midnight black Dire Wolf with hardly any effort. His change was so quick, he moved from skin to fur in the blink of an eye. His pile of clothing rested next to the largest pine in the woods behind their house, and he gazed over at it, checking to make sure all was right. He lifted his lupine head towards the room where Lucy was.

Safe. Inside. Mine.

Turning around, he prepared to run. His Alpha Wolf ready to scout the area, make sure it was secure for his mate and his Pack. It was another one of those Dire Wolf things, an instinct as old as time to care for and protect what was his.

The property they'd bought was bigger than he'd hoped for, with almost five acres' worth of land surrounding them. Putting their mark on all three structures, the house, bar, and garage had settled something in his beast, and over the past few weeks, he and his Pack had roamed these woods and marked the lands that belonged to them, warding off any other predators in the area of the wild and supernatural persuasion.

Security was extremely important to Derrick and his Pack. They'd had run-ins before with other supernaturals who thought taking on a Pack of beasts as powerful as Dire Wolves would give them some sort of up in the paranormal world. The problem was, there were not many who could take on a full grown Dire Wolf and live to talk about it. As he'd gotten older, Derrick had found he'd lost the taste for blood and vengeance. He had nothing to prove to anyone.

His black Wolf took off at a run, leaping over the roots and rocks that littered this part of the forest floor. It was early spring, and though the days were pleasant, the nights were cold. But the wind felt good against his thick, dark fur, and Derrick relished running through it.

His animal refused to stray far from the house, knowing his mate was inside, Even with Sheila's reassurance that she would stand guard, Derrick wasn't comfortable leaving Lucy for long. He imagined it would get worse after he claimed her.

When? Soon. Soon. Soon. Please soon.

Shaking his impatience off, Derrick leaned down to drink the cool, clear water that bubbled from a small brook a few hundred yards behind his house. Lions roamed the other side of his property, but this watering hole was used by both. A neutral ground they'd agreed upon after he'd met with the Blue Valley Pride's own Lion king.

Interesting times, he mused as the refreshing liquid slid down, soothing his beast's throat. The constant growling ever since he'd met Lucy was the reason for the ache there and the water felt good, healing the mild hurt he couldn't help inflicting on himself. But there was only one thing that could soothe the fire inside his blood.

Lucy.

Just thinking her name seemed to conjure that wildly enticing scent of hers as if by magic. He closed his eyes and took a moment to savor the fragrance. His chest rumbled and Derrick felt as if he were being watched. Eyes snapping open, he turned in the direction of something rustling in the brush behind him. Then he came face to face with the cutest damn thing he ever saw.

Lucy's she-Cat slunk forward, bathed in moonlight, her fur glowing in golds and platinum. His lupine eyes memorized her in an instant. From the tips of her pointed ears to her short, powerful legs, cute, stubby tail, and razor-sharp, claw-tipped paws—*she was beautiful.*

The thing he loved most was her eyes. They glowed bright like amethysts in the darkness. He could not believe she was really there, with him, in her fur. Lucy approached with the same air of regality she maintained on two legs, and he chuffed appreciatively as he watched her smooth gait. Purring loudly, she shocked the shit out of him when she rubbed her smaller body along his left flank.

Derrick's Dire Wolf froze. He stood there soaking in the pleasure of her presence while she continued to mark him with her scent. Unsure of what to do next, he waited for her lead. He did not want the meeting to end. So, he remained still and quiet, allowing her animal to sniff and rub and swipe her rough tongue over his snout until she lay before him and closed her eyes. Derrick's Wolfen gaze blazed gold with pleasure at the ease with which her animal half seemed to accept him.

He only wished her human side was as accommodating. Then again, maybe not. There wasn't a thing he would change about her. Lucy was perfect as she was.

Derrick watched her, wondering what he should do next, wishing she would tell him, but he needn't have bothered. With her next breath, Lucy's form began to twitch and shimmer with that same familiar magic all Shifters used to merge back and forth from fur to skin. Naked and bare in front of him, she waited a beat, purple eyes still glowing before reaching forward and touching her warm hands to his fur.

"You're so big," she whispered. "Much larger than any of the Wolves I've ever seen before."

At that his Wolf growled, and she smiled, a small sound that seemed to shock her as it escaped her lips.

"No need to get jealous. You're much more handsome, too. So strong and soft. So beautiful. I heard you, you know. When you were talking to Sheila."

So that was it, he mused, and allowed her to continue petting and stroking his fur. She'd been listening when his cousin had approached to speak to him.

"Will you turn back for me?"

It was all the invitation he needed. One second, he was his Wolf, the next, he was a man. Fuck, she was stunning, and he could not help himself, he had to touch her.

"Did you get the potion?" he asked, unsure what else to say.

"I did."

"You know, I left to give you space, Lucy. Following me out here is making me think all sorts of things, so tell me now if I have it wrong," he whispered, baring his soul as he ran his fingertips lightly down her forearm. Fuck, she was so soft.

"I got the potion, Derrick. But I didn't take it," she whispered, eyes going to half-mast as he traced the curve of her elbow next.

"Lucy, if you want to wait still—" he tried to warn her, hearing his voice raw and rough with his animal. Fuck, it was barely more than a growl, even to his own ears. Husky and deep, ripe with need, as he took in her luscious body in all its glory.

"It was the most thoughtful thing anyone has ever done for me," she explained, and her eyes swelled with tears. "You tried to help me keep my power. You could have forced the decision, using my heat to stake your claim, but instead you found a way to quell it."

"I didn't mean to overstep, darlin', but I couldn't bear to think of you in pain, he confessed, heart breaking at the sight of her tears.

"You didn't overstep. You did good, Derrick. So fucking good, and I am damn lucky you're mine."

"What are you saying?" he asked, fearing to hope.

"I'm saying I've got no secrets left, Derrick. You've completely surprised me at every turn. When I expect you to act one way, you go and do something else. You've been patient, caring, understanding, and I want—" she paused, stuttering, and wiping her face.

"What do you want, Lucy? I'll give it to you. Anything you want, darlin', it's yours," he vowed.

"I want the impossible. I know you and I are mates, I can feel it, my Cat can too, but I did not want to do this because of my heat cycle. I wanted to make the choice," she said, and he could see the vulnerability clear as day in her violet gaze.

"I gave you the potion, take it, and the choice is yours, Lucy. I know my choice. My Wolf chooses you, and so do I."

"Even if you don't know everything about me?"

"I know all I need to. You're honest and loyal, tenacious too. You don't take handouts, and you've worked for everything you have. You're sassy, badass, and I fucking love your hybrid Cat. You're beautiful, kitten. You are the sexiest woman I have ever seen. Your body, your lips, your hair. And those incredible eyes. They slay me every time," he said, going for broke now.

"I want your eyes to be the first thing I see every morning, the last before I go to bed, and when I am done with this world, I want those eyes to be the last thing I ever see. I am yours for the taking, Lucy. You own me. Looking at you is heaven, but breathing you in, touching your petal soft skin, is pure ecstasy."

"Derrick," she moaned his name.

"Lucy, I'm about half mad to have you. Go now, take the potion, I'll wait. However long it takes. I will wait," he promised.

"What if you get tired of waiting?"

The cool grass felt good against his heated body as he raised her face by her chin. He wanted her to look at him when he said what he had to next.

"I mean it. I will wait as long as you need me to. But know this, I know my own heart, Lucy. I *love* you. I *need* you. I *want* you. Only you. Whatever is going on in that pretty head of yours, understand this. I *know* you, Lucy."

He held her chin when she would've turned her head, firmly yet gently, between his thumb and forefinger. Truth time.

"I know you've never had a real home. I've got that in common with you. I know you've never had a Pack or people you can trust. I know you've never trusted a man before, but I swear here and now, in front of the whole damn world, if you take that risk, if you trust me, I will be your home, Lucy."

"Dammit, Derrick," she gasped, but he was relentless. He needed to get this out, needed her to listen.

"If you stay with me, if you have faith in us, I will be everything you need. I'm it, darlin'. I'm your home," he growled.

"That's what I'm afraid of. You'll be my whole world and if you leave, what will I have?" She ducked her head back down, and he wanted to burn her doubts to the ground, kill whoever it was that made her feel this way.

"I can't say I will never hurt you, because I'm bound to fuckup, but I swear it won't ever be intentionally. I will never leave you, Lucy. I couldn't. It would be like cutting off my own leg. We are fated mates. You would know if I was lying. I can't lie to you, kitten. I love you, Lucy. I want to claim you as my mate, take you as my own if and when you will let me. But first, let's get one thing clear, when I say I am your home, you need to understand, you are mine too. And I will always fight for my home."

"Yeah?" Her whispered question stroked his skin like hands ghosting over his soul.

"Yes," he said, and pushed his will into the word, unable to resist trying to make her feel the strength of his vow.

"Alright. Yes."

"What?" He almost couldn't believe what he was hearing, then she smiled.

"I said yes, Derrick. No potions. No more waiting. Yes. My answer is yes."

"Yes?"

"What are you waiting for, Alpha?" She smiled and bit her lip.

Passion and hunger exploded inside of Derrick's blood. He reached out, his Wolf right there with him, as he stroked the rose petal soft skin of her throat and face with trembling hands before lowering his head and crashing his lips to hers.

"Open your mouth," he commanded, dipping inside the hot cavern and penetrating the warmth with his tongue in a mimicry of what his body longed to do.

He eased between her legs, bearing down on her with all his weight, yet careful not to crush her. This was everything good and right with the world. He knew when he'd come here, this place was for him. Felt it in his bones that he was somehow meant to be there. With the forest floor as their bed, the grass cushioning her body beneath his, Derrick was finally about to make Lucy his. He couldn't have pictured a more perfect landscape for their first time.

Lucy's eyes widened and he could read astonishment and apprehension as his sex came into contact with hers. More than that, she was afraid. He realized, and it dawned on him that his sassy little mate was not used to this kind of intimacy.

Made him wonder what kind of men she'd known before, but he quickly shut the thought down. As far as his Wolf was concerned, she was his period. No one came before and nothing else mattered. Just the two of them. Lucy whimpered, and he made sure she was looking at him before he spoke.

"You think this will be over fast and easy, I see it in your face," he whispered as he dropped kisses along her throat, then looked up to meet her gaze. "You're wrong, kitten. I want you to get used to my weight, to feel how this is going to be. I want your body to know mine before I take you."

"You're so big, Derrick," she said, as if it were a secret. He smiled against her mouth, savoring her precious innocence.

"I promise I will never hurt you like this," he whispered, and he took her mouth with his, kissing her until she softened beneath him.

"You're gonna beg for me before you get me," the huskiness of his voice penetrated the night air.

"Cocky," she whimpered, but already she was unfurling beneath him.

So responsive. So sexy. So mine.

Born from the same desire that had clouded his mind the last few days, sheer delight and tender amusement flowed through him at her innocent whispers and soft hands. Understanding dawned and the prehistoric animal he shared his soul with howled against the night sky. Imagine, under all that sass, his little she-Cat was demure and shy. His Wolf growled deep inside the recesses of his mind, his every Alpha instinct demanding he mark and claim her now. He would wait not one second longer.

Mine.

CHAPTER NINE

DIRE WOLF MATES

When Sheila knocked on her bedroom door after Derrick had left, Lucy did not know what to think. She had heard their whole conversation. Knew about the potion he'd procured for her. Her heart had almost trampled her body to death when he'd vowed to give her all the time she needed.

"You did that on purpose?" Lucy asked Sheila.

"Yes, but not to butt in. Derrick is my cousin, Lucy, but he is also the Alpha. What he feels affects us all, and he's been on edge. So, I want to know, are you gonna put him and us out of our misery? Are you gonna let him claim you?"

"Yes," she'd said, knowing full well she was. Sheila handed her the vial and Lucy looked at it in her hands. It seemed so small, but the gesture was huge.

"Yes, I am going to let him claim me. And I am going to claim that big man right back," she proclaimed, and wondered what the hell she was waiting for.

"Lucy!" Sheila had screamed when she opened the second-story bedroom window and vaulted out.

She looked up and laughed at the stunned Dire Wolf female. Sheila looked horrified, but Lucy just laughed.

"Cat's always land on our feet," she chided, then grabbed the hem of her nightgown and tossed it over her head, shifting from skin to fur in an instant.

Seemed forever ago, but it was only minutes. Now, she was here, with him, her almost-mate, in their makeshift forest bed. Lucy's entire body was a shivering mass of nerves. She felt new, untried, and totally at his mercy. But to her utter shock and delight, Lucy trusted him to take care of her.

She couldn't quiet the moans and pants escaping her lips as Derrick pressed his immense body onto hers, crushing her into the soft cool grass with all his delicious weight. Her she-Cat hissed and clawed inside of her, wanting to take part in this mating dance they were beginning. But what did she know about claiming a mate? For the first time in her life, she was trusting herself with someone else. Derrick was kind and good, and hers. All hers. Her instincts demanded she let him steer the way, and once she gave herself over to his control, she knew she'd been right.

"So beautiful," he growled, kissing her with deep, deliberate strokes of his tongue.

There were no half-ways or maybes about it as he plundered her mouth and ran his rough hands over her skin. Lucy couldn't hide behind her sassy mouth here. She had no armor to protect herself, and her all too vulnerable heart was pounding inside her chest like mad.

"That's it, kitten. Touch me," he grunted as her trembling hands slid up his tattooed arms and down his muscular back. Up, down, all the way to his firm ass as his clever mouth sucked on her neck, then down, down, down till he reached the tops of her aching breasts.

"Just like that, darlin'. Drive me crazy with those nails," he groaned, taking her nipple into his mouth.

Lucy raked her claws back up to his shoulders and held his head to her chest as he did unimaginable things to her. Her body tensed and moisture pooled between her legs, she felt her stomach tense as her heat started right then and there. Derrick's mouth was driving her insane. Her body ached and heated, her cycle prompted by sex with her mate, making her ready to receive him.

Derrick's growling never abated as he licked, sucked, and nipped at her tender skin. He was marking her even now, in this small way, making her Cat yowl inside her head. A deep, dark, burning need born of desperation and the absolute certainty he was her mate began to throb throughout every single inch of her body, heart, and soul.

"Mine," he growled, and she nodded.

Every single part of her longed for him, wanted him in new and exciting ways. Frightening ways that would have mortified her had it been anyone else. But this was Derrick. Her mate, who was fated by the universe to be hers and hers alone. *Mine.*

Their sweaty bodies writhed against each other in a dance old as time. Intuition took over, and though her body was on fire for him, her mind was right there with her every step of the way. No more doubts, no more questioning whether this was right. Lucy was very aware of every single thing happening, and she welcomed them.

There was something about acting on impulse and feeling instead of hashing through everything a million times in her head that made her pulse quicken, sweetening every kiss and caress. She wouldn't have to wonder what it felt like to be possessed by this sublime specimen of a man for much longer.

Lucy moaned as his head dipped lower still, licking a trail from her belly button to her thick thighs. This was not like anything she'd ever felt in her limited experience with men. Derrick was not just claiming her body, he was staking claim to her very soul. Gold eyes met hers, his heated breath warming her skin.

The moment was intense, maybe because it was long overdue, but she was glad she'd waited. Glad she'd held onto her heart like it was a precious gift she could only give once. Glad even more that it was his to receive. She only hoped she could satisfy his hunger, sate his need.

"You are all I ever want. Everything I need," he said, and she realized she'd spoken aloud.

Lucy's body beat with a wildly throbbing ache that was scary and yet so damn sweet she wanted to cry. He was powerful and enormous, with hard planes and curved muscles—a creature of pure masculine beauty. She quivered and shook as his lips explored every silken inch of her.

Mouth wide in a soundless moan, she gasped and watched stars explode in the night sky above as Derrick licked his way down her body, eliciting pleasure from nerve endings she had no idea even existed. His shoulders spread her legs wide, and she moaned his name, crying out as she watched him take her sex in a hot kiss that left her begging for more.

Her eyes rolled back as he continued to lap and suckle her plump nether lips, causing moisture to drip down her thighs as he coaxed her body to unimaginable heights. To say she'd never felt this way would be a gross understatement. Lucy was a Shifter, and as such, she was aware of her body in ways no human could ever begin to know.

As his fingers dipped into her sheath, Lucy tensed. Two long, thick digits pushed and pressed inside of her tightness. Their way made easier by the moisture from his tongue and her own body. Tight, tight, tight, and he was big. So big. Even his fingers were large.

"So pretty and pink. Taste so good, kitten. You been saving this for me, haven't you?" he moaned and held her down with one hand when she would've shied away.

"Derrick," she whimpered and gasped, wanting him to finish it, to take her all the way.

"Hold on, love," he growled, and looked at her, his eyes glowing gold with his Wolf.

Lucy nodded, trusting him, she spread her legs wider and watched fascinated when instead of plunging between her folds, he went back to using his tongue and lips to suck her into the most intense pleasure she'd ever felt. On and on, wave after wave of pure, unadulterated bliss blasted through her. Lucy cried out in pleasure, made that much more intense when he slid up her body and pushed his thick, hard shaft into her.

"Mine," growled Derrick.

He moved over her, staying his hips as his thick, beautiful cock pulsed, buried deep inside her. Her gaze found his, fascinated by his intense gold stare. His Wolf was showing, taking part, and yes, she gloried in it.

"Tell me," he demanded, pulling all the way out, leaving her empty, clenching on air. "Say you are mine."

Heat and desire filled her stomach as she looked down to where he stroked himself. Yes, he was denying her his body, but at the same time she was hypnotized by the vision of him touching himself. His mushroomed head leak a perfect pearl of precum, and Derrick's eyes blazed gold fire.

Her mouth watered. Lucy wanted it, wanted him so badly. She needed him filling her mouth, her pussy, everywhere. Wanted his bite, his claim, now more than ever. Some long forgotten primal instinct was driving her now.

"Tell me," he ordered again, and his voice broke through the haze of her brain.

"Yours. I'm yours. Only yours," she replied.

Derrick grunted, satisfaction in his gaze as he dipped his head and claimed her mouth, and pushed back inside her. Thank. Fuck. She tasted herself on him, and it was wild and erotic, and only when she opened her mouth, and he plunged his tongue inside did he move his hips.

Thank. Fuck.

"Make me yours. Claim me," she begged as her pussy clenched, her next orgasm already starting.

The cocky Wolf grinned wickedly, his eyes glowing and she realized he'd been right. She was begging him. At the moment, Lucy was too far gone to care. Her entire body was on fire. She'd been empty and raw before, and she needed him to fill her, to bite her neck, make his claim, complete their mating.

"Derrick," she growled, thrusting her hips in hopes of enticing him to hurry.

He merely smirked and grunted as he moved his body, switching angles with deep, deliberate strokes. Cupping her face, he made sure to capture her eyes with his own as he kissed her again, tongue pressing into her mouth at the same time his cock moved inside her tight channel.

Magic man. Sex god. Mine. Mine. Mate.

Derrick's smoky, woodsy flavor teased her senses as he coaxed her muscles into relaxing for him, accepting every single bit of his enormous, magnificent cock. He ground his hips, thrusting deeper and deeper into her. Every second that passed brought new waves of arousal, increasing her need and her pleasure.

So much pleasure, almost too much, she thought as she gave control of her body completely over to him.

Derrick seemed to know, seemed to understand what she wanted before she did. He stroked and caressed her, pressing deeper inside of her in one long sliding move till she couldn't tell where he ended and she began. His husky voice seemed all around her in the darkening woods. He whispered naughty phrases of praise and celebration while working them both towards the same goal.

Guided by instinct and the fierce need to claim her mate, Lucy rolled her hips, trying with all her might to pull him deeper, to suck the cum from his body. Her body trembled, blood burned, and heart pounded with need. She wanted it all. Every last drop.

Loosening his hold on her face, his hands roamed down her neck and shoulders to caress her breasts and tweak her nipples as he started moving in earnest. Faster and harder, his deep thrusts became more frantic. The scent of their combined need was thick and potent in the air.

Lucy could hardly breathe as pleasure wrapped around her like manacles, chaining her to him. The imagery just as arousing as the act itself. And she would do it, too. She would willingly place chains around her arms and feet and slide the lock closed herself. Yes, she wanted this mating. Wanted him and the pleasure he brought her, longed to be connected to him, bound to him, mated to him forever.

"Yes," she cried out as the pleasure grew.

The warmth started in her belly, making her feel heavy and hot with the impending explosion that promised to be even better than her first orgasm with him. Claws out she scratched his shoulders, marking her the way felines do as her gums ached with her fangs. She saw the same need, the same instinct, reflected in his gold eyes.

The Wolf was watching her, waiting for the moment their stars aligned. It was the perfect time to seal their mating, a gift the Fates had set in motion eons ago. Blessed, they were both blessed to have found each other. She fully believed that now.

And, suddenly, she was there. Stars exploded behind her eyes as her sex gripped his cock in the most magnificent culmination she'd ever imagined. Derrick roared as his seed coated her womb, he turned her head and bit down, staking his claim where her shoulder met her neck, marking her as his one true mate.

Lucy roared her joy, then she struck in a mirror image of her own mating mark. Lucy bit Derrick, piercing his skin and swallowing his essence with pride. He tensed and squeezed her to him as he spilled even more cum inside of her, triggering another orgasm until the evidence of it was running down her thighs.

Several minutes later, Derrick lapped at her wound, closing the bitemark with his healing saliva. He held her close while she did the same. They were both breathless, boneless, but he still found strength to kiss her head and caress her back as if she were precious, coveted. The thought warmed her as she felt him lift her. She moaned and snuggled, not expecting the cold, as he plunged them into the brook's frigid water.

"What the heck?" she screamed as he sank them both down into the shallow and ice-cold stream.

"Come here, mate," he whispered, smiling as he caught her lips with his own. "Feels good on all that overheated skin, right?"

"Yes, but you could have warned me," she said, smiling back reluctantly, and kissing him to help soothe her shock.

Lucy closed her eyes, allowing him to take all her weight as he tended her and bathed them both in the clear water.

"I didn't know you had a stream," she said.

"You didn't know *we* had a stream," he countered.

"That's right, *we*," she replied and smiled, unable to stop once she started.

He lifted her out of the brook, carried her back to the house, up the staircase to their bedroom. The hallways were empty, and she smiled, knowing that *their* Pack must have heard them in the woods and made themselves scarce. Privacy was a luxury amongst Shifters.

She'd expected Derrick to strut a bit, but in all honesty, he seemed more concerned with caring for her, and that touched her deeply.

Good mate. Strong. Loving. Fierce.

"Derrick?"

"Hmm?"

He settled her on the bed after they'd showered in the bathroom with actual soap and water. Her mate had been so lovingly gentle, kissing her silly and patting her skin dry. Her heart squeezed and warmed, and looking at him, she felt like she'd won the damn lottery.

"Are you happy?"

"Are you kidding? You made me the happiest man in the world."

"You still want me after that. No regrets?" she asked, biting her lip. Derrick grinned and took her hand, placing it on his dick. He was long and hard and pulsed beneath her hand.

"Feel this? This happens whenever I am near you. Fuck yes, I want you."

"I'm glad. I want you too," she confessed before straddling his waist.

"Fuuck," Derrick grunted as Lucy kissed his neck, running her tongue over the mark she placed there.

She lifted her hips, placing his head at her ready entrance, and lowered herself on him. They moaned in unison as she rode him. Derrick was sweet and patient with her fumbling.

"So sexy," he growled, squeezing her breasts with his big hands, and licking every inch of skin he could reach. Lucy could hardly keep up, and finally, she allowed him to guide her into a rhythm that satisfied them both.

"More, I want more," he growled, and lifted her, flipping her over onto her hands and knees.

Her inner kitty went wild, yowling as he stroked her cheeks, slapping one hand down on her ass as he found her with his cock, filling her with one hard thrust. This was the claiming her animal wanted, *no*, demanded. She pushed back instinctively. Hissing, she looked over her shoulder and saw his Wolf glowing gold in his eyes.

"Take me hard, Derrick."

"Mine," he growled, and did just that.

Her mate had more moves than she could have guessed, and he rocked her world with them. With his clever fingers thrumming over her clit and his long, girthy cock filling her so good, it did not take long before she was screaming his name. Then they were both coming. And Lucy felt their bond strengthen even more before he turned her over and kissed her slowly and carefully.

Sweet, tender mate.

"Derrick?"

"Yeah, love?"

"I love you, *mate*," she said before sleep took her.

CHAPTER TEN

DIRE WOLF MATES

The next few days were like something out of a dream. Derrick's Wolf had stopped pacing and growling. He watched Lucy all the time, wondering at the hole she'd filled inside him. His mate was so beautiful and tough, the perfect combination of sweet and sassy. She fit in with his Pack, with him, and he was just so damn proud to call her his.

Right now, she was laughing at something Cole said, but he was not paying any mind to their words. He was too stuck by her beauty. Her hair was shiny and thick, long like he liked it. He imagined it as it had been that very morning, spilling across his pillow like a bolt of silk.

He'd had those tresses wrapped around his hand when she'd surprised him with a morning BJ. In his wildest dreams, Derrick had never imagined he'd be waking up to find his cock buried deep in Lucy's succulent mouth.

"I guess cats really like cream," he'd mused aloud, and winced at the slap she'd given him right on his ass after that remark.

They'd had a spank war then, and just thinking of his pink handprint on her luscious, rounded ass made him hard. Oh yeah, his little hellion was definitely into spanking. Something they'd be exploring together in the near future.

Grrr.

"When are you gonna let me bring your car over here, Luce? You know Big Tom isn't gonna take care of it like I would," Cole stated.

"Well, he already started the repairs. I feel bad about taking the work from him," his surprisingly tenderhearted mate returned.

True, he'd tried several times to get her to allow him to bring the old Ford here for Cole to fix, but she wouldn't hear of it. His sassy little mate insisted she pay for it too. Damn stubborn woman.

Isn't she great?

He noted the dark pink blush that swept up her face when he caught her gaze, and his heart damn near stopped beating inside his chest. So pretty. Beautiful with milky white skin and crazy gorgeous purple eyes. They reminded him of wild bull thistles, the kind he passed a million times on the open road.

He'd seen his share of wonders in the world, but looking at her was better than any ocean shore, desert sunset, or mountain view. Yeah, he'd missed the open road, but this was home now, in more ways than one. Lucy bit her lower lip before flashing him a smile, the one that drove him wild, and he felt his body respond instantly.

He loved her sweet innocence, headstrong retorts, and responsive nature. He'd worried his hunger for her would scare her, but not his mate. Her appetites were as insatiable as his. Lucy was a firecracker in bed. Fantastic in and out of it. Her desire was more than a match for his own, as was her heart.

His mate's loving nature was so big, she could more than take her place at his side. Lucy might be a tiny little feline hybrid, but she was the undoubted Alpha fem of their Dire Wolf Pack. Caring for each of them in her own way. Getting them total, and joke when they'd been worried and nervous about settling. She was a tonic for them all.

"Hey there, kitten," Derrick called as he walked over with a cold bottle of sweet tea in his hand.

"That for me?"

"Yes, ma'am," he drawled, and held the bottle to her lips.

Hunger flared to life as he watched her small, pink tongue lick a drop of the brown liquid from the rim.

"Okay, you two, I'm out," Cole muttered, and the smart Wolf walked away.

"Missed you," Derrick said, pressing her against the wall of the garage, and lifting her in his arms until he could comfortably settle between her denim-clad legs.

"Hmm, did you?" She smiled and mashed her mouth to his.

"Yeah. I fell back asleep, and you left. I don't like waking up without you," he said.

"Sorry, I, uh, had an appointment," she replied, and he frowned.

He'd been getting used to waking up with his arms full of his mate's luscious curves. Today he'd missed that. Only the note she'd left on the pillow stopped him from losing his mind and taking off after her. As it was, he'd still called her cell.

"What was the appointment for?" he asked with mild interest as he nibbled that sweet spot under her chin where her neck met her chest.

"You know that shop in town where Sheila got my, *uh,* uniform?"

Lucy sighed and tilted her head back to give him better access as his tongue traced the line of her ample cleavage. His Wolf had developed quite the appetite for her berry-pink tipped delights. He wanted them again. Now.

Grrr.

"Yeah, what about that shop?" he inquired, as he tugged the neckline down and lifted one sweet mound out for his lips to catch and suckle.

"Oh gods," she moaned, but continued to talk.

It was a little game they played. To see how long either could go with a conversation before they lost their minds in each other's bodies.

"I, uh, had to order a few more things," she hedged, biting her lower lip and pulling on his hair to get him closer.

He laughed and bit down gently, loving the way her smile peeked out at him. Derrick frowned then as her words filtered in through his lusty haze, and he pulled free of her glorious breast.

"What things?"

"Oh, well, I needed some tops in larger sizes."

"What for? I told you, kitten, you look gorgeous in everything," he said, and kissed her lips again just because.

"I know. There is a reason, though."

"Such as?"

"This," she said, and tilted her head. "Breathe here," she commanded gently, and pushed his head down against her neck.

Derrick went willingly. God, he loved that part of her. Her mate mark had healed already, but the pink scar was visible. He'd been a little rougher than he'd meant to be, and the resulting mark was rather large.

He ran his nose over it and breathed deep, loving the mingled essence of both their scents that now made up her fragrance. There was something new there, something different. Alarms sounded inside his brain, and he stiffened. Derrick pressed his nose against her neck, eliciting a giggle as he sniffed her skin deeply.

Could it be? Holy. Shit. YES! Warmth and pride filled him at the revelation.

"Lucy, for real? Are you sure? Already?"

He held her closer, eyes wide with wonder. Tears welled in her violet eyes as she placed her hand over his and brought it to her soft lower belly.

"Are you angry?" she asked, and he realized he still had not spoken.

"Angry? Oh my gods, darlin', no, of course not. You have no idea the gift you are," he told her. "A baby. Our baby. Fuck, I love you," he whispered, breaking down a little.

He let her see his emotions overflow for a moment before he kissed her again. Softer, slower this time, with his hand pressing the button that would shut the garage door, closing them in and away from the rest of the world.

It took less than a second before he lost control and crushed himself to her front. His claws sliced through her clothing until she straddled him as he leaned back on the seat of one of the classic Harleys he'd bought to work on before she'd arrived in his life.

"I've been wanting you to take me for a ride on one of your bikes," she moaned as he lavished attention on both her breasts while one hand spread her dripping slit and he found her hidden bundle of nerves.

"How about you ride me instead," he groaned as he freed himself from his jeans and entered her in one hard thrust.

Derrick could not seem to get enough of his mate's amazing body. He never would either. With this news, he needed to be inside her, to show her the depth of his feelings. Violet eyes wide and glowing with her Cat, Lucy moaned as she rocked her body, taking him deeper and deeper. Hands gripping the plump globes of her sexy as fuck ass, he lifted and dropped her hard onto his engorged sex. Fuck, he needed her, wanted her all the time.

"Oh fuck, kitten, you feel so good. Like a velvet vise wrapped around my dick, squeezing me so fucking tight," he growled as he took her mouth and rode the wave of overwhelming pleasure until they were both roaring with it.

Her wicked sharp claws scratched at his skin and his Wolf howled with joy. He loved wearing her marks. Pride and possession flowed through him as her pussy gripped his cock, milking him of his cum.

"Mine," he growled, sucking the skin over her mating mark, causing another series of mini orgasms to rack her sweet body.

Cradling her close, he kissed her head, her eyelids, and every bit of her that he could reach as he lifted her, and himself, off the bike and carried her to the back door. He grabbed a clean drop cloth and placed it over her body before taking her across the yard to the house.

"Oh damn, my eyes," growled his Beta, Brock, who had just dropped the carton of milk he was holding to cover his eyes with both hands.

Lucy giggled from underneath the drop cloth and Derrick

growled. After all, it was his ass on display for Brock, Cole, and Thor, who were all sitting in the kitchen. Brock was groaning like an idiot, but the other two simply kept their heads down.

Smart asses.

"Hey Lucy, how ya doin'? Congratulations are in order, then?" Cole asked.

Derrick growled again but stopped once Thor smacked the younger Wolf in the head. At least someone was smarter than they looked, he thought grimly. After a warm bath, he settled his mate in bed and ordered her to take a nap. Not that she listened, but after spending a little time on his knees, enjoying a bit of his favorite snack, he finally wore her out enough to send her to sleep.

Cubs. My cubs. Imagine that?

He dropped a kiss on her brow before heading downstairs. It was Friday night, their busiest night of the week, and he wanted to make sure everything was ready.

"Fucking Weylin. You hide my gauges again?" Thor growled, lifting the younger Wolf off the floor by the neck.

By the time Derrick walked into the sprawling living room, Weylin's face was the same ruddy shade as his hair. He smacked against Thor's grip, shaking his head and blinking rapidly before the much bigger man let go.

"Fuck, Thor. No! I learned my lesson last time," Weylin gasped and choked.

Derrick walked over to the bookshelf and held up an empty whiskey glass in Thor's direction. He shook it and waited for the beast to drop the younger Wolf.

"Looking for these?"

"Oh, yeah. Thanks, Alpha," Thor grumbled, and took the glass with his Australian Bloodstone plugs.

The giant, bald Enforcer sat down and began the process of cleaning then inserting them into his lobes, not even looking at Weylin who was gasping, face still pink from lack of oxygen.

Derrick had plenty of tattoos, but few piercings. In fact, he'd largely neglected his body art for a while. It was time to begin the process once more, and he waited until Thor was finished before approaching him with the subject. By then, all of his Pack was there, either standing or sitting in the living room.

They'd been seven for so long, and he was about to change that. It was tough for their kind, living longer and predominantly solitary lives, cut off from normals and other Shifters alike. But Derrick was shaking things up. Setting them up in territory of their own. Claiming a mate. He was making waves—for the better, he hoped.

Yes, it truly was with the best intentions. He wanted to move forward for the good of them all, but most especially, and selfishly, for his own good. Lucy was his salvation, his reason, his everything. Finding a mate, getting her with cubs, was like a dream come true, and he was humbled that she'd chosen him as well. Just as he was humbled when they'd picked him to lead.

Mine, growled the Wolf inside him.

The Pack. Lucy. His babe. All his. Imagine a prehistoric beast like his Wolf completely devoted to his Pack and female. The tiny little she-Cat sleeping upstairs held his heart in his hands even as she carried their cubs beneath hers.

Cubs? He wondered why he was referring to her pregnancy in multiples, but the Wolf inside him merely grinned.

Cubs, the animal responded knowingly.

The atmosphere seemed to sizzle and crack with anticipation. Each of his Wolves knew about his mating, and yet they'd been waiting for him to make the official announcement. This was the way of his kind. A sacred culmination of events that had begun eons before he was even an idea. It was time to seal the mating bond.

"Well, you gonna spit it out or what?" Sheila asked, breaking the tension as she usually did.

"Sheila," grumbled Brock.

"We all heard you two in the woods the other night, and if we were dumb enough to miss that, we've been hearing it in here the last few days. I'm really glad we went with the soundproof insulation," Phoenix added.

"You gonna tell us or what?" Sheila prompted, grinning wider.

"Tell us what?" Weylin asked, grunting when Thor thumped him on the head yet again.

"You all know Lucy is my mate. Yes, I have given her my mark, and she's given me hers," he waited a beat for the ruckus to die down before continuing.

All the whooping and congratulations they showered on him felt good and right. Derrick looked each one of them in the eye before speaking, so they knew he was focused on them as their Alpha should be.

"You know, we've been searching for a place to settle, and you also know I chose this spot on nothing more than a gut feeling. I am proud to say Blue Valley is the official home of the Dire Wolf Pack and MC. Now, I have to do something else. Thor, it's time," Derrick said, and looked over at the Enforcer.

Thor was a man of few words, but the deep pride on his face made Derrick glad inside. Pack emotions were channeled through their bonds, and theirs was such it was built on friendship and trust, maybe even more than the usual Shifter dominance hierarchy.

Derrick stood up and stripped his shirt off. It was past time he did this. Adrenaline pumped through him as Brock moved the coffee table, and Thor gathered his things. His Pack gathered around him, and Derrick's chest felt tight with feelings.

Arms clasped, the Dire Wolves formed a circle around Derrick and the big, bald man. They nodded as one and Derrick, the Alpha, dropped to his knees in the middle of them. This was a show of trust, of devotion, of their dedication to each other. Alphas did not go to their knees for anyone.

Thor chanted quietly in an old, forgotten tongue. He removed a jar from a small metal chest with the ancient glyphs of the original Dire Wolf Pack engraved on it, a sacred relic from their past. Inside was a special ink, magicked by friends of the Dire Wolves to use on their otherwise *tough to penetrate* skin.

This was an old custom. A rite of passage every mated Dire Wolf throughout the ages had gone through. Especially the Wolves who wore their patch. To them, DWMC meant history. It meant brotherhood. It meant a bone deep devotion to one another that no other Pack in existence could claim.

They were descendants of the original wanderers and had lived nomadic lifestyles for generations together. Always together. Occasionally, their Pack broke off into smaller MCs, as Derrick and these six had—but they were still DWMC.

That was who they would always be at their core. That meant loyalty to Pack and family, and in this moment, he was telling his Pack, *his MC*, that Lucy was his family. With this ink, he named her as his true home, just like he told her when he'd claimed her as his mate.

Thor closed his eyes, repeating the sacred prayer in the old language. He then took a long, thin bamboo needle and dipped it into the bottle of ink that never dried or ran out. With smooth efficient moves, he sliced Derrick's skin with the sharpened wood and imprinted the symbol and words of his commitment to Lucy as the Fates willed it through the large male's fingers.

"What's going on?" Lucy's voice reached him from the stairs. His Wolf tensed as he scented her fear and anxiety, but Derrick remained still.

"It's alright, Lucy," Sheila said, and he made a note to thank his cousin as she gestured to Lucy to join their circle at her side.

He followed her movements through the room with his ears. His mate, *his pregnant mate,* stood between Brock and Sheila now. He inhaled her sweet scent, made sweeter now that he could pinpoint the subtle notes of the cubs she carried. He wondered if she was aware she was having multiples yet and allowed a small smile to settle on his face as he thought of her and their young.

"It's almost over," Sheila told Lucy.

"What is he doing?"

"Dire Wolves' tattoos tell our story. The story of our Pack and MC. Our backs are left bare until we find our fated mates. I'm sure my cousin has informed you that you are his, sweet Lucy. This is our way of marking the occasion and recording it for all to witness."

He heard Lucy's intake of breath and noted again the subtle change in her scent. Anxiety and fear became gratitude and, yes, there it was. His favorite scent of all. The scent of her love.

Hope rose in him, as did his love for the woman he'd claimed as his own. He would make sure she knew how he felt every day of their lives together.

Mine.

He was so focused on her he barely felt the pain of Thor's movements as he cut through his tough skin again and again. The smell of his own blood was thick in the air. The wet, warm towel Thor used to wipe away the gore felt good as he worked. Some several minutes later, Derrick felt the bamboo needle stop.

With a grunt and a great intake of breath, Thor sank down onto the floor. As one, the dire Wolf Pack bowed their heads and said their own private thanks to the gods and the Fates alike.

Thor was what the old graybeards of the original DWMC called *favored by the gods,* meaning they sometimes spoke through him. Visions and messages were only part of his special talents. He was also the only one of them to be *touched by the Fates.*

The ritual of the claiming tattoo was sacred among the DWMC. Derrick gave thanks to the Fates for his friend and Enforcer. Thor's gifts went far beyond being the biggest and baddest amongst them, but sometimes they took a lot out of him.

"Thank you, brother," Derrick said, standing up and meeting his Enforcer's gaze, "If you need the night off, take it. We will handle it."

Thor blinked, too drained to do more than that, and Derrick squeezed his shoulder and pressed his forehead to his. A gesture of affection and a way to let him know he was Derrick's to keep safe. As Alpha, it was his duty and privilege. He turned to his mate as Cole ran to the kitchen to bring water and tea for the man who'd just performed the ritual that sealed his claim for life.

"Lucy?" Derrick found her standing on the bottom stair.

"Hey," she said, wiping tears. She touched his shoulders gingerly.

"Turn around," she ordered, once more reminding him she was a sassy little thing.

"Why the tears?" he asked as he turned to show her his mating tattoo.

"Oh, Derrick, it's beautiful, and it's already healing," she exclaimed.

"Tell me what you see," he whispered. He had yet to see the image, only felt its path as Thor carved it across his back and shoulders.

"Your Dire Wolf is laying down on the forest floor, body bent in a semi-circle like around a, a—" She gasped, and he knew she was crying, the need to comfort warred with the need to hear what she had to say.

"Don't turn yet," she told him. "You're lying with your body tucked around a she-Cat. It's me," her voice trembled.

"That's good. My Wolf is protecting you," Derrick answered.

"There's more," she said, and this time he felt her wonder. "Three cubs are playing between us two Wolves, one red and one black, and one she-Cat. She's got one of her brother's tails in her claws." Lucy laughed, and Derrick grinned, picturing it already.

"There's writing, but I can't read it," she told him, as he turned to her.

"Those are Dire Wolf glyphs. Show me what they look like?"

"One is kind of like a circle, but there are two lines twirled around each other inside—"

"That is the symbol for fated mates."

Derrick touched her face hesitantly. Her tears left tracks down her face, and he bent forward to kiss them away.

"I love you, Lucy," he said, and felt his Wolf rise when she pressed her lips so sweetly to his.

"I love you too." She sighed against him, and he wrapped her up in his arms. The new tattoo stretched his skin a bit, but he'd be fully healed in another hour. Thor would've cut deeply to make the ink last.

"Sheila said you're only allowed to have this done once in your life."

"Yes. Unless Fate blesses a Shifter twice with his or her perfect mate, but once is all I need, kitten."

"Yeah?"

"Yeah. You are it for me, love," he said, and his voice dropped to a husky whisper as her violet eyes blinked away a fresh wave of tears.

"Derrick," she whispered and kissed his lips again with all the sweetness and heat she had bubbling up to the surface. "I love you so much."

"I love you back, darlin."

Derrick tugged her closer to him, fierce yet tender. In a short time, this woman had become his entire world. Now everyone would know it.

"You two about done?" Sheila asked, breaking the moment.

"What time is it?"

Lucy asked and looked around for the wall clock. Derrick stopped, finally noticing her outfit.

"Hey? What's this?" he asked and nodded to her short shorts and tank top.

"It's my uniform, Derrick," she explained slowly, like he was an idiot.

"I know that, but why are you wearing it?"

"Because we open in an hour. Did that ink hurt your brain or something?"

"You're not working tonight," he said, and realized his mistake the instant her eyes glittered at him like amethysts.

"Lucy, I mean, um, well, you're carrying our cubs—"

"Don't you call them pups?" she interrupted, and he shook his head, grinning.

So little was common knowledge about his kind. But that was okay. He'd teach her everything she needed to know. Besides, according to the image Thor had seen and tattooed on his back, they would have two Wolves and one she-Cat. Gratitude filled him, followed by a serious wave of protective instinct.

"Actually, we call our young cubs like cats do," he said and nuzzled her neck with his nose and dropped a kiss there.

"Mm, that's nice," she replied and nodded. "Come on, let's go to work."

"Kitten," he said, trying a different tactic. "Don't you think you need to sit this one out?"

"Derrick, I'm like five minutes pregnant. This is going to go on for another six months at least, and I will not sit around like a damn cantaloupe waiting to ripen."

"I think you're perfect, kitten. Let's go to bed," he growled and nipped her ear, wondering if he could maybe entice her to stay home.

"Listen up, Fido, I may like that tongue of yours, but if you want to get it near my body again, you will not try to tell me what to do. Got it? Now, I'm not an idiot, I am not going to risk hurting myself or my cubs for anything. We're just going to the bar."

"I know, but I worry—"

"Derrick, I'm a Shifter," she said, ignoring the snickered *"more like a house cat"* comment from Sheila. She tossed her blonde hair back and flipped the younger woman the bird, while not taking her eyes off her mate.

"We're still looking for more staff, plus I need money to pay for my car. Now, are you gonna stand there with your mouth hanging open, mate? Or are you gonna shake that ass and come with me?"

"Damn, Derrick! You are one lucky Alpha. That is one sassy as hell mate you got there," Brock said, grinning at Lucy in a way that set Derrick's teeth on edge.

A sharp elbow to his stomach had Brock bent over and gasping for air before he understood the undercurrents. His eyes widened as he hightailed it out of the house. Just in time, too.

"Sorry, uh, excuse me Alpha, Alpha fem," the man said, burning rubber to get outside.

Derrick couldn't stop his rumbling growl, but Lucy just rolled her pretty purple eyes, turned her back, presenting him with a perfect view of her delectable ass in those soon to be torn up and thrown out cutoffs. Then she stomped out the door.

Fuck, Shit. Grrr.

CHAPTER ELEVEN

DIRE WOLF MATES

Serious Moonlight was at full capacity by ten o-clock and Lucy's feet were killing her. Perhaps Derrick was right, and she should have stayed home. Not that she would tell her overprotective mate that. No need to inflate that big head of his. Besides, she could finish out the night.

A full moon hung low in the sky outside, and the place was overloaded with Shifters who were feeling the power that came with the change in the lunar phase. Without Thor there to wrangle the customers, who were a bit enthusiastic, the job had been mostly left up to Derrick.

She watched him when she could and there was no doubt about it, her Alpha was one tough mutt. Still, something was off. She'd been on edge all night. Her thoughts kept drifting to Derrick and his amazing new ink. She took a pic of it with her phone and held it up to him so he could read the glyphs to her.

"It says, 'For each Wolf there is a perfect mate, the road was long and lonely, but the destination complete. Lucy is for Derrick, and he is for her, their hearts forever entwined, a home for each other, united until all the stars burn up in the sky', Then this here is the symbol of my house. Rand literally

means 'wolf shield', see that there? There's a feline paw print inside of it now. It means I'm your shield, kitten. I'll protect you and our cubs from the whole damn world."

His words had turned into moans as their mouths crashed together in a long, drawn out kiss Phoenix had interrupted with a fake sneeze. *Idiot,* she smirked and shook her head. The entire Pack was a lot more easy-going than she would have expected of a bunch of tough bikers, who happened to also be giant, prehistoric Wolves.

"Can I get a drink here?"

Lucy turned and faced the same angry customer who'd been tossed out her first night on the job. She stared the man down, but there wasn't much she could do by herself.

"I said, I want a beer. I'm a paying customer," the sour-faced man grumbled.

She couldn't ignore him any longer, but she was uneasy. He should have known better than to come back. There was not much she could do now. Everyone was busy and she could not catch Derrick's eye.

"Okay. One beer, then you need to leave," she told him as she slid a domestic bottle across the bar and took his five-dollar bill.

"I'll leave when I'm ready," he mumbled under his breath, but Lucy still heard him.

She needed to find Derrick, but a group of young human women snagged her attention next, and she spent the next fifteen minutes mixing a bunch of Cosmos. Her thoughts drifted back to the tattoo ritual and Thor. Derrick had explained a little about his gifts. That Shifter certainly had a mystical way about him, despite being enormous, tattooed, and pierced. Or maybe even because of it.

Lucy happened to like the Pack's propensity for ink. She'd have to ask Derrick about acquiring some of her own. That was the thing about Shifters. They tended to heal quickly, and tattoos faded away a lot quicker than they did on humans, but he'd also explained about the special ink they had.

The sound of glass breaking brought her head up, and she watched Weylin vault over the front bar, broom, and dustpan in hand. He efficiently cleared the mess while Derrick made his way from the front door, a concerned expression on his face. Weylin gestured to the slinky blonde woman who'd made the mess and made quick work of the clean-up. Derrick walked the woman around the spill to the bar and got her another drink.

The woman was already tipsy and did not seem to understand what *no* meant. She kept running her hands up his shoulders while he efficiently removed them and frowned when she reached for him again. The woman giggled and tried tugging him back to her side when he replaced her drink, and Lucy growled. Her mate's golden stare found hers, and she closed her eyes for a second. Her feline was turning into a seriously possessive bitch.

She sighed and opened them to find him staring, the female customer happily attached herself to another male, and all was right in the world. He cocked his head to the side, and after a minute, Lucy was surrounded by her mate's wonderful embrace.

"Kitten, you need to stop flashing those gorgeous eyes of yours at me if you want to keep working," he growled, and dropped a warm, quick kiss on her mouth before turning to fill an order.

"Yes, Alpha," she said and nudged him with her hip.

"Need help back here?" he asked softly, and she felt their bond pulse and beat in time with her heart.

Damn, she'd missed him. Craved his touch, His scent. It was silly. They'd only been right here. Separated by a few measly feet, working for just a few hours. Derrick Rand had officially turned her into some clingy, mated female. Eeek! But she would not have it any other way, she thought as he touched her hip to reach past her for a bottle of booze.

"Are you finished with the door?"

"Brock's on it."

"Then, yes, please. Stay and help me," she replied, loving the smile that lit up his handsome face as he nodded.

Derrick hadn't wanted her to come in tonight, but that was him being protective. Besides, she was glad she did. She enjoyed working beside him. The band tonight was all female, a group of Fox Shifters from Philadelphia calling themselves the *Stealth Vixens*. They were good. Loud, but good.

She liked their country rock rhythm. Brock had closed the kitchen early, and had taken over as Bouncer for Derrick, so the Alpha could join her at the back bar. He'd spent the last few days working alongside her, and she loved it. Lucy decided then that she was going to work as long as she could fit behind the bar. If Derrick wanted to work beside her, she'd welcome it, but that was up to him.

She had a car to pay for. Not that she needed it for anything since she wasn't leaving her mate obviously, but still. It was hers. She and Buddy—*that was what she called her car*—had been through a lot together. She tried to be angry at Derrick when he unceremoniously bent down and retrieved a case of beer faster than she could, restocking the rear coolers, but she just couldn't.

Really, she wanted to yell at him, to stand up for feminism, but he was just so darn sexy. And that Alpha male attitude of his kind of turned her on. Okay. It seriously turned her on. How had she gone from being nothing but a vagabond, to being claimed and mated to the sexiest damn man, and one of the most powerful Shifters she'd ever met, all in a week's time?

Maybe Fate had finally thrown her a bone, or Karma had finally caught up with her. After being on the road alone for most of her adult life and, if she were interested in looking back, most of her youth, Lucy had finally found a home.

In him.

"You alright?" Derrick asked.

"I love you," she said, feeling the words to her marrow.

"Love you too, mate," he said back, no hesitations.

His warm hands cupped her face and neck, and he dragged his lips across hers in a kiss that screamed of possession. Her stomach tightened and pulse raced. She felt her heart explode with emotion. Lucy could have spent all night kissing him.

She was still lost in his touch when the first scream broke out.

Derrick's Wolf snarled and snapped to attention just as all hell broke loose., He shoved his mate gently behind him as not one, but five men, wearing masks, came busting through the doors waving actual fucking torches and screaming profanities.

"What the fuck is going on?" Sheila asked, running over to them from the back room where she'd been getting some bottles to restock the front bar.

"Lucy, stay down! Sheila, protect her!" he ordered.

"I'm fine, Derrick. Go," his mate said, anger and worry making her scent sharp.

"I can't see anything," Lucy said to Sheila, who was already grabbing her hand and pulling her to safety.

"Sheila's got you, Lucy."

"I'm fine, Derrick. Go, get everyone out—"

Smoke billowed, stinging his eyes, and making it difficult to see. Forget about hearing anything. The crowd had begun to stampede at the first sign of trouble. He pushed back against the throng, trying his best to reach the first masked male who was holding what he realized wasn't an old-fashioned torch, but rather was some kind of a homemade holder for a smoke bomb.

"Motherfucker," he roared.

Derrick punched the guy in the face, knocking him out cold, and grabbed the device, ripping it from the hands of the stupid human fuck who thought this would be a good idea.

Another approached, but the fucker went down fast. Weylin ran to him, covering his mouth to stop from choking. He grabbed the torch and took off for the side door with it fast as his Shifter legs would take him. Derrick had another offender by the throat as Brock handled one by the front door. He didn't see the other man until the bastard was on him with a blade of some sort.

"You filthy animals. I know what you are. Get out of our town!" He screamed and slashed at Derrick's forearm.

The fucker cut him, and Derrick's rage boiled as he scented his blood on the air.

"You shouldn't have done that," he growled, dropping the man he'd been holding hard on the ground.

That dick would just have to wait. Derrick turned and faced the man with the huge hunting knife. The human swallowed, the stink of fear and liquor coming off him in waves. This was the same asshole from their opening night. The one whose name he'd given to the Council. Derrick frowned, they should have caught up with him by now.

"Come on, then. You're nothing but an animal. You belong on my wall," he sneered, and Derrick's Wolf pushed forward.

"Oh, I wouldn't do that," the stranger gestured behind him, and Derrick saw another guy with a video camera pointed at him.

"I'll expose all of you for what you are," the asshole sneered. "And I'll hurt your bitch too."

Derrick turned to see his worst nightmares come true. One of the assholes resurfaced holding some kind of homemade pipe bomb in his hand, and he had Lucy. Sheila was crumpled on the floor, bleeding from her head and Lucy's hands were covering her stomach. Her wide purple eyes met his, and he realized she wasn't afraid. She was waiting. For him.

"That was your last mistake," Derrick growled.

He watched the stupid fucker laugh right before Derrick jumped on him. In an instant, Derrick's Wolf lent him fangs and claws without needing to swap skins. He heard scuffling behind him, recognizing Sheila's snarl as she whooped the would be Spielberg's ass.

Fuck these assholes, he growled and squeezed the man's throat snapping his neck like a twig. Lucy was holding the wrested pipe bomb in her hand and Derrick ran to her, taking it gingerly before running to the door and tossing it hard as he could away from everyone. The explosion was loud and sharp, but small. Still, the entire bar went quiet.

Everyone had started clearing out the moment chaos erupted, and only a handful of people, Shifters, had remained to round up the bad guys. Eight in all, two dead in the struggle, the other six subdued and waiting for authorities.

The video camera had been wiped and destroyed, no evidence of the Shifter secret would remain for police to discover. Derrick sat on a stool with his arms wrapped around his mate while the investigators finished working the scene. He could have lost her tonight, but his mate had remained levelheaded and calm. She'd trusted him to protect her, and he did his best, but his fierce little she-Cat had really saved herself.

She's safe. Safe. Mine. Protect.

"So, what can you tell us?" asked the lead detective, a Lion Shifter, named Leonard Crowley. Derrick and Lucy went over the incidents again, and the detective took notes.

"We won't be pressing any charges against any of you, as it seems these guys were unhinged and looking for trouble," Crowley said. "The bomb was real. Unfortunately, crimes like this happen from time to time. We got an email earlier and some anti-government organization claimed responsibility for the attack."

"And Derrick won't be charged, you're sure?" Lucy asked.

"No ma'am. He was acting purely in self-defense. He's a hero. Had that bomb gone off, dozens of people would have died."

"Thank goodness," she said, and slumped against him.

"Detective, my girl is tired. I'd like to take her home. If you have any other questions, you can talk to my staff or wait to get in touch with me."

"Will do. Thank you."

"Oh, when can we reopen?"

"Soon as we're done. Shouldn't take more than a few hours," he nodded and walked away.

"Come on, kitten," Derrick rumbled, and scooped Lucy up in his arms.

"You don't have to carry me," Lucy said as she lay her head against his shoulder.

It was just like her to deny she was dead on her feet. He smiled his response and kissed her hair, holding her even closer as he walked them home.

"I saw him sitting at the bar earlier. The guy we threw out on opening night. I am so sorry, Derrick. This is my fault. I just forgot when you came over. I should have told you. I am so sorry," she repeated, and he hated that she blamed herself.

"Lucy, look at me. There was nothing you could have done to stop that lunatic. None of this is your fault and look what you did. You kicked his ass, broke the camera, saved us all from exposure."

"You're not mad?"

"At you? No fucking way. You are a total badass. I am proud of you."

"I just feel responsible—"

"You're not," he insisted.

"Is your arm okay?" she asked softly.

"All healed, kitten," he said, and bent so she could turn the knob on the front door.

Thor stumbled into the kitchen from his room, and Derrick could tell the man was still out of it.

"Something happen?"

"Don't worry about it, brother. We're fine."

"You sure?" he asked, voice hoarse.

"Yeah. Go on back to bed," Derrick commanded.

The big man nodded, and Derrick took the stairs two at a time, taking them straight to the shower. He wanted to wash away the smoke, blood, and the stink of fear at seeing that man holding a bomb on his mate.

"Hey, I'm alright," Lucy said, and stepped under the spray of warm water with him.

She wrapped her arms tightly around him and he felt himself tremble. Fuck. He could have lost her tonight. It was unthinkable.

"I'm alright, you protected me, your Wolf protected me. My mate, my good mate," she said, dropping kisses across his chest and shoulders until she reached up with small hands and tugged his face down to hers.

Lucy could not believe everything that had happened over the last few hours. Her strong, protective, amazing mate had taken down a bunch of lunatics who'd wanted to cause real harm to them. Humans were not supposed to know about Shifters, but that angry customer sure seemed to know too much. It was a huge problem, and she hoped the Council acted this time instead of sitting on their hands.

But none of that mattered right now. The only thing that concerned her was getting her big, sexy mate to reaffirm their connection. After their warm shower, where Derrick had insisted on washing her body from head to toe, he'd wrapped her up in a fluffy towel and carried her to the bed.

"Lucy, I need you. Sweet mate," he growled, laying her down and teasing her with his whisper light kisses and gentle hands.

She didn't want him to be gentle. She wanted him rough and fierce, like he was when he'd defended her tonight. Boldly, she reached for him, taking two hands to encircle his girthy length. She squeezed and stroked, loving the helpless groan that escaped his lips at her ministrations.

Sexy, sexy mate.

"Mine," Derrick growled and crouched over her body on all fours.

"Show me," she demanded, lifting her arms wide and running her hands up his forearms to his biceps, and then his massive shoulders, skimming the top of his back, touching the tattoo that branded him as hers forever.

"I want one like yours," she said suddenly, stopping him short.

"What?"

"A tattoo. I want one too," she replied.

Derrick's eyes glowed gold and for a second she thought he would refuse, then a smile broke out on his face, and he was crushing his body and mouth to hers. Pleasure blossomed everywhere he touched. Arousal spiked, need grew, and love, so much love flared to life that it left Lucy breathless. He moved so slow, too slow, she tried bucking her hips, but he was immovable.

"Patience, mate," he growled deep and low, and her whole body quaked.

It was like his voice had a direct line to her clit, the needy little bud throbbed and twitched, practically begging for his touch.

"Gonna go slow, but I'll tell you what I'm going to do as I do it, okay? You want that, mate?"

Lucy nodded.

"Tell me."

"Yes, I want that. Please," she pleaded.

Hell, she was begging already, and he hadn't even started yet. Lucy didn't care. She wanted him more than she wanted to breathe.

"First, I'm going to lick your nipples, suck your breasts into my mouth," he growled and lifted her breasts in both hands, kneading the flesh and pinching her just enough till he sucked one plump mound into his hot mouth.

Her pussy throbbed, moisture flooding between her legs as he continued to tend to her breasts. Lucy begged, but he wouldn't budge. Only when he was satisfied did he lift his head.

"Got to taste you, mate. Gonna lick this pussy until you're ready for me. Want that? Want me to lick your pretty pink pussy?"

"Yes, Derrick, yes," she moaned as he slid down her overheated body, licking a trail from her navel to her inner thigh as he went.

Derrick pushed her legs open, his face level with her sex, and just looked. Lucy felt exposed. So open and vulnerable, but she trusted her mate to take care of her.

"Look at you, so wet and ready, kitten. So mine," he growled, then dipped his head, spearing her heat with his long tongue.

"This is mine," he growled and spread her lips open with his fingers, sliding his digits across her swollen flesh. "You are all mine, kitten. Say it."

"Yours," she moaned with no more prompting.

She was desperate for him. Lucy could hardly think with wanting. She needed his mouth on her, his hands, his cock filling her. Now. But he was in no rush. She watched the smile spread across his face as he took his time teasing her. Derrick's fingers lightly breached her opening while his lips dropped soft kisses to her weeping slit. Finally, his gloriously rough tongue snaked out, and he lapped oh-so-slowly at her.

One stroke, then two. A finger. Then two. A graze. A nip. Another lick.

Fuck. Fuck. FUCK.

"Don't stop," she begged. She was so tense she could have snapped.

"Don't stop what?"

"Don't stop eating me," she moaned, rocking her hips to try to force those slick digits deeper inside of her, but he would not be budged. It was like he wanted her out of her mind with need.

"Love your taste, mate. This is my cream, isn't it? My pussy. And it tastes so good."

His tongue moved faster, with longer, harder swipes. Lucy couldn't be still. She bucked her hips, fucking his face with gusto, riding the wave of pleasure until she was screaming his name. When his head finally emerged, she was completely wrung out. Didn't think she had it in her to do more than blink and breathe.

"Mine."

His husky growl sent shockwaves of pleasure through her sex, and she throbbed with need renewed. He slid his hand out of her and brought the soaked digits to his mouth. One by one, he sucked them clean while she watched. Was there anything sexier?

"Need you," she said and reached for him, but still he would not be rushed.

Derrick slid slowly up her body until he was perfectly aligned with her heat.

"Watch baby, I want you to see how we become one. Mine," he lifted his chest and stomach so that she could see the view of his cock kissing her velvet wetness.

"Mine," she echoed, and felt her fangs lengthen and claws extend. She knew she pierced his skin with them as she pulled, but still her mate would not be rushed.

Inch by inch, he slid inside her until he filled her to the brim. So fucking hot and hard and heavy, his length stroked places she never even knew existed deep inside her.

"Fuck, you drive me wild, kitten. Love you. Mate. Mine. Mine. MINE!" he shouted in time with his moves.

Slam, withdraw, slam, withdraw.

Before they'd made love with the new wonder of mates finally meeting, but this was different. This was raw, dirty, Shifter fucking, and Lucy loved it.

"Gonna fuck you till you can't move," he snarled through his own fangs and she could see the Wolf in his eyes.

"Yes," she said, wanting it, needing it, needing him to confirm that they had both survived.

They were both here. Together. Harder and faster, Derrick pumped inside of her. Sex was good, she realized. She'd never trusted it, never wanted it before, but she would always want it with him. Sex with her mate was fucking amazing.

"Derrick, need, please," she growled, the need to come building and building until she was bucking and moving in earnest.

"I got what you need," he roared and flipped her onto her knees.

Ass out, he pressed her head down and spread her cheeks, teasing her hole before slamming his thick, long, glorious cock deep within her pussy. Derrick dropped forward, caging her in with his enormous body as he pounded her slick heat from behind.

"Come for me," he growled, and she wanted to.

She really did. So close. Almost there. He reached around with his thumb and found her clit. Strumming that tiny little nub, he flicked and fucked until she was hissing and roaring like the animal she was.

Pure bliss thundered through her as his cum filled her inside. He squeezed her ass with one hand and thrust again, egging a second slower, but just as powerful orgasm to rush through her.

"So beautiful, mate," he grunted and withdrew from her, covering her with his arms even as she turned into him. They lay like that for hours, unable to move or speak, only capable of breathing and holding each other close.

"I love you, Derrick."

"Love you, mate. Mine," he answered.

"My home," she returned, and his responding smile was all the affirmation she needed.

EPILOGUE

DIRE WOLF MATES

"Are you shitting me?" Sheila practically howled with outrage as Detective Leo Crowley walked into *Serious Moonlight* and took his usual table in the dining room.

Now that they'd started opening early for lunch, they'd been seeing a lot more of the Lion Shifter, much to his baby cousin's consternation. Derrick nodded at the cop and winked at his cousin even as she grumbled and snatched a menu from Susan, the new human server and bartender they'd recently hired.

After the attack, the community really seemed to rally together, and support for *Serious Moonlight* was booming. Of course, they did not know about the supernatural world, but no one liked a terrorist and that was how the public viewed the attack as a war against a friendly MC that had been ostracized and mislabeled by the townies. No one wanted to be seen as politically incorrect these days, so yeah, they had more customers than ever. Either way, things were good.

"Derrick! Where are you?"

He turned as the front door opened and his mate strode in. His eyes went right to her stomach and the beast in him rumbled. True, her belly was only slightly swollen, but he couldn't help the possessive way he watched her. She was carrying their cubs, and he'd never seen anything so damn beautiful.

"Hey there, kitten. I'm here. Where you off to in such a huff?"

He lifted her to him and dropped a kiss on her mouth, loving the blush that spread across her face and the way her purple eyes glittered with her Cat. The sassy little feline was always asserting herself, especially in bed, and fuck, if he didn't love it.

"Derrick, Cole got Buddy towed here from Big Tom's, and now he's saying the car can't be fixed!"

"Now, darlin'," he began, trying to figure out how to broach the subject with his mate.

He'd wanted, no, he'd needed to make sure she was safe and driving that little junker with his cubs was just not happening.

"I see. So, you went and did this, didn't you?" she asked.

"Now, Lucy, I just want you safe, all of you," he explained. Picking her up so he could swipe his tongue across her lips.

Fuck, he loved it when her little pink appendage came out to play with his. The woman had one magical tongue. Matched the rest of her.

Lucky Alpha. Lucky man.

"Well, that's fine, I suppose. But I have an appointment at the doctor's office, so I guess I'll just take your wheels."

She'd been kissing him so sweetly, he didn't notice her hands searching his back pockets. By the time he did, she'd already snagged the keys to his bike and was jiggling them. Brain still foggy, thinking of ways he was going to make his mate scream his name, Derrick didn't move until he heard the roar of his twin engines come to life outside the bar.

"What the? Lucy!" he bellowed.

He was already too late. Pregnant and all, by the time Derrick ran outside, it was to see his sassy mate speeding off down the highway on his Harley.

Fucking hell.

He looked around the lot, sensing he was all alone, and ran to the woods, shucking his clothes and bundling them into the knapsack he had stored there. With the straps secure in his mouth, he shifted to his Wolf and started pounding the asphalt to catch up to her. Hopefully, she'd wait inside her doc's office for him to dress and meet up with her. With a short howl, he pushed his legs harder. Fuck, he loved her. She was his match in every way.

No buts about it.

Derrick growled and used his power to run faster. If he wanted to catch his quick little mate, he needed to shake that sass.

Afterwards, he was taking her car shopping.

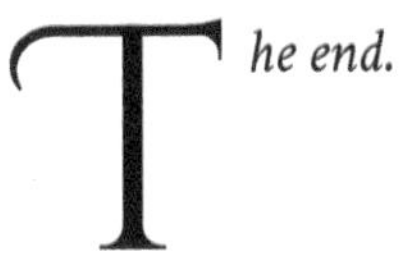*he end.*

Liked this story? Want more Dire Wolf Mates?
Grab the next book, Breaking Sass, at
https://www.cdgorri.com/books/breaking-sass.
Or
Follow the whole series at https://www.cdgorri.com/seres/dire-wolf-mates.

Thank you and happy reading!

BREAKING SASS

DIRE WOLF MATES

BLURB

DIRE WOLF MATES

What happens when a sassy Dire Wolf, with a penchant for breaking rules, and a Lion, who's in love with the law, clash?

She's a sassy Dire Wolf with a fondness for speed, and he's a lethally sexy Lion who knows how to lay down the law. Get ready for fireworks when these two dominant personalities clash!

Sheila Rand is the only female member of the Dire Wolf Motorcycle Club. Rare and powerful Shifters, the Dire Wolf MC has decided to make Blue Valley their permanent home. As the Alpha's cousin, Sheila's outspoken nature, and habitual defiance are overlooked by her Packmates, but not by *him*.

Mr. Law and Order thinks he can break her, but he doesn't know who he's dealing with. This she-Wolf does not want a mate. Especially not a puffed up pussycat!

Leonard Crowley is one of Blue Valley Police Department's only Shifter Detectives. He's worked hard to keep the Shifter secret, doing his utmost to blend in with mainstream life. With his father ailing, Leo is called home to confront certain issues that have popped up in the Blue Valley Pride. The elders insist he name one of their females as mate to assume his rightful position as King of the Pride, but Leo has a surprise for them.

Leo has already met his mate. He just has to claim her.

Will the feisty couple discover breaking sass is much more fun together?

PROLOGUE

DIRE WOLF MATES

Damn. Damn. DAMN.

Sheila Rand pulled her Harley Softail Convertible over, coasting to a slow roll and eventual stop on the shoulder of the four-lane New Jersey highway. She'd been out for a spin on her bike alone after closing the bar tonight. It was nothing she hadn't done a dozen times or more since they'd opened Serious Moonlight in the South Jersey town of Blue Valley.

She tore off her helmet and tossed her mane of fiery red over her shoulder, huffing out an angry sigh. All she'd wanted was some time alone. A few minutes with the wind rushing all around her so she might try to weed out the negative thoughts and worries that had plagued her throughout the long and surprisingly busy day.

Business was good. Her Alpha was happily mated. The female he'd chosen was a real spitfire, and Sheila thoroughly approved of her. Lucy Corwyn was the name of the now pregnant feline Shifter Derrick was completely smitten with. They were downright cozy and wasn't that annoying in an adorable sort of way?

Grrr.

Easy, girl.

Sheila's inner beast prowled inside the metaphysical plane where she rested till called. Her evening rides usually helped settle her animal, but of course, tonight was all wonky. Her favorite thing about Blue Valley, the new place of residence for the Dire Wolf Motorcycle Club, was its easy access to the highway. Sheila could really cut loose on the miles of smooth, sleek asphalt in the wee hours of the morning.

Her Pack was off doing whatever they did when they weren't working or riding. She'd chosen to run with Derrick and his boys when she'd still been young enough to appreciate their wild ways. Oh yeah, their branch of the DWMC had started as a real ragtag group of renegades and nomads. Like all Dire Wolf Shifters, she supposed.

Only they were different. Very recently, Derrick, the boys, and Sheila had all decided to end their time on the road. Dangerous for their kind, but necessary if they wanted to lay down roots, build homes, have families. Her stomach clenched with butterflies, thinking about Derrick and Lucy's cub.

Lucky, lucky couple.

Sheila didn't know if it would work in the beginning, them staying in one place. But now that Lucy was growing her cousin's baby inside her belly, well, it gave all of them a reason to settle. A reason to protect their land and their business. That cub was the future heir to the throne, and the entire Pack couldn't wait to meet the little blessing.

The fact their kind usually attracted unwanted attention in the form of challenges and brawls with other Shifters didn't worry Sheila. Because of their size and strength, Dire Wolves often kept their Packs small, but that did not make them any less tough. The elusive Shifters usually stayed on the road to avoid altercations, but they'd staked their claim and they would defend it with their lives.

She liked Blue Valley, contrary to popular belief. Sheila wasn't trying to leave or missing her old life when she went on these runs. It was just, *well,* riding a motorcycle was a lot of fucking fun, and she was fond of fun.

Hell to the yeah.

She trusted Derrick, and not just because he was her cousin and Alpha, but because the man had a nose for things. When he'd announced his plans to settle, the whole lot of them had agreed to join him. Tired of life on the road, they all agreed to make a claim on some land and build a home, a Pack house, together.

So, here they were. And here she was. But there was something else in the air Sheila hadn't counted on when they'd landed here, and that was a restlessness she didn't want to name.

Shit.

She was no coward, and it was time to face facts. With their Alpha just mated, hope had sprung eternal. The rest of the Pack had started mooning around and looking outside, all of those big, dumb boys wondering if they too would find their fated mates in the small town.

All except for Sheila.

This spunky little she-Wolf was perfectly fine on her own. She didn't need a man to complete her, or whatever horseshit the graybeards from her old Pack had tried to convince her of when she'd been just a cub. What could a man do for her that Sheila couldn't do for herself?

Puhleeze.

She was stronger, smarter, faster, and worked harder than most of the guys she knew. Sheila could out cuss, out ride, and shoot more whiskey than half the Shifters she knew, and that was saying something.

Plus, she already knew where her g-spot was. The last guy she dated couldn't find it with a hand-drawn map or satellite guided assistance, for fuck's sake.

Pack house was getting stuffy with all the sighs and whines of the lovesick men she'd pledged to ride, *and land,* with. Overgrown cubs, the whole bunch of them, crying in their beers about needing a mate. Still, Sheila could deal with them. With her Pack.

They'd picked Blue Valley and that meant she did, too. But she'd never ever, *never ever* signed on to deal with *him*—that butt-sniffing, post-scratching, lazy feline pain in her ass.

Nuh uh. Not her. No way.

She looked in her rearview mirror at the sedan that had pulled over onto the shoulder behind her with one end sticking slightly into the traffic lane, to protect the person being hassled, of course. The customary siren was perched on the roof, lights flashing. At least the bastard hadn't turned on the sound.

Silver lining.

Oh, whatever.

He'd been waiting for her to ride by, of course. Crafty fucker. Darn speed traps should be illegal, in her humble opinion. What harm was she doing, taking her frustrations out on the road when no one else in their right mind was out and about at this time? It was the witching hour, after all, and Sheila was feeling mighty crafty.

Should make a big, fat voodoo cat and stick pins right in his you-know-what, she thought with an annoyed snarl. Would be a shame, though. Truth be told, the boy was quite good looking. Nice, big, hard body, and from the semi bulge in his pants, Sheila would bet the Lion was packing something mighty girthy behind his zipper.

Grrrr.

Hush up, she told her horny she-Wolf.

The man certainly was taking his time, but finally, after a few minutes, Sheila's supposed *fated mate* stepped out of his vehicle. She watched as he straightened up, and up, and up—he sure was big. His gold eyes flashed in the darkness, and was that a purr coming from his chest as he raked over her body with that possessive gaze of his?

Sheila frowned. She was not an object. He did not own her. And furthermore, she refused to let her inner beast dictate her reactions to this, this—*really hot fucking guy*. Her she-Wolf could be somewhat pushy at times with her invasive thoughts.

Ugh.

"Put your helmet on the ground, please, and show me your license and registration," Leo Crowley said in his usual gruff voice.

Gives me goosebumps every single time. Bastard.

"Make me," she countered.

"Sheila." His tone held a warning note, but she didn't give a fuck.

"Detective," she replied, tossing her hair arrogantly.

"You know, you were doing ninety-five. It's dangerous on the road at night," he started.

"For you, maybe. But I was born on the road, detective. Just one more difference between you and me. Now, are you giving me a ticket?"

"Not tonight," he said, hands on his narrow, rodeo cowboy hips.

"Then can I go?"

Leo growled deep in his chest before nodding sharply, staring at her with those big, golden eyes of his.

"Get home safe, Sheila."

She ignored his parting words, revved her engine, and shot off like a bat out of hell. Inside her, a storm was brewing, and the reason was that man. Why couldn't he just walk away? She'd told him now a hundred times.

So, what if her she-Wolf was up in arms over the man? Sheila the human was decidedly not. He was all wrong for her. A cop, for fuck's sake, when she'd been raised to flout the law.

No, no, no. Leo Crowley was not for her.

Mine.

No.

Grrr.

Quit it.

Fate might have decided Detective Leo Crowley was her mate, but Sheila wasn't about to go down without a fight. She was going to break that crush right out of that man, one sassy comment at a time. Then Sheila would have what she'd always wanted above all else.

Her freedom.

CHAPTER ONE

DIRE WOLF MATES

"Leo, come home," George whined over the phone.

The grating sound his younger cousin had perfected at seven years old still made Leo's Lion hiss in annoyance. His inner animal seriously did not care for George's manners or attitude.

It's not that he was blatantly disrespectful, but George was a bothersome prat. A pest. An annoyance. An irritation. But he was still his cousin—something Leo would very much like to forget.

His beast chuffed in response to the whining imbecile on the other end of his smart phone. If he were here, Leo would have already shifted and played a little game of cat and mouse with the much smaller male.

Grrr.

As it was, he had to count to three before replying. A little technique he'd learned in kindergarten to help him reassert his self-control. After all, it was unseemly for the future King of the Blue Valley Pride to lose his shit at a subordinate. Especially over the phone.

"I have a job, George. I cannot just come home when summoned. If you have an issue, tell the King."

"That's just it, Leo. The King is not seeing anyone these days," George whined.

"What? Come on, that can't be true. Dad is always available to the Pride. Besides, I'm on a case investigating an attack that could lead to a possible leak in our *organization*," he said, alerting his cousin to the fact some humans had gotten wise to the Shifter secret.

If word spread about the existence of the supernatural world, it would be pure chaos. Every Shifter, Vampire, Witch, and whatever would be under fire. There was a reason they kept hidden. Humans did not respond well to the unknown, and paranormal creatures would suffer grave consequences if discovered.

"Officially, I am investigating the bombing at *Serious Moonlight* that occurred last month. Unofficially, the Council has me poking around to try to find the mole. They want me to shut this shit down, George. It's important," Leo said, working hard not to let his Cat override his sense of serenity.

"So is the Pride."

"The Pride can wait," he snapped at the younger man, his beast's growling growing louder by the second.

Shit.

There were too many humans milling about. Leo closed his eyes and rolled his shoulders. He gazed out over the horizon outside of his small kitchen. He'd chosen this house for one reason only, and that was the view.

Magfuckingnificent.

The structure was small and cramped, but its location was sound. On the edge of town, his home was far away from the hustle and bustle of the otherwise idyllic community of Blue Valley. Sure, he missed the Pride sometimes. Conversations with his father, and the small patch of woods where he used to roam as a cub, but Leo had a different life now—a new purpose.

"Leo, please," George whined again.

"Rroarr!"

"Eeek!"

Leo roared into the phone, unable to hold on to his patience any longer. Thank fuck he was home. His idiot cousin actually squeaked in reply, and the sound made his animal want to hunt.

No. No. NO.

"Christ, George, enough," Leo grumbled and rubbed his hand over his face.

His Lion was a damn nuisance. Being born dominant meant always battling the beast within. His Lion was violent, bloodthirsty, volatile. He liked to growl, hiss, bite, and claw—tear into anyone who even thought to challenge him.

His list of enemies now, unfortunately, included George, his idiot cousin. The fool obviously thought it was a good idea to try to order him around. But Leo's dominance was a real thing, even over the phone. He looked around quickly, making sure no one had heard his little slip.

Fucking hell. 1, 2, 3...

"Sorry, Leo," George mumbled. "I mean you no disrespect, your majesty. But your father, *the King*, is not doing well. His illness is progressing, and the elders have called a circle—tonight, Leo."

"Tonight?"

"Yeah. It's serious. You really need to be here for this."

This time, George's whine was coming from his animal. The difference sounded distinct over the phone, and Leo knew he was agitated. His Lion growled softly. The beast was a natural born leader. He wanted to soothe the younger male, while maintaining his position as the stronger, more dominant Lion. It was all part and parcel of being born the next true King of the Blue Valley Pride.

Other Shifter groups had *Alphas, Netas,* and *what-have-yous* to guide them, but Lion Shifters were led by either a King or Primus, depending on their Pride. The Blur Valley Pride had Kings and Queens to rule them.

Leo Crowley had flouted tradition by leaving to become a cop, but it did not matter. His future had been set in stone the day he was conceived. It was easy to forget since he'd moved away from the

Pride. But George was right. Leo had a duty, a responsibility to his father, and the Pride.

No, he was not particularly fond of politics. The slimy, greasy, double talk of the Pride's circle had never sat well with him. Hence the reason he chose a profession where he kept law and order, not talked about it.

There was another reason he wasn't feeling particularly gracious at the moment. Everyone knew the best Kings had Queens by their sides. Fate often played a hand at bringing Shifters together, but Leo's own potential mate had found some pretty unique and off-putting ways to turn him down.

Telling him *no* was a favorite pastime of Sheila Rand's. One of her favorite methods was, of course, the one-fingered salute she waved whenever he even walked into the bar her Pack owned and operated, which was daily, since—*stupid fuck that he was*—Leo couldn't seem to stay the hell away from the ornery female.

Sassy, sexy, fiery-tempered woman.

Leo's beast chuffed whenever he pictured the voluptuous Miss Rand. The Lion grunted, baring his teeth where he rested inside the metaphysical plane where all Shifter beasts existed till called. Leo had a special connection with his Lion, and he could see and hear him quite clearly inside his mind's eye. The Lion was annoyed at his human side's fretting, but whatever. Leo had plenty of things weighing on his great leonine mind.

Curvy, redheaded, sweet-smelling things.

"Well? Leo, will you come?" George interrupted.

He'd forgotten he was still on the phone with the annoying male. Leo sighed heavily. The younger Lion had a point about the elders calling for a circle on such short notice. It was unusual and suspect. But he had no desire to be sucked into Pride politics. Not at the moment.

His Lion wavered. The primal need to take care of those weaker than him was strong. Right up there with his need to crush anyone who dared challenge him. Instinct won out. His Lion was riding him hard, urging his human side to offer comfort to his Pride and kin.

Years of practice pushing his dominance aside in order to get things done, Leo tapped the countertop and exhaled slowly. Working with one foot in the human world and one in the supernatural world required balance. But if he was any sort of son to his father, *the King*, keeping tabs on the Pride was a matter of familial obligation and duty. What other options did he have?

"A circle, you said. And it is taking place on Pride territory tonight?"

"Yes. It's not good, there's been talk of a coup," George replied quickly.

"A coup?" growled Leo.

Bad enough they were calling a circle, but if this was a plot to overthrow the King without a direct challenge, heads were going to roll. A circle usually just meant the elders were getting ready to announce something. His guess was it was something big, and possibly annoying.

These things did not occur for no reason. Leo's experiences on the force and his heightened supernatural senses made him superb at finding out people's motivations. Leo was his father's heir. Whether or not he wanted to rule, Leo would have to accept formal challenges for the title once he ascended the throne.

Anyone trying to flout that law would be dealt with. Lion laws were complex and intricate, dating back to ancient times. The elders knew this. If they were plotting a coup, what did they have to gain by trying to circumvent their own traditions? That was the real question.

"I'll find someone at work to cover for me."

"You mean, you'll come?"

The younger man's excitement made Leo wince, and he growled into the phone loudly before he stifled the sound.

"Yes. I will be there, George," he returned.

Feelings of duty, honor, and loyalty welled up inside Leo as he tapped the end call button on the small screen. They were strong character traits of any Lion of worth, in his opinion—any person, really. He had a strict view of his responsibilities, and the Pride was both duty and obligation at the very least.

With over sixty adult members, the Blue Valley Pride was one of the largest Big Cat groups in the northeast. And that was not luck. No way. Leo's father, the current King, was a total badass with a reputation for being strong and decisive, while maintaining a gentle paw on the pulse of his Pride mates. Happy Lions meant a happy Pride, and a happy Pride was a fruitful one. The Blue Valley Pride was extremely productive in that respect.

Eat Well Live Proud, their import and export business, worked with the finest organic meat products in the world. The business was profitable and kept the Pride's coffers healthy. They had business dealings with top sheep, goat, bison, and of course, cattle ranches around the world, including but not limited to Colorado, Texas, New Mexico, Brazil, China, Australia, and of course, Argentina. Not to mention their fish and poultry connections.

EWLP products were shipped to all the top supermarkets, specialty stores, hotel chains, and restaurants. They even had a *ranch to table* delivery service where families could order top quality meat in bulk. He knew the importance of this business and its connection to the Pride, and Leo was proud of his father's success in making it all happen.

The US Department of Agriculture's Animal and Plant Health Inspection Service had been a constant figure in young Leo's life. He still kept tabs on new regulations and requirements and made sure his father and his advisors were aware of any new laws and rules that crept up on them.

Eat Well Live Proud kept the Pride in the black. Every one of his Lions shared in the profits of the company with quarterly dividends. Most of the adults in the Pride worked for the company, and those who retired did so with excellent packages and still kept a portion of the proceeds.

Donovan Crowley was no fool. His father had always been crystal clear during his reign that greed had no place within the Pride. He was a philanthropist, using most of his own wealth and his share of the proceeds to see to his community's needs.

King D had built an entire community of houses for his people. A gated community where he managed to separate his Lions from the normals who would likely shit themselves if confronted with a couple of changed adults from the Pride.

Smart. Very smart.

It was the duty of every Shifter to keep their secret. Leaders had to be strong, decisive, and capable of keeping the peace. King D was all that and more. The Blue Valley Pride's gated community, called *Blue Valley Homes,* had three recreational parks for their cubs, several grassy knolls, and over fifteen acres of surrounding forests to roam.

There was plenty of room for Pride members to move about. He also reinforced their sense of fellowship with scheduled runs and Pride meetings. Yes, Leo's father was a good King. And yet, the elders were calling a circle.

Grrrrr.

Of course, Leo had been absent lately. He didn't have much hands-on experience with his father or the Pride since he'd been elbows deep in doing his job—not to mention *other* distractions.

Redheaded, big-bosomed, sassy, sexy as fuck distractions... Prrrrrr.

The truth was simple, if a little embarrassing to admit aloud now that he was an adult—but here it was. Donovan Crowley was Leo's personal fucking idol. The King had always been larger than life to his son. A true example of the best of what their species had to offer. Powerful, just, fair, and stronger than any other Lion Leo had ever seen.

True, he'd been distant. But he was a caring father. He just always put duty first—something his son had learned to emulate. One thing was certain, the Pride sure loved Donovan Crowley, and his people were loyal.

There just hadn't been much room for Leo in his busy life. But that was okay. Leo understood all about duty, and he wasn't whining about it. He was never mistreated. Nothing could be farther from the truth.

If anything, Leo was a little spoiled. Growing up Lion royalty had given him the best. He had an excellent education—best that money could buy. As for the whole Dad being too busy to toss around the old pigskin, well, Leo had plenty of friends and buckets of affection from his dearly departed mother, and the other Lionesses in his family.

He literally had dozens of female relatives, all doting on him throughout his child and young adulthood. He had been afforded all the benefits a man of his position was entitled to. And when he was old enough, he'd left home for college. That had been a very turbulent time in Leo's life.

At the end of his first semester, he'd returned on a weekend visit to find his human mother ill, and his father tending her bedside alone. He'd been stopped at the door, told by his father's loyal valet—a man who was a pillar of the palace—that his father thought it best if Leo did not visit during that time. The King needed his Lion settled before he could handle the dominant male his son had become.

Of course, seeing his mate decline in health had upset his Lion, and Leo mourned the loss of both mother and father during that time. He hated not seeing his mother, but he managed a handful of visits when his father was away from the palace, during her illness, before she'd finally succumbed to it.

Yes, he resented his father for keeping him away from his mother for all those years. Partly why he'd become so distant. Donovan Crowley had ordered his son away from the palace and kept his mate to himself, denying Leo access to his mother, and that broke something between them. It damaged the bond Leo should feel to his King and father. He knew it. The King knew it. But both ignored it, pretending everything was okay over brief emails and even briefer phone calls.

He did not want to deal with all this Pride business right now. Fucking George. Why couldn't he just leave Leo alone? Being heir to the crown was simply a fact he did not have time for. But Leo knew his duty. Even if he'd conveniently forgotten it as he'd set about making a life for himself outside the Pride.

He'd always known he would have to return one day. Leo just wasn't prepared for it to happen this soon. He stood looking at nothing and thought long and hard about his position.

A Crowley had reigned over the Blue Valley Pride since the late 1790s. His father was a firm believer in the old ways. Donovan Crowley followed those old beliefs to the *t*, including alienating his only son.

He'd even kept a *circle of elders*, a sort of council of advisors to help keep the Pride on a healthy track. Their job was not to dictate, but to ask questions and to make suggestions. Should a King not be able to perform his duty, they had the power to call for a challenge for new leadership.

That meant they would have to pick a challenger who would then fight the King in a battle to the death either on two feet or four. Those were the only rules. And it had never happened. Not in the history of the Blue Valley Pride. At least, not as far as Leo knew.

Born with the Crowley lineage's powerful streak of dominance, Leo's Lion was strong, a true Alpha male. It was logical for Leo to leave the Pride until the time came for him to lead it. No one wanted a challenge between father and son. Heartbreaking though it was to be parted from his mother, Leo understood his father's reasons for keeping him at bay. Sometimes a King had to make difficult decisions.

"Son, I have no wish to harm you, but the elders say it is inevitable. When two dominant males, each with the predisposition to be King, are locked inside of the same Pride, one usually winds up dead. I will not have any harm come to you. I owe your mother that."

His father's voice echoed in his ear on the day of his mother's funeral, and he realized it had been one of the last times he'd actually talked to the man face to face. Leo knew stories of Lions killing each other, of sons and fathers at each other's throats to claim the throne. According to his father and the elders, this happened when dominant males could not control their natural urge to rule.

His grandfather had been killed in an accident before his father had cause to test this theory himself. Leo understood he did it out of love for his son. But understanding and accepting it were two different things. Would he change the past if he could? Maybe. But that was not within his power.

Pride life was bloody and complicated. Keeping the Shifter secret by working alongside human law enforcement and covering up those incidents that would have leaked the truth had become his duty and obligation in place of the Pride. It had been hard, very hard, to stay away when his mother had become ill. But he did. For peace.

He'd tried to forgive his father. Tried to patch the bridge. Even made the best of it when he'd been told to leave and not return in that hated letter Montgomery, his father's valet, had given him. But Leo was loyal and good at following orders. He did as he was commanded by his King and father. He moved on, only visiting a few times over the years. Of course, ever since his mother had passed away, the visits had lessened.

According to George, he had to return. His father's health was declining, the Pride at risk. Shame filled him as he thought of all the time he'd allowed to pass. The gap between him and his father growing wider all the while. Leo walked outside of his house, into the warm night breeze that greeted him like a blanket against his skin. It was not balmy, just mild. Agreeable for the season.

Kind of like the warm air that blew from the expensive dryer he'd ordered through his barbershop. Like most Lion Shifters, Leo was big on maintaining his mane. He wore it a little shorter than most males in his Pride, but it was thick, glossy, and golden and he treated it well with conditioners and organic, sulfate free shampoos. Good hair care was a Lion thing.

He shook his head at the errant thought. He'd need his wits about him if he were to enter the *elder's circle*. Those felines were cunning and slick as most hunters were, and everyone knew Lionesses ruled the hunt in any Pride. Four women from the oldest, most loyal families made up the circle. He'd been away long enough to lose sight of their agenda, but not of the fact that they were dangerous.

Distance can be good, his Lion grunted, *they will have forgotten who we are.*

"Well then," he said aloud.

"Let's remind them."

L*ater that night...*

The sky seemed lit with thousands of stars, and he took a moment to look at them before he sat down in his custom 1965 Corvette Stingray. The red convertible was pure cherry, in his not so humble opinion.

It took him a few years to track down that particular model of his favorite sports car, but it had been worth it. He'd spent weeks rebuilding the engine, adding perks, and modifying the interior to fit his larger than normal frame. Leo was a big fucking Lion, and he needed the extra room.

He'd tried to maintain the original body, right down to the accents. The color was not just simple red. It was the original *Rally Red* made by GM with the same luster and deep shine the car would have come with brand new from the factory.

It was the best of both worlds. Classic car, modern comfort, and fuck, he loved the damn thing. Especially the way the powerful engine felt beneath his hands and feet. The sleek automobile had taken a long, long while to hunt down. But Leo was a patient Lion when it came to things he wanted.

The image of a certain seductive she-Wolf flitted through his head, and his Lion growled, rising within him to contemplate the object of his current hunt.

Sheila Rand. Beautiful, dominant, sexy as fuck Dire Wolf.

Mate. Mate. MATE.

Leo's growl rose and rattled the interior of his ride. He closed his eyes and counted, trying to rein in his inner beast. Fate sometimes played a hand in bringing Shifters together. Leo had never really thought about it. At least, not until the day he'd met his in a curvy little package who wanted nothing to do with him.

Fuck. Fuck. FUCK.

The confounded woman knew they were mates. At least, he was 99% sure she did. For whatever reason, she was completely unwilling to talk about it. So, he did what any self-respecting Lion would do. Leo visited her at her job. Waited for her when she left for her nightly rides. Watched. Protected. Lusted from afar.

Fine. He was stalking her. What the fuck choice did he have? The animal would not let him leave her alone. He tried for patience. Wanted to take his time, to woo her with his charm, wit, and looks, which were not half bad—if he did say so himself.

Sheila Rand was worth it. And Leo would not, could not, rest until she was by his side.

Grrrr.

But first, he needed to focus on what lay in wait for him at the Pride house. Afterwards, he'd worry about the sassy woman who'd already laid claim to his fierce predator's heart.

Mine.

"Yes," he agreed with his beast.

"Mine."

CHAPTER TWO

DIRE WOLF MATES

Sheila heaved out a sigh and wiped up yet another spill on the otherwise gleaming bar top with a clean rag. Normally, she liked her job, but tonight she was a bit preoccupied.

He walked in a half hour ago. Stupid Lion, with his stupid, thick, glossy hair, tempting her to walk over, straddle his lap and run her fingers all through the perfectly tousled golden locks. It was ridiculous for a man to have such good hair! He looked like he hardly did a thing to it, but it was way too perfect for no effort. She'd bet half her tips he spent an hour on that head every damn morning.

Fucker.

Cute fucker.

Whatever.

It was all Sheila could do to keep her animal away from the dumb pussycat—tempting, dominant beast of a male. He'd been showing up daily for weeks now. Just pranced on inside her bar every damn day, like he owned the place.

Irritating, heavy handed, sexy, muscular, gorgeous—wait, what?

When did she start complimenting the big pussy? Nuh uh. Sheila wanted nothing to do with that badge-wearing overgrown house cat!

Leo Crowley was law and order, and Sheila Rand was anything but. She was a ripped jean wearing, motorcycle riding, fierce as fuck Dire Wolf Shifter. She did not need some Alpha male Lion in her life. Hell, she knew all about those ridiculous males, needing females to do all the work, wanting her to pander to his every wish and need.

Hard pass. Seriously.

Sheila leaned down to pick up a speck of invisible dust, needing the break from the rather intoxicating view of his golden-eyed stare—yes, he watched her. She felt those eyes on her like hands. Secretly, it thrilled her. She wondered what it would be like to give in to the undeniable attraction she felt for him, but no! She was so not falling down that rabbit hole.

Her inner Wolf whined, the beast barking a sharp, sad sound that echoed in her mind's eye. The animal wanted Sheila to greet her mate. To rub her fur on him. Mark him with her scent.

He is not my mate.

Yesssss. Mine. Mate.

Shut it, she growled at the beast.

This was ridiculous. She was not one big, throbbing hormone, for fuck's sake. She had to concentrate. Sheila tilted her head to better hear the conversation taking place on the other side of the front bar at *Serious Moonlight*.

A lifelong David Bowie fan, Sheila had enthusiastically approved of the name immediately when Derrick, her cousin and Alpha, had come up with it. After some debate with the ornery fucker, she'd been granted permission to come up with the logo.

Sheila had taken great pleasure in designing the logo and overall theme for *Serious Moonlight*. After all, this was the first official home of the Dire Wolf Motorcycle Club. Blue Valley had welcomed them with a healthy flow of patrons courtesy of Rafe Maccon. That powerful Alpha of the Macconwood Pack had come in with his mate and infamous Wolf Guard during their first week in business. After that, he'd sent plenty more customers over to them.

She'd been nervous at first. Had heard the rumors of the powerful male and knowing how other Wolves often reacted to their small, but potent Pack, she'd worried about her cousin. Challenges would, of course, be directed at him as Alpha. But Rafe, and his mate Charley, had surprised Sheila. They were not interested in fighting. Charley, a human, had been more intent on discussing the logo Sheila had designed, to her great pleasure.

The curvy little Alpha fem had loved the brash, hot pink scrawl Sheila chose to go on top of the glowing image of a large, white, full moon. It was both eye-catching and memorable. Sheila had liked the neon incarnation of the design so much, she'd ordered a mini sign for behind the front bar. She'd also slapped the logo on custom ordered black t-shirts, tank tops, and aprons for the staff.

Only recently, their order of printed napkins and place mats had come in. Sheila could not wait to use them. It was a branding thing. Guaranteed to make their customers remember their time at *Serious Moonlight Roadhouse & Bar*.

The Pack had plenty of start-up money, and though they each had their own bank accounts, there was one central business account that detailed their gross earnings before they got their shares. Some of the Pack had bitched about the pink neon, but after a few months of raking in the crowds, they'd shut up.

Jerks.

She snorted at the thought. They might be jerks sometimes, but they were her Pack, and she loved them. Not like *loved* them loved them, but they were all family. Derrick was a good leader, and she supported his decision to settle down. It was not easy for their kind to do—nomads, the lot of them. But they managed.

Derrick was smart for a boy. He doled out jobs and responsibilities as evenly as he handed out shares of the proceeds, keeping their minds focused and their Wolves too busy to notice their surroundings. Money was good, but it was not everything. They had a few regular bills, but other than that, little use for money. Most of their cash went to motorcycle maintenance, and the rebuilding of whatever old school bikes they found, of course.

None of them had any particular love for material things. Too much time on the road was good for that, at least. Stuff was stuff. The important things in life were free. Sheila knew that deep inside her heart and soul.

Not that she wasn't loving the little conveniences living in Blue Valley offered. Having a house with running cold and hot water beat sleeping in the dirt and washing in a cold stream any day of the year.

Hell yeah.

She was more than glad they'd found a place to settle, but just lately she'd felt a little anxious. Of course, it wasn't Blue Valley or her Pack that was making her restless. It was more likely the six-foot something hunk of man, staring at her from the other side of the bar, driving her bananas.

"Can I get another beer, baby?"

Sheila's attention snapped to the older customer, who'd interrupted her train of thought. Blue eyes flashing their annoyance, she frowned at the too familiar male, disapproving his use of a term of endearment with her. Sheila growled a little, grabbing a bottle of his preferred brand from the cooler, opened it, and placed the bottle on the bar top in front of him.

"The name's Sheila, Irv. Not baby. Not honey. And not sugar tits. I told you that already," she said curtly and made change for the twenty he'd put on the bar.

"My bad, Miss Sheila. But you sure should be somebody's baby," he grinned widely, showing off the big gaping hole where a tooth should have been.

"You flirtin' with me, Irv?"

Sheila smirked, shaking her hair back off her shoulders. It was hot inside the bar, and she'd have to adjust the thermostat, so she didn't start sweating.

"Heck yeas, I am. I'm old, not dead," the man replied readily.

Irv's eyes gaped, his head dropping as he stared at the way her tight tank top outlined her curves. Sheila rolled her eyes. Men were so damn predictable. Her tank top was useful for tips, but the truth was, she had zero hangups about her body. Yes, the uniform was tight, but the material was soft and stretchy, and she enjoyed wearing it. Fuck what anyone said about her.

Yes, she had curves. She also had muscle. Tattoos. And five piercings in her left ear. Sheila was a motherfucking Dire Wolf Shifter. Her body was hers and she wore whatever the hell she wanted when she wanted.

Period.

Were it not for the fact he was seventy years old, if he was a day—Sheila might have popped old Irv right in the jaw for smacking his lips together like she was a slice of pizza. Extra cheese. Lucky for him, she was feeling gracious.

"Irv, you leave that young thing alone," one of his companions butted in.

"Oh hell, now don't you go embarrassin' me in front of my boys, Miss Sheila. Tell him we're just talkin' here," Irv said, taking a pull from his beer and blushing all the while.

He met her eyes for a second, averting his gaze almost immediately, which was just as well. Her Wolf was riled. Of course she was. Leo's eyes were trained on her and Irv.

Nosy pussy.

"I would never think of embarrassing you, Irv. Next one's on me, okay?"

She winked at the older man, whose blush turned even redder. Sheila laughed and Irv waved before taking his beer and turning to chat with his buddies. She dropped the change he'd given her in the tip jar and went back to wiping the counter and eavesdropping on an unhappy couple in the corner.

Always be nice to the customers.

It was an unwritten rule all entrepreneurs adhered to. Sheila more than most. She was tough, levelheaded, and business oriented in ways that even managed to surprise her. But there was something going on in the corner she didn't quite like.

Sheila was manning her station solo tonight. Her usual cobartender, Weylin, was busy covering the back bar for Lucy, who was taking time off for the next couple of days because of her ever-growing abdomen. The she-Cat was pregnant with Derrick's young, and Sheila could not be happier for them.

Cubs, her inner Wolf whined.

Just thinking of them terrified Sheila. They were so tiny, so delicate, and fragile. How could anyone take care of something so small? It gave her the willies just thinking about impending motherhood. And if that was not frightening enough, how about dealing with some overbearing Alpha breathing down her neck?

Ugh. Poor Lucy—though, truth be told, she did not look like she minded. Thank fuck for the new soundproofing insulation the boys had installed in every room. Last thing she needed to hear was her cousin and his mate getting it on night after night.

Sour grapes much?

Fuck off, Wolf.

Anyway, Sheila was working her station alone, and typically, that would be fine. Sheila was no slouch. Besides, if Derrick had his way, the Alpha fem would be off every night, but Lucy was a stubborn kitty. Sheila's new cousin-in-law, a Bobcat Shifter, was fiercely independent. It drove Derrick nuts, which, of course, amused the rest of the Pack to no end.

Sheila liked Lucy very much. She respected the woman's natural grit and her determination to work by her mate's side. Tonight was a special occasion—Sheila had it direct from the source. Derrick was finally going to pop the big question over dessert. He'd chosen to take Lucy on a picnic, complete with a fancy supper prepared for them by Brock, their Pack Beta, and head chef at the roadhouse.

It sounded romantic and sentimental—just perfect for the couple, as far as Sheila was concerned. Not that she went in for mushy shit most of the time. Sheila was more a get it on and get out the door kinda gal. Even if it had been a hot minute since the last time she'd felt the need to get sweaty with a member of the opposite sex.

Sheila was not the *settle down with a mate* type, and it surprised her to find her cousin was. Good for him, though. She supposed it helped that Lucy and Derrick were so much alike. The little hybrid Cat Shifter loved the outdoors as much as the giant Dire Wolf did.

Yes, this was good news. Important too, for the whole of them as a Pack. It was about time Derrick claimed the female in a traditional if old-fashioned way. Lucy had already started showing, and Sheila was definitely in favor of their cubs bearing the Rand name.

Of course, Lucy was going to give him hell. Sheila grinned, thinking about it. Ha! Poor big cousin. But she knew the little she-Cat loved Derrick like crazy. Besides, they were already mated. Marriage was just a nice way to tidy it all up. Not that Sheila wanted to get married. Like ever.

Never ever. Not me. No way.

Even if a certain pussy kept prowling around the bar, trying to get her attention. She was having none of what that tomcat had to offer. IN fact, Sheila pointedly ignored Mr. Law and Order every single night. She would've thought he'd have gotten the hint already. But no. He still came strutting through those doors like clockwork.

The damn man had even stopped in front of her tonight, giving her one long, thorough look before heading over to where Weylin was working the back bar to grab his usual IPA. He was wearing fitted slacks and a neat, button down that made her want to run her hands all over it, wrinkle him up good.

There was just something about his good boy clothes and bad boy hair that was so damn appealing to Sheila. He was a series of contradictions—tiny little mysterious quirks she wanted to work out and discover for herself.

Grrrr.

Watching him walk away, fine ass outlined in his tight pants had set her Dire Wolf into immediate annoyed mode. Her beastie was pissed he'd gotten his beer from Weylin—but she was not mad at him. Oh no. Never that. Snarky, territorial female that she was, her she-Wolf was pissed off at her human side, at Sheila, for driving their mate away with her off-putting manners and sassy nature.

Oh well. This is what I wanted, anyway. About time that overgrown throw rug left me alone.

Mine.

Shut it.

Sheila heaved a sigh, frustrated with her inner arguments. She told herself over and over again that pussycat was not hers. And yet, every time she caught sight of his golden hair gleaming or heard his raucous laughter boom out from the other side of the room, her Wolf snapped to attention.

Her Pack mates were fond of him. They enjoyed his stories about working as a detective and often had a joke or two for the Lion when he came in. Ever since he'd helped out with the little bombing incident, he'd earned the respect of the DWMC, and maybe a little loyalty, too.

Fine. He was alright, she supposed. Leo had helped them identify the culprit behind that attack, and he saw to it Derrick was not charged. Afterwards, her cousin had announced that Leo Crowley's money was no good at *Serious Moonlight*.

In other words, the big ol' pussycat was not to pay for a single beer as long as he lived. Of course, that didn't stop the *by the book* Lion Shifter from leaving a couple of bills on the counter every night.

What a hard ass!

He couldn't even accept a beer without getting his tail in a bunch. Sheila's stomach clenched. Her pulse raced, and she found it hard to focus on her current task, which involved tossing a few empties into the recycling bin. He was just so, so—*what was the word she was looking for?*

Gorgeous? Sexy? Ours?

No. No. NO.

How about infuriating, annoying, and ridiculous?

Bingo. Those would work. The man was all those things, mostly though, he was distracting. Leo the Lion and all his steady persistence were proving to be something more than just a nuisance. Everywhere she looked, he was there. Stopping her when she was speeding. Showing up at the bar at all hours. Insisting they were mates.

Grrrr.

She ignored her Wolf's unhappy growl. Whatever the Fates had decided, Sheila was convinced they'd made a mistake. She was not the one for that uptight pussycat. Pushing the man out of her mind, she inched closer to the couple sitting at the end of the bar.

They'd had her attention from the moment the pretty, young woman came in about twenty minutes to join the man, who had been drinking beer on tap steadily for over an hour. She'd been happy, smiling, confident, until the moment she sat next to him.

Sheila had walked over to take her order, but the man waved her away. She left to take care of someone else. After all, it was none of her business. But Sheila kept one ear on their conversation—not picking up any words, just the overall tone. The woman was silent, but the man, whose face was longer than average with thick gray side-burns and matching salt and pepper streaked hair, was speaking in furious undertones to the no longer smiling female. She looked near to tears now. Her face was flushed with embarrassment, and that was not at all cool with Sheila.

"Fucking good for nothing, leech," the man sneered at the woman. "You didn't pick up my stuff, even after I told you I needed it."

"But you know I don't get paid till Friday. Besides, I don't like that man, he scares me—"

The woman tried explaining, her soft voice catching at the end. But the man cut her off, slamming his empty glass down on the bar angrily. Sheila frowned hard as she eavesdropped.

"You're just a selfish, lazy bitch," he snarled.

"Al, you don't m-mean th-that," the woman stuttered.

"You don't do a damn thing 'cept sit on your fat ass while I work hard every day. Shit, at least you used to look good. Now look at you. Saggy tits, fat stomach, stretch marks all over you, fuck. I could do so much better than you," he said, not even bothering to turn his head while he belched in her face.

"Al, please, people can hear you—" the woman begged.

Sheila growled low and deep. Her Wolf was getting mighty pissed off at Al. She handed another customer his change, listening, waiting, and wondering where the fuck Thor was. Usually, she could signal her Pack mate and bouncer when something was going to go down, that way they could nip it in the bud before it grew out of control.

"Shit, woman," Al, the charmer, continued, and Sheila was really getting angry, now. "You're lucky I invite you here at all. You don't bring my shit. You look like a fat mess. And then, you come up in here, start acting like I'm supposed to buy you a drink and shit. Hell, no! You don't earn shit. You don't get shit! Fuckin' waste of space."

Mr. Boyfriend of the Year slapped his hand on the table and signaled Sheila. Oh, this motherfucker wanted another round, did he? She narrowed her eyes. The cheap fucker had ordered plenty of beers for himself ever since he'd first sat down. He'd paid, too, so she knew he had money.

Whatever it was he wanted her to get for him, Sheila had a feeling it was not savory. The woman looked down, unable to hide the tremor that ran through her at the man's harsh words. Sheila hated bullies. She walked over with a glass of water for the lady.

"Hey, I need another," he said, but Sheila ignored him, speaking to the woman only.

"Can I get you something, honey?" she asked gently.

The female looked up, shocked. She bit her lower lip, looking like she wanted to cry, and it was all Sheila could do to not let that jerk have it with both fists. She was too far away, and there were too many scents for her to make out if they were human or supes. Not that it mattered. Mistreating your significant other was a shitty thing to do whatever your species.

Al the asshole glared. He was clearly pissed Sheila was not serving him, but *whatfuckingever*. Dumbass should be grateful her attention was focused elsewhere.

"Oh, um, th-thank you," the woman replied, and Sheila nodded her understanding.

Sometimes, kindness was a foreign language to people who'd been denied it too long. Sheila understood. She offered the stranger another smile before walking away, adding something before she turned to help other customers.

"If you need anything at all, just let me know. I'm Sheila."

"Hell, Sheila, I need something. I need a fucking beer," Al said, trying to get her attention, but Sheila ignored him.

"Rudeness will get you nowhere here, mister," she said, and walked away, giving him a hard look that had Al squirming in his seat.

The man was a dickhead and a bully. His eyes glowed a little, so yes to being something other than human. He really ought to know better. Sheila let off a low growl, and Al the asshole gulped.

Poor woman. Stuck with a mean man. Sheila was not judging her. She was sure she had her reasons, but if she needed help inside this bar, Sheila's Dire Wolf was there for her. She'd grown up with strong female role models. Her mother, her aunt, and the other women of her Pack who'd broken off, forming their own MC had taught her many things. Mostly, to have other women's backs.

She was proud of those she-Wolves, even if her place was not among them. And Sheila took their lessons with her wherever she went. Female solidarity was alive and well in the Shifter world. Male dominance could go fuck itself. Sheila was a motherfuckin' badass. Anyone in her bar was hers to protect.

It was the Wolf in her that demanded. Her beast was a protector. Derrick knew it and loved that about her. It was why out of all the other Wolves, whether bigger or stronger, he had selected her as his mate's Guard. Sure, they were not as formal as other Packs, but Sheila understood her role.

If and when shit went down—and it always did—her job was to get Lucy to safety. She could do that. To protect her own, no ask was too big or small. And right now, as she sat at the bar Sheila was tending, that woman was hers. Even if only temporarily.

If the lady had said yes to a drink, she would have bought her a damn beer herself. Maybe she still would. Sheila finished with her present customer and turned to head back in the bizarre couple's direction, but someone beat her to the punch.

There he was. Mr. Law and Order to save the day. Damn interfering pussycat. She grumbled but could not stop her feet from heading over there. She was curious at how the straight as an arrow detective would handle Al, the dickless wonder.

Sheila continued to edge closer to the trio. Okay, maybe she was curious as to how the lawful Lion would handle the situation. True, the Pack might like the detective, but something told her they would be right pissed if Leo went around arresting their customers.

Shit.

She had better stick close to him then. Just in case she needed to intervene. No other reason.

Yeah. Right.

Her enormous, red-furred Dire Wolf snorted from inside her mind's eye, and Sheila shook her head to clear the sound from her brain. She was getting a little tired of her irritating animal's snide remarks.

Pfbbbbbtt.

Crap. Did Dire Wolves even know how to blow raspberries?

Apparently, was her only response.

FML.

Sheila growled and wiped the bar once again. It was an endless exercise, but a necessary evil. She refilled shot glasses, served a couple of cold longnecks to the good patrons of her Pack's establishment. All the while, she kept tabs on what was happening between the three people at the end of the bar.

Leo, the pain in her ass Lion himself, was one persistent pussy. Al was showing signs of completely losing his shit, and his female companion was biting her lip, eyes huge as Leo struck up a conversation with her. The man just couldn't take a hint, from her or anyone else, it would seem, but if she were being honest, Sheila would admit the big, furry butt face was growing on her.

Kind of. Like a fungus. Ha ha!

CHAPTER THREE

DIRE WOLF MATES

The band was playing a rock ballad, and the flow of customers was steady for a weeknight. Food was coming from the kitchen in spades. Their new hires were hustling from table to table, making sure everyone was happy.

All in all, Sheila could not complain. It would have been just like any other night if only the volatile moron at the end of the bar had used his brain and walked away. Leo was perhaps the most gallant and chivalrous male she knew. There was no way he would walk away from Al the asshat, leaving that female alone with the man who'd been ripping her a new butthole in front of everyone.

Sheila inched closer to the trio and listened intently as Leo flashed one of his patented, panty-melting smiles of his. Al was shaking, frowning hard at Leo's invasion, but the woman, his girlfriend or whatever, seemed happy at the intrusion. Who wouldn't be? She was blushing a bright, pretty pink under Leo's attention—*as any red-blooded female would.*

Sexy, hot, golden boy. Kissable lips, hard body, and that delicious spicy musk wafting off him in waves. Yummy. Sooooo yummy.

Grrrrr.

Sheila stopped short, almost dropping the bottle of vodka in her hand. Leo's gaze flashed over at her, one brow raised in question, but she ignored him. Replacing the bottle on the shelf with the others, Sheila pretending to concentrate on wiping the bottles and making sure the labels faced front.

What the heck was she doing? Getting jealous of the attention he paid that poor mistreated woman?

He was just being kind. Probably heard the hell the man was giving her and wanted to make sure she was safe. But did he have to be so good-looking while he maintained order?

Down, girl.

Sheila never said she didn't find him attractive. Leo Crowley was a Shifter. That alone ensured he was physically fit and attractive. Exceedingly hot. Hell—she'd have to be dead to think otherwise.

He was a straight up eleven on a scale of one to ten. The detective's pearly whites sparkled in the dimly lit bar, his platinum-streaked blond hair was pushed back off his forehead, making him appear approachable and friendly even. He had tanned, flawless skin beneath the scruff of facial hair that was already showing, despite his having shaved that morning. Yes, she knew of his impeccable grooming habits.

Truth was, she knew more about Leo the Lion than she cared to admit. He was model hot. And, sad as it was for her to admit, this was the first time he'd even looked at another woman, and she was jealous. Embarrassingly so.

Jealousy simmered beneath the surface, but she knew better than that. A woman was being mistreated by her male friend, and the good detective was doing something about it. Smile trained on the little lady, he opened his mouth and spoke.

"So, Marilyn, now that we have been introduced, what will you have?" Leo said, picking up on where he'd left off.

He was speaking loud enough for Sheila's Shifter hearing to pick up on the conversation, and she bit back her smile.

Cheeky fucker.

OMG. Did he know she'd gotten slightly miffed?

Sheila cleared her throat, trying not to grin while Leo completely ignored the blustering male beside the now openmouthed woman. Al the dickhead was turning beet red, but Leo did not seem concerned in the slightest.

"Oh, um," the woman, Marilyn, replied.

Her big eyes went round in surprise, and she blushed prettily. Sheila spared a glance at Leo, but his gaze was on the shorter woman, even if his attention was on the man beside her.

"Hey, she's spoken for," growled Al, the ass, who, as it turned out, was an actual Ass.

Sniff.

Huh. Why hadn't she noticed that before? Sheila's nostrils flared as the Donkey Shifter brayed at Leo. The hair on the back of her neck spiked, and her inner Dire Wolf pressed at her skin. Her inner Wolf didn't particularly like the way Al was speaking to her mate.

Shit.

There was that word again.

Mate.

That itty bitty little word was something she'd been denying herself for weeks now. Fate had a plan, but Sheila was fighting it tooth, claw, and nail.

Mate? Nope. No fucking way.

Yes way. A whole lot of fucking way.

Her inner bitch had a way of really getting on her nerves. But now that she'd admitted the word to herself, it was all she could think about.

Mate. Mate. Mate.

There it was, flashing in her brain like the pink neon sign she'd craftily concocted.

MATE.

Ever since she'd scented his rain-washed scent, her Dire Wolf had known what he was to her. Sheila's denial was about to end.

Well, fuck me, she thought.

Yes, please, inserted her Wolf.

Exhaling slowly, she prepared herself for the moment his scent invaded her nostrils. It was pure Shifter biology. Easily explained, but every time she caught a whiff, her hormones threatened to go completely crazy. Her ovaries were working triple time, going off like roman candles around the man. She could feel her heat simmering below the surface, that primal biological instinct that ensured the propagation of the species when one fated mate ran into another.

Not now. Think about something else, Sheila.

Immediately, her brain flashed back to the first time she'd caught sight of him. It was the night those humans had tried to set off a bomb in *Serious Moonlight*. Detective Crowley had been the lead investigator on the scene. One sniff of the Lion Shifter's fresh scent, and Sheila's Dire Wolf had gone gaga for the big pussy.

He smelled the way a grass field did after a good, cold, crisp rain. Clean and untainted, tinged with ozone and budding with life. It was her absolute favorite fragrance. One she wanted to roll around in and coat herself with. *Damn biology,* she grunted and ignored the flash of gold from his eyes as they landed on her for a second before returning to the other female.

Grrr.

Awareness raced through her veins. A wave of his scent hit her again, stronger this time. She closed her eyes, willing herself to calm down. But how could she when he was so close and smelled so damn tempting? It was all she could do not to throw herself over the counter and attack him like the animal she was.

Sheila had a little bitty reputation for being reckless. Derrick had given her hell for that for as long as she could remember. Especially for her habit of riding her Harley during the fiercest rainstorms.

When she could, she'd take off in her fur, but that hadn't been too often when they'd lived on the road. Blue Valley was their last chance to find a permanent place in the world, and so far, so good. She couldn't wait for the next storm. She'd get to run through it in the safety of the woods they'd claimed behind the Pack house. It was nice to think she could do that anytime she wanted.

Strange. Different. Good.

The house was big, yet a little crowded for a Pack of adult Dire Wolves, in her not so humble opinion. Still, it was theirs and she had space that was just her own. Finally—and wasn't that awesome? She wasn't ready to give it up. Did not want to lose herself to anyone, mate or not. And no, not even to the yummy smelling pussycat.

"I said she's spoken for," the Ass said again.

Sheila watched Leo's golden gaze find the imbecile. She waited a beat, ready to smack the Donkey down if he got out of hand. Protectiveness welled inside her. She'd deny it in the light of day, of course. But just then, every fiber of her being was attuned to the heated situation developing. She'd started wanting to protect the woman, but she had a bigger mission now.

Protect her pussy—and not the one between her legs. She meant the six and a half foot tall Lion Shifter whose golden gaze haunted her dreams. The Donkey narrowed his eyes, blunt teeth bared, as he tried unsuccessfully to hold Leo's predatorial stare.

Good boy.

Leo growled low and deep, but his body was too relaxed. He could get hurt if he was not battle ready. Now, he might have to follow the law as a cop, but she didn't. Sheila Rand was a law unto herself. A fierce Dire Wolf, Sheila could more than handle the situation. She waited and watched, surprised when straightlaced Leo moved so quickly, she barely caught it. He had Al's hand under his, pinned to the bar top, and that was when she saw the switchblade.

"You brought a knife to my bar? Oh Al, you imbecile," Sheila muttered, taking the thing from his hand, and tossing it in the trash.

Leo nodded at her, gold eyes flashing briefly, then he curled his lip in disgust at the man. Sheila's inner Wolf was practically tripping over herself to get closer to him.

Sexy, powerful, dominant.

Fine. So he could take care of himself, she admitted reluctantly.

Leo wasn't done either. He revealed his long, wickedly sharp canines in a not-so-friendly reminder of what he was. A predator. A Lion. King of the beasts.

Normally, she would snort at the thought. But not now. Not when he was flexing his badassery to protect a strange female while keeping it secret from the humans in the bar. The Leo she knew was a cut and dry kind of man. But not this side of him. He practically oozed dominance, and she had to admit it was sexy as hell.

Gulp.

Sheila was getting a little hot around the collar at this hint of Leo's baser, ferocious nature. Okay, so she had a thing for dominant males. She had always known she could not settle for a submissive. Sheila was too damn sassy for that. She would kill any lesser man's spirit with her snark, not to mention her thighs. Her strength had been a slight problem once or twice with past lovers, and she really fucking hated holding back.

Not Leo. He can handle us.

Her Wolf was very dominant, and the beast inside her enjoyed the byplay between her would be mate and the lesser male. Especially when the Ass actually started shaking in his seat. Sheila couldn't help it when her belly tightened, and her skin grew heated. Leo was hot as fuck when he was being all growly.

"Marilyn, are you spoken for?" Leo asked the woman, eyes trained on Al.

"Oh, well, I um—"

"Dammit Marilyn, I'm your husband!" Al shouted, wincing when Leo appeared in a blur on his other side.

He had Al's collar in his fist and was snarling deep in his throat as he pulled the fucker off the stool to stand in front of him.

"Do. Not. Speak. Unless I talk to you first, understood?"

"Yes?" Al whispered.

The word came out more like a question. He whimpered and Sheila's nostrils flared. The Ass might have just peed a little. Oh, fuck no. She was not cleaning that if he made a puddle. Eyes narrowed, she leaned over the bar to check, but thank goodness, the floor was clear. His piddle was still in his pants.

Gross. So gross.

"I think you've worn out your welcome, Al. Why don't you get on out of here?"

"No, uh, well, I can't. She's my ride?" Al squeaked.

"Your ride?"

"Well, yeah. Marilyn is my wife. We, um, live together?"

"This lovely little woman is your wife? A slovenly, foulmouthed, foul smelling Ass like you? Marilyn, is he lying to me?"

"Um, sadly, no, he's not," the female whispered her reply.

"Do you always mistreat your wife in public?"

"Sometimes. Mostly he just does it in private," she told him, her eyes gaining some of that confidence Sheila had spied when Marilyn had first come inside the bar.

"I-I'm sorry, Marilyn. It's just, well, you know how I get when I don't have my, *uh,* medicine," the Donkey whispered, eyes wide, pleading with his wife to understand. He still couldn't quite meet Leo's predatory gaze.

"What medicine?" Leo asked.

"Oh, he means drugs. He's a Duster," Marilyn said with distaste, referring to a type of bespelled drug that could give supernaturals an unnatural high—Shifters included.

Sheila frowned hard. She didn't want any Dusters in *Serious Moonlight.* Making a mental note to tell Derrick and the boys to look out for dealers, she clenched her jaw angrily. There was just no excuse for Al's behavior. He could blame it on magical drugs, but ultimately the fault was his own. He needed help, but before she could speak up, the Ass was sticking his foot in his mouth.

Again.

"Wait! Don't tell him that, he's a cop! She can't say nothing about me. She's my wi-wife," Al stuttered and swallowed as well as he could with Leo's hand wrapped around his throat.

"A Duster, huh? What was it you called your *wife* a moment ago? A leech?"

"I, well, uh, that is—"

"Do you know what a leech is? It's a parasite. An amorphous bloodsucker who lives off others. Does she look like a leech to you? Using Witch Dust is a disgusting habit, very dangerous too, Al. I'll need to call to the Council," Leo muttered.

"Oh, you don't have to do that," Marilyn began. "He's really not worth it."

Sheila was standing right in front of them now. Her eyes and ears were attuned to the surrounding crowd. There were mostly Shifters, but some humans in the mix. Best to keep things friendly. She ran her hand over Leo's arm, and he dropped his hold on Al, gold gaze flashing to hers.

"Shut up, Marilyn," hissed Al, turning to stare at Leo with wide eyes. "Sorry, uh, sir. Look, we will just be going. This isn't your business, anyway."

"Al, because you know I am a cop, I do not have to tell you this is very much my business. Domestic abuse is a punishable offense," Leo growled. "Give me your phone. I'm installing a tracking app, try to remove it and you will have a dozen of the Council's Enforcers on your ass faster than you can say the word help. Now, until someone from their office contacts you, I suggest you go home and wait—"

"Okay, fine. Thank you," Al mumbled, standing to go, eyes flashing at Marilyn.

"Before you run away, Al, listen carefully. I need you to understand this female of yours is a treasure. She deserves a worthy mate who makes her feel special, protected, loved, and cherished. All females do. This second number I am putting into your phone is for a counselor, someone like us who can help you with your addiction problems. Now, I am also putting my number in Marilyn's phone. I will check in with her about your progress and cooperation with the Council."

"What? You're gonna spy on me?"

"You're damn straight, I am, Al. This is my town. You do anything wrong, and I will find out. Now, tell me, Marilyn, do you have children with this person?" Leo ignored the man and spoke to his mate once again.

"Yes, we have t-two. A boy and a girl," she said shyly.

"I see, and you take care of them?" he asked.

"She's supposed to!" yelled the harried looking Donkey Shifter.

"Interrupt me again, and I will remove your ability to have any more children, understood?" Leo's quiet threat had more effect on the man than if he had yelled.

Sniff.

Sheila almost gagged as the scent of urine grew thicker. She looked once more at the floor, but it seemed Al's jeans were soaking it all in. It was the only thing saving him at this point. Leo looked down, disgust etched on his handsome features as he snarled at Al.

"Will you man the fuck up, please?"

Sheila was impressed. She'd expected the Lion to strut and roar, to announce his dominance and flash his badge with all the suavity of a fucking parade, but he didn't. Surprising both her and her she-Wolf, who watched the byplay with keen interest. The man nodded. His long face went ashen, and Sheila approved.

Asshole.

"Sorry about the interruption. Now, do you cook? Clean? Care for your children and your mate?" he'd turned his attention back to the female.

"Yes, but I don't have a job, so it's fair," Marilyn said.

"No, you don't have *a* job," Leo said.

Sheila narrowed her eyes at him. What the hell did he say? Was this it then? The moment he revealed his true leonine assholery? Leo Crowley was a secret chauvinist—something did not feel right, but she did not have to wait long to see where he was going with this. With Leo's next sentence, he redeemed himself and Sheila released the breath she did not know she was holding.

"Sounds to me like you have three jobs, Marilyn. Probably more if you count chauffeuring the children to school and extracurricular activities. Not to mention the shopping and million other chores that crop up every day, am I right?"

"You're not wrong," the woman replied, and yes, she was blossoming under Leo's praise and acknowledgement.

Sometimes that was all it took. A little recognition, a modicum of respect, and some affection. Those three things could save any failing relationship be it romantic, business or whatever. Everyone liked to feel needed, valued, and appreciated. It was human—*and not so human*—nature.

"You do it all, don't you, Marilyn? Unappreciated, unrecognized. And you," Leo's quietly intimidating voice was aimed once more at the Donkey Shifter, whose expression had gone from angry red and confrontational to *shitting his pants* green.

Oh, he better fucking not, her Wolf chimed in, and Sheila snorted. Leo's head tilted, so he heard her, but he did not miss a beat.

"You have one silly little job compared to all she does, and still, you think you're more important. You really think you are the irreplaceable one. How delusional are you, Al?"

"Well, I, I mean, I bring home the money."

"So. Fucking. What? Do you even know how to care for your children? Do you cook, clean, wash the clothes? Would you know what food they prefer if you even bothered to do the shopping? Hell, do you even know what day the trash gets taken out or when to change the lightbulbs or the smoke detector batteries?"

"I do, well, *er,* no, but still I have a job," Al said, but he didn't sound so sure anymore.

"One job. You *pathetic waste of space*—sound familiar? I heard what you said to her. All of us did," Leo growled, and when he jerked his head, Al looked around, Sheila too, and saw every male Shifter glance their way, their golden eyes flashing anger at Al.

Leo had rallied every male in the bar without raising his voice even once. And all to protect a stranger.

Fuck. That is so hot.

"For your one job, Marilyn accomplishes dozens, and she gets them done without a hand from you. You called her the leech, you sorry excuse for a male. She is way too fucking good for the likes of you, *Duster*. Now, apologize to her, or so help me, I will drag you outside, and show you three good reasons why you should."

The Donkey Shifter swallowed loudly. He looked from Leo to his wife and then back again. Sheila waited. Would the man prove smarter than he looked? Or would she get to find out what those three good reasons were?

"You really don't want to argue with me, son," Leo growled. "Apologize. Now. Or I will forget my job is to uphold the law, not break it."

"Okay, okay! Look, uh, I'm sorry. I won't do that Dust no more. I swear. I will call that counselor. Marilyn? Baby? I didn't mean nothing by it. I'll get help. Um, here, let me get you a glass of wine, and some buffalo wings too," he said, scratching his head and raising a hand towards Sheila.

"Thank you, Al. That would be nice after the day I've had," the smallish female said.

Marilyn straightened her shoulders and nodded at her husband. Her whole outward appearance seemed to have risen along with her self-esteem in the last few minutes. She turned back and looked at Leo, smiling at the big ol' pussycat like the sun rose and set on the man. Sheila might have found it a tad annoying, but she could not blame her.

Pretty damn impressive, pussycat.

"Just remember, you deserve respect. You don't have to take attitude from anyone. Society might not place high value on the roles of females who stay home to raise their families, but Shifters should know better. Don't hesitate to call. Especially if he doesn't straighten up his act."

"Alright. Thank you so much, officer," she said.

"It's detective, actually," Leo replied, and the woman smiled even wider.

Sheila slapped her rag on the bar in front of the cozy pair and placed the empty glasses in the sink.

"Can I get anyone anything?"

Golden eyes flashed at hers, causing an unwanted reaction deep within her core. Fucking Shifter biology. She tried not to notice the smirk on the corner of Leo's handsome face and focused her eyes on the smallish female. Far as Sheila could tell, the woman might be a Squirrel or Chipmunk Shifter. That would account for her large, round eyes, and that cutesy, vulnerable little overbite.

Grrr.

What was it about men who just loved a damsel in distress? Sheila wasn't a damsel, never had been and never would be. She could handle herself. The way *Ms. Chipmunk* here was batting her eyes at Leo wasn't something she could ever mimic. And if that's what he wanted in a mate, well, he wouldn't find it here. Wasn't that just too damn bad?

Ugh.

Acting weaker than she was simply wasn't in her. All the harmless flirting was causing a serious side effect that she wasn't at all prepared for. Her furry side was getting beyond agitated. Sheila's fingertips itched with the need to flex her claws. Her gums burned and Sheila had to bite her tongue to keep the snarl from slipping past her lips.

Leo was just being a good guy. Of course, he would fall for the simpering helpless female routine. Then again, it wasn't like the little Chipmunk Shifter was putting it on or anything. Al was a total dick. She felt like an idiot for thinking bad thoughts about the female.

The woman's mate had been acting like a jerk to her, and in public, too. Leo was doing what she herself was about to. Of course, she probably would've just upended his beer over his head, and maybe had Thor, or one of the boys, drag him outside.

Leo's way was probably better. Not that she'd tell the arrogant pussy all that. Her head turned at the deep, resonating chuckle coming from her mat—*er,* from Leo. Dammit, that four letter word floated through her head again.

Mate.

Marilyn laughed too, and Sheila realized again, the tiny woman wasn't entirely unattractive. That fact only pissed off her Dire Wolf just a little bit more.

"Oh, wow. Thank you, Leo. I think Al is going to be better now. He wasn't always this way. That Dust is affecting his attitude, and well, I have to believe he is not a bad man," she said.

"I promise, Marilyn, I'm not," Al walked over, looking contrite. "I won't do that stuff no more. It's just I've been under pressure lately with lay-offs at the job and all. I know I was wrong. I am sorry," the Donkey Shifter said, and he looked pretty damn ashamed.

Serves him right.

"Al, if you feel you are hitting a hard spot, and the counselor isn't working, I want you to call me at that number, too. I know places that can help you," Leo said.

The fact he was being helpful, and not judging the man anymore, was just astounding to Sheila. She still wanted to kick Al's ass, but maybe Leo's way was better.

Interesting cop. Decent Shifter. Good man.

"Thank you so much. It was really nice of you, stepping in like that. You're a real hero. You too, Sheila," Marilyn said and waved goodbye.

Sheila watched Marilyn and Al move some stools down. Al was looking suitably apologetic and offered Marilyn a soft smile. Sheila still thought Marilyn should bop him in the nose for all that name calling, and maybe she would. But ultimately, it was not her business. If Marilyn wanted to give him a chance, that was her right. All she knew was Leo had done well.

"Hey."

"Speak of the devil," she murmured, catching Leo's unerring gaze as he focused on her.

She schooled herself not to react. Not visibly, anyway. Keeping a tight lid on her emotions, even the somersaults her stomach did whenever the big man's eyes locked onto hers, was getting to be second nature. Sheila adopted a bored faced, careful to loosen her clenched jaw and ignore her suddenly dry mouth. She couldn't speak. Not yet.

Awareness flared to life, little sparks of electricity, like lightning, flitted across her skin wherever his golden gaze landed. Right then, Leo the Lion was focused on her face, bringing a warm, possibly horrific, blush to her cheeks. Damn her redheaded complexion. It was tough on her vanity, being pale as milk with outrageously bright locks. She'd been teased mercilessly as a cub and had to learn to fight at a very young age.

Sheila might be good at pretending disinterested, but on the inside, she was building steam like a volcano ready to blow. Now and then, Leo's gaze would drop, sweeping up and down her body in a slow, steady move that made her pulse race and her panties wet. It had been sixteen months since Sheila had last felt the touch of a man. A long, dry spell, for sure. And Leo was not just any man. He was hers.

No. NO. NO!

"What time are you finished?" he drawled the question like no born and raised Jersey boy should be able to.

She closed her eyes, willed her body to stop its telltale trembling. Leo leaned closer, inhaled her scent and she knew he was getting a whiff of the millions of pheromones coming off her.

Shit. Shit. SHIT.

"Closing time. Like always, detective."

"Will you meet me then?"

"Nope."

"Why not?"

"Can't you take no for an answer, cop?"

"From you? Nope," he retorted, giving her back her own words.

Damn, he was cute. And he knew it too. She shook her head, tossing her hair behind her shoulder as she grabbed some disinfecting wipes to clean the same spot on the bar she'd wiped a hundred times in the last ten minutes.

"Why do you insist on doing this?" he asked, voice betraying nothing of the heated emotion she saw in his eyes.

"Tending the bar? It's my job, officer."

"When are you going to admit the truth?"

"You just won't quit, will you, pussycat?" she asked, sucking air behind her teeth.

"Pussycat? Only for you, Sheila," he growled, and the deep, rumble resonated throughout her body, sending chills racing down her spine.

She could almost imagine what it would be like to hear him whisper naughty, delicious things in her ear. In the dark. With their clothes off. And nothing at all between their hot, writhing, bodies. Good Gods, she needed a drink.

"You know, I never took you for a coward," Leo casually remarked, and his smirk was really starting to irritate her.

"Excuse me?" Sheila snapped.

"Are you ready to talk about us, yet?"

"There is no *us*, and what do you mean, calling me a coward?!"

"Tell me you aren't running scared, little Wolf," Leo murmured.

His rumbly growl grew even deeper as he threaded his fingers through his golden locks and pushed them back, away from his handsome face. He could have been a movie star, she mused. That sound he was making had her inner beastie panting and rolling over, belly up. Her Wolf yipped and howled, wanting to get closer to him.

Hot boy. Sexy cop. Wonder if he takes those handcuffs home?

No. NO. NO!

Have some self-respect.

"Look, you might be some hotshot detective, but you better be careful throwing words like that around me," she growled.

"What words? Coward? I'm just calling it like I see it. And what I see is a beautiful, tough as nails she-Wolf running away from the very thing she should run towards."

"What's that, huh? You? Ha!"

"Your fate, little Wolf. You're ten kinds of sexy, Sheila Rand, and that dominant Wolf inside you is hot as fuck. But you run scared every time you see me—"

"I don't know what you're talking about, *detective*," she snarled, angry at the fact he read her so well.

"Leo. My name is Leo," he growled, and for the first time she caught his Lion peeking at her through his glowing gold eyes.

Sheila bit her tongue to stop herself from moaning in response. He was just so big, looming over her, larger than life and a million times hotter than the sun. When had he come behind the bar, anyway? She inhaled his spicy musk, loving the mix of fur and man

Wanna roll around in that scent. Cover my skin with it. Let everyone around me know who I belong to—grrrrr.

No. I belong to myself.

"I am talking about us, *mate*," he continued, snapping her out of her inner argument with her Wolf.

"I am not your mate."

"The hell you're not," he growled, eyes flashing their frustration.

This was it. The time he finally acted like the jerk she knew he was. But as the seconds ticked by, Sheila realized he would not behave the way she expected him to. Not here. Not now. Maybe never.

She couldn't just check off a neat little box that said *alpha asshole* and be on her way, like she'd done with other males over the years. Leo did something she'd never witnessed in a male other than her cousin before.

Control.

Leo turned off his innate machismo and grinned lazily instead.

"You know you're mine, little Wolf. Why are you so scared of admitting it?"

"First of all, my Wolf is not little, and second, I'm not afraid of a damn thing."

Sheila glared at the smug Lion Shifter. She did her best to ignore the attraction sizzling between them. It wasn't easy with his immovable stare, the tension that vibrated from his powerful body, and the slight flare of his predator's nostrils as he picked up on the heightened state of her emotions.

He was so close. But not close enough. Fucker wanted her to make the first move, but she wouldn't. Even if it killed her, Sheila was going to hold her ground. She would not give in. Not one single inch.

"Hey, detective," Phoenix greeted Leo, nodding at Sheila.

Her Pack mate sauntered over and took the seat Leo had vacated, eyes wide at the two of them standing so close to one another. He probably had no idea he was busting in on a battle of wills between Sheila and the Lion. Then again, the wily Wolf might know exactly what he was doing.

"Phoenix," Leo replied, eyes still glued to Sheila.

"I was hoping you had some time for me. I've just installed a new *Draco Fortis* system on the grounds here, and wanted to go over it with you when you have the chance?"

"Sounds like a good idea, Phoenix. When were you thinking?" Leo answered.

Sheila wanted to turn her back on him, but the damn pussycat was holding her gaze. He had it locked on his, and fuck him if he thought she would break first. She would never admit how close she was to climbing up his body and claiming the sexy man's lips in front of the whole damn bar. She flinched, her elbow sent a bottle crashing to the floor and shards of glass flew up, slicing her calf.

Shit.

"Sheila," Leo growled, lunging forward, to look at her cut. It was already healing, and she really could not have his hands on her right now.

"I'm fine," she snapped, stepping back to grab the broom.

He looked pissed, but she ignored him and swept up the busted fragments, tossing them into the trash. Sheila just wasn't cut out for mates. Having a mate meant having cubs, and Gods knew she wasn't the least bit maternal.

How could she be? Growing up in an MC meant a shit ton of time spent on the road, and zero chance of a typical childhood. Even by Shifter standards. She just wasn't a good risk for a male like him—one who'd undoubtedly want cubs.

Gulp.

Lots of little red and golden-haired cubs. She could just see him now, letting them climb all over him like a jungle gym. It was enough to make her ovaries work double time.

Grrr.

Her Wolf growled and snapped inside her. Furious with Sheila for not claiming him, and their future babies, already. To her randy wee beastie, the sooner she got knocked up by the powerful male, the better. Leo was good mate material. He was strong and powerful. He'd make an excellent protector. And then there was the little bitty fact that the man was positively freaking gorgeous, too. Add to that already winning combination, the determination he'd already shown her, and, dammit it all to hell, the lawful Lion was the perfect candidate for a mate. He was more appealing by the second, which, of course, scared the shit out of Sheila.

Dammit.

Leo was right. She was a coward. Her admiration for him, her physical attraction to him, and the crack in her determination to stay away from him, all grew by the second. The big pussycat didn't need to know any of that. He was already conceited.

So, what if she was fiercely attracted to him? There was no shame in that. Any Shifter worth his salt could scent her arousal. And if they couldn't, well, the constant damp state of her panties whenever he was near was proof enough. Not to mention, the mountain of dead batteries in her bedside trash can, all triple As, like the ones that fit inside her vibrator.

Sigh.

Maybe she should just jump him and get it over with?

About damn time, agreed her Wolf.

Mine.

CHAPTER FOUR

DIRE WOLF MATES

"Leo, are you paying attention?" George tried to get his attention as Leo sipped his coffee.

It was just the way he liked it, stronger than his father's second—a big, badass brawler who was Beta of the Blue Valley Pride—and hot as his *soon to be* mate. Fuck. He couldn't go two minutes without thinking of her. That feisty female had blown him off again last night.

He felt as though he'd made some headway with her, which was always good in his book. Slow and steady. That was Leo's new motto. His campaign to win over the beautiful redhead involved spending most evenings at the bar she and her Pack mates owned, admiring from afar, and engaging whenever she was near.

Serious Moonlight had drawn plenty of attention from locals and out of towners, Shifters, and humans alike. Imagine, an honest to fuck roadhouse in South Jersey. It was a risky idea, but so far, so good.

Leo saw the appeal. The place offered unique amusements, such as local entertainment, which was mostly live music, excellent fare, and craft alcohol and beer from local microbreweries. And of course, there was the view. Every single one of the Pack was an eleven in their own right. Straight or not, Leo recognized good looks, and the Dire Wolf MC had it in spades.

Of course, Leo was only interested in one of them. Still, it didn't hurt their bottom line any that the owners and operators of *Serious Moonlight* were all perfect physical specimens. All of them were fit, attractive, and their MC status gave them an air of mystery and intrigue many found irresistible.

Leo appreciated a nice motorcycle, even if he was more into his Vette. Whenever he saw Sheila atop her Softail, his pants grew uncomfortably tight. The little Wolf was a total boner inducer. He wanted her so damn badly. More with each growing day, and not just cause of her perfect ass, and sumptuous tits.

He wanted to know all about her. Found himself wondering what she liked and didn't like. Hell, he even drove to the city to research rare breeds in the library at the Shifter Council of NYC for information on Dire Wolves. He only found the basics, but he would take what he could get. Beggars and choosers, and all that.

They were very elusive creatures—large, prehistoric species of Wolf, extinct in the wild, but still around in their Shifter cousins. He counted himself twice lucky that he would be fated to have one as a mate. Not that he'd care if Sheila was a Wolf, Wildebeest, or Walrus. He just wanted her.

"Leo, I said the elders want an answer to their requests. Otherwise, they're calling for an open challenge to the leadership of the Pride."

"George, I'll tell you what I told them at the circle the other night. Back the fuck off. I need time."

Leo's mind went back to the elder's circle he'd walked into a few nights ago. The Lionesses had gathered, as they were permitted to, under the King's laws, and had presented him with some otherwise unknown quandaries. It seemed Leo's father was no longer seeing audiences nor was he answering his correspondence.

Leo had asked for time to investigate, and he left right away to talk to the old man only to be turned away at the door. He'd had to leave a message with Montgomery, his father's valet, and still had yet to hear from him. The King was absent, and that was not a good look for the Pride. But even worse, Leo was worried about his father. Absentee dad or not, Donovan Crowley deserved his loyalty, and Leo was determined to give it.

Fuck.

"You know the laws, Leo," George said.

"Of course, I fucking do. I'm a cop, George. I study laws. I enforce them," he growled, turning on his heel and pacing. Fuck. He was agitated.

"You are still single. If you don't choose a mate, your claim to the throne will be questioned. Look, the elders are willing to give you first choice at the crown, but they want you to meet with the unmated females this week," his cousin told him.

"I know what they said, George. I was there."

How old was his cousin, anyway? Twenty-one, twenty-two? Whatever. Leo was not about to spill the entire story of why he was still unmated. It was neither his, nor the circle's business. He needed to talk to his father. To clear up this whole disastrous matter. The sooner, the better.

"I have a mate. I won't meet with the pride females. My mate is just not ready to accept me yet," he admitted, grimacing at the sting those words caused. "She requires patience, and I will give it to her."

"What? You have to meet with them, Leo! It's the only way to stall them till Uncle D snaps out of whatever funk he's in. It's not like it's cheating. You have no claiming mark, Leo," he pointed out, unhelpfully.

Would anyone really miss him if we snapped his neck and tossed him in the woods?

The Lion's question was a good one, but the answer was an unfortunate yes. Leo would have to watch the ambitious younger male. Good thing his Aunt Patricia, who was also George's mother, and all his female cousins, the real movers, and shakers behind *Eat Well Live Proud*, the hunters of the Blue Valley Pride and so on and so forth, had his back in so far as assuming his rightful role as his father's only son and heir.

"I will get to it in due time," Leo replied.

He left the younger Lion sitting in his car and sped away down the highway. Traveling just under the speed limit, of course. The sight of George's face still sputtering inside his vehicle grew smaller in his rearview mirror as Leo drove away.

Twenty-minutes later, he found himself outside of *Serious Moonlight*. Again.

Fucking pathetic.

Just grab the female, hoist her over your shoulder, take her home, and bite her, for fuck's sake. She will thank us later.

No. She really wouldn't, and Leo had to count to three just to keep the gold from showing in his eyes. He was only going to grab some food. Just a bite, he told himself.

Brock Laurent, the Beta of the Dire Wolf Pack, was an outstanding chef. His dishes constantly surprised Leo. But the truth was, he would have kept coming back, even if they only served peanuts. Maybe he really was pathetic.

Grrrr.

Leo was standing beside his Vette, chest rumbling way too loudly. A couple of humans passing told him he left his engine on, to which he nodded and pretended to shut the car off. Fuck. He needed to control himself. He should not be this riled over one tiny, albeit feisty, redheaded woman.

Sheila.

Her name began as a whisper inside his mind. The animal within him stood up, waiting to catch a glimpse. His hunter's instinct ever ready, ever waiting. The whisper built up in speed and momentum. Louder and faster until his beast roared the two-syllable moniker inside his mind's eye.

Sheila.

SHEILA.

SHEILAAA!

Rrrroooaaaar!

Control, he needed control. But it was difficult, and he was getting antsy. The animal had waited, albeit impatiently, for Leo to stake his claim. Lion didn't understand what was taking so long. In the wild, a dominant male pursued the female until he claimed her. Fast, simple, boom. But Leo was playing a different sort of game.

Truth was, he wasn't playing at all with his intended mate. Sheila was more than just a roll in the hay, *er*, grass, or whatever the fucking metaphor was. It didn't matter. She was no casual fling. She was everything.

Leo would pounce when he was good and ready and not a moment before. Even now, his beast demanded he give chase. He pressed his human side, demanding he actively pursue his claim of the sexy she-Wolf. She was his fated mate. It was destiny, after all.

She might not be ready for what Leo really wanted, but the she-Wolf could handle lunch. Hell, she could handle anything. His mouth salivated at the thought of grilled wild-caught King salmon with a side of spicy candied bacon cooked Brussel sprouts.

Grrrrr.

His stomach growled. Or was that his Lion? Whatever. The meal was Leo's favorite. Brock was a fucking magician in the kitchen. He did wonderful things to fish, meat, even vegetables. Any person—human, Shifter, or whatever—could and did readily appreciate the man's efforts.

Brock was a culinary genius. He made the best grilled steaks, monster-sized burgers, ribs, and chops to die for. But his salmon. Fucking. Perfection. The man's salmon was better than beef, or even chocolate, as far as Leo was concerned. And that was saying something.

Serious Moonlight's menu was small, but perfectly executed. Quality over quantity. And because he was a proud member of the Blue Valley Pride, Leo had met with Brock, and he'd gotten the ornery Pack Beta to sign with *Eat Well Live Proud*. They were taking on smaller accounts now. And why shouldn't they? Plenty of caterers, restauranteurs, and people in the food industry were clamoring for better products.

EWLP could deliver what they wanted. They boasted the finest quality meat, poultry, and fish available. Fresh from the range, ranch, or sea, directly to the table. The fish import business was just one of the Pride's latest endeavors on top of the meats they already dealt in.

Leo's cousin, Ariella Golden, was in charge of new client acquisitions. The Wild Fish division was currently on the hunt for some, and Leo was hoping she could drop by to catch Brock's ear. EWLP was the Pride's top enterprise, and Ariella was a very savvy Lioness.

Even if George was her brother.

George had obviously been shorted in the whole genes department. Maybe his Aunt Patricia had been stepping out on her mate, or something. He thanked his lucky stars there were no shared genetics there. The Goldens were not blood related, though he called them cousins.

His Aunt Patricia was no relative of either of his parents. She was his late mother's best friend from childhood, and their families were very close. He supposed he was lucky. To be fair, George really didn't have a shot at standing out.

He had four older sisters, and each one of them was phenomenal at something. Poor George was just average. Leo supposed he had time. A little bit of it, anyway. After all, Aunt Patricia had only forbidden her daughters to mail George to Saskatchewan when he was a cub. He was a man now, and he thought he saw Ariella checking the rates of international shipping for live animals the other day. No, it was not business related.

Leo smiled. Memories of life with the Pride had been coming back to him in bits and pieces. More so over the last week. Ever since he'd been forced to think about his father and visit with the elder circle. He had to admit, he missed some of his Lioness cousins' shenanigans. Pride life was never dull, he'd give them that.

Of course, he stayed in touch as much as his job allowed. He was still, technically, the Prince of the Blue Valley Pride. He also sat on the board for *Eat Well Live Proud,* holding the most shares of any Pride member, just under his father. Duty and responsibility were a key part of his makeup. Before he exited his car, Leo pushed all thoughts of Blue Valley Pride to the back of his mind. Sure, the elders had given him an ultimatum.

"Leo Crowley, you will either announce your mate by the week's end or this council will seize rule of the Pride as your father is unfit and until we can find a formal challenger for the title," Ruth Cunningham had stepped forward and made the announcement on behalf of the circle.

It was all he could do not to Shift and go after those haughty females after she'd made that pronouncement. How dare they! The elders had gone too far this time. He'd told them to back off, let him try to fix this. They reluctantly agreed to give him a week, and he intended to use every second of the time he'd won to try to sort it all out. So far, things were not looking well.

First, he still hadn't reached his father. Second, he already had a mate and the idea of looking at the Pride females parading through the palace was downright distasteful on several levels. Not to mention it was horribly offensive and sexist. Third, good manners aside, those old biddies needed to be taken down a notch or three.

Leo had no intention of being bullied into making any announcement or proclamation, and he sure as fuck was not pretending to choose a mate from a bunch of women who probably did not want to be there. Leo had a mate. His Lion wanted no other.

And he was not about to rush her, either. Despite what the little she-Wolf thought, Sheila Rand was his one and only—his absolute fated mate. His Lion had felt it the moment he laid eyes on the sexy, fire-kissed female. His beast paced angrily inside his mind's eyes.

Right, he needed food. First, he'd eat. Then he could think through his next move. At least he could sate one of his appetites. The bar's pink neon sign was lit, though it appeared much duller in the daylight. Still, it made him grin.

Brock might be gifted when it came to Leo's favorite cut of Pacific caught chinook salmon, but Sheila was a certifiable marketing genius.

She'd come up with the design and plans for the logo for the Dire Wolf Pack's bar and roadhouse herself. Something her cousin and Alpha, Derrick, had told him. So many hidden talents. And he wanted to discover them all.

Grrrr.

Both his stomach and his Lion grumbled hungrily. The beast was salivating for a Lion's portion of the perfectly cooked fish—the scents of hickory and applewood smoke wafted over to him on the breeze. He knew every flaky pink morsel would be seasoned to perfection, a veritable delight for his senses. He had it at least three times a week, and each time, it was outstanding.

But there was another, even more appetizing fragrance on the air. Like sweet cherry wine and habanero heat. Summer breezes, and winter fires. Sugary spice, and more tempting contradictions. It could only be her.

Mate.

Leo sucked in a breath, his Lion's tongue tasting the air, savoring each hint of her. His sexy, reluctant little Wolf. That was a misnomer, of course. He'd glimpsed Sheila's animal once, and the beast was enormous, magnificent, fucking perfect.

Dark, red fur, she stood as tall as a small horse. He had wanted to change with her so desperately, but before he could move, she'd appeared back in her skin. Naked and glorious, chin high as she leveled him with one of her patented, *I dare you* looks. Leo held her gaze that day. He didn't know how, but he managed it. Used his hand to bring himself to oblivion that night to the memory of his ten second glance at her perfect, ripe breasts, and the red curls that shielded her sex from his hungry gaze.

Fuck, her image was burned into his brain, and Leo would do anything for another glimpse of her soft, pale skin. And there went his boner. Fucking hell. He sucked in a breath of air and could have cursed himself for catching her fragrance again. That sure as hell would not do a thing to relieve his hard on. No hope for him now. He followed the heady scent hanging in the air, marking the way like a lighted trail straight to its heavenly source.

Spicy sweetness.

That was Sheila. Only she could combine those two contradictory flavors and make them work. Like honey and cayenne, caramel and salt, whiskey, and chocolate—all that but more. Her flavor held all those notes and yet, there was something else. Something elusive.

She'd made him a shot one night, called it a *wake-up call.* Sassy little Wolf said he might as well try it since he sure as fuck needed one. Damn, she was amazing. The drink too. She'd made it with cherry moonshine with a concentrated dollop of iced espresso, in a habanero sugar rimmed glass with crushed cacao nibs floating on top. Fuckin' hell, that innocent looking motherfucker had burned going down, but it had been worth it. Best damn shot he'd ever tasted. And it left him wanting more. More of the drink, and more of Sheila Rand.

She'd barely glanced his way as he walked into the bar, and yet she called to him. Tempted him, like a fish hooked with a single lure, her scent, the sway of her hips as she moved unhurriedly about her business, even the curl in red hair—all of it, *all of her,* pulled him forward before he even realized he was walking towards her.

She made his Lion chuff and his pulse race even from across the large room. She was here, and that was all that mattered. Just a few yards away. His mate. The only woman who'd ever made his blood buzz in anticipation. His muscles tensed at the ready. Even his heart thundered like a freight train inside his chest. Leo needed to be near her, to touch her.

Now. Now. Right now.

Sheila.

Her name whispered through his mind. She'd been giving him the cold shoulder for weeks, but he kept coming back. Waiting patiently for her to see reason. He'd figured that in time the pull of their mate-bond would grow too strong for her to resist. It was there now, a living, breathing thing, weak and sickly though from neglect, but they would fix that. The second she said yes.

So far though, his plan was an utter fucking failure. The she-Wolf had proven marvelously resilient. Not exactly great for his self-confidence. He believed his patience would be key. But that didn't mean the ugly mug known as self-doubt didn't pop up every now and again.

What if Sheila really was not interested? What if she found fault with him as a prospective mate? Maybe she didn't like the way he looked. Or smelled. Or the fact he was a Cat.

No way. We are fucking awesome, his inner beast chuffed.

And true, the animal had a point. Lions were one of the fiercest predators in the land. And Leo was also honest, loyal, and handsome if he did say so himself. Obviously, he had no shortage of ego, but what could he say? Cats were King. And so was Leo.

Literally.

He'd gone too far last night, calling her a coward. Leo regretted his choice of words. Maybe his plan to wait her out was a little cowardly. And maybe he'd been projecting. Shit. He should apologize. Sheila was strong and dominant. She would respect strength, not weakness. Apologizing was not weak, it took a strong man to admit he was wrong.

He could show her strength, reveal himself as the Prince of the Blue Valley Pride, but he had a feeling that wouldn't impress her much. It wasn't a secret. Not exactly. He just wasn't sure how she'd react. The fact she wasn't too thrilled with him to begin with fucking chafed. He didn't want to use his position to gain her respect or admiration.

His Lion chuffed and snarled. The beast was being pulled in two directions. One, towards his mate. The other towards his Pride. Leo had a duty to fix whatever was going on at the Pride, and to see his father. He was a problem solver at heart.

But his heart was the reason he was still here. He did not want to go without speaking to Sheila. He straightened his back, waited for the server to seat him in his usual spot. His eyes continued to hunt for Sheila. She'd walked to the back a few moments ago and was nowhere in sight.

"Your usual, Leo?" the waitress asked with a wide grin.

"Sure, Kelly, thanks.," he replied respectfully.

The waitress was a Wolf from the Macconwood Pack. She'd been a little too friendly, but he was good at shutting that kind of thing down politely. With a shrug of her shoulders, she led the way to his table and left to grab him a cold iced tea.

Where are you, little Wolf?

The predator in him was riled. But that was to be expected when a male stalked his female. This was natural. It was the most primal chase of all, pursuing his mate. Leo stilled, looked up, and saw her coming up from the basement.

Beautiful.

Stunned, he merely watched Sheila, in her badass ripped jeans and tank top with all her curves on blatant display, wearing a pair of leather boots with big steel toes and two-inch heel in the back. They weren't *fuck me* boots, but Leo was changing his mind on what he thought about feminine footwear and quick.

He'd never gone for this kind of woman before, but everything about Sheila Rand turned him on. She was a match to his kerosene. And every time she refused to acknowledge the building lust between them, he wanted to pull her against his body and see if she was really as immune as she claimed. Fuck, he wanted her.

He knew she wanted him too. Could smell her arousal, despite the words she spouted. His Lion was a beast, but Leo was not that kind of monster. He would never force or finagle his way into her tight as fuck jeans. Leo was going to have to wait for Sheila to ask him. He was not, by nature, patient. But he would wait. Even if it killed him.

Today, he'd put in his paperwork for some overdue vacation time from his job with the Blue Valley Police Department. He'd locked his service weapon and badge in his safe at home, cleaned out the fridge, and packed a few things in his duffel bag.

It felt good to be wearing a pair of jeans and a simple cotton t-shirt. Much different from his usual day-to-day clothing. Typically, he wore a suit and tie, tailored to fit his larger than average frame.

Perhaps his new attire would win him some points with his reluctant mate.

His little Wolf was definitely a leather and denim fan. As a member of an MC, Sheila's usual attire was enough to make his Lion go cross-eyed with lust. Followed directly by an intense jealousy and fierce possessive streak. The animal wanted her for himself only.

Possessive? Yep. But that was Shifters for you. Until he claimed her, his Lion was bound to be pretty fucking proprietorial. The wide, heavy bar top made a loud thud as she swung it open, carrying a case of something or other in her arms. He watched her carry her heavy load, knowing she needed no help. Yeah, she grunted and groaned, made like her arms were wobbly, but that was for the humans. To hide her supernatural strength from them.

Leo watched her, the patient hunter, and breathed in her hot spice and honey sweetness. He was going to miss this the next few days. Fuck, he was going to miss her. No, she never talked to him unless he initiated the conversation, but still. Being near her helped soothe his animal. If nothing else, it was going to be hard on his sanity, being away.

"Salmon plate, Leo?" Kelly asked and he nodded.

She was asking him something else but couldn't hear her. All his attention was on his mate's sweet, glorious heart-shaped ass as she rounded the bar and bent over to retrieve something from the floor. That ass was one of the many subjects of Leo's dreams lately. Especially the way it filled out the tight ripped up denim. Holy fuck, two slits under her ass had the bottoms of her cheeks coming out. The smooth, pale skin making him wild.

His dick pounded, balls tightened, and fuck, when was the last time he wore those jeans? The denim was thick and stiff, and currently strangling his dick. Fucking hell. He looked around and quickly readjusted himself.

A few customers had noticed Sheila, too. All males. All staring at her assets appreciatively. Leo had to bite his tongue to hide his snarl.

He was going to fucking burn those pants—as soon as he got them off her hot little body.

Holy fuck.

"Leo? Sides?" Kelly repeated, snapping her fingers in his face.

"The usual."

"Okay—"

"Uh, Kelly? Can you ask Ms. Rand to join me for a second?" he asked.

"What? Sure," she replied, looking at her notepad.

He was still watching Sheila, and almost swallowed his tongue. Red hair down and loose in a messy tangle that told him she'd been out riding. He loved her hair. It was sexy and wild, like her. The black cotton tank top she wore hugged her impossibly curvy frame, dipping low in front to reveal the most excellent cleavage he'd ever seen. And that meant others could see it, too. Other unmated males were right now staring at the precious treasure that was his mate's sublime body.

Hell. No.

Fuck.

What was wrong with him? He'd been coming here for months, knowing she was his, but had never acted this way. It was enough to set his Lion to roaring. As if finally sensing him, Sheila's entire body stilled. She turned and inhaled, whipped around to where he was sitting. Her red lips pulled back in a snarl. She looked ferocious, spitting mad, and hot as fuck, with her hair whirling around her face and her electric blue eyes flashing like lightning. She walked over to him, graceful and sleek, like the huntress she was.

"What do you want?" she snapped.

Leo opened his mouth to speak, then closed it. Eyes narrowed, he took a step closer, wondering at the increase in the pulse at the base of her neck. She wasn't repulsed, as she often pretended to be in his presence. The sharp scent of her arousal reached him, and Leo's beast chuffed.

Fuck waiting.

Before he could stop himself, he stood up, hands reaching out, and he captured her wrists gently, *always gently*, but firmly, too. Sheila's blue eyes widened, and he pulled her closer to him, close, so close, right until she was smashed up against his chest. His usual table was a closed off booth, and because it was early, there were only a few people inside. No one near them, though. It was why he liked that table. Against the wall, a perfect view of the room, and no one could see him.

"What are you—"

"Shhh," he whispered, leaning down, giving her plenty of warning, ample time to push away.

Sheila swallowed, gaze trained on his lips. She licked hers, anticipating what he was about to do, and fuck control, he just lost his. Leo pressed his lips against her closed mouth.

He ghosted over hers at first, testing, teasing, until he felt her surrender with a deep, beautiful moan. He wrapped his arms around her body, binding her to him, licking the seam of her lips with his tongue, begging entry.

Fuck yes. He could have roared aloud in victory when his sexy little Wolf finally opened for him, meeting his kiss with a need that matched his own. The blood in his veins turned to molten lava with the strength of his desire. Passion flared between them, igniting fast and furious like rocket fuel and a spark.

She felt so good right there. Better than good. She felt perfect. In his arms. Kissing him back like he was the only man in the world. Sheila clung to him, nails piercing through the thin cotton of his shirt.

Grrrr.

Yes, the beast liked that. Liked her marking him with her claws, like that she was leaning on him, taking strength from his body. Her arms wound around his neck and she held on all the while kissing him, and kissing him, and fuck, yes, kissing him some more.

No more games, no more hiding. This was raw need. Sheila's mouth opened wider for him, her tongue tangling with his in a battle for dominance, but neither would give in. Was she all sweet and submissive? Maybe for a second, but then his little Wolf was hot and demanding. She parted her lips, angling her head and forcing him to follow, ruining his shirt with her claws, and making his dick hard with the way her tongue drove deep inside his mouth.

Leo opened his eyes. He needed to see her, needed to know this was really happening. Of course, hers were already open, the electric blue glowing with her Wolf. Sheila grinned wickedly. Wrestling with him. Maybe for dominance, or maybe pure pleasure. Hell, maybe both. All he knew was she was pure fire in his arms, giving as good as she got. Nobody had ever kissed him like Sheila Rand. No one ever would.

Fuck. Leo was man enough to admit she was making him weak-kneed, but he'd never let her fall. Never ever. It was his job to hold her up, his pleasure to be the only man to bring that lust-glazed look to her eyes. He stroked and teased her tongue with his, reveling at the feel of her nipples biting through their shirts. The feel of those two hardened pebbles aroused him all the more. From the sounds she was making, Sheila felt it too. Leo purred, a satisfied sound deep in his chest, swallowing her moans greedily.

Her hands released his shirt and ran down his back, over his hips, and his ass. She was a true queen, taking pleasure in his body, giving only what she wanted to. Fucking perfect for the King of the beasts. Leo's cock pulsed inside his pants, a steady tattoo slowly rising in tempo and potency.

Pulse. Pulse. PULSE.

He wanted more. Needed more. Wanted everything.

"Mmm," she groaned, still trapped in their kiss as he lifted her clear off the ground.

He walked with her in his arms, out of view, to the office next to Derrick's which they used for breaks, or whatever, backing her into the wall. Never once did his lips leave hers. He pinned her there with his body, shielding her from the still open door while he kicked it shut. All the while, he was devouring her mouth, sating his soul, losing himself to the heady intoxication that came with kissing Sheila Rand.

Plump lips caressed his while her long tongue drove him crazy.

Her spicy flavor burst on his tongue. Today was pineapples, but those habanero peppers still stung beneath that sweetness.

Sugar and spice, and so fucking nice. Leo's hands squeezed her ass, and Sheila rewarded him with a hiss, clutching at his shoulders while he rocked his hips into the apex of her thighs. She squeezed him with her legs wrapped around his waist, grinding her hot core against him. He could no longer contain his growl.

He wanted her. Needed her. Here. Now.

A jolt of desire spiked through his blood. She was his mate. His. Mate. He was going to claim her. Here. Now. He didn't know or care what else was going on. All that mattered was Sheila, all he cared about was her, and that she never stopped kissing him.

"What the fuck is going on here?" a man—*no,* a Wolf, a *soon to be dead* Wolf, bellowed from behind them.

Leo turned his head, lips pulled back. The fucker had slammed open the door to the office, and Leo took exception to that. He loosed a mighty roar, like the beast he was. Dropping Sheila carefully to her feet, he turned, keeping her behind him as his claws extended from his fingertips and fangs descended from his gums.

He was ready for battle at a moment's notice. He was a Prince. A Lion. And this was his mate. His vision was red from the sheer strength of his anger at being interrupted. He'd take care of this.

Sheila tried to sidestep him, but Leo tucked her behind him protectively, as a good mate would. He had to shield her from harm. It was his duty. But did she appreciate it? No! Of course not. His sassy little Wolf was pounding on his back, yelling something at him. He could not hear, the blood was still roaring in his ears, but he moved when she started kicking, albeit reluctantly.

"No! Bad pussy! Heel! Sit! Where's a fucking water gun when you need one?" she yelled.

"Fuck, Leo! Sheila, you alright?" Derrick Rand growled.

"*Ohmygawd,* Derrick! You are cockblocking your cousin," Lucy mock screamed.

The tiny, yet very pregnant female, pushed into the now cramped office, giggling as she did, and was eyeing Leo and Sheila like a sorta disapproving-approving big sister. Then, she was pushing her big Alpha mate back, and Leo finally realized what he'd been doing, and with who.

Holy. Fuck.

"Ow!"

Leo ducked his head to stop Sheila from beating on it. But he could not blame her. he was equal parts frustrated and confused. Yes, he wanted her like no other, but claiming his mate in a cramped office within ear range of who knew how many people was not his ideal.

"Bad kitty!" Sheila raged and continued slapping him on the shoulder.

"Please stop hitting me, and put those away," he whispered.

"What? Sorry. Oh, shit," she muttered, clearing her throat as she tucked her fantastic bra-covered breasts back inside her tank top.

"Lucy, that overgrown house cat is mauling my cousin in the middle of the goddamn day in my bar!" Derrick pleaded with his wife, who'd just smacked him in his head.

"Housecat? Really," she hissed. "You have a problem with Cats, do you? Well, good luck seeing this pussy's pussy ever again! You flea-bitten hound dog," she raged, and pushed away from him.

"Fuck, kitten. I didn't mean that. I'm sorry!"

Derrick was quickly trying to backtrack, and Leo couldn't blame him. Even if he thought it slightly hilarious to see the big bad Alpha groveling at his five foot nothing mates feet.

Good luck earning her forgiveness, buddy. A feline scorned...

"Ouch! What did I do?" Leo asked after getting another whack from Sheila.

"I don't know, you used your Lion magic to make my brain stop working or something—"

"Lion magic? Really? Just admit it. We're mates. You want me and I want you, dammit—"

A shrill whistle filtered through the air and every Shifter in the entire bar covered their ears and whimpered. Especially the four that were trapped inside the office.

"That's enough," Lucy growled, ceasing that horrible noise.

"Okay, okay. Derrick, I am an adult. Thanks for your concern. Lucy, my cousin is a butt hole, but thank you for putting up with him. And you," Sheila said, glaring at Leo as she stepped out from behind him. "I don't know what to say to you, but honestly, Derrick, Leo and I are good here."

She turned her blue eyes on him, narrowing them angrily. Then she exhaled and made an impatient face, like he was doing—oh, yeah the growling. He should probably stop snarling at the man in his own establishment.

"Sorry," Leo said, voice still husky with his beast.

Leo turned to Sheila to see if she approved, but that redhead was not easy to please. Still, it would be fun trying, he mused. Sure, Derrick was her Alpha and her cousin, a big fucking Dire Wolf too, but his Lion seemed pretty sure he could take him.

Wait. What? No, this isn't right. Derrick is a friend.

Leo shook his head, trying to clear out some of the noise. Sheila stood next to him, talking to Lucy in a low murmur. He was too riled up to relax, and as if she knew and understood, the sexy little she-Wolf pressed her side close to his, allowing him to place his hand on the small of her back.

Just like that, he was calm. Like magic. The faintest touch of her skin soothed his savage beast long enough to stop his grumbling. Then, she went and placed her small hand on his stomach, a sort of half embrace, and the damn Cat inside him started purring.

"I still don't know what's going on," Derrick mumbled.

"Oh, honey, when we get home, I will tell you all about the birds and bees. Though, considering you're the one that gave me this freaking forty-pound basketball under I've been hiding beneath my shirt, you should know all about it," Lucy grumbled.

"TMI, Lucy," Sheila groaned, and Leo smiled at her silliness. He liked her playful. It was just another side to the woman he wanted to know more about.

"Anyway, you two can go now. I'm fine. This was all kind of, um, unexpected," Sheila said by way of explanation and shrugged her shoulders.

"Oh, don't you two worry. We understand. We have to be going anyway," Lucy answered and embowed her mate to get him moving.

"Ooof! Seriously? Fine cuz, but next time find a fucking room, not inside my bar, or the Pack house," Derrick grumbled.

"Hush! Bye Sheila! See you later, Leo!"

"Dammit, Lucy, you pinched me, and now you're gonna pay," the Alpha Dire Wolf bent down and lifted his pregnant mate off the floor like she weighed nothing at all.

He spun her around until she was giggling and kicking like mad, before taking off with her for the Pack house. Leo and Sheila watched them for a moment, and he was already dreaming of the day Sheila looked at him like that. With love and trust glowing in her pretty eyes.

Someday.

"Oh, hell. Well, I guess I better tell the boys to steer clear of the Pack house for a few hours," she mumbled and shot off a text on her cell phone.

"So," Leo began, watching Sheila's cutesy little frown as she sent that message to her Pack mates.

"So, what?"

"You kissed me," he said, not bothering to hide his grin.

"Oh, bullshit! You kissed me. I was just reacting."

"No, no," he replied, shaking his head. "You kissed me, Sheila, and I want you to admit it."

"Oh, for fuc—you know what? Fine. I kissed you. What do you want, a cookie or a sticker or something?"

"No. I want lunch. With you. Right now."

CHAPTER FIVE

DIRE WOLF MATES

Sheila huffed out a breath and sat down at the booth with him. Leo the lunatic Lion.

You mean Leo the luscious, lip-smacking, long-tongued, lengthy if the bulge in his pants can be trusted, loquacious because yes, she had heard the man speak, limber, lithe, lusty, and lucky sonovabitch who made her panties wet, her heart race, and her she-Wolf howl like a banshee.

Shit.

She couldn't think straight. That kiss had certainly thrown her for a loop. Loopy for a certain loveable Lion. Dammit to hell. Sheila was turning into Motherfucking Goose with all this rhyming and alliteration.

Grrrr.

She'd vowed to steer clear of the man, but here she was, sitting in a cozy little booth with him. After she'd spent the last fifteen minutes making out and letting him feel her up like they were a couple of horny teenagers. The man had moves. She would give him that. And yeah, maybe this was long overdue. Sheila listened to him order, and with surprising ease, she gave herself permission to enjoy this opportunity to just eat lunch with the man.

Kelly was staring, but one sharp look from her, and the female yelped and hustled to the kitchen. Good thing too. Sheila did not need an active audience. She was simply going to eat with the man. An idea that was surprisingly appealing to her.

True, she'd been actively avoiding the big ol' pussycat ever since she'd gotten his scent. A fated mate. Her. She could not believe it. What were the Fates thinking? Pairing her up at all, never mind the fact he was a Cat Shifter.

She grinned and shook her head. She'd tried to keep her distance, hoping she'd gotten it wrong and the by the book detective wasn't really hers. But there was no chance of that now. This was no mistake. Fear turned her stomach until she felt queasy. That kiss, that wonderful kiss, had definitely pulled the plug on any hope she'd been holding onto that he was not her mate.

Gulp.

So, yeah, she'd agreed to lunch. Maybe they could come up with a viable solution for this thing. Some kind of temporary fix, or something that wouldn't end in ruin and heartbreak for the two of them. Also, as a little bonus for herself, maybe Sheila could spend part of this lunch date covertly studying his new look a little.

Tight jeans. Big muscles. Hot, hot man.

She had to admit, Leo the Lion looked good as hell in regular clothing. She'd only ever seen him in suits and ties. Yes, he looked good in those too, but something about a man in a threadbare t-shirt and tight jeans that molded to his powerful frame, showing off his carved muscles and the sheer size of him to the best of their ability, really whetted her appetite.

Sheila's Wolf approved. Her human side was having one heck of a hard time keeping her eyes and hands to herself. She pinched her leg under the table and shook her head.

What the hell am I doing? Eating lunch with this arrogant male who thinks he can sweep me off my feet just because he threw on some blue jeans!

Hell. No. Stay strong, Sheila. Do not give in. This is how girls get got!

Her she-Wolf snapped her jaws in annoyance at Sheila's wayward thoughts. According to her other half, this big ol' pussycat was most definitely her mate, and her inner bitch thought it was about time Sheila started acting like it.

Roll over and assume the position.

Fuck that.

Yes, please.

Not what I meant, Wolf.

Sheila growled softly, but Leo's attention snapped to her. Pussycat had really good hearing. Good eyes. Good mouth. Hot body.

The better to listen, see, eat, and fuck you with...

I'm the big bad Wolf here, not him.

Potato, potahto.

Sheila had just about had it with her inner Wolf. She didn't want a mate. Not now. Not ever. And definitely not him. Right?

Not that there was anything wrong with Leo. He was a good man, honest, hardworking, with a moral compass that seemed to pass most Shifters. Plus, he seemed genuinely interested in more than getting into her pants. Or he usually did.

What was up with him, anyway? This was probably the longest he'd gone without pinning her with that golden stare of his. Just the thought made her shiver in anticipation. He had the thickest, longest eyelashes she'd ever seen on a boy. Dark too, despite his blond hair. There was just something about that long, unblinking gaze that melted her in certain spots. Not that she would tell him that.

But for some reason, Leo was not looking at her at all. He'd already ordered but was still looking over the menu. What the actual fuck?

He's not going to just sit there and ignore me. That's my shtick.

Sheila wiggled in her seat. Next, she fluffed her hair. Then she licked her lips. Finally, she adjusted her *tatas* in her bra, dipping her shirt low enough to flash him. But the bastard still didn't look up. Not a peep. Not one fucking glance.

She glared at him with her lips pursed and eyes narrowed. She tapped the table with her long, hot pink painted fingernails. Nail polish was her one vice when it came to expensive grooming habits. It was a weakness of sorts.

Her mama had always told her material things would weigh down her soul. Best to keep the load light when you lived on the road. But things were different now. Sheila had a permanent place to lay her head, and finally she could indulge.

So, maybe she went a little wild with the old one-click button. Thank fuck for Prime delivery options. Her first online shopping expedition landed her a professional quality manicure set complete with all the tools and instructions she'd needed to care for her supernaturally enhanced nails. That meant only the best stainless steel files and clippers—the kind zoologists used for predators.

Of course, she'd added a dozen top quality polishes to go with it. She liked the stuff so much, she now boasted over two hundred premium bottles of paint in every shade, from *daffodil yellow* to the *hot crush pink* she was wearing.

Thor, the Dire Wolf Pack Enforcer, and total sweetie on the inside, had merely grunted as he'd lugged the brown cardboard box full of goodies to her bedroom door. Phoenix had laughed, Brock too. Their teasing had grated on her nerves, but it stopped right after they'd both woken up to aqua-colored nails on their feet and hands. The hard to get off kind. Neither of those boys had anything further to say on the subject.

So, what if she spent an entire month's wages on the stuff? A girl had to have some fun now and then. Why the hell shouldn't it be on something that made the rough and tumble Dire Wolf Shifter feel pretty? It might have shocked her Pack mates, but there was more than one side to Sheila. Besides, she didn't have to explain herself to anyone.

Especially not this usually prim and proper police officer. Who did he think he was, wearing sexy jeans and a t-shirt, messing with her very staid view of him? He was supposed to be a stuffed shirt. For fuck's sake, this was silly. Truth was Leo filled out anything he wore to perfection with that hard, muscular body and ruggedly handsome face of his.

He was hot as sin and the bastard knew it. Usually, he was the one begging for attention, not her. Sheila raised an eyebrow. Yes, he was hot, but so was she in a curvy girl, badass kind of way. Being good-looking was kind of mother nature's way of ensuring survival of their species. Not that all Shifters were graced with pretty faces, but hers was more than okay.

Her red hair had mellowed from the flaming days of her youth to a darker, more sultry shade of auburn. Her blue eyes were still big and bright, framed in long dark lashes. She had an okay nose, a little bigger than she would have liked, but whatever. Nicer than average lips. And her body, while a bit chubbier than most Shifter females, was still good to look at, and even better to touch.

She was not embarrassed by her size in any way, shape, or form. Sheila had long ago made peace with the softness of her belly. Her long legs, which made it easier to ride her Harley, firm breasts, and squeezable butt more than made up for it in her opinion. Yes, she had a couple of belly rolls, but fuck it, a girl had to eat.

She didn't believe salads and celery counted all that much when it came to meals. Sheila's Wolf was a carnivore, and right then, this meat-eater was getting angrier by the second. It annoyed her that Leo wasn't looking at her. The man who claimed to be wildly in lust with her was calmly perusing the menu, in the midst of all her rapping. He didn't even flinch when she raked her nails, scoring the hard wood of the table.

Oops.

Derrick was gonna be pissed. Sheila shrugged one shoulder up. She would deal with him later. The damned pussycat was going too far this time. Why was he even bothering with the menu? He'd already chosen the grilled King salmon with Brock's spicy cilantro sauce. It was the detective's favorite dish. He typically paired it with a cold micro-brewed IPA or, when he was on duty, a tall glass of iced tea with a slice of lemon.

She blushed at the fact that she knew so much about the man. Okay, so maybe she kinda, sorta spied on the big pussy whenever he came in. Which was often enough.

Cause he's ours, her Wolf supplied.

Whatever.

Sheila wasn't stupid or blind. Yes, she noticed him. She'd have to be dead not to. He was just so big. Massive really. With wide shoulders and rippling muscles cording his tall frame. He walked with the slow, self-assured swagger of a Cat who knew he was hell on women no matter how old or young.

Damn females practically drooled at the mere sight of him. All of them stopped to admire and stare whenever he came to *Serious Moonlight*. It was all Sheila could do not to unleash her beast and smack down on those bitches.

Mine.

The enormous animal inside her paced back and forth on that metaphysical plane where she resided, while Sheila was in her human skin. Her Wolf's agitation was enough to make her start picking at her nails.

Fuck no.

She liked that polish too much to chip it. It was just that she felt uneasy. She'd never had her Dire Wolf so pissed at her human side. The two of them were usually completely simpatico. But not lately. Not since he showed up on her radar.

Grrr.

Sheila mentally gave her she-Wolf the finger and stuck her tongue out for good measure. It was just too damn bad. She might not be able to fight this whole fated mates thing forever, but she wasn't claiming him. It just wouldn't be fair to him or to herself.

Sheila didn't want to face those demons just yet. She'd much rather busy herself staring at his chiseled features while he wasted time reading today's specials. She snorted at the thought. Whatever. It was his time to waste, she supposed, but sooner or later, she'd have to get back to work. Might as well enjoy the scenery.

She'd never gone for pretty boys, but Leo was definitely that, in a strictly macho way, of course. Sheila couldn't have abided anything less. Her personality was just too damn strong. It was a turnoff for most men she knew, Shifters too, to have a woman be so dominant. So far, Leo didn't seem bothered. Time would tell, she supposed, that is, if she were to give it to him.

Maybe she would, Leo was a hottie. Leave it to the Fates to send her a man after her own heart's design. She had a thing for faces, and his was near perfect. Bodies were one thing, but if Sheila couldn't swoon at a man's face, he wasn't worth her time. Leo was worth it.

His nose was straight and long, but it didn't dominate his face. Still, it was nice, with no sign of ever being broken. Unlike several of her Pack mates. He had a broad forehead, and thick eyebrows two shades darker than his light gold hair. Her fingers itched to run through the smattering of stubble along his square jaw and back to those full lips she'd nibbled on just minutes ago.

His face was good and honest. Okay, fine. She liked it. Very much.

Her curiosity about Leo grew stronger by the second. This was the first time she'd been next to him for so long. Minutes, but they were ticking by so slowly, she felt like hours had passed. His hair was getting long, she mused. The ends were starting to curl around his neck and hang over his forehead. He was usually neater than that. Staid and proper, like the lawman he was.

Nice, she thought. Sexy, too. She'd have something to hold on to now, she thought, picturing him settling those massive shoulders between her thighs, lapping at her sex with his long tongue. Fuck, yes. Nothing like a Big Cat licking between a girl's legs, in Sheila's opinion. Leo would be good too, she could tell. He'd have her screaming his name, gasping for air.

Eeep!

Had she lost her mind? Sheila clenched her thighs tight on the wave of moisture that drenched her panties. Daydreaming about smexy times with the big pussy was not okay. Shit. She'd been just a second too slow to react. The scent of her arousal had already drifted across the table to Leo's extremely sensitive nostrils. His chest rumbled and gaze finally met hers, glowing gold with his beast.

"You know, we can postpone lunch," he growled, his voice deep and sexy as fuck. "—until after I've eaten."

Sheila's mouth went dry at the barely veiled innuendo. Her sex throbbed and pulse raced. She could think of a dozen different ways to get them both to her room in under five minutes so they could continue their, *er*, conversation in private. She shook her head and went with annoyance instead.

"Fuck off, kitty," she returned.

"Anytime you want, little Wolf," he replied with a smirk.

Sheila signaled for Kelly.

"Can you tell Brock to hurry up with our order? I have to get back to work," she grumbled.

"Sure thing, Sheila," the young woman said, and giggled when Leo looked at her, smiling.

"What?" she spat, glaring at him.

"Impatient."

"You usually have your food ten minutes after sitting down, and we've been sitting here in silence for fifteen."

Leo grinned at that, and Sheila felt her cheeks burn.

"What?" she demanded.

"You watch me when I come in."

"You come in everyday, Leo."

His response was to grin even wider. The damn pussycat was not even trying to hide his pleasure. So what? She let one little fact she'd picked up about him slip. Big farting deal.

"I don't have to be a detective to keep track of customers."

"True, little Wolf, but you are keeping track of me and that's a win in my book. Maybe I'm wearing you down," he teased.

"Shut up." Sheila snorted. "Okay, so what's with the outfit?"

Leo looked down at his clothes, then back at her, eyebrow raised.

"You never wear jeans or t-shirts," she pointed out.

It was bad enough seeing him looking so good in his work clothes, but having him sit next to her smelling all good like freshly laundered cotton was making her mouth water. Sheila had a thing about soap, too. Had always loved the clean scent growing up. It was one she readily welcomed, especially after what was sometimes days on the road.

"I'm officially on vacation," he replied and interrupted her train of thought.

"So, what are you doing here?"

"Well, I came to see you because I have to leave—"

"You're leaving?" she asked, stunned by how hard that hit.

Sheila should not care if Leo left town for a few days on vacation, right? Shouldn't bother her one bit. And yet.

"I'm gonna be gone for a few days, and I wanted to say goodbye—"

"Oh," she whispered.

"But after that kiss, there is no way in hell I can just leave now."

"That didn't mean anything," she lied.

"Lie. But I won't argue with you, Sheila. Anyway, I have a proposition for you. If you're not chicken, that is."

"Oh, you didn't just call me chicken."

Grrr.

"Hey, Leo, Sheila," Brock greeted them.

He sauntered out of the kitchen with their lunches in hand and placed them on the table.

"Damn girl, easy on the growling. We have a lot of *normals* in here this afternoon."

"Oh, don't mind Sheila, Brock," Leo inserted. "I might have taunted her a little."

"Oh, yeah?"

"Well, I may have called her a chicken."

"No way! Ha! Sheila a chicken? Damn Leo, you must want your ass handed to you sideways," Brock replied and laughed.

"Is that so?" Leo asked, his eyes dancing with mischief.

"She's pretty tough, *for a girl*." the Beta added.

"Gods, save me from arrogant men," she mumbled, and felt herself getting angrier by the second.

It was bad enough she let herself get roped into having lunch with a damn feline, but now she had to take shit from her Beta, too? What the hell?

"I wasn't exactly calling Sheila out. You see, Brock, I have a little situation going on within my Pride right now. I could use Sheila's help, but I understand if she's not comfortable entering an all-feline community."

"What?!" she sputtered.

"I see," Brock answered Leo, talking like she wasn't even there.

"I suppose it might be intimidating for a she-Wolf. What seems to be the problem anyway, Leo? Can I help?"

That dirty, lowdown, ass-munching traitor.

"The fuck?" Sheila snarled at her Beta and the Lion.

The two of them ignored her, chatting away like the old biddies they were about to become, once she was done slicing their balls off. Holy hell. She needed to calm down. There was no reason for her to be this riled. Only, she was.

Relax. They can take their stupid taunts and shove them up their furry butt holes.

"Thanks Brock. Appreciate the offer. I don't know who I can trust back home. It's been a while and there's been a troublesome development. You see, the King's health is bad, and the elders are looking to replace him. I need Sheila here to act as my mate while I go home to the Pride for a few days to investigate."

"Why?" she asked, curious now.

"Lions are all about breeding. When word gets out that an unmated, breeding age male is around, I won't be able to get anything done. Every family with an eligible female will be shoving them at me. I'll be drowning in unwed Lionesses, some of whom will be in heat, and I need a way to effectively fend them off, preferably without insulting anyone."

"A whole Pride of horny Lionesses, huh? That seems like a good problem to have," Brock replied, enjoying Sheila's discomfort.

Lionesses prowling around my mate? Fuck. No. Grrr.

Crap. Now was not the time to go all possessive. She was supposed to remain separate and aloof to Leo's charms. She couldn't go strutting around pretending to be mated to the man.

"You would think that, but I need to focus on the King. Problem is with Lionesses in heat, and me still unmated, my Cat will feel a biological imperative to service those females, and well, I don't have the time—"

"Don't have the time?" she growled, deep and low.

Two-timing tomcat.

"I have a duty to my Pride, Sheila, and I am asking you to help me root out whatever is going on there by running interference for me. It would be a big help. And I will owe you a favor," he said, sweetening the deal.

"Damn, Leo, Pride politics sound intense," Brock interrupted her thoughts.

His easy going tone belied the intelligence she knew he possessed. He was the Beta for a reason. The man had an unending supply of patience and understanding.

Prick.

"So, Sheila," he addressed her. "Are you afraid to play a Lion's mate?"

"It's not that simple, Brock," she sputtered, still on the fence.

What did he know about it, anyway? She didn't tell anyone that Leo really was hers. How could she just pretend? The Lion knew damn well they were fated mates, and being in such close proximity would drive her nuts.

She'd find herself good and claimed before the weekend was finished. Maybe that was his plan. The dirty rat!

"Well, I suppose I could find some other woman to help me out. Maybe Kelly, our waitress, wouldn't mind pretending to be my mate while I investigate things. That will cause a significant delay, of course, while I teach her what she needs to know about Pride life. I'll also have to mark her with my scent," he continued despite her growing growl.

"I was really hoping your Pack mate here would find it in her heart to help me out, Brock, but if you could just call Kelly over here—"

Leo spoke with just the right amount of inflection to suggest he was really understanding, though presumably put out by her rejection.

"Now, wait a minute—" Sheila was positively incensed at the idea that she was not honoring her Pack's obligations. Okay, there was the itty bitty little fact that the idea of him marking anyone but her with his scent was turning her Dire Wolf into a homicidal maniac.

"You know, I don't see why you won't help a friend of ours, Sheila. That isn't like you," Brock interrupted. "Or is the good detective here right in thinking you're afraid of tangling with a couple of Cats? After all, Lucy whooped your ass at arm wrestling the other night."

"I let her win! You know, I did," she replied, shocked he would stoop so low.

"Sure you did, honey." Leo agreed condescendingly. "Now about Kelly?"

It was obvious he was just placating her about the arm wrestling thing, and that was bad enough. But then to ask for their waitress to act as his mate? No way was that going to fly with her or her she-Wolf.

The nerve of that milk-lapping jerk!

Anger coursed through her veins, and some other green-eyed emotion she'd rather not admit. That big pussy might have laid out this trap for her like an angler dangling a worm on a hook, but at least she recognized it. Too bad, idiot she was, Sheila was grabbing onto the damn thing faster than a hot knife sliced through butter.

"So, if I come home with you and chase those females away, you owe me a favor, right?"

"Yes," he replied, tensing a little.

"You will do anything I say?"

Leo's eyebrows furrowed as he thought about the implication, but she saw something click right before he nodded. There was no going back now. If she did this for him, Sheila could tell him to leave her alone. She could remove the temptation to be subservient to a man and get on with her life.

It was the perfect plan.

"Fine. I'm in," she said smugly.

Leo eyed her suspiciously, and Brock chuckled as he walked away. He might be bigger than her, but she was smarter.

Wily little Wolf.

"So, when do we leave?" she asked nonchalantly.

"How fast can you pack?"

CHAPTER SIX

DIRE WOLF MATES

Leo was smiling like the Cat who got the canary, and he didn't care who knew it. His tousled hair was blowing in the warm breeze, and he was tapping his thumbs in time to the classic rock blaring from his high quality sound system. He didn't have a care in the world.

Bastard.

Sheila huffed silently in the passenger seat, wondering if she had really gotten the better end of this deal. She watched him maneuver his slick car expertly and cursed herself for admiring the sleek classic sports car. But she couldn't help it. The Corvette was gorgeous, much like the man driving it.

Golden boy opened his lips and sang a few bars of a familiar and pleasant rock ballad. Covertly, Sheila sighed, relishing the deep timbre of his voice. He sounded good. Singing was something she couldn't do on a motorcycle. Nope. That kind of thing resulted in a mouthful of flies. Nothing Sheila wanted to experience, for sure. She pictured Leo on the back of her bike and bit her bottom lip. Seeing him in jeans for the first time had put him in an entirely different perspective.

Racing down the highway in his Corvette, windows open, rock

music blaring—Leo was hot as fuck. His Alpha attitude would probably keep him from letting her drive his sexy ass car, but damn, if he was up for it, she would take him for a ride. He'd look good sitting on her bike, those big arms of his snug around her middle and his muscular thighs wrapped around hers.

Oooh la la.

Sheila was getting all hot and bothered just thinking about it. She was getting to see a side of him she hadn't known existed and all in a short space of time. It was unnerving.

Exciting.

Frightening.

All of the above.

Shivers raced up and down her spine as the Corvette zipped down the lane. Leo drove past other cars like a big Cat cutting through the jungle, taking turns like a motherfucking pro. She admired the car and his handling of it. Never pictured him in the low slung, sexy as hell sports car. He usually drove a staid sedan. But that was his work vehicle. Detective Crowley was a rule-following kind of guy. The kind she'd typically avoid. But here he was, chipping away at walls and breaking down barriers.

Chip. Chip. CHIP.

This wilder side of him was making it more difficult for her to keep her resolve. He turned his head and winked at her, using his signal to exit off the highway. Her hands were itching to get hold of his vintage teak steering wheel—and no that was not a euphemism. She wanted to feel the powerful *vroom* of the rebuilt and boosted horsepower engine Leo had installed. Right then, that machine was positively singing beneath the hood. Sheila appreciated the sound.

It was a good, strong rumble that did not interfere with the stereo. In fact, it enhanced it. The leather bucket seats hugged her curvy frame, and she had plenty of room to stretch her long legs. Good car. Good man. Sexy, too.

Sheila bit her lip, hoping to hide her grin of excitement each time he expertly shifted gears. His maneuvers were smooth, while remaining sharp, on point, and fast. Only a maniac or a Shifter would drive like that. She bit her lip as her pulse raced.

Excited as she might be about his choice of automobile, it didn't change the facts. Sheila needed to keep a level head, else she might lose herself to this man. Hell, she was still trying to figure out how she wound up in his admittedly awesome Corvette Stingray with her saddle bags packed and snug behind her.

What was she thinking agreeing to play his mate? And for his Pride no less. Shifters would sniff out a lie, but he already knew that. There were ways to get around lying, of course, but she didn't expect the detective to employ such means. Surely, he wouldn't use these circumstances to press his suit. Hell, if he even thought about it, she'd just have to show him that Wolves had claws too.

What did he think of her giant beastie? She refused to give in to the unease that threatened to creep up. She was used to intimidating others with her animal. It was hell on relationships, but she was not ashamed of her animal. Her she-Wolf was a thing of motherfucking beauty. With thick red fur and the same electric blue eyes she had in her human form, her prehistoric animal was roughly the size of a small horse and ten times as strong.

Over eight-hundred pounds of pure muscle lived inside of her and her animal radiated energy, loyalty, and the primal instinct to protect what was hers. Those things and more drove Sheila's actions. The strongest at the moment was the need to claim her mate. The Wolf wanted it. Desperately.

It was her human side who was not as sure. Sex was easy. She'd have no problem getting down and dirty with the golden-eyed cop. It was the rest of it that was complicated.

She exhaled slowly and concentrated on the yellow stripe running down the black pavement as it zipped past her window. Only fifteen minutes from the roadhouse to the Blue Valley Pride, but it felt longer. She was surprised to learn the woods behind *Serious Moonlight* eventually led to the woods owned and protected by Leo's Pride.

The trees opened up to a low, grass covered valley that was visible just behind the *Eat Well Live Proud* headquarters, which was, of course, also owned and operated by the Blue Valley Pride. She looked at their large stately sign and snorted. She much preferred pink neon to the gold block letters, but she supposed it wouldn't have made sense there. Leo drove past it, eventually turning into a beautiful large gate.

Blue Valley Homes was scrawled across the wrought iron in big gold letters. It was an entire community just for the Pride, she realized. After he punched a few numbers into a keypad and swiped a card, the gate opened. Leo pressed the gas pedal and drove straight to the largest home in the entire complex. It was an enormous sprawling ranch with columns and statues outside.

Sheila had never seen anything quite like it. It was huge, not to mention fancy. Like one of those ridiculously expensive homes, television dramas of the 1980s and 90s loved to flaunt. Might as well hang a sign up that read *millionaire inside,* she thought, and snorted at the imagery. She balked, realizing Leo was parking right outside the opulent mansion. This couldn't be Leo's childhood home, could it?

Sheila swallowed hard and tried to calm her nerves. Noise from a large koi pond out front caught her attention. He had a fountain. His own fountain. And, of course, the shrubs and lawn were all trimmed to immaculate perfection. Though, in her opinion, Sheila always thought those tallish bushes seemed trimmed to look like dildos, for whatever odd reason. Maybe a secret landscaper joke, or something.

"Are you okay?" Leo asked, eyes intent as he waited for her to answer.

The driveway was laid with expensive pavers. Each one had a symbol in the middle, but she couldn't make it out from inside the car. The smell of fresh cut grass filtered in through the open windows and it helped settle her anxiety. What the fuck were they doing there? She turned to him.

"I thought we were going to your childhood home?"

"We are. This is it," he answered, hopping out of the car, and opening the door for her.

His face was grim as he walked around to her door. Once opened, he didn't bother to hide the fact he was eyeing Sheila up and down with a certain familiar glitter in his amber gaze. She had to admit she loved the way he looked at her. Had hated those minutes in the bar when he'd steadily ignored her. She'd never had a man pay so much attention to her before. Usually it was her saucy mouth that earned shocked stares, not so much the rest of her.

She'd changed into a pair of fairly new, un-ripped, black jeans in an effort to look presentable. She paired the tight-fitting bottoms with a cream-colored peasant blouse. The thin, gauzy material was fun and flirty, and it felt soft against her skin. She'd always been hypersensitive to clothing. Even her leather cut was lined with a special breathable cotton blend that her skin didn't object to. She'd applied some mascara and lip gloss, but that was as far as she took the makeup thing. She didn't like the way it felt.

Leo's golden stare reached her eyes, and suddenly she wished he'd look away. Goosebumps broke out on her arms and a tiny, almost unnoticeable shudder sped through her. She felt exposed and vulnerable. Maybe it was the clothes. Hell, she'd never felt so soft and feminine. She'd thought she maintained her edge with her carefully broken in leather boots and her hair hanging in loose waves down her back, but she'd been wrong.

She was completely undone, and it made her want to lash out, to hit something, to grab the man and kiss him for all she was worth. Fuck. She was in a tornado of emotions. She wasn't finished with one before another threatened to sweep her away. Her hair blew around her face with the breeze and she was grateful for the respite. It allowed her to break eye contact without losing face.

She usually wore her thick red tresses in a ponytail or braid. Harleys were made for that sort of thing. Tied up hair, little makeup, tough denim, and leather on her body. She didn't mind it, either. The badass she-Wolf in her might not like to admit it, but she was almost scared of how exposed she felt in front of him just then. Leo was looking at her with heat and approval in his stare, and she was shocked at how much she liked it. She wondered what his eyes would express if he saw her nude—*when he saw her nude.* Her mouth went dry, and she licked her lips. Leo followed the small movement of her tongue with rapt desire clear in his honeyed gaze. Her heart squeezed inside her chest.

"If I didn't tell you earlier, you look beautiful," he murmured, and she heard the truth in his words.

Sexy, sexy male. Mine.

Uncertainty made her tremble. She knew what fated mates were. Was aware what they meant to other Shifters. But her kind was different. Her parents had proved that. A quick affair that led to her birth. Absentee parents. No idea who or what her father and his real family were or if they cared. Sheila had long ago made peace with the fact she wasn't cut out for family life. It just wasn't in her genetic makeup, no matter that her body wanted more from Leo. More of those sultry looks and dynamite kisses, like the one they'd shared earlier that afternoon.

It wouldn't be fair to either of them. Her mind understood that, but her heart didn't care. That reckless muscle wanted her to throw caution to the wind. Heat and desire vibrated from his powerful body in steady, constant waves as he leaned closer to where she leaned against the car, stroking, and teasing her with promises of better things to come. Hopefully her. His emotions seemed to wrap around her. Lust, desire, absolute certainty that she belonged to him, and more, so much more. She wished she had a tenth of his resolve.

Her Dire Wolf whined, the animal wanting to get closer to him. To mark herself with his scent, his energy, until every one of her senses was filled with only Leo. Both sides of her, Wolf, and human, were completely focused on the man. Awareness buzzed around her like bumble bees swarming their hive.

"Sheila," he whispered her name, his body hovering so close, but still not touching.

She could feel the tentative pulse of their barely there *matebond.* That tie that urged and called her to claim him as her own, to solidify what the Fates had decreed eons ago. Want became demand, and need became essential. It rose more and more with each passing moment.

No.

Sheila fought against it. She knew better. Knew from her own mother that she wasn't made for permanent things. Her dame rode with Derrick's mother, the older Alpha fem, and her band of twelve Dire Wolf widows. They'd claimed their own Pack and had formed an MC decades ago. Though Sheila's mother had never married, she still rode with them.

Her so-called mate had been married to another when Denise Rand had met him. She'd never lied to her daughter, told her all about the one night of passion she'd shared with him. That was, of course, when Sheila had been conceived. The she-Wolf had left the next day. The call of the road was too strong for her to stick around and watch while he stayed with his family.

At least, that was the way she'd described it. Aunt Mabel, Derrick's mother, had welcomed her sister into her Pack no questions asked. Together, they'd traveled the North and South American continents from Alaska to Cape Horn, and back again, over the past forty years. Dire Wolves aged slower than normal Shifters. Their lifetimes lasted a bit longer.

Sheila was only thirty-two years old. She had plenty of time left. Plenty of time to disappoint Leo. To prove she was not good enough for the golden boy. It was that thought that scared the shit out of her.

"Did I mention you look good enough to eat?" Leo remarked, shaking her from her unpleasant daydreams.

"After all that salmon, I can't believe you'd have any room," she joked.

"Aww, little Wolf, I always have room for you," he promised, eyes flashing heat.

Leo stepped closer. He was crowding her with his big body. She gasped, not quite liking the fact that he was above her since he was so damn tall. His gorgeous face broke out in a smile as he continued to reach and reach behind her, until she realized he was trying to move around her to get to her bags.

"Nice trick," she said.

"Thanks. I always liked that I could reach the trunk through the back seat. Handy if anyone ever tried to stuff me in there."

"You? In the trunk of this thing? You barely fit behind the wheel."

Leo frowned, pretending to be affronted, and Sheila responded with an unladylike snort. Next, he grinned, and her heart went crazy.

Bum-bum bum-bum.

"You know," he said and straightened to his full, glorious height. "I had them customize the car to accommodate my greater size."

"Yeah?" Sheila cleared her throat. "Must have taken years," she teased. "Seriously, though. It's a sweet ride. No wonder you take such good care of it and don't use it for work."

"My work car is different. Needs to blend in. This is special," he confided with an edge to his voice that went straight to her core. "When something is made specially for me, little Wolf, I treat it with the utmost respect and care."

"Yeah?"

"Yessss," he hissed.

His eyes glittered like yellow diamonds and Sheila felt an echoing tremble rack her soul. Beautiful, dangerous man. He was doing things to her heart she hadn't counted on. Scary things.

"I cherish the things I'm lucky to have in my life."

"You still talking about your car?"

"You tell me, little Wolf. And when you're ready, I'll prove it to you."

He backed up a step and she immediately missed his heat. His Lion blinked back at her from behind thick lashes. He could mesmerize her with that slow, unblinking stare. The realization stung.

Golden boy. Dangerous beast. Sexy, handsome man.

"Come on, let's go inside."

Sheila tucked a lock of hair behind her ear and stepped carefully beside him. She wasn't sure what just happened, but it felt like his

Lion had announced his claim on her, and her Wolf really fucking liked it. She tried to shake the feeling that something big was about to happen. Something that was going to change her life irrevocably.

Fuck it.

Sheila narrowed her eyes. She was no coward and she sure as shit wasn't going to back away from a challenge. She focused instead on the man next to her, and the heat emanating from his powerful body. It warmed her, chasing away the chill she didn't even realize she'd felt.

Spring was strange like that. The winds blew hot and cold with no rhyme or reason. Kind of like her emotions, she frowned. That wasn't entirely true. Sheila knew how she felt about Leo. She just didn't know if she would ever be ready to share it with him.

He's our mate, her she-Wolf, insisted. But Sheila still had her reservations.

She wasn't mate material. Anyone could see that. He was calm and steady where she was riotous and loud. They couldn't possibly mesh together. It would not work.

Yes. It will.

"You ready?"

Leo cocked his head to the side, his steady gaze unwavering as he waited for her response. It touched her somewhere deep that he seemed to understand her trepidations. Sheila played it off like it was no big deal, rolling her eyes and sashaying past the big pussy.

He's the pussy?

Her Wolf seemed to have it out for her today, so Sheila just kept on as if the animal wasn't having a dig at her. There was no point in fighting all the time. Leo opened the front door—apparently, he did have a key.

Inside, the sprawling mansion was even more stunning than the exterior. Every inch of it seemed to sparkle and shine brighter than a new penny. Fucking Lions loved their gold. Sheila's eyes widened as she took in the gleaming marble floors in the hallways that gave way to an enormous round living room with not one, but two huge fireplaces and thick, plush carpeting covering every inch.

There were two large sectional couches that faced each other in that same circular pattern, with a large round marble coffee table in the center. Everything was beautiful, but it all seemed so clinical to her. Maybe Cats were different from Wolves in that respect.

All the Pack and Clan houses she'd ever been in were filled with several members of that Shifter group. There was always noise, mess, and signs of life. But not here. This was super classy, and yet, where was the heart?

This was not the typical middle or even upper class home she'd expected of Leo Crowley. Perhaps she should have done some more homework on the good detective. Still, it surprised her to find not one single Lion on the premises.

"It's, uh, nice."

She raised an eyebrow, but he didn't respond. The immaculate entryway and living room area were just one section of the imposing structure. It reeked of money and class, but she could sense from his grim expression that all was not right in this house.

Hell, she was running through the entire myriad of emotions herself, just standing there and taking it all in. Paintings hung on the walls, huge carved bookshelves with what had to be first editions covered one enormous section of space, there were glass curios with what looked like ancient relics, dozens of awards, and some historical photographs on display. She'd never been one for pomp and circumstance, but she couldn't help but wonder if she should remove her leather boots. Maybe she should take off her socks, too.

"This place is like a museum," she said, and he grunted his reply.

Money had never been a big deal to her, but this place reeked of it. What the hell did Leo say his family did for a living, anyway? That's right, he didn't. She'd assumed he had something to do with that export company. Maybe his dad was the CEO or something.

"What?" Leo asked and turned around when he realized she wasn't following him down the hall.

"Is this really where you grew up?"

"Sheila, there are some things we haven't discussed," he began, but the sound of footfalls speeding closer had Leo's attention.

Sheila turned when she saw a man in a three-piece suit come rushing up to him, head bowed, neck bared. What the hell was going on?

"You're here early," the older man gasped and dropped to his knees.

"Montgomery, please, stand up. You know, you don't have to do that," Leo replied, and offered the man a hand to help him stand up.

The Lion refused. He shook his head, insisting on staying in that strange, bowed position for a full three beats before slowly rising. Still, he would not meet Leo's gaze.

"I knew you would be back. I told the King, you would not leave us," Montgomery took Leo's hand and pressed it to his forehead, bowing in subjugation.

"How is he?" asked Leo.

"As good as can be expected, sir."

What the hell? OMG. Wait—was that a blush spreading across Mr. Law and Order's face? Sheila would have laughed if she wasn't so confused.

"Um, Leo? What's with him?"

"I am sorry, sir, I did not see your, *uh*, friend. Shall I make up a guest room?" Montgomery rose to his feet, looking anxiously at Sheila.

"No, Montgomery, that won't be necessary. This is my mate. Sheila, meet Montgomery, he's been the caretaker of the Blue Valley Pride house for as long as I can remember."

"Longer, sir. My father was the caretaker before me, and his before him," he said with an air of pride that had nothing to do with him being a Lion Shifter.

Montgomery leaned in just a fraction, and Sheila thought she saw him sniff. Weird. He looked confused, but turned before she could gauge his reaction. Surely, the Pride was not prejudiced against mixed species matings? But who knew? Maybe they were. Montgomery's eyes flashed briefly, before he turned his attention to Leo.

"Apologies, sire. I had no idea you were mated," the man replied.

"Is there a problem, Montgomery?" Leo's quiet question held an air of authority that sent shivers of excitement rippling through Sheila's body. She always did like a man with a little bit of bite to him.

Grrr.

"No, of course not, sir."

"Good, then you will see to my mate's needs while we are in residence."

He stated the fact without a single doubt in his voice, and that made Sheila's stomach clench and her sex moisten. Her body recognized her mate, and the following desire was only natural. Especially when he spoke about her like that.

So hot.

Of course, her rational brain's reaction was something entirely of its own making. She'd agreed to play Leo's mate through this thing, but she wasn't prepared for the thrill that zipped through her at his proclamation or his ready defense of her.

"Sire, um, she's a Wolf," the man mumbled, confusion evident in his face.

"Yes, Montgomery. Sheila is a *Dire Wolf*, and she is also *my mate*," Leo growled with authority ringing in his tone. Sheila watched as the man backed up a step, eyes locked on the floor.

"Yes, sir," he returned.

"No worries, Montgomery. I trust you will act accordingly. Now, I will see us to my room, and after we are settled, we shall go see the King."

"As you say, sir."

Sheila followed Leo quietly as she tried to make sense of that little exchange. Leo had seemed stiff and unlike himself. In fact, the further he stepped into the sprawling Pride house, the less she recognized the serious detective.

She watched him maneuver down the long hallway carefully and with purpose. His back straight, head high, confidence bubbled over like water from a boiling kettle. He was just this side of conceited.

Fuck, he was cute. Sexy and with an air of authority that called to her wilder side. Would he be bossy in bed? Would he try to tell Sheila what to do? Maybe even spank her if she was naughty.

Yes, please.

She swallowed loudly. If she didn't get her hormones under control, she was going to jump him the second they were behind closed doors. She just couldn't help it. Lying and pretense didn't sit well with her, she might as well just admit that she wanted him. Really wanted him.

Standing up, lying down, on his knees, on a train, on a plane—she didn't give a fuck where. The only thing that mattered was Leo. He could have all her fucks. Every. Single. One.

Mine.

Sheila shook her head. Wolves did not always experience a heat cycle, but because of the nature of Dire Wolves, and their rarity, her kind did. Sheila had never experienced it, but there was no other explanation. It was the only thing that made sense. Too much time with her fated mate, and her primal instincts were bound to kick in.

Her eyes roamed over him from head to toe as they made their way to his room. The unfamiliar jeans and t-shirt revealed a side of him she wasn't ready for. A human side perhaps. It was so easy to dismiss him as nothing but a big ol' pussycat, but not when he wore soft cotton that clung to his every muscle and outlined his rock hard abs.

He stopped at a set of intricately carved wooden doors and raised his hand in the air. Leo hesitated, almost as if he was afraid to touch it. But it wasn't fear, it was resignation on his face. She frowned. Why should he look like that?

Her Wolf whined inside of her, and Sheila was caught unawares by the need to comfort him. Again she tried to stem her instincts, to ignore them, and she focused on the beautiful doors instead. She recognized images in the wood. A full moon, a lion's head, a crest of some sort, and other symbols that were lovely yet unfamiliar. Running her pink polished fingers over the smooth surface, she stopped and looked up. Amber eyes glittered at her in the dimly lit hall.

"What does this mean?" Sheila traced one symbol that looked like a series of circles, starting with a small center, and growing larger with each ring until it spanned two of her hands.

"That is the symbol for greatness. My mother had it carved on my door when I was born."

"Why?"

"Because she had high hopes for me, Sheila."

"Why? Who are you?" she repeated.

"You know who I am."

"I don't think I do. What are we really doing here, Leo? Who are you really?"

Leo frowned, and it was the first time she saw no humor in the big, golden man's gaze. She wanted to erase that severe expression, replace it with something lighter, something good. And that scared the shit out of her.

"Come inside, little Wolf," Leo replied, eyes begging for something she was not sure she could give.

"Come inside," he repeated. "And I'll tell you everything."

Sheila nodded, and she walked into the room, knowing everything she had ever thought in her entire life was about to change. Leo was important. He was big. He had secrets.

And Sheila wanted them all.

CHAPTER SEVEN

DIRE WOLF MATES

Leo growled softly. His Lion snapped his jaws inside his mind's eye. The beast was on edge. He'd been that way since the second he'd stepped over the threshold of his ancestral home.

Five generations of Crowleys had lived and ruled under this roof. Five Lion Kings born within these walls. Inside the Palace was duty, obligation, resignation, and responsibility.

I am not ready yet.

Leo had his own life to live. His own mate to claim. A career waiting for him. This was not his time to rule. Not yet.

His grandfather had ruled for sixty years. His father had sat on the throne for only half that. Of course, after his mother's death, his father had experienced a tremendous suffering. Their people had expected a slight change, but not this. Something was wrong.

For the King, the pain of losing a mate was unimaginable, but Leo would never have anticipated this. The Palace was empty. The King absent. For his father, the mighty Donovan Crowley, to simply give up, was completely out of character. All Leo's detective's instincts were on high alert. He saw red flags everywhere. Something was not right. Not at all. The Pride house, or the Palace as it was sometimes called, used to be teaming with Lions. Now, it was empty. A cold shell of what it used to be.

The elders should have told him this when he'd gone to the circle. They'd kept this from him. When he'd visited his father that night, he'd assumed it was empty simply because of the late hour. Kings needed their subjects. Alpha's needed their Pack. And Primus' needed their Lions.

Having his lions around would give the King's beast something to care about, rather than dwell on the loss of his mate. This isolation was poison.

Yes, Leo had been angry at their ridiculous demands regarding his mate. As if they could force him to claim some unwitting female in order to inherit the throne from his father. That was just a little too pushy, in Leo's opinion. They'd wanted him to choose from a list of females they'd already vetted. As if.

He'd surprised them with his demand to back off. George, too. Only when he'd told his cousin he had already found his fated mate had the younger Lion finally shut up. It was not a lie. Not in the least. Sheila Rand was the only one for him. He knew that for truth. The she-Wolf was beyond his wildest dreams in so far as beauty and personality. His perfect companion. The one person in the universe who understood and completed him.

It didn't hurt she was the sexiest little thing he'd ever seen with those cornflower blue eyes of hers, that shiny red hair, and her killer body. She was more than enough to tame his inner Lion. Thoughts of her constantly filled his mind. Hell, he wanted her all the time, even when he should think about other things. Like the Pride and his father's health. He couldn't help it. The Lion wanted to claim his mate.

Roarrrr.

At the very least, he planned on kissing her the second he got inside his room. Leo couldn't wait to take that sassy little mouth under his again. That small taste he had of her at the bar wasn't nearly enough to satisfy his hunger. He wanted it all, but only when she was ready. A kiss would have to be enough.

The hesitation he felt coming from her both hurt and confused him, but he tried to understand. He was a patient man. Unusual for Shifters, but not for him. Trained as a detective, he understood the importance of timing. Raised as a Prince, he also knew it was necessary, and rewarding, to be compassionate with others.

Sheila would be his. There was no doubt in his mind. He just had to wait. Things were complicated and messy right then, but Leo would convince her soon enough to take the plunge. He had other things to do while she figured out for herself that he was a Lion of his word.

Leo needed to explain it to her. All of it. The fact his father was the King, that he was actually the Prince of the Blue Valley Pride might be a tough pill to swallow.

Shit.

He was nervous. Then there were the circumstances he was there to investigate. And finally, the real reason he needed her with him. Not because he wanted to trick the elders, but because she brought his Lion peace and purpose.

Mine.

He followed her inside the room, eyes riveted to the fiery redhead as she turned to face him. Everything about her commanded his attention.

Beautiful, strong, sexy woman.

"Spill."

Sheila tapped her booted foot against the gleaming marble floors of his bedroom. She should have looked out of place among all the riches, but she didn't. Not in the least. Sheila belonged there. With him.

He looked around and tried to see it from her perspective. He knew Sheila was not materialistic. But this world, though far removed from his daily life, was still his. Leo was royalty, whether he wanted to be or not was inconsequential. But his mate had grown up on the open road. Literally. She'd been loving every moment of her wild and free existence, riding her Harley from town to town since she could sit on one.

What if his sassy little mate was not happy with him? What if the road called to her once more?

Easy peasy. She goes, we follow.

His Lion was right. The Big Cat had provided the only possible answer. Leo would follow Sheila Rand out on the open road, and off into the sunset each and every time. No contest. He would follow the woman he loved anywhere.

Fuck. I do love her.

The knowledge hit him hard enough that the room seemed to spin out of focus. He'd only just put a name to the feelings he'd been having. How would he feel once they consummated their mating? The thought sent a shiver down his spine, but it wasn't of fear. Not at all. That slight tremor was wholly born of anticipation.

"Well?"

"This is where I was born. I haven't lived here in a while, but my father still does."

"Your father? What is this place?"

"It's the Pride house, some call it the Palace."

"Okay," she murmured, a frown on her pretty face.

Leo did not like that. He wanted her to smile. Wanted to be the one to make her smile. Her blue eyes widened as he stalked her across the room, and Sheila froze. She knew better than to turn her back on him —hunter, predator, beast.

Smart, sassy, little Wolf. Go ahead and run from me. I'll catch you.

"You trying to distract me, pussycat?" she asked, eyes narrowed as she took a tentative step to the left.

She could do that, but he would cut her off with a single bound to the side. Just imagining her tight little body snug against his made Leo feel ten times frisky.

Yes. Do that, his Lion urged.

Already his cock throbbed, and his heart went wild inside his chest for the sweet, spicy Sheila. The beautiful she-Wolf who called to his

Lion. Yes, she belonged to him, and he to her. Claiming her would only increase the desire he felt, and that idea was getting more appealing by the second.

"Come here," he said in a gravelly voice thick with his Lion.

"No."

"Scared of a Lion?"

"I'm not afraid of you," she replied, narrowing those beautiful baby blues. "You're nothing but a big pussy."

"The only pussy in this room is right there, soaking in sweet honey, begging for me to take a lick. Mine," he growled the word, breathing in deep, his chest vibrating with need.

Sheila bit back a moan and he growled deeper. Her eyes glowed bright with her Wolf as he backed her up into the wall.

So close. So hot. So mine.

"Wait," she whispered, and he stilled. He would do anything for her. Anything at all.

"Explain. Now."

Was it wrong that he liked the fact he'd reduced her to one-word sentences? Maybe, but who cared? She was cute when she was pretending to be outraged. He could scent her reciprocal desire, and it was making him hungry. The notes of an old eighties classic rock song filtered through his brain, though Leo changed the lyrics a bit.

Hungry. Hungry. I'm hungry for the Wolf.

"Are you afraid of the big bad Cat, little Wolf?"

"First of all, it's the big bad Wolf. You are just an overgrown tabby," she replied, poking him in the chest with her hot pink painted fingernail, scoring the cotton tee he'd worn just for her.

Damn.

She was so fucking hot. Soft, feminine, vulnerable on one hand, and completely fucking badass and in control on the other. Standing there in her jeans, those shit-kicking leather boots, and that see-through gauzy top. Leo rubbed his body on her, meeting her gaze, the predator in him gaining satisfaction as she stood her ground.

A challenge.

Yes, but a good one. Win or lose, he still wins. Whoever came out on top, Leo would still consider it a victory. His muscles tensed, ready to pounce on a moment's notice. He needed her fiery lips against his, had to taste that spicy sweet flavor that was all her.

Roarrrr.

He swallowed her surprised gasp, mashing his mouth to hers, and finally, he tasted the fire from its source. Her lips were plump and soft, exactly right for savoring.

Leo was drunk on kissing her. Her contradiction of flavors burst on his tongue. First spicy, then sweet. Always provocative. Stimulating. Tempting him to sin. The taste of her stamped itself on his brain, like a permanent tattoo he never wanted to erase or forget.

Just having her in his arms changed the course of his life forever. Fuck. It wasn't enough. Never enough. He wanted more. Needed more. Never had he felt such desire for a woman. He was desperate to have her naked in his bed, writhing beneath his touch, buried balls deep, coating her walls with his cum, filling her to the brim.

"Leo," she said his name, and ran her nails down his back until she lifted his shirt and touched his skin.

His already hard cock grew even harder. The thick length throbbed and pulsed, threatening to burst the seam of his jeans. He would've gone with fucking sweatpants if he'd known his body would have such a severe reaction to her. Leo groaned as her hands found him through the denim, and he wrapped his arms around her curvy frame.

He fucking loved the feel of this woman's body pressed against him. Her drool-worthy curves filled his searching hands. She was perfect for him. Perfect size. Height. Everything.

Leo was big all over, especially those parts that mattered most, hands, tongue, cock, and heart. He needed a woman who could take all of him in stride. Sheila could do more than that. She was the ultimate match for him. Unsurpassed by any other female. She topped them all. A true mate who could take on every inch of his powerful frame.

Mine.

Kissing, touching, squeezing her in his bedroom made everything better. He didn't forget why he was there, but for a little while, Leo could push it all aside. Sheila was everything to him. But he would not claim her until she asked him to. She was much too important to him and his future to fuck things up by acting like an unlicked cub.

He had her in his arms, and that alone was worth celebrating. For months she'd been fighting him, but not here. Not now. Finally, Leo could savor his mate. He lifted her onto the edge of his dresser, and Sheila immediately brought her legs up and around his waist. She tangled her hands in his hair while he lifted her shirt high, and then off, revealing a pink lace demi-bra, barely large enough to contain her. His lips twitched and his breathing increased. He wanted her, ached for her.

"Beautiful," he growled, then dipped his head.

"Leo," she moaned his name as he brushed soft kisses on the bits of flesh that were revealed to him.

"So soft," he growled and lifted his head, meeting her eyes as his hands traced the tops of her breast.

Her blue eyes seemed to glow, and he knew it was her she-Wolf joining them. His own animal approved and rose to meet his mate. Leo's chest vibrated with a low, rumbling growl as he slowly caressed the delicate skin of her ample breasts with his work-roughened fingertips. This was dangerous. Touching her like this was pure madness.

But he couldn't stop. He wouldn't. Not unless she said to. He pulled the fabric down gently, allowing her ripe nipples to spill out. Leo couldn't contain his groan. So pretty and pink. Her tip-tilted breasts were perfect for his hands and lips, and he traced them *oh so carefully*.

Slow and steady.

He wanted this to be better than good. He wanted to raise her temperature to match her fiery sass. Leo growled at the apt description. The redheaded seductress was just that. Fire and sass, mixed with a little bit of sugar just for him. Together they'd break bad, raise hell, see the stars, and bring mountains to their knees with the height of their passion.

At the very least, he'd make sure she never thought of him as a pussy again.

"Leo," she moaned his name again, arching her back, offering him better access to her succulent body.

Only a fool would refuse, and Leo was far from that. This was what he'd wanted, what he'd been chasing for weeks. Sheila's willing submission to his desire, her need for his touch. It was what he craved, what his beast demanded, but that wasn't all. He wanted more from the sexy she-Wolf.

He didn't just want her ready, willing, and waiting, he wanted her panting, begging, and demanding. He wanted her to feel the same way he felt about her. He'd been lusting after her like mad. Ever since he'd first laid eyes on her, but it was more than that. Leo was head over heels for the little Wolf. He wouldn't rest until she felt the same.

"Tell me what you want, baby," he growled and nipped her earlobe between his teeth as his hands made short work of her bra.

Finally, completely freed from their confines, Leo took both her gorgeous breasts in his large hands. He kneaded the supple mounds, pushing them together, and tweaking her nipples with his thumbs and forefingers.

All the better for him to kiss, lick, and suck each plentiful bud and that valley between. Visions of sliding his cock between the two mounds had him growling almost nonstop.

"More," she demanded, gripping his hair, and pulling his head closer.

He did not disappoint. He couldn't. He sought her pleasure as if it were his own. She might be one sassy little Wolf, but in this, in the bed, *or* dresser, Leo was the maestro and she, his orchestra. He would coax her to symphonic precipices until they both tumbled off together into sheer bliss. His beast would accept nothing less. Nothing, save her utter and complete surrender to the pleasure he dealt.

"Bed now," she said, and shoved against his chest.

The blue fire flashing in her eyes had a direct and almost painful effect on Leo's cock. His member, already swollen in his need, throbbed painfully in the strict confines of his pants. Fuck, he needed her.

Sex was important to Shifters. It was necessary. An outlet, a means of expression, not taken lightly, and yet indulged in sometimes a little too haphazardly, in his opinion. Because of his status, Leo was not one to take women into his bed lightly.

Hell yes, sex was fun, but no youthful experimentation, none of the meaningless unions of his past, nope, not a fucking one could have prepared him for his reaction to having his mate shove him down hard onto the mattress while she stripped for him. Leo almost swallowed his tongue whole.

"Ffuucckk, Sheila," he growled.

Leo's eyes bulged as Sheila kicked off her leather boots. She winked at him, wiggling her tight jeans and panties down and over her ample hips, kicking them off after her boots. She stood there in all her naked glory, proud and sexy as sin. Then she unzipped his jeans and ripped them clean off his legs. Leaving him naked and standing up, tall and straight as a fucking May pole.

"I've been waiting for this for a long time, detective. You better not let me down," she growled the words, eyes flashing blue fire.

Leo hardly made a sound before she was already jumping on top of him. Fierce, proud, gorgeous woman.

My woman.

"Mine," he growled the possessive word as he caught her delicious body.

If he thought he had seduced her, he was wrong. Sheila Rand was not one to be manipulated into anyone's bed. She chose him, here and now, and the feeling was the best kind of high. Only to be superseded by the bliss he was bound to feel when he finally claimed the sassy little Wolf as his own.

Automatically, she wound her arms around him, lips going to his neck for a biting kiss that made him shudder. His hands reached between them, dipping between her slick folds. So fucking hot and wet for him. Perfect.

He was grateful his quick Shifter reflexes allowed him to catch his feisty female before she could land. Hot, naked flesh felt like heaven against his skin. Even better was the wicked smile on her face as she held herself just out of reach before mashing her lips to his.

Leo's heart hammered in his chest like a herd of wild horses, his gums ached, and fangs threatened to lengthen. He was holding on to his Lion by a thread. The heady scent of her arousal made him salivate as he strummed her clit with his thumb, testing to see if she could take him.

Leo was big, and he would not risk hurting her. Sheila moaned, twirling her tongue with his as he fingered her with two thick digits. Her legs were wide as she sat astride him, her sex tight and wet. She felt so good, squeezing his fingers with every thrust and withdraw.

So sexy, hot, and wet for him. Good girl.

Her hips rocked against him, and Leo's cock ached to replace his hand. He was completely invested in this, in her. Needed her hotter, wetter. His cock slid up behind her ass and he kneaded one globe with his other hand, while fucking her with his fingers. He fucking loved her response to him. She moaned and moved, letting him know exactly where she wanted it, how hard, and how fast. They devoured each other with their lips.

Fuck.

Desire bubbling over, Leo waited for the first signs of her orgasm to hit. He was ready, and he wanted to feel her squeeze his fingers tight before he swapped them out for his dick. Hell, he wanted it all. Wanted to bathe in her sweet scent. Get her juices all over him. Coat her walls with his cum. Wanted to taste her cream right from the source.

Some stereotypes were true. Cats liked cream, and this pussy sure as fuck did. He was dying to lick her. Wanted to bury his head between her luscious thighs and swallow down every drop.

Later.

Yep, that sounded like a plan to his Lion. He wanted all of that and more of her. Wanted to take his time to enjoy every smooth inch of her soft, smooth, delectable flesh, but his mate had other ideas. Just when she almost came, Sheila backed off his hand, taking hold of his more than ready cock. Leo hissed. Fuck, she was killing him.

She took his hard length, placed him at her slick entrance. She held him there, her wet pussy dripping, kissing the tip of his dick. But she waited, eyes flashing blue fire at Leo. His balls tightened as he held her gaze.

Fuck, she was so sexy, and she held all the cards. Literally, held him by the dick. Her predator's gaze unblinking, and dammit all to hell, Leo was desperate for her to sink down and swallow him deep inside her heat.

Why the fuck wasn't she moving?

The Lion clawed at him, but it was obvious she wasn't ready. Not yet, and fight though his beast did, Leo held himself still. Sheila looked him in the eye, making sure she had his attention before she spoke.

Fuck, she has more than that, he thought.

"No biting, Leo. Promise me. Sex only. Fucking only. No claiming. Or we stop, right now. Agreed?" she asked, her voice husky with need.

He wanted to roar and demand, but fuck, she had him good. Sheila raked one hand down his chest, not hard enough to break skin, but definitely hard enough to rouse his beast.

"Sheila," he started, unable to do anything while she held his cock in her firm hand.

"Agreed?" she asked again, dropping a fraction of a centimeter onto his pulsating shaft.

Ffuckk. So tight. So hot.

Leo was going to go permanently cross-eyed if the woman didn't finish, but he wasn't hard of hearing. He'd already promised himself he would not claim her until she asked. It was going to be hard, but so what? The best things in life did not come easily, and he already had plans to make his mate work for it. Puns intended.

"No biting. I understand, but it will never ever be just fucking. Not with you, *mate*,"

His growled words ended on a groan as Sheila impaled herself on his cock. Sinking down hard, she swerved her hips and took him even deeper inside of her incomparable heat. Sexy little Wolf, she'd rendered him speechless with her body.

Roarrrr.

Leo's Lion threatened to burst forth as his mate's tight pussy sheathed his cock, covering him with her heated, wet flesh. He growled aloud as her molten walls stroked and squeezed his steel length.

"Oh fuck, Leo. You feel so good," she murmured and rocked her hips.

His little Wolf growled low in her throat as she rocked slowly along his thick length. She wanted control, but Leo couldn't not move. He simply could not be an impassive party to this poignant culmination. For weeks, he'd dreamed about this. Days, hours, minutes that seemed to stretch into eternity just picturing the moment he finally had Sheila Rand in his arms.

Finally, his waiting was over. The little Wolf wanted no strings, but she had no idea what this meant to him. He had her now, and he wasn't letting go. Sitting up straighter, he moved with her, thrusting upwards to meet her downward grinds with sharp, precise motions. They marked the time with a rhythm all their own, the steady thudding of the mattress music to his sensitive ears.

Sheila was glorious, a thing of pure beauty. Her tight channel stroked him good and hard. Deep, so deep—he moved within her sex, stroking her like he was born to. Leo had never felt anything like this, had never loved anyone like her.

"Sheila," he growled her name, holding her head behind her neck and crashed his mouth to hers.

He had to kiss her again. Just couldn't stop himself from kissing this woman. She was everything he'd ever wanted and never realized. A conundrum of opposing actions and ideas. She didn't want to be mated, and yet she lay claim to his heart with every swivel and slide of her luscious body. She kissed him like she was born to, but still refused his claim.

Not yet.

That was the key phrase. Her eyes locked onto his, and Leo felt his Lion's growl answer the call he saw there. If he tried, he'd see the tentative bonds of their mating growing stronger. Those magical ties that bound every fated mate together existed even now. This consummation solidified theirs just a fraction more. She might not want to face it just yet, but they belonged to one another like they never would to anyone else.

Leo was as sure of that as he was the sun would set each night and rise again the next day. Awash in that star's fiery rays, his Sheila practically glowed in the golden-hued beams that filtered down from the skylight above them. He was mesmerized by her beauty. She was a goddess.

Woman. Warrior. Mate. Fierce Dire Wolf.

Her flame-kissed hair swirled around her shoulders, the deep red color more pronounced against her flawless ivory skin. Sweat beads dotted her forehead and her body was slick with it. Sheila panted and moved with increased vigor, taking him deep, riding him hard, and fuck, if he didn't hold on tight. Leo's heart squeezed, ready to explode with the strength of his feelings. The muscle tightened almost painfully inside his chest.

He always used to laugh whenever he'd heard people described as having the *heart of a lion*. What normal man or woman could know a Lion's heart? What Shifter, for that matter? But Leo knew. At least, he did now.

He had been unprepared for the powerful wave of emotion that started with that muscle housed inside his chest. Right then, it beat with the strength of his thousand pound beast, filled to overflowing with all the love he had to give this fiercely beautiful woman who rode him so expertly.

Sheila's mouth opened in a soundless scream. She raised her arms high over her head, rocking her hips in time with his thrusts with all the grace and fire of a Valkyrie charging into battle. Untamed and dazzling, she reached for him and crashed her mouth to his, controlling the kiss, and in turn, the pace of their fucking. Each tug on his tongue seemed to echo all the way down to his cock. It was marvelous, poignant, and so fucking hot he almost came right then.

How did this happen? When did she become the master in this exchange?

He didn't give a fuck as long as she kept moving. Her sweet, succulent pussy squeezed and sucked his cock, bringing him to heights he'd never imagined. Sheila moaned in her pleasure, and he felt her pulse and ripple around him. Her walls tightened, gripping him like a velvet vise. She rocked her hips harder, faster. Leo grunted with the effort. He was close, so close, but she needed to come first. He still had that much control.

"Faster," she ground out, her movements becoming more and more erratic and disjointed as her orgasm neared.

"Sheila."

"Leo," she panted.

He understood what she needed. He grabbed her waist, nipping her lower lip between his teeth, he held her in place until she opened wide and allowed his tongue entry. If they were going to fall apart together, he wanted his mouth on hers. He wanted every single one of her groans and gasps. They were his, dammit. Leo lifted his sweet mate and dropped her down hard, impaling her on his cock.

Up, down, grind, swerve, harder, faster, again, and again.

"Yes," she moaned, and this time she nipped his bottom lip between her sharp teeth.

Leo growled. His Lion loved that little bite, wanted her to break the skin, mark him, claim him. He pumped his hips, thrusting upwards and into her faster and harder from underneath her sweet body. Together, they moved, grunted, and rocked. He kneaded the flesh of her plump ass. Loving the way her globes filled his large hands.

Sheila clawed at his shoulders as the pressure built and became almost overwhelming for her. His Lion hissed inside of him, encouraging him to strengthen his mate's pleasure. He dipped his head, releasing her lips so that she could moan as he licked and sucked on her neck, teasing the spot he would one day mark with his claiming bite. Hopefully sooner than later.

With one hand still on her waist, directing her movements, the other spread her cheeks apart. Sheila growled and tensed as he teased the sensitive, puckered skin surrounding her forbidden hole before finally testing the thing itself. Steadily he continued to increase the speed of his thrusts, swallowing down her moans, one after the other greedily as he slipped one thick digit inside her tight, trembling orifice. Leo had found it. Her breaking point. That edge she needed in order to completely surrender to the pleasure only he could deliver.

"Mine," he roared the possessive word, and tasted victory in that moment when her orgasm claimed her.

Pride filled him as Sheila threw her head back, howling out loud in her ecstasy. He'd done that. He'd brought her there. That was, of course, his last coherent thought as her pussy clenched around his cock, squeezing him tight while her forbidden hole did the same, tightening around his finger.

She continued to howl her release, her nails scratching at his shoulders, and finally he let his own magnificent climax take him. Leo roared. Loudly. He came long and hard, coating her walls with his seed and marking her with his scent.

"Mine," he said, despite his fangs.

The words would have to suffice in calming the beast when all he wanted to do was bite down and claim her.

Mine.

CHAPTER EIGHT

DIRE WOLF MATES

Holy. Deliciousness.

Sheila blinked slowly. A wide grin cracked her face as she stretched her well used body. She throbbed and ached in places she'd forgotten she had. She was exhausted, deliciously so.

Good dream. Sexy.

The ache in her muscles was a good ache. A welcomed one. Who knew a pussycat had moves like that? Speaking of, where was he? Sheila shot up like a rocket and looked around. His scent was everywhere. That thick, spicy masculine musk was in the sheets, the pillows, on her skin. That was no dream.

Oh. My. Gods.

Sheila had done the dirty with Leo the Lion. Holy. Fucking. Hell. She'd *made the beast with two backs, knocked boots, shook the sheets, got down and dirty, shtupped, rutted, balled, boinked, bumped uglies, got laid, got lucky*—no matter how you said it, she did it and done it with the pussycat.

Slightly panicked, she realized Leo was gone. Well, at least she did not have to face him first thing. Squashing the tiny bubble of disappointment that threatened to rise, she got out of bed and made her way to the connected bathroom.

"Is that a bidet?" she murmured, shaking her head as she took care of her business, trying to wrap her mind around what had happened during the night.

And with Leo. Her pretend nemesis.

So much for keeping him at arm's length. She'd actually jumped him. And hot damn, the man was a monster in the sack. He'd truly matched her every inch of the way. She washed her hands and face, looking in the mirror at her reflection.

For the first time in like ever, Sheila looked content. Happy. Satisfied. And she was. Imagine that? She ran her hands along her neck, but he hadn't betrayed her. True to his word. no claiming bite marred her skin.

Sheila did not want to dwell on the feeling of disappointment that sprung up on her suddenly. Instead, she looked around the ornate bathroom and opened the door to the bedroom. He had not returned, her Wolf hearing would have told her if he had.

This space was just as fine and expensively decorated as the rest of the huge house. Not what she imagined Leo's childhood home would look like. He was a detective, so she'd pictured normal, middle-class suburbia for the pussycat. Not this Palace, which was also the dwelling place of the Lion Pride's current King.

Sooo…. what did that make him? Was he the son of an Enforcer? A Guard? Whatever the fuck these pussies had for hierarchy? She really didn't know a thing about Prides. Maybe he was involved or related to the head honcho, somehow?

It was sort of bizarre they had an actual King, but whatever. To each his own. She'd been in such a fury of hormones last night, her body and emotions both went haywire, and Sheila had gotten none of the answers she needed. But he sure made her feel good last night.

Yes sirree. Really, really good. Grrrrr.

Grabbing her cell, Sheila balked at how many hours had passed since they'd arrived, and she'd basically attacked Leo. Had she really slept that long? Sure looked like it. But in her defense, she'd had the best sex of her entire life, so yeah. Some good, all through the night, sleep time was well earned. Seriously, she had never come so long or so hard with anyone ever before.

And you won't with anyone else. He is ours. Mate.

OMG. Can you just let me enjoy this? Sheila growled at her Wolf's inner bitchiness.

From what she knew of mates, the need to consummate their relationship, to lay claim with fang and claw, would only grow until they finally went through with it. Afterwards, there would be even more amazing sex. That's how it went with Shifters.

Sniff. Insta-lust. Sex. More sex. Claiming marks. Then even more sex.

Not bad, if you didn't mind the whole out-of-control lusty sexy times, followed by bitey claiming marks, then forever stuck together, and finally, the almost always pregnant thing. Hell, even swollen like a cantaloupe, there was still the sex, right? At least, according to Lucy. She'd already told Sheila, with way too much TMI than any cousin-in-law should share, that sex with her mate got better every single time they did it.

But it was not the need to be with him that scared Sheila. It wasn't the sex. Or even the pain of the bite marks, and sometimes clawing, that went along with claiming your mate. Sheila would stick like glue to someone she was loyal too. After all, she'd stuck with Derrick and her Pack since she was a teenager.

But the possibility of motherhood, being an actual mom to a fragile, needy little cub—that scared the shit out of her. And for good reasons. Sheila had no real parental role models. Derrick was about as close to having a parent as she came.

What if she sucked at it? She loved her mother, but the woman was no kind of actual parent. Sheila had grown up with the other cubs, hanging around the graybeards of her old MC when the others went with their moms and dads. Those old Wolves had been patient when it was called for, and stern, too, when she needed it. She earned diplomas on the road. Got her real education from life. And any milestones were achieved with and witnessed by her cousin and friends.

When she left the Pack of her birth to follow the Pack of her heart, Sheila felt positive she'd made the right decision. Being the only female was tough, but she liked having a bunch of honorary brothers. They had her back, and she had theirs. Her Pack mates were loyal and tightknit, but not exactly demonstrative about their feelings.

Fuck.

Sheila would make a terrible mother. But even acknowledging her greatest fear didn't stop her body from reacting to the mere idea of being with Leo. Wearing his bite mark. Bearing his young.

Shit.

Her heart started pounding, and pulse raced up just thinking about the big, sexy Lion. Where was he, anyway? She grabbed the sheet and inhaled, breathing in his musky scent. Want, need, longing filled her. She missed him. Even though it had only been a few hours, she missed him. Her Wolf whined, beast in agreement.

It was sort of like nature's way of ensuring destiny didn't fuck things up. That attraction, that never ending need to be with him. Wow. She really didn't appreciate waking up to an empty room. One night of good sex, and Sheila was turning all clingy, dammit. What the heck had happened to her life? Sheila was out of control and all because of one overgrown, presently absentee, tabby.

The fucker.

One minute she was all aloof, handling the whole pretense of their mating just fine with no *howdy dos* about the whole damn thing. She'd agreed to this ruse not to be near him, but so he could solve the mystery of whatever the fuck was happening here. Still, that didn't explain why one minute she was touring the sprawling mansion, and the next minute she was butt ass naked, and wrapped around the big pussy like a cheap suit.

How was that his fault? Her snarky she-Wolf seemed to laugh as she asked that question.

Fine, she admitted.

That was all on her, even if he didn't exactly resist. Leo made no secret of his desire for her from the beginning. It was flattering, but also pure biology. Fated mates and all that jazz. Whatever. Sheila knew just how to get her swerve on. So, what if she was horny? The big ol' pussycat had the goods, and he wasn't shy about using them.

They'd both had fun. It didn't have to mean more. She'd help him with his Pride's issues, then she could move on. Fuck it, he could move on too, with whomever he wanted. Find a nice Lioness to settle down with, have some cubs, live a good, settled life.

GRRRR.

Her she-Wolf was really not having any of that. She closed her eyes and shook her head. Tears welled in her eyes, and she punched the mattress. What the heck? She did not do crying. Ever.

Shit.

She wiped her face.

Goddammit.

She was crying.

Sigh.

Way to stay strong and resist the mating fever. Not. She rolled her head on her neck and then her shoulders, stopping the tears and stretching her exhausted body. Sex with Leo was better than good. It was fanfuckingtastic. But she couldn't let it happen again.

She'd almost bitten him. Then where would she be? Mated for life. And that could only be disastrous. Okay, so it was a near thing. A one off. Done and done. She had just made up her mind, sitting down on the large luxury bed as a hurricane in the form of two waspish felines came crashing into the room.

"Alright, you hussy, where is my nephew?" the older one with silver hair, and a cute as fuck pair of printed capri pants topped with a gold, off-the-shoulder blouse, demanded haughtily.

"*Oh my gah*!" The younger of the two snapped her chewing gum and pointed at Sheila. "Mom, she's a Dog!"

"What?"

Sniff.

"You're right! She does smell like a canine, doesn't she?" the older woman addressed the younger, as if Sheila wasn't even there.

"Excuse me?" Sheila asked.

She was starting to get more than annoyed with these two intruders. Not bothering to cover herself, she worked to rein in her she-Wolf, the beast definitely didn't like them, until she knew who and what they were. For all she knew, these could be Leo's relatives.

"There is no excuse for humping my nephew in his childhood bedroom without even introducing yourself to us," the older female said.

Sheila's eyebrows disappeared into her hairline as she watched the two felines lay down and settle on one of the two sofas in the bedroom. Sheesh, this room was fucking huge. Four times the size of her own bedroom at the Pack house. Still, how had she missed the gold-trimmed pieces of furniture? Probably because she was too busy attacking her mate's sumptuous body.

EEEP!

She really had to stop calling him that. She looked around again and tried to ignore the tingle of anxiety that shivered up her spine. Everything in the room was of the highest quality. Looking down at the crumpled sheets, she recognized the checked pattern of the mattress beneath it.

The Vividus was a luxury mattress upwards of fifty-fucking-grand. What the fuck kind of money did Leo have? The hand carved dresser, mirror, and chairs all reflected the same top quality craftsmanship. Like most Shifter wares, it was specialty built to withstand the antics of a growing Shifter. In Leo's case, a Lion cub.

Shifter furniture artisans responsible for pieces such as these would undoubtedly charge tens of thousands of dollars for each one. They were beautiful works of art, and they were well-cared for. The entire mansion was full of them. Everything was top of the line, cleaned and polished.

Void of Lions, though. Sheila frowned. It was odd, seeing a Pride house empty like this one.

The plush carpets were spotless, the furniture shiny. For a she-Wolf who'd slept under the stars on an old bedroll for most of her life, this place was over the top grand. It was way out of her league.

Sheila didn't react outwardly—the Lionesses would be all over her if she did—but she couldn't stem the tide of panic that welled up deep inside. She was good at keeping her crazy to herself, and she would have to do just that right now.

Once she got hold of that sneaky pussycat, she'd let it all out. What was he, anyway? Some rich flunky of the King's? How could he not tell her? She thought he was just a detective, and that had been bad enough, but finding out he was rich too.

Ugh.

Sheila did not belong here. This place was top shelf, and she was more a dollar drafts kind of gal. She didn't want an audience for this little breakdown she was having. Did not want to reveal too much to these two strange Lionesses. That would be incredibly foolish, and Sheila was not that.

Nope.

She needed to think. She needed to know more about their agenda, at the very least. The two felines watched her with that same steady glare of house cats, and Sheila's Wolf snarled. Should they prove to be enemies, her animal wasn't opposed to using them both as chew toys.

Grrr.

"What I want to know is what was that hairbrained nephew of mine thinking bringing a Dog inside the Palace?"

"Well, she has good boobs, Mom," the younger said, and Sheila looked down.

Shifters were usually comfortable with nudity, and Sheila was no different. The fact they called their Pride house a Palace was something only a fucking Cat would do—haughty little shits.

"Thanks. I need to shower," she told the females, who seemed perfectly fine just lounging around.

She needed answers, but her pussycat ran away. It was a sneaky move. Definitely not straightlaced, and she didn't know whether to be angry or proud of him. Leo always followed the rules, as far as she knew. It was kind of sexy to see a mischievous side of him. OMG, she really was sick. How could him hightailing it out of there turn her on?

"Easy there, Spot," the younger Lioness said, sniffing the air and picking up on the effect Sheila's naughty thoughts had on her body. "We don't swing that way."

"I swing a lot of ways actually, but incest is not my thing. Seems like my nephew has finally been having some fun with—say, just who are you, anyway?" the older Lioness asked.

"Yeah, what's your name, Doggy?"

"Okay, first, I'm a Dire Wolf Shifter, not a Dog, so you're going to want to watch it with the insults or you two kitties are going to lose your tails," Sheila replied.

She turned away from the bathroom door to face them, naked as a jaybird. The two blonde-haired females slunk further into Leo's sofas and eyed her with casual interest. Nothing icky, eyes on her face, but they definitely knew something she didn't. Best to make friends, she decided.

Lounging lazily like the haughty felines they were, Sheila wondered just why they had presumed to simply walk in. Were these relatives allies of Leo? They were definitely nosey. Sheila reached for her jeans and top. She did not do confrontations naked—unless they were with Leo.

"A Dire Wolf, huh? That's kinda cool, but you didn't answer the other question. *Who* are you?"

"Second," Sheila continued, as if she hadn't been interrupted. "You don't get to just walk in here. Not anymore. And you certainly don't get to snap questions at me."

"And why not?"

"Because," Sheila continued as she turned around and entered the bathroom, closing the door unhurriedly. "I'm Leo's mate."

"Holy butt-sniffers!" the younger woman squeaked and practically choked on her bubblegum.

"Ariella, I don't know about you, but I like her," the woman with silver streaks threaded through her stylishly short blonde locks said loud enough for Sheila to hear her with the bathroom door closed.

Yay, Sheila! She smirked and turned on the shower. Sixteen minutes later, she was cleaned, and dressed in fresh jeans and a t-shirt. Sheila opened the door to see the two Lionesses still there.

"You clean up nice," the younger one said.

"Gee, thanks," Sheila said, rolling her eyes.

"Well, since you are Leo's mate, I figured we'd stick around for formal introductions. I'm Leo's Aunt Patricia. Guess that makes me your auntie, too. This here is one of my daughters. Ariella, stand up and say hi."

"Hi," Ariella said once she stopped choking. She grinned wickedly, and peaked at her mother.

"George is going to shit himself."

"Ariella! Don't talk about your brother like that. He is though, isn't he!" Auntie Pat said, smirking before she laughed wickedly.

"You see, my little brother Georgie has been lining up all the eligible Lionesses for Leo to choose his mate. In fact, they should be parading through the Palace interviewing room in about an hour," Ariella informed her.

"Oh, really?" Sheila growled.

"Yes, really," added Aunt Patricia. "Forgive me, but how do we know you're actually his mate?"

"Surely, you can scent what happened in here?"

"Sex is sex, dear. But where is your mating mark?"

"My Pack prefers to hold all claiming ceremonies for the night of the full moon," Sheila replied.

It wasn't a lie exactly. Dire Wolves did prefer to mate by moonlight. Afterwards, the ritual of the claiming tattoo would take place in sight of the Pack. Odd, she did not really think of them as an MC now, since they'd retired. But some shit was bone deep. In fact, she grabbed her cell phone and shot off a text to Brock. The bastard owed her one after that shit he pulled in the bar yesterday.

"So, you know, the full moon is tonight, you know," Ariella supplied, and Sheila's heart immediately started beating overtime.

Hmm.

She wondered if Leo would mind getting a tattoo. She hadn't noticed one on him earlier. His wide shoulders and broad chest would be perfect in her opinion, and with those muscles, he'd only look hotter with a bit of ink.

Whoa.

That would only be an option if Sheila was thinking about making this mating real, and she was far from doing that. Her emotions were all over the place, but her Wolf was consistent. She wanted Leo to be hers, regardless of her human fears.

"You ladies up for a ride?" she remarked casually when she was feeling anything but.

"You're changing the subject," Aunt Patricia said.

"Yep. You pussies riding with me? Or are you a couple of scaredy cats too timid to follow a badass Wolf?" Sheila baited them, sliding her boots on, and tugging her hair into a low ponytail.

"What kind of ride?" Ariella asked.

Just then, the sound of a couple of Harley's revving their engines echoed in the room. Ariella bounded over to a row of long curtains lining the wall. She pulled a switch, revealing double, glass terrace doors. Sheila gasped her surprise before Ariella opened said doors, that led out to a stone patio leading to a path that split off to different areas of the massive yard. One path went to the side of the Palace, to a fence the other side of which sat her ride.

Wowza.

Leo had a fucking terrace in his bedroom. This man was way too good at hiding bits and pieces of himself from her. Some goody-two shoes he was turning out to be! It was like he was leading this whole double life. Leo was a bad boy! And that just made her she-Wolf swoon and sigh dreamily over the big puffed up pussy, for fuck's sake.

Just think of the midnight runs! We could find our fur together and come right to bed.

Sheila rolled her eyes at her canine's imagination.

"Well, ladies? What do you say? Want to burn some rubber with a couple of Dire Wolves?" she asked, and the two Lionesses looked at each other, mischievous grins on their faces before joining her on the patio.

"We talkin' tires, or other kinds of rubber?" Aunt Patricia asked and wagged her eyebrows.

OMG. The older Lioness had just made a condom joke. Ha! Sheila snorted.

The woman was old enough to be her mother, but hey, Sheila wasn't judging. People had sex because it felt good. Sex was fun. Sheila was not going to hold her suggestive and hilarious questions against her. That Lioness was funny as fuck.

"Just a ride on a Harley, Auntie P," she said and winked.

"Oh pooh! Well, I suppose I could be persuaded. I'll take the big, bald one," she purred.

"Um, Sheila?"

"Yeah, Ari?"

"Who are these guys?" Ariella asked and blinked slowly as she took in Thor, Brock, and Weylin.

The latter was riding Sheila's custom pink, and black painted Harley Softail Convertible. She watched her Pack mate pull up to the fence along the side of the rock wall that partially closed off the garden and opened to the field and forests behind. Fucking place was amazing, she thought while admiring the view.

The back of the property seemed to begin as a manicured lawn with all the customary entertaining doodads that crazy rich people always seemed to have in their yards. There was a large swimming pool, a fountain, a gazebo, tennis courts, and a huge grassy lawn. Maybe that's why these Lions called it a Palace.

There had to be some good explanation for why her Leo lived with the King of the Pride. She swallowed hard and pushed the thought away. She wasn't ready to hear her own ideas on that situation, much less whatever these two Lionesses had to say about it.

Sheila eyed the high rock wall separating the property from the small side road where her Pack mates were currently idling on their bikes. She could clear that on her two legs. No problem. A sharp whistle reached her ears, and she turned to see Brock signaling to her. Right. The Beta had a kitchen to run, and it was almost lunchtime. Sheila's pulse raced as she got closer to her motorcycle. Her blood hummed with the need to ride.

"Those are my Pack mates," she finally answered, noticing Ariella's still and unblinking stare. The Lioness had her golden gaze on Brock, and the Wolf seemed unwilling or unable to break eye contact.

Hmm. That's interesting.

She'd save her curiosity for another time, though. Right then, Sheila had better things to do. Like maybe get herself away from the weird situation she found herself in so she could mull it over.

Grrr.

Her she-Wolf was not happy about this at all. But she shut down her animal with a sharp command. Her human side was in control, and she had some thinking to do.

Relax, she told the beast.

She needed to beat it, even if just for a minute or thirty. Not like she'd run out on the big ol' pussycat without telling him. Not now that she'd let him in. Sheila couldn't walk away cold if she tried. And for once, she did not want to try.

Also interesting.

It had only been a few days since she'd jumped on the back of her Harley and cruised the open road, but she could use the clarity right about now. There was something about miles of black asphalt that allowed Sheila to just think.

Oddly enough, that sweet moment of peace she got whenever she went out for a ride, no matter how long or short, was even sweeter now that she had a permanent place to land. For a she-Wolf who'd never had a room, much less a home of her own, that was something alright.

But was she really destined to live in a Palace? The thought stuck in her throat like an un-popped piece of popcorn.

Shit.

She didn't want to have those thoughts. Not when she was still feeling so good after her sexy little romp with Leo between his silky sheets. Fuck, they were probably real silk she realized with an unsteady breath. Her fingers itched to get ahold of his hot and hard body once again, but for now she'd settle for gripping the handlebars of her bike.

She'd had Weylin repaint the trim a few months ago. It kind of went with her nails now, and their logo. She grinned excitedly at the hot pink lines and flames that covered the custom body of her ride. The other two boys were on their own rides. Brock on his FXSTB Night Train and Thor on his VRSCA V-Rod. All three Harleys gleamed in the setting sun and the men on them with their leather cuts and dark helmets looked pretty dang good, even if they were her family.

"Well, ladies? Let's go!" Sheila laughed and took off for the wall at a run with the two felines right behind her.

"Hey there, Sheila girl. Dang, you stink like Cat—*ouch*!" Weylin rubbed his arm where she'd punched him.

"Shit, Sheila, you know I bruise easily!" he complained.

"Oh, shut up, you big baby. Now, scoot out of the way, I'm driving. Ladies, this here is Weylin. He's just a grunt," she teased despite his scowl. "That's Brock. He's our Pack Beta. And that giant over there is Thor, our Enforcer. Guys, this is Aunt Patricia and Ariella. They want to go for a ride, what say you?" Sheila asked grandly and grinned wickedly as the humor left her Pack mates' faces.

"Ma'am, I'd be happy to take you for a ride," Thor said and offered his hand to Aunt Patricia, who slapped it away.

"I can get on myself, big guy. You just keep this thing straight, and I'll hold on to the good parts," she replied and grinned wickedly. With a throaty little purr, the older Lioness mounted behind the big man.

"Ooof!"

Thor's eyes bulged out of his head, and he actually squeaked as the feline wrapped herself around him and clung like a vise. She nipped his ear, and Thor revved his engine, taking off like a bat out of hell.

"Mom!" Ariella blushed as she gingerly got on the seat behind Brock.

Sheila pretended not to listen as the Dire Wolf Beta instructed her to scooch on closer. He handed her his helmet, turning to latch it carefully beneath her chin before telling the little kitty to put her arms around his waist. The lust in the air was pretty hard to miss, but Sheila was much too worried about herself to tease her Beta about it just yet.

Very interesting.

It seemed like it was open season on the DWMC. She supposed Cats and Dogs could get along if circumstances were right. Maybe this was a sign of some sort.

Fuck it.

Sheila might not be able to stop fate, but she'd go down swinging. That was a guarantee.

"Let's ride," she said before taking off with Weylin clinging to the seat and cursing for all he was worth.

Sheila's laughter was swallowed by the wind as she sped away from the Blue Valley Pride, and from Leo. Her she-Wolf growled and snapped until she reassured the beast she'd be returning within the hour.

Make it fast.

Grrrr.

CHAPTER NINE

DIRE WOLF MATES

Leo squeezed his father's hand and looked into the older man's sightless eyes. It's not that he was blind, the Lion King had perfect vision. And yet, he knew his father was not seeing him.

It was as if he was somewhere else, locked away inside his mind. The old King seemed caught in his past somehow and judging from his expression and the occasional moan that escaped his thin lips, it was not a pleasant experience.

"Car! Car!" Donovan Crowley repeated the nickname he'd given Leo's mother a long time ago.

It struck a chord deep within Leo as his father called out for his mate over and over again. Caroline Crowley, Leo's mother, was a human woman, a *normal*, as their kind referred to them. Fate had dealt his parents quite the hand, but it all worked out. His human mother fell in love and got mated to the Lion King of Blue Valley.

Their story was legendary in a time when prejudice and hatred for humans had run rampant among Shifters. Things had settled down some, but there was always that fear of being discovered to make human supernatural pairings uncomfortable. The Pride had not wanted to allow such a mating. But his father had not backed down an inch. Donovan had claimed his human bride, and the massive Lion had torn down every doubter in his Pride.

Leo knew the tale well. He'd cut his teeth on it. Hell, he was in awe of them both. His parents had succeeded despite the naysayers from the Pride. Leo was proud of them and of his heritage. It saddened him that Leo didn't know his father that well anymore. They'd drifted apart over the years. It was a hard truth.

Still, he loved the man. Respected him. But this frail shell of a man was not the father he knew. It was not the King he remembered.

"I'm going to figure this out, Dad," he whispered into his father's ear, and kissed his withered cheek.

The old man turned with a speed Leo didn't expect. Hell, he didn't think his father still had it in him. Hope sparked deep inside his chest. His father clutched his arm, and when he finally spoke, Leo saw the cloudy white film of disease leave his eyes and the golden amber of his Lion leaked through.

"Car! It's Car," he growled.

"Dad? No, Dad, it's Leo. Mom is gone. I'm sorry, Dad, but she's gone."

"Caroline? Gone? No, no!"

His father released his hold on Leo's arm and clutched his head. The once mighty King rocked back and forth, sobbing in his hands. He muttered to himself, and Leo noted the cloudiness had returned to his eyes. His heart nearly broke at the sight.

Something was not right. How did a once robust King suddenly turn into this? It was unnatural, but Leo was too close to the situation to see it clearly. Damn. He needed Sheila. She could help him. Both his Lion and human sides were at peace when she was near. He needed his mate. Now.

"My Prince? What are you doing here?" Montgomery entered the room with a wheeled cart filled with food and his grandmother's tea service.

Leo's cousin George was hot on his heels. His Lion growled, and both men stopped in their tracks. He didn't want them to witness his father's weakness, but he was helpless to stop them. Montgomery was a trusted attendant and George was being groomed to fill the position of advisor once Leo ascended the throne.

Fuck.

Dread filled him. He wasn't ready. Not yet. He nodded his head, and both men moved cautiously into his father's room. He had to keep level to find the truth.

"Leo, it's good you are here. Please, come into the interview room and we will begin—"

"I told you, do not discuss those things in here," Montgomery hissed, surprising Leo and George.

"Excuse me, but what do you have to say on the matter?" George responded.

"Oh, sorry, I was just thinking of the King. He needs his rest. Excuse me," the man said and continued to prepare the tea.

"Okay," George replied, eyes wide. "Well, Leo, there are a few items on your agenda you need to see to immediately. Maybe something that will cure whatever ails you," the younger Lion said and wagged his eyebrows.

Unfortunately, Leo was in no mood for games. His father was worse off than he'd thought.

"George, I want to speak to the Pride healer. Now," Leo grumbled, turning back to cup his father's neck, pressing his forehead to his sire's in a show of deep affection and respect felines were known for before heading out of the room.

"Now? Why? He isn't going to say anything new, you know," the younger man replied, trailing after him, and looking puzzled.

Leo turned around and barked an order to Montgomery. The older man stopped what he was doing and followed George, though he did not look happy about it. Well, wasn't that too fucking bad?

"George, Montgomery, when the two of you entered my father's room, did you show him the proper respect befitting your King?"

"What?" George sputtered.

"Pardon, sire?" Montgomery balked.

Leo's Lion growled deep inside of him, the sound filling his stomach and chest until it reverberated throughout the tiny hall between rooms. Leo wasn't King yet, but he was the strongest Lion there. Immediately, George and Montgomery dropped to their knees, baring their throats under the heavy weight of his dominance.

Both males averted their gazes, neither daring to look at Leo with his Lion so close to the surface. It was a good thing. A smart thing to do. Leo felt raw and angry. His beast wouldn't like the challenge their direct stares would pose.

Still, he did not like feeling this out of control. It was unbefitting a man of his station, and Leo was all about the rules.

"I apologize, sir," George replied.

His voice sounded strained under the force of Leo's alpha Lion's will. That sort of power was inherent in certain Shifters. Wielded by those who would lead, the alpha gene was inherited, but that extra bit of Pride magic was only granted to those few chosen strong enough to be Kings. The Crowley family bred such Shifters and George would do well to remember that. What it all meant was fairly simple. Leo was not to be fucked with.

It was clear some members of the Pride had forgotten that one little thing. Leo would have to correct that. He'd been gone too long, but he was not going to make that mistake again. Leo pressed his will on them for just a moment longer, then he released his hold.

They stayed on the ground, unsure of what to do next. His Lion gleaned satisfaction from their submission. Sick? Maybe. But he was a predator, a dominant, a born Primus. It was his natural power and position within the Pride. His due if you will.

"Thank you, sir. May I tend my duties now?" Montgomery gestured to the door where Leo's father waited.

"My father is still the King, Montgomery. That means you, and everyone else, needs to afford him the respect he is due at all times. Is that understood?" Leo asked, barely holding onto his beast.

Power pulsed through him, and it was all he could do to fight his Lion's urge to dominate these others into the ground.

They are of our Pride, he reminded his Lion. Finally, the regal animal relented.

"Yes, of course," Montgomery spoke with his forehead still pressed to the cold, hard marble floor.

Guilty for his bullying tactics, Leo nodded for him to rise. The man had been around forever. He had always been overeager to please, and exceedingly efficient in his duties.

But Montgomery had always made him a tad uncomfortable, even when Leo was just a cub. His mother had told him about Montgomery's family's history, and stories of the Clover males and the fact they had been employed in the Palace for just as long as a Crowley had reigned. Those stories softened Leo's point of view.

The man simply took his job seriously. Nothing wrong with that. In fact, Leo could relate. How many cases had he brought home with him over the years? His supervisors had one constant reprimand, and that was for the number of hours in overtime Leo worked in his search to bring justice to the people he served and to hunt down any criminal who dared transpire in his territory.

Hell, he'd stopped reporting those long overtime hours years ago. He didn't care about the money. He had plenty. It was the thought of leaving a case unsolved that haunted him.

"Of course," George gasped. "I know Uncle Donovan is our King. Look, Leo, I am sorry, I just got excited. I have a surprise, that's all."

Leo lessened his Alpha will, and George rose hesitantly from the floor. His eyes were still averted, and Leo realized he was being an ass.

"Okay. Sorry, bro, I'm just tense. Get the healer anyway, and I'll meet you in the interview room," he growled, and walked away from his sputtering younger cousin.

It seemed like George was always upset about something or other. Leo didn't give a rat's ass at the moment. His cousin was an adult, he could handle his own problems. Right then, he had his own Lion to worry about. The animal was on edge.

In fact, he was seriously pissed at Leo, and not because he wouldn't let him snack on those two less dominant males. Heck, those Lions were not even on his radar at the moment. No, the beast inside him was angry at Leo for leaving their den with Sheila still asleep. His animal was livid he had not claimed his mate.

He was still reeling from the fact that Sheila had taken the reins from him almost immediately after he'd instigated a kiss. Sexy little she-Wolf had stripped her clothes, then his, teasing him with glimpses of her pale, silky smooth flesh. She was the hottest thing he'd ever seen.

His cock hardened at the memory of her delightful sexual aggression. She was so damn confident, so sublimely seductive with her ivory skin, sapphire eyes, and that mane of wild red hair. He was positively enamored of her. Leo swallowed, clearing his throat. He could admit it to himself.

He loved her. He was in love with her. The feelings were right there, and dammit, they felt good. It was just a shock. He knew he adored her, cared for her, and wanted her. Hell, he worshipped the feisty woman, or he wanted to, but she hadn't given him the opportunity yet.

Next time.

Next time, Leo would have his fill of her the way he'd dreamed about. He'd start with that sassy little mouth of hers. It made him smirk when he thought of her kickass comebacks. She was so damn cute.

Yeah, he'd start with that mouth of hers alright. Kissing Sheila was like trying to hold on to the wind. She was everywhere at once, filling his senses and haunting his dreams. Wild, untamed, and fucking glorious. He'd claim that spitfire's mouth with his alright. Then, he'd leave a trail of kisses down her smooth neck until he could savor the plump berries that tipped each of her splendid breasts.

He'd lick and nibble his way further still to the curve of her belly, over the flare of her hips, to that delicate smooth skin of her inner thighs. Finally, he'd find paradise in between those gorgeous legs of hers. Her short-cropped auburn curls hid the passage to absolute glory that Leo was destined to claim as his alone. Just thinking about her made his dick hard and his mouth water. He wanted his little Wolf with him.

Here. Now. Always.

Roarrrr.

Leo really needed to calm his beast before the Lion claimed her without permission, and he'd already promised to do no such thing. Some alpha Shifters ruled with big shows of strength, but Leo had always appreciated a quieter, more subtle approach. Reining in his beast was difficult, but he would wrestle his Lion down every single time if it brought him closer to his ultimate goal. And of course, that was claiming Sheila.

His Dire Wolf mate had made her position clear. She would help him with his mission to solve the source of his Pride's issues, but she wasn't sticking around forever. Or so she thought. Little did she know he had no intention of letting her go.

The sound of motors revving got his attention, but he was needed in the interview room. Besides, he'd left her snug in his bedroom. He would join her as soon as he finished with the Pride. First, he'd have Montgomery cook them a few porterhouses as a late lunch. He'd feed her, make love to her, then he'd bring up their future. That sounded like a helluva plan to him.

His Lion would never be satisfied until she was truly claimed. Difficult with her insistence that this thing between them was temporary. He just had to get her to change her mind about mating him. Shouldn't be too hard.

Yeah right.

He entered the King's interview room and immediately went on high alert. This was where he would conduct Pride business acting in his father's stead, where the King normally sat to hear his Pride's concerns, and to rule on things that needed ruling on. Apparently, stuff had been left to slide this past month and there were many issues that needed his attention.

Leo stopped short at the sight awaiting him inside. What fresh hell was this? No less than a dozen Lionesses stood in a line, each of them with what looked like a file folder in hand.

Fucking George.

He snarled. Were those resumes? He bit off his growl, noting the shocked gold stares eyeing him like some prize. Leo straightened his shoulders, grateful he'd donned his at home uniform. The navy blue suit with the Crowley crest on his cuff links acknowledged his position. It also happened to be one of his favorites with a thin pin strip and a silk shirt underneath. He'd foregone his usual tie but wore the medallion of his station. A thick gold chain with a single Lion claw hanging from it.

Should he need to shift, it would be both large and strong enough to withstand the power behind his change. And if that younger cousin of his didn't watch himself, Leo was sure to go all fierce and furry on his ass. Maybe take a bite out of the cheeky male's hide.

Fuckface.

He had already told George no to the whole Lioness thing. Leo raised an eyebrow as he sought his cousin. Ah. There he was. George tried to herd the females into a line, swatting down the hairs on the back of his neck that were undoubtedly standing up because of Leo. He was pissed.

What was his idiot cousin up to now? He took out his phone and shot a text to Sheila, wondering if she was up. He asked her to respond the minute she woke.

Dammit.

He missed her. Yes, he needed her too. Not for the reason he told her. Not to dissuade these griping females. He needed her to settle his animal, to make him feel whole—because fuck knew she did.

Beautiful, tempting, sassy seductress.

"Leo! Excellent, sit down and meet the most eligible females the Pride has to offer!"

The females stood at attention. Some he knew from when he was a cub, others he did not recognize. They were all dressed up, like this was some kind of pageant, and George, the idiot, had the nerve to smile at him. Leo was going to murder him.

Grrrr.

"George, I asked you to bring the healer to me," he said instead.

"Um, yes. I called, but he is delivering a set of cubs right now. I assured him you would be fine for a few hours. Besides you have other things to tend to, my Prince," George whispered and nodded to the first female in line.

She was wearing an expensive suit that showed off her best assets. She had her blonde hair piled on her head in some sophisticated, and painful looking updo. Her nails were neatly trimmed and polished a staid beige color. She was attractive, sophisticated, a bit boring, truth be told.

The blonde woman flashed him a toothy grin, and Leo nodded politely. His Lion snapped and spit in revulsion. The beast wanted nothing to do with this or the other tawny-haired females. This was exactly the type of female he'd thought he would end up with when he was just a cub. But not him. Not now.

Adult Leo found his tastes ran much different from Leo the cub. What he really liked was dazzling redheads with hot pink nail polish. Sexy biker chicks in leather and ripped jeans. One in particular with bright blue eyes, skin pale as milky, and a Harley between her legs when he couldn't be.

Yessssss.

"George, when did you notice my father started feeling ill?" he asked, ignoring the female.

"What? Oh, I don't know. He has not been himself since Aunt Caroline passed away, but he didn't start showing these signs till a few months ago, I think."

"I see. And had his habits changed?"

"Really, Leo, I don't know. Look, you should at least hear them out," George said and tilted his head. Leo noted a group of older Lionesses had entered the room from the other side.

Fuck.

All of them were elders. He knew well that the females of any Lion Pride were the backbone. Even in the wild, the females were the hunters, the providers. They had the numbers and the strength, but a male was King. It was simply their way.

After the circle he'd attended a few days ago, Leo had expected some backlash, but even he could not have predicted this. The four Lionesses included Maribel Clover, Ruth Cunningham, Margaret Donner, and Evangeline Mayers, all present and accounted for.

These Shifter females were cunning, sharp, and determined hunters. Strong despite their silver hair and the signs of age on their once unlined faces. Leo's father had allowed the elders to have a say in the way things were done within the Blue Valley Pride by listening to their council on more than one occasion. He would not undo all of his father's work, but that didn't mean he would go into this blindly.

Leo had spent years as a detective, he knew better than to trust people's motives. Especially when they had their own agendas. These women would not approve of Leo's announcement that he'd found a mate without their counsel. For one thing, his mate was not a female of their choosing. For another, she was not a Lioness.

Either way, they were going to be pissed. Something that would have worried younger Leo, but again, not now. Neither the elders nor the Pride would have a say in his choice of mate. He noted several of the females George had gathered for this introduction belonged to these Lioness' immediate families.

Well, fuck me again.

There was just no graceful way out of this. He had to do his duty and at least allow them to present themselves. George was still smiling, idiot that he was. He nodded his head at the Lionesses once more, knowing full well Leo was not happy.

"The way I see it, cousin, this is the way our Pride has always conducted such things. You have a duty, you know."

"I have found my mate, George. This will not change that."

"Maybe you're wrong," insisted the younger male.

Leo growled unhappily. Of course, he wasn't wrong. His Lion

chuffed and snorted. He would not be happy about it, and he sure as fuck wasn't changing his mind, but there were rules, and he had to at least appear willing. He had a protocol to follow.

Leo sat in his father's chair and nodded for the first woman to present herself. He would pretend to listen, and maybe he would find out just what the fuck was going on here.

"This is Taylor DeBlume," George said, smiling at the first boring blonde.

Leo huffed out a sigh. It was going to be a long morning.

CHAPTER TEN

DIRE WOLF MATES

"You are so right, Mom. Leo picked good."

Ariella giggled and fluffed her hair as they stumbled through the front doors of the Palace. They were all a little windblown, but no worse for wear. Besides, that ride had given Sheila exactly what she needed. Time to clear her head.

"Ladies! What are you doing here?" Montgomery sputtered at them.

His eyes raced wildly as he looked back and forth from one female to the other as if their presence were somehow blackening the polished floors. Sheila did not know what the fuck was wrong with this guy, but she wiped her feet on the rug, for fuck's sake.

"Look, it's cool, Monty. I wiped my feet," Sheila told him straight out.

She winked and opened the door wider, lifting each of her leather-booted feet into the air and holding her black and hot pink helmet under one arm.

"Montgomery, why do you always look like that?" Aunt Patricia asked and narrowed her eyes at the man. "You know, I've been trying to get in to see Donovan for weeks now! What is going on, anyway?'

"You should not be here, madam. Your presence is unwanted," he growled the words between clenched teeth.

"Whoa, tone it down there skippy. I don't think Leo will like you talking to her that way," Sheila growled. "I sure as fuck don't."

"How does he look, Mom?" Ariella asked.

"Oh, like someone farted right in his face," Aunt Patricia barked out a laugh that even a Dire Wolf could be proud of.

The two drunken kitties giggled, and Aunt Patricia leaned heavily on the wall. Okay, so, maybe Sheila shouldn't have stopped at Serious Moonlight with Leo's aunt and cousin for a couple of pitchers of mimosas. Of course, those had turned into margueritas, and from there it was shots all around. And it wasn't even dinner time!

Sheila bit her lip guiltily. But what a time they'd had. Sigh. She recalled Aunt Patricia's bar-top dancing while guzzling a bottle of eighty proof tequila like a motherfucking champ. It took Thor and Brock both to get her down. Shifter metabolism was such that alcohol burned off within minutes and by the time she left, she was not even buzzed. Ariella and Patricia were, but that's because they were still drinking.

Her stomach fluttered. The butterflies inside waking up now that she was closer to him. She'd expected to feel better, less anxious, once she'd hopped on her Harley with her Pack mates and her two new friends, but truthfully, that familiar calm she'd sought had proven elusive. Her she-Wolf had been seriously pissed at her for leaving Leo. She'd done her best to shake it off. Had some drinks, checked in with her Pack mates, and talked to some friendly customers. Including a certain Ass and his mate.

"Hey! It's you? Where is that amazing man of yours?" asked the Chipmunk Shifter Leo had rescued a few days ago.

"He's working, how are you?" Sheila had replied to the one and looked from her to where her mate was standing with one hand on her waist in a protective and possessive gesture. Sheila approved.

"We're good, never better," she'd returned with a twinkle in her eyes.

"Ma'am," the Donkey Shifter, Al, nodded at her and whispered something in his mate's ear that had her blushing like a schoolgirl.

"Um, we better go. Tell him, thanks again for me," the woman winked and left with her mate wrapped around her.

Sheila had felt a pang of jealousy as she watched the pair hurry on through the crowd. Probably on their way home, together. There was something about mates and being Shifters that meant when things were good, sexy fun times often ensued. Sheila could get used to an arrangement like that. But it was more than sex that appealed to her. Leo was simply perfect.

He was outrageously handsome, had an impeccable moral compass, was good to talk to, and possessed an air of power and strength that her Wolf wholeheartedly approved of. He was her ideal everything. How could she ever measure up? And, as if that wasn't bad enough, her new buddies had spilled the beans in a very bad way.

"You know, you're gonna make one helluva queen," Aunt Patricia slurred her words after she'd tipped off the bar when she'd finished the first bottle of tequila. The woman had taken a header into the unwilling arms of one particularly unhappy Pack Enforcer.

"For fuck's sake," Thor had muttered and glared at Sheila. Still, he was gentleman enough to drive them home after.

"My bad," she'd apologized to her Pack mate, but she was more concerned with what the Lioness had just said.

"The old Palace could use a little livening up. We haven't had any fun since Caroline passed. Leo's mother was one helluva queen, I tell you, and Donovan was so in love with that woman. She was my best friend. You're a lucky Dog, Sheila! The Crowleys are good Cats. Ha! A lucky Dog! That works even better cause you're a canine! Ha ha ha!" The matronly feline had snorted and laughed at her own jokes.

A few more shots, a couple of dances, and some indirect questions were all it took for Sheila to get the truth about Leo Crowley from the mouth of that swaggeriffic feline, Aunt Patricia. And when she finally pieced it all together, Sheila was fucking furious.

That lying', no good butt-sniffin' mother-humper!

Grrr, even her she-Wolf was pissed.

Sheila had not been prepared for that little tidbit of information he'd been holding back. Talk about a shock. He lied. After her initial fury had settled, Sheila was pissed to discover the real reason she'd stayed away much longer than she'd intended when she'd taken off earlier. Hurt flared up inside of her and fear.

Yes.

That's right. Sheila was afraid. What did a foul-mouthed ex-biker Wolf know about being a queen? Fated mates or not, she didn't see this working out for either of them. No wonder the strait-laced, law-abiding pussy was so uptight.

Apparently, every one of her Pack mates, even Derrick, her Alpha and so-called cousin, had known or suspected the entire time. They'd all been privy to that tiny factoid, and no one, not even her dear mate, had bothered to tell her.

Fuckers. Each and every one of them.

And what had her cousin's reply been when she'd confronted him with the news? The dumb Alpha had gotten all snarly with her.

"So, Leo's a Prince. Big fucking deal, woman."

"But Derrick, why the fuck didn't you tell me? How am I supposed to face him now?"

"What the fuck are you on about, girl? You're no damn slouch. We Dire Wolves have our own hierarchy as you well know, cousin, and the Rands are top fucking shelf. He's a Prince and you're already a Princess around here, so go make it official already. Claim your mate and stop your snarling."

She'd been spitting mad, but in the end, she knew Derrick was right. Her Alpha cousin was usually right. The jerk.

So, Leo was a Prince among Shifters. And not because he was charming and handsome, or because he wore a badge, or because he was a hero to Chipmunk Shifters and women everywhere. No, he was an actual, honest to goodness heir-to-the-throne Prince like in a fairytale. Sole successor to the King, and the current ruler of the Blue Valley Pride, while his father was incapacitated by illness. Her Leo. Her fated mate.

And that made her what, exactly?

A fucking idiot.

At least that was how she'd felt. Leo was a Prince, and he hadn't trusted her with that information. Hurt by his betrayal, she'd stayed out longer than she'd planned. Why hadn't he trusted her? That was the question.

Anger and pain warred with each other for dominance throughout most of the night, but Sheila still walked away, confused and a tad annoyed.

"Sheila, I wanted to ask you at the bar but did not have the chance. Um, are all your Pack mates, uh, single?" Ariella hedged as she took off her high-heeled shoes and rubbed her feet.

"Do not do that here! Have you no decency?"

Montgomery was trying to sweep some imaginary dust and was definitely close to losing his shit for no reason that Sheila could see.

Talk about an uptight pussy.

Sheila narrowed her eyes at the man before turning to the striking, yet shy Lioness. Unlike her extroverted mother, Ariella had behaved in a more staid fashion at *Serious Moonlight*. One might have observed her actions as a sort of recon mission, instead of just hanging out. She'd chosen to nurse her margarita from her barstool with her eyes trained on a certain Pack Beta.

The finicky feline had dismissed the attention she'd garnered from other men at the roadhouse, and that had been quite a few, in Sheila's humble opinion. Brock, the object of her interest, had also behaved strangely. In fact, he'd disappeared entirely when it was time to leave, and Ariella had to ride in the sidecar they'd hooked up to Thor's bike.

Strange indeed.

"Far as I know, only Derrick has a mate," she answered the pretty Lioness.

"And you. You have a mate, don't you, Sheila?" Aunt Patricia snickered.

Sheila swallowed. She nodded and tried to stave off the feeling of dizziness that statement brought on. Holy shit. She did have a mate. A big, strong, seriously hot one, if she recalled correctly. Maybe it was time she started acting like it?

She sucked in a deep breath, suddenly needing a quick infusion of oxygen to clear her foggy brain. Crap. If she didn't know better, she'd think she was drunk. Alcohol left her system fairly quickly, as it did with most Shifters, but still. She would have passed for drunk right then. She felt unsteady on her feet, a little nauseous, and was she sweating?

Of course, she never would have ridden her bike home if she was actually intoxicated. There was just no way. Besides, Sheila was not impaired by the shots she'd thrown down with these two felines. And yet, suddenly, she found it difficult to form a coherent thought other than one, single word that kept popping in and out of her brain.

Mate. Mate. MATE.

Goosebumps broke out over her skin and her throat felt dry. Sheila licked her lips and tried to count to ten inside her head. Anything to still the churning in her stomach and the heavy pounding of her heart. She was wobbly and tense, uncertain and clear, she felt everything and nothing all at the same time.

It had absolutely nothing at all to do with alcohol, and completely everything to do with the scowling mountain of a man who was right then stalking down the hallway towards her. Leo wore a pair of navy blue suit pants with a lighter colored silk shirt. His sleeves were rolled up, revealing powerful forearms that ended in large, long-fingered hands.

Her skin itched with need, she could almost feel those hands on her body. His tailored shirt was unbuttoned down to his navel, exposing hard muscles and scandalous inches of golden, tanned skin that she longed to touch. Sheila's body responded to the sight, heating, and readying for her fated mate. The she-Wolf inside of her growled and panted.

Her inner beast wanted her to claim and be claimed. Suddenly, she couldn't remember why she'd said no in the first place. Everything about him called to her, beckoned her to him in every single way.

Desire swelled, as if the need to have him was a living thing. It grew and grew until she felt like her skin was on fire.

It itched and burned, and Sheila wanted to strip. To tear off her clothing, hell his too, but their audience prevented that. Her Wolf was a tad bit possessive when it came to sharing her man, and relatives or not, Leo's sexy body was for her eyes only.

She shivered as another powerful wave of desire swept through her. Her nipples hardened, clit throbbed, and she damn near salivated down the front of her shirt. So this was what it felt like to be in heat, she thought as her pussy dripped moisture, drenching her panties.

Her stomach clenched as he drew nearer. Leo's long legs ate up the distance between them quickly. She couldn't help but admire her leonine lover, this Lion Prince, whom the universe had decided was for her.

Mine.

Fuck.

Really, though? Was he? Could the Fates be wrong? She couldn't possibly mate a Prince.

Yes. We can, her she-Wolf insisted.

She swallowed hard and raised an eyebrow. He wasn't exactly playing the besotted lover at the moment. No, he was not happy at all. His stride was angry, less calculated than normal, and his breathing was heavy. Sheila's eyes widened as she realized something was different about him.

Oh shit.

Leo was pissed. And the giant, sexy as fuck pussycat never looked hotter.

"Where?" he growled the word at her, not even bothering to finish his sentence.

"What?" she asked, arching one eyebrow, and cocking her head to the side, fascinated by the change in him.

"It's late."

"I can tell time," she responded.

The two feline females nearby looked back and forth between Leo and Sheila with mischief glittering in their golden eyes. They reminded her of observers at a tennis tournament.

Well, fuck her sideways. Like hell was she going to be fodder for their entertainment.

"Not here," she growled, and stepped forward, hoping to get him to move this out of the hallway. But the big dumb cat thought he made a better wall than a man. "For fuck's sake, Leo, move."

"Where?" he asked again and refused to back up an inch.

"Hello, nephew," interrupted Aunt Patricia in her current drunken sing-song-y voice. "Sheila here was kind of enough to take Ariella and me out for a ride and then we had lunch, and then some drinks, and some more drinks. Then a band came, and there was dancing, and drinking —"

"Yes, she brought us to *Serious Moonlight*," Ariella supplied. "We were only gone for a few, *er*, hours. And she introduced us around."

"What are you doing?" Sheila gasped as he leaned forward, lightning quick.

Pressing his nose to her neck, Leo sucked in a deep breath. His lips were so close to her skin, she could practically feel them, but he did not touch her. Leo retreated as quickly as he'd closed in, and she was left reeling. Why hadn't he kissed her? Didn't he want to? But no, apparently not. He just breathed her in. Sheila swayed involuntarily.

Her heart was pounding in her chest, so hard he had to have heard it. Her Dire Wolf whined. The animal inside her wanted him closer. She wanted Sheila to leap into his arms, to press her lips to his, wrap her legs around his waist, and get on with the claiming already. Despite the lies and omissions, she'd missed him. Even more stunning, she wanted him. Like really wanted him.

Sheila wasn't known for her public displays of affection. She was tough as nails usually. Hell, even her Pack mates knew better than to fuck with her, but for him her Wolf went belly up. She bit her lip to keep from grinning. Hell, it was all she could do not to jump him right there in the hallway for all to see.

"Aunt Patricia, Ariella," he said, acknowledging the females.

But his gaze never left Sheila. He nodded towards the other hall.

"I had George make up extra rooms. Montgomery here will get you anything you need."

"But sir," sputtered the man.

"Roarrrr!"

The sound of Leo loosing his beast's roar erupted through the hallway. Every Lion in the small space looked to the ground, and Sheila's heart thumped heavily.

Sexy, powerful, hot male. My mate.

Chip. CHIP. CHIP.

"Thanks."

Aunt Patricia sniffed and giggled while keeping her eyes averted.

"Well, the sexual tension coming off you two is making my Lioness want to yowl at the moon, so you better get on that. We'll just head off to bed now, and leave you to it," Aunt Patricia replied. She winked at Sheila, then sashayed down the hall.

"Mom! Sorry," Ariella whispered and gave Sheila an apologetic smile before chasing after her mother.

"If that is all, goodnight, *sir,*" Montgomery said without a glance to Sheila, who at that moment did not give a fuck.

Prince Leo nodded his head and turned around, leaving Sheila no choice but to follow. And follow him she did, noting the hard, straight line of his spine and the ripple of muscles beneath his shirt and slacks as he walked away. She recalled something funny the boys used to say and thought it fitting as she watched his fine ass walking away.

Hate to see you leave, but I love watching you go.

And boy, did she ever. Her little pussycat had quite the gluteus maximus. Sheila licked her lips and closed the door to his bedroom behind her. She watched him as he looked out the terrace doors. A Prince overlooking his Kingdom, but no, there was more to it. Something was bothering him. Something more than her staying out all day.

Right away, she wanted to comfort him, to share in his pain, to take it away, but she paused. Uncertain of the reception she'd receive.

Leo opened the sliding door and allowed the evening air to rush inside the room.

It teased her sensitive nose and made her think of youthful days spent on the road. Of course, the air was cleaner here than some places she'd stayed when she was young. Better company too.

Leo moved in that liquid way Cats had about them, jogging her from her reverie, and she watched as he started removing his clothes. She swallowed down her desire for him and simply watched.

This was not a striptease. He was angry and agitated, but she couldn't help but admire him, anyway. His physique was sublime. The power rolling off him, seductive.

"You know, I never was much for museums, but I swear if I was a painter or sculptor, I'd make works of art around you, Leo Crowley, Prince of the Blue Valley Pride."

Sheila's voice had been clear, quiet, and maybe a touch whimsical. She meant every word, too. Knowing full well, he would hear the lie if she'd been fibbing at all, which she was not. He stopped and waited a beat, absorbing the hand she'd just shown him. Leo had taken a gamble by not telling her everything, and she wanted him to know she knew, and she was still here, waiting for him to own it.

This was it, she supposed. The moment of truth. Leo turned to look at her. His eyes glowed with his beast in the darkness of the night that seemed to seep in from the outdoors. He did not try to talk around the truth she'd had to learn on her own. Didn't apologize yet, either. That made her curious.

"Is that why you left?"

"You mean because you lied?"

"It wasn't a lie, little Wolf."

"Lie by omission, officer."

"I didn't mention it, because it doesn't matter," he stated.

"Well, that one little thing that doesn't matter to you is the fucking difference between night and day, Leo, You're a fucking Prince and I'm an ex-biker bartender."

"You are my mate, Sheila. After last night—"

"No. That was sex. This, this won't work," she said, gesturing between them.

Fuck. She was panicking, crying too. Tears streamed down her face. There was a difference between thinking something and saying it aloud. For fuck's sake, she was no princess. She turned around, wiping her face on the back of her hand as she grabbed her saddle bags.

"I just came back to grab my shit. I won't be able to stick around to help you do whatever it is you're doing," she said casually, trying to play the part.

Fuck. What was she thinking? She'd honestly thought for half a minute that she could do this, but she couldn't. They were too different. Sheila hated her weakness. She was disgusted at the tears that pricked her eyes. She felt him then at her back, but she refused to face him, refused to let him see her like this.

What the fucking fuck, Sheila? You don't cry, and you don't do feelings. Ever.

"*Shhh,*" his deep gravelly voice touched a chord inside of her and she trembled with it. "Please, Sheila. I'm sorry. I am so sorry. Swear on my life, I was not lying to you. I didn't think it mattered because I never wanted the throne. I need you Sheila, please. Stay. Don't cry."

"I can't be what you want," she said and shook her head as pure misery filled her soul.

Sadness on the heels of arousal was fucking draining. She didn't know what to do. She felt tired, but mostly miserable at the thought of a life without him.

"You are the only thing I want."

"I should go."

"Don't go. Run with me. Now, tonight, please."

Leo was so vulnerable like this. So honest and unsure, and fuck, it made her fall for him just a little bit more. He wasn't the cocky Lion tonight. He was just her Leo as he dropped his forehead down till it touched the back of her head and she shivered at the contact.

"Leo—"

"Please, mate."

Sheila turned at his whispered plea. His amber eyes were so big, so focused on her. It made her feel like she was the only person in the world. The only one who mattered, well, to him, anyway. But how could that be when he was a Prince, and she was a nobody?

"You are not a nobody," he growled, and she knew she'd spoken aloud by mistake. "You are the most important thing in the whole fucking universe to me, Sheila Rand, Dire Wolf badass, most beautiful woman I have ever seen, sassy, sexy queen. I love everything about you. Now, will you run with me? Please."

"Okay," she answered, stunned by his admissions.

Leo smiled then, and it was like the sun coming out after a storm. Sheila's pulse raced as he backed up one step, and another, until he was a safe enough distance away. She noted the change in his stance, and the scent of ozone fill the air as Leo switched his skin for fur. The transformation was almost instantaneous. His powerful body accepting the shift from man to Lion in the blink of an eye.

"Beautiful," she whispered, her eyes widened with awe.

Leo stood before her majestic and proud as only a Lion could be. His mane was thick and lush, his entire body covered in golden fur that did nothing to conceal the lines of muscle and strength within him.

"But you're still just a big ol' pussy," she said and grinned at his shocked expression.

With her next breath, Sheila shredded her clothes and swapped skin for fur as she went from woman to Wolf. Together, the Dire Wolf and the Lion stalked through the night into the forest beyond the Palace. Imagining this little slice of heaven tucked away in the beautiful, quiet town of Blue Valley, New Jersey, made Sheila want to laugh.

In her Wolf form, it came out a yip, and the Lion beside her chuffed and swatted her on the rump with his long tail. She growled playfully and followed him down a path. The woods were noisy with new life. The song of Spring filled the air, and Sheila reveled in it. The woods began to thicken around them, and she felt peace the likes of which she had never known. It was a sort of meeting between two worlds. The two of them were so different, and yet, they were fated to be together.

Leo and Sheila ran and stalked each other through the acres of tall grass, and thick copses of trees, to the stream that cut between both lands. As a Dire Wolf, she was huge with reddish fur and long black claws, but Leo was even bigger still. His Lion was the largest she'd ever seen, with a thick, glossy mane of dark gold circling his head like a crown, announcing to one and all that he was meant to rule.

He was gorgeous and lethal, more than capable of protecting even a fierce Dire she-Wolf. The beast approved, and she wanted him to claim her as soon as possible. Sheila's human side agreed. Her feelings were too strong to deny, and why should she even try to?

They stretched out along the bank after playing like a couple of cubs. Sheila panted with glee, it had felt good to run. They both lapped up some of the cool water before settling beside one another. It was unusual for her to share her space with someone in this shape, but it felt natural and good.

Her Wolf was perfectly at ease with Leo. Like everything was right with the world as long as he was beside her. Then again, she always could see things a little clearer when she wore her fur. Her Pack bonds pulsed dimly and told her she was close to them. In fact, the Pack house lay just beyond the stream and the next stand of pines.

She would always be a Dire Wolf and a member of the DWMC no matter what. She didn't need Derrick to tell her that, though he had. The Pack house would also be there waiting anytime she needed it. Sheila could stand up and stop this thing with Leo right now. She could walk through those trees and go home, tell Leo to forget it, but that wasn't what she wanted.

Her eyes found the Lion's glittering gold stare, and she knew she wouldn't leave him. Not that night. Not ever. His intense gaze was focused on her, as it always was, but she didn't feel rushed or trapped. Looking through her she-Wolf's eyes, Sheila no longer saw things in terms of money, class, or circumstance of birth. She only knew one thing as truth. This Lion was her fated mate, and she wanted to claim and to be claimed by him.

Now.

Her Wolf was ready, and she decided it was about time Sheila did something about it. The full moon shone down on them from high above, and Sheila knew the time was right. Turning to face her Lion, she allowed her Wolf to recede into that plane where her beast rested until called upon, and Sheila found her skin.

Her nudity aside, she was nervous for other reasons. Tremors ran up and down her spine because tonight, she would claim her mate as her own for all time, and with any luck, he was going to claim her right back.

"Leo," she had just finished his name when he completed his shift.

"What's wrong? Are you okay?" he asked, and the concern on his handsome face warmed her.

"I'm fine," she smiled.

"Then what?"

"I think it's time we stopped playing around. I think it's time we mate, for real."

His entire body vibrated with power. The lines of muscle that corded his tall frame seemed to tremble with barely restrained intensity, and Sheila felt an echoing shiver race through her. She wanted him more than ever. She craved his touch, his kiss, his cock, his bite.

All of them. Now.

"Be sure, Sheila, because I won't be able to stop once I get my hands on you," he said.

His words made Sheila bold. She inched closer until all she could see was him. Sheila pressed her naked body to his and reached for his hands. She took them and placed them on her body with more certainty than she'd ever felt in her entire life.

"Who's asking you to stop?"

Mate.

CHAPTER ELEVEN

DIRE WOLF MATES

E*arlier that evening...*

Mate. Mate. MATE.

Leo was about to lose his fucking mind. After he'd listened to the endless parade of Lionesses, and their overachieving mothers sing their praises, he wanted nothing more than to get the fuck out of the Palace with Sheila.

She had ignored his texts, was not in his bedroom when he went to search for her. And yes, he looked. He'd stalked out of the interview room, leaving a dozen angry Lionesses waiting, but she was gone.

His unclaimed mate was nowhere to be found, and his Lion had nearly shredded him from the inside out. He felt raw fear for a full minute till it almost crippled him. Then, after he'd regained his senses, Leo made a few phone calls.

"Yeah, she's here, man. Everything cool?" Derrick Rand had picked up his phone on the second ring.

"It will be," Leo had answered.

The Alpha of the Dire Wolf Pack had been a good friend ever since he'd introduced himself. He was someone Leo trusted. Now that he knew Sheila was safe, all he had to do was wait. And wasn't that a kick to his ego?

Most females, a whole fucking gaggle of them in just the last couple of hours, pursued Leo relentlessly. And yet, his one true and fated mate acted like he didn't fucking exist.

Sure, she enjoyed what physical pleasures he offered, but even then, she'd cut him loose. Only taking the very tip of the iceberg of what he had to give. Leo had so much feeling brewing inside of him for the woman, he was about to explode. He just needed the opportunity to show her.

Shit.

He had it bad. For a normally patient man, he'd assumed it would be easy to wait her out. After all, how long could Sheila resist the mating call? Apparently longer than his Lion. The Cat was beyond lovesick. He was agitated as fuck now that he knew she was not there, safe and sound in his den.

Any dominant male, no matter how sure of himself, was liable to lose his shit, knowing his still unclaimed female was out on the town. Even with a couple of his own Lionesses at her side, it was all he could do not to give in to his Lion and race over to get her caveman-style. As in, toss her sweet ass over his shoulder, then fuck her until she couldn't get out of bed. Sounded like a good plan to his inner animal.

Leo ran a hand over his face and worked instead. His father's illness meant a massive amount of correspondence had gone unanswered. It took him three hours to sort through it all, and he still had dozens of emails to go through.

Eat Well Live Proud, the Pride's major concern was doing very well. Their new expansions were right on the money, and he felt confident with those Lionesses, mainly his cousins Ariella, Annabella, and George running things.

The elders were another matter. Those older felines had a whole lot to say about how things were being run and not all of it was within their purview. In fact, after the parade of eligible women he was forced to sit through, they'd tried to get him to agree to hand over a percentage of the corporation for them to run.

That was a hard no, to which they'd all grumbled and complained. He'd finally had enough, and when he stood to leave, it was with one parting statement.

"Might I remind the elders that your job is to simply advise the King on the health of the Pride? You have nothing to say about our corporate interests. I am not the King yet, but when I rule the Blue Valley Pride, I shall disband this circle, as it is clear you have lost sight of your purpose. Good evening, ladies."

That had not gone over well. In fact, George had to restrain one of them almost physically after they'd been dismissed. Leo had certainly stirred up the litter box. Wasn't that just too bad for them?

The police department never put up with shit like that. He'd only been back with the Pride for a day, and he already missed his old life. Being born to rule didn't necessarily create a desire to rule. He would do his duty, always, but his mate came first. As she should.

Fuck.

He was flustered. His Lion snarled and hissed inside of him to where Leo could hardly think. The sound of motorcycles pulling up outside reached his ears, and his feet hit the marble floor before he thought about what he was going to do or say. The Lion in him snarled.

Fuck decorum. He wanted his mate. Now.

It was all he could do not to pounce the second he saw her standing in the vestibule. Sheila's eyes glowed with her Wolf as she took him in. He scented her conflicting emotions over the distance between them. He twitched with the need to go to her, to soothe and kiss away any remnants of whatever upset her. Only his will stopped him from doing so.

There was so much unsaid, and he needed her to hear him first. He wouldn't just go at her like some lovesick animal, but he wanted to. Gods, how he wanted to. She was beautiful, standing there like a siren in ripped jeans and that gauzy top.

Her windblown hair had come out of its braid. Long waves spread around her like wildfire across her creamy shoulders. One errant curl dipped into the rounded collar of her shirt, finding a home nestled between her ripe breasts, making Leo jealous of her own precious locks.

He was a fool. A lovesick fool, and he didn't give a shit who knew it. His animal was aware of others in the hall with them, but his full attention was on her. After a brief interaction, where he couldn't even recall enough words to form sentences, Leo embraced his fur and running into the night with his mate.

If hearts could burst from happiness, then his Lion's heart surely would just from having Sheila running at his side. She was magnificent with fire-kissed fur and sharp claws digging into the ground with each leaping bound they made deeper into the woods.

Her noble Dire Wolf stood almost as high as his massive Lion's head. She had long, razor-sharp claws, enormous fangs, a powerful body, and eyes as blue as when she walked on two legs. Gorgeous, formidable, and perfect.

They ran and played like the wild things they both were. Leo roared into the night sky. It was his Lion's way of telling others to be wary of encroaching on his space when he was out with his mate. He heard a few answering calls, and his beast chuffed, content because his Lions would obey.

He might not want to be King yet, but some things were beyond even a Shifter's control. When the time came, he would be ready. First things first. He had a mate to protect and to cherish. They'd shifted back into their skin as they lay side by side on the mossy bank of the stream and Sheila had just said the words he'd been longing to hear.

"Who's asking you to stop?" Sheila's voice echoed through his brain as the seductress mashed her mouth to his.

Had anything ever felt more right? Never. His Dire Wolf mate stole his breath in every way, shape, and form. Kissing her was like touching a star, she burned so hot and bright, but Leo could take it. He was made to take it, and he wanted more. He wanted all of her.

Once he had his hands on her, Leo's mind flashed to every single fantasy he'd every indulged in since the moment he'd laid eyes on the sassy little she-Wolf. But this was no fantasy. This was the real thing.

Even the taste he'd had of her before was nothing compared to the things he was going to do with her here and now, before nature, fate, and the gods themselves.

Leo pulled her down onto a soft bed of moss that lined that part of the forest's floor. The spongy greenery made up the perfect place for what he had in mind. Sheila sighed and laid back, her trust humbled him, and he dropped his forehead to hers kissing each eyelid, then moving to her slightly upturned nose, her plump lips, that stubborn chin he loved so much, and further still.

Leo sat back to better admire her beauty. He ran his hands gently over the many curves and valleys, up and down the sweet and sultry delights of her sumptuously soft flesh.

"You're so beautiful," he said, catching the slight flash of her big blue eyes.

Leo licked his lips, holding her gaze for one more beat. He noted the hitch in her breath with satisfaction as he skimmed his fingers over the peaks of her lovely, pink-tipped breasts, teasing the tiny buds until they were hardened pebbles under his hands.

"Am I?" she breathed the question.

"Yesss." His voice was raspy even to his own ears.

"Perfect, mate. Let me show you how beautiful you are," he growled and leaned down, the better to savor each pebbled nub with his lips, tongue, and teeth.

Sheila moaned aloud, the scent of her pleasure increased, and Leo growled. He suckled her sweet flesh, loving the sting as she reached up to grab hold of his hair and pulled. She was all ivory limbs and bountiful curves, acres of smooth, flawless skin for him alone to discover. She was a goddess in the forest, on a bed of moss, trembling beneath his touch.

Leo was one lucky Cat. She moaned his name, heightening Leo's own desire as he licked a trail between her breasts down to her navel.

Kissing her body was like taking a shot of honey and Tabasco laced whiskey. Sweet and fiery, and guaranteed to warm him inside and out.

His cock throbbed painfully, and Leo reached down with one hand to give himself a good, long tug. Fuck, he was like a steel rod and more than ready, but first he wanted a taste. Needed it. He'd dreamed of this, of sampling her tantalizing cream from the source plenty of times, but nothing prepared him for what he felt being so close to his goal.

His fangs descended, and Leo's beast pushed forward. He'd never hurt her, of course, teeth were just another way Shifters expressed passion. And his Lion did so enjoy a good lengthy nibble. His Shifter eyesight enabled him to see despite the darkness and what a sight.

She was glorious, completely nude, and bathed in moonlight. Sheila's plump, pink pussy lips were just ripe for the tasting. They gleamed with the evidence of her desire and his Lion purred in anticipation. All that cream, his for the taking.

Mine.

Leo moved between her legs, bending them at the knee. He parted them, spreading them good and wide until he was face to face with those glistening copper curls and the treasure beneath. Breathing in her honeyed musk, Leo's Lion surged forward, claws tipped his hands as he carefully held her thighs wide. He had to work to push the beast aside, but eventually his Lion understood.

"This is mine," he stated, catching her eyes before opening his lips and sliding his long tongue out of his mouth and towards glory.

Fucking hell.

He groaned as her flavors burst across his tastebuds. A feast for his senses. Sugar and spice, and Leo groaned as he lapped at her.

"Yes," she moaned, and bucked her hips, but he stilled her with his hands,

"You're driving me crazy," she pleaded, and he grinned while he slowly tasted her from asshole to clit with the flat of his tongue.

"So sweet," he groaned and watched her desperation etch into her face.

It mirrored his own, but this was something he simply refused to rush. She tried to move again, but he held her still. It was his turn to dominate. Her turn to submit. And she was going to love it. He could make sure of that.

"Patience," he said, enjoying her musky taste, imprinting it on his tongue and his brain.

"To hell with patience, fuck me already," she growled.

Leo smirked, holding her thighs down. Then he dipped his head and pierced her core with his tongue, loving the frantic growl that escaped her lips as he started moving slowly, then faster, then slow again. Her moans held a mixture of satisfaction and frustration, of anticipation and desire, and he reveled in them. In his ability to bring her to this state.

He would always give her what she wanted, what she needed, but when he said, and not a moment before. Sometimes, you just had to be patient. Sheila whimpered, arching her back and wiggling her hips as much as she could under his strong hands, and finally, he relented. He let go briefly, only to replace his tongue with his fingers. He slid between her folds, stretching her channel with two thick digits. He pumped them slowly in and out of her welcoming heat.

"You taste so good, mate, so sweet and hot," he said in a voice barely recognizable.

"Leo, need you," she moaned, and he felt her walls contract around his fingers.

"What do you need, mate?"

"You. More," she pleaded with him.

What man could resist that? Especially when it was his destined mate who was asking. Fuck yeah. He was going to give her more. He was going to give her everything. His balls tightened in anticipation as he felt her shudder around him.

"I'm gonna make you come, little Wolf," he promised.

"All over my hand and in my mouth. Then I'm going to fuck this sweet pussy of yours, fill you with my seed. I'm going to have your ass, too. I'm gonna fill that tight little hole, make it good for you. You want that, don't you?" he whispered.

Sheila whimpered. His sassy little Wolf loved hearing all the naughty things he was going to do to her. She nodded her head, bucking her hips, and trying to get him to move. But Leo wasn't ready yet.

"I'm gonna take every inch of you and stamp myself on it. Make you mine, gonna bite you, mate. Going to claim you every way I can. Here, now, tonight. Tell me you want that," he growled. It was his turn to demand. She whimpered and nodded her head, her Wolf growling. His Lion chuffed and grunted. The animal was impatient to claim what was his. But first things first.

"I need the words, little Wolf."

"Yes," she mewled. "I want that. I want you. Mate."

Leo growled and his chest vibrated with the force of it. He added a third finger to her tight channel, circling her forbidden hole with his pinky. He teased and tested the tiny, puckered entrance. Licking around her tiny bundle of nerves and pressing, until finally, he had both orifices full of him. Then he latched onto her clit, giving the swollen nub long, hard pulls from his mouth.

Fuck, she tasted divine. His own personal flavor of cream.

Me-ow.

"Oh my gods!" she cried out.

"No, baby, it's just Leo. Say it. Say my name," he commanded.

"Leo. Leo. LEO!" she cried out as she fell over the edge. Both holes squeezed him while she bucked wildly in her release.

His balls tightened as her sweet pussy rippled and fluttered. He was desperate to be inside of her, filling her with his cum, claiming her in every way possible. First with his mouth, then with his cock inside her pussy, and finally he was going to claim her sweet ass. He needed to.

It was raw. It was primal. And it was meant to be.

The desire to fill her with his scent, to mark her as his, in every way, so there was never a single doubt about it, was the only thing riding him at the moment. His beast roared inside of him. She'd moved in time with his ministrations.

Sheila's head whipped from side to side. Searching for a little bit more and Leo knew instinctively what she needed. He hummed against her mouth, purring with his beast, the vibrations going from him and straight to her clit. Sheila came then with a long, hard howl, bucking wildly against his lips.

"Now, need you now, now, now," she moaned the words, and grabbed his shoulders, pulling him up her body.

Kneeling between her splayed legs, he crashed his mouth to hers in a hard kiss that forced her to taste herself on his lips. It was raw and sexy and fucking perfect. Just like she was. Sheila opened wide, both mouth and legs, tugging his hips until her wet pussy kissed the tip of his cock.

"What do you want, little Wolf?"

"Claim me as your mate, Leo. Do it now."

That was all he needed to hear. Leo pushed inside of her molten heat. His thickness stretched her walls as he slid deeper, and deeper into her tight channel until he was buried all the way to the hilt. His engorged cock pulsed and throbbed once he'd slid home, but he did not move. Not yet.

"Feels so good, mate," he grunted.

"Yes," she moaned, and her hands came down on his ass in a hard slap that stung so good.

"Fuck," he growled.

"Yes, fuck me, now," she demanded, squeezing his cheeks almost painfully, until he started moving.

"Thank the gods," she growled and slapped him again.

Leo's beast roared, the animal approving of her aggression. He grunted. The slap had smarted, but it made the pleasure that much sweeter. She had desires and as her mate he loved giving in to her needs.

His Sheila was fucking sublime. Wicked and sexy as hell, her tight pussy sheathed him perfectly. She was his other half, designed for every inch of him. She squeezed him and he moved faster, harder, deeper with every thrust.

Every inch of silken heat was like a glove wrapped tightly around him. His balls tightened, he was desperate to come, but he needed her with him. Her sex rippled and caressed his length. So fucking good, Leo had to fight to keep from spilling his seed too soon.

Did he say he was lucky before? He didn't know then just how lucky. His little Wolf was a hellion in bed, *er,* on the moss-covered ground. She wiggled and worked him so fucking good from beneath his heavy body. His Wolf could take it, she could take all of him. She murmured sexy little taunts and phrases, raked her long pink nails down his spine and nipped his earlobe between her teeth.

How the fuck had he ever looked at another woman? Everyone else paled compared to her. Together they grunted and moaned, each seeking the other's complete release. He could lose himself completely in the pleasure of his mate's body. She was so fucking incredible.

He opened his eyes, catching her lust-glazed ones and holding them there while he pumped harder. *Swivel, grind, withdraw, slam, and repeat.* Leo lifted her hips, and she wrapped her legs around his waist, allowing him to sink even deeper.

"Right there," she screamed, and he knew she was close.

"Come on, baby, come," he grunted, fucking her at a furious pace.

Her sheath tightened, their breathing increased to rapid pants, sweat slicked their bodies. Silver moonlight bathed them both, seeming to stroke them in the magic that only mating with your fated other could bring.

"*Sheila,*" he thrusted.

"*Sheila,*" he withdrew.

"*Sheila!*" he pounded home again, saying her name like a litany to the whole fucking universe. She was his to worship, to praise, to cherish. Only his.

Mate.

"I'm gonna," she moaned, scoring the skin beneath her nails.

"Now, now, now," she cried out in ecstasy, and Leo struck.

He sunk his teeth through the soft flesh between her neck and shoulder, swallowing down her life's force, and solidifying that unbreakable bond between a Shifter and his mate. His balls tensed, and finally, Leo came deep within his mate's sweet sex.

Pain exploded on his right shoulder, followed by an even longer, harder orgasm as Sheila reciprocated the claiming bite.

Holy fuck!

That sting of pain gave him the edge he'd never knew he needed, and pleasure erupted from the very bottom of his soul until man and beast both felt it.

Roarrrr!

Still, he did not stop thrusting his hips, he fucked her through her orgasm and his, and soon she came again, longer this time. Sheila's mouth opened, and she loosed the longest, loudest howl he'd ever heard. Her blue eyes glowed with her Wolf, and his Lion rose to meet his mate. Slowly, he eased out of her, lapping at the wound, sealing it with his special Shifter's saliva.

"Mate." Sheila smiled as she tried to catch her breath, and Leo's heart pounded heavily inside his chest.

"Mate. Love. I love you, Sheila," he said as she grabbed his head and claimed his lips in a hard, poignant kiss.

His dick responded immediately to his mate's touch. Hardening as she sat up and pushed him down until he was flat on his back. Fuck, he was ready again. It would always be this way. He was insatiable for her.

"Mine," he grunted as she scratched his thighs and pushed them wide.

"My turn," she smiled as her lips closed over him, sucking him deep and down her throat. Passion flared to life and mischief twinkled in her electric blue gaze as she took him deeper.

"Oh fuck, baby, that's it. Suck me," he grunted and took hold of her head, holding her in place while he thrusted in and out of the hot, soft cavern.

He couldn't take much more without exploding, and as promising as that sounded, his Lion had other plans. He needed to fill her one more time. To mark her once more.

"Come here, baby," he said and pulled her to her knees, taking her mouth with his, "Gonna make you come, little Wolf, you want that?"

Sheila whimpered, nodding her head, and holding on to his shoulders. Leo kissed her hard, then turned her around. He eased her head down and moved in behind her. She thrust her pert ass up in the air and he growled.

In that position, she was fully exposed to him. Her virgin asshole on display, and those swollen pink pussy lips pursed as if waiting for a kiss. He could not resist placing one right there. Leo bent and dropped a hard, open-mouthed kiss on her slit, working her until more of that sweet cream flowed down her thighs. With his fingers, he worked her natural lubricant around her slit and into her asshole, easing the way for his passage. She grunted and moaned against his invasion.

"Shh, s'okay. Need you, mate. Gonna fill this sweet ass, make it mine," he growled, noting the flare of arousal his words elicited.

More cream coated his fingers. Yes, she wanted him. Was more than ready and willing for him to take her in this way too. It was the way of Lions, and perhaps Wolves as well, he thought. Sheila's trust humbled him, her submission turned him on so fucking much. All musings left and instinct took over. He'd marked her once, but the mating wasn't done.

Leo moved closer, teasing her clit with his fingers, and massaging her asshole with his thumb. He pressed the thick digit in, moving it in and out of her tight hole, stretching, and readying it for his cock. Finally, when he thought she could take it, he nudged her hole with the head of his dick. He was big and long and needed to proceed with caution.

"So fucking sexy," he growled as she moaned and pressed back, sucking his cock deep inside.

"S'mine."

"Yes, yours," Sheila moaned.

His sexy little mate liked it when he got all possessive about her, and that was fine with him. Leo couldn't help it. She was his, and he was desperate to mark her again.

"Mine," he growled again, kneading her clit with his fingers until she pushed all the way back, taking his cock even deeper into her sweet, heart-shaped ass.

Fuck, she was so tight, so good. Leo caged her in, holding where he needed her as he worked his thick cock back and forth, in and out of that tight hole. His passage was made slick by her own natural lubricant, but he was careful to keep it that way, rubbing her moisture on his cock and in her hole. He heard rather than felt the crackle of her bones and knew her Wolf was coming out to play.

Naughty girl. My girl. My woman. My Wolf. My Mate.

Leo squeezed her hip and pushed in deeper.

"Fuck, yes, mate. Need you," Sheila shouted and pushed back.

"I know what you need," he growled.

"Yes," she grunted.

Leo fought his orgasm back. He would not let go, not until he felt her begin to slide into the abyss of pure pleasure only a fated mate could deliver. Yes, he knew what she needed, and he would give it to her if it killed him.

Grunting and groaning, sweat poured down his back as he worked her good and steady. Strumming her clit with his hand, Leo fucked her ass until her orgasm began to rage through her. He fucked her still until her pleasure echoed through Leo as well.

"My Sheila, mine, my mate," he roared as they both tipped over the edge, slicing his fangs into her other shoulder.

He bit her again, sucking on the wound while white hot lights of ecstasy exploded behind his eyes. Hard jerks turned to slight twitches as they collapsed in a heap on top of their mossy bed. The night was silent, as if everything had just taken a deep, long breath and was holding it in. Sheila turned and cuddled into him, her face a study in satisfaction and wonder.

"Mate," he whispered and kissed her head, unable to stop the rumble of pleasure from his Lion at her cuddling.

"Mmm, mate."

She smiled, still panting, and dropped a kiss on his chest. Leo held her to him, and they dozed together as the sounds of crickets and the bubbling stream filled the night.

Finally, he thought and sighed.

Sheila was finally his and his Lion had never been more content.

CHAPTER TWELVE

DIRE WOLF MATES

"Are you nervous?" Leo looked concerned, and Sheila couldn't help but shrug guiltily.

"I never met a King," she said.

Like duh.

What was wrong with having some issues about it? The man was royalty, even if he was sick.

"Actually, the King of a Lion Pride is no different from a Wolf Alpha," he tried to assure her, but Sheila had her reservations.

No Dire Wolf Pack had ever lived in a Palace with servants. They certainly didn't stand on ceremony. Wolves ruled by might and loyalty. Anyone could challenge for the position, though Dire Wolves argued against that. As a mostly nomadic species, they could simply leave if they did not favor a ruling Alpha.

A challenge was a profoundly serious thing. Not at all the same as in a Pride, after Leo had told her of the elder's threats, she'd been outraged. Her own Dire Wolf was fiercely loyal to her cousin and would not tolerate anyone who dared make such flippant remarks about him. Now that Leo was her mate, he topped her list of males she was devoted to. As a result, her canine had a few choice words for the nasty bitches who dared threaten him with a challenger!

He'd assured her it was simply politics, but she was not impressed with that excuse. The haughty Lionesses needed to be taken down a notch in her opinion, but that was up to the King. The King she was about to meet. Leo's father. Her mate's dad.

Holy shit.

Her mate was a Prince, and he'd said he'd loved her last night. Fated mates were one thing, love was something else. She'd heard of couples who were mates but felt no such affection for one another. Of course, perhaps they weren't fated exactly, but she had no way of knowing that.

Did she love him? She felt strongly for Leo. Maybe she cared deeply already, but the words were hard for Sheila. Perhaps she would grow to feel love someday?

We already love him, her Wolf insisted.

One step at a time, Sheila growled back.

She'd taken the leap and mated with the Lion Prince, but she still felt that same fear deep inside of her. What if she felt trapped? It terrified her to think she could hurt him. That she would be the one to let him down. Like her mother and the man who fathered her. What if Sheila had no staying power?

"Hey, it's alright. If you'd rather not meet my father today," Leo said and rubbed her shoulders, and Sheila leaned into him.

Her sweet mate was a good and kind man, a powerful Lion Shifter, and fiercely loyal. She was truly blessed to have him, she realized.

"We're gonna be okay," she said, verging on tears.

"Of course we are," he stated, with no doubts at all evident in his words.

Knowing that, she vowed she would never hurt him. How could she? It would be like hurting herself or worse.

"Good, I'm ready," she smiled, and she meant it.

Thunder sounded and lightning flashed just outside the terrace doors. New Jersey Spring was a psychotic bitch if you asked her. Glorious one minute, and downright mean the next.

"We beat the rain back," he laughed, and she nodded.

That they had. He'd carried her back to the Palace sometime around five o'clock in the morning. Of course, she could have walked, but he'd insisted. Like a proper wedding night, he'd said, and secretly, Sheila loved it. They'd showered together and made love some more. Hunted down some food somewhere in between. It was wonderful.

She loved the play of muscles across his wide shoulders and chest as he buttoned his shirt and Sheila reached up to smooth it over his back. She had never felt so cherished, loved, and content.

I've never felt so happy.

It was like a switch had gone off inside of her and suddenly all the pieces clicked into place. Last night was simply amazing. Their claiming was beyond anything she could have ever imagined. Right then, all her doubts washed away like the rain washed away the grit they'd tracked onto the terrace. She sighed.

Shelia really loved him. It welled up in her slowly, a new feeling, bright and fresh. Just like his scent, that clean grass after a storm scent that drove her Wolf crazy with need. Her emotions grew and grew, a fountain, a pool, until they turned into a flood.

"I love you," she blurted, and turned her startled blue eyes to him.

Leo's gaze glittered with the gold of his beast. He reached for her, one hand on her waist, the other on her cheek as he lowered his mouth to hers and pressed a soft kiss there.

"I love you too, mate," he said, and tugged on her lip with his teeth.

She moaned and stepped back, looking up at him with all her feelings in her gaze.

"Let's go meet your father," she smiled and took his hand.

She'd donned the one dress she thought to pack with her. It was long and flowy, feminine, and soft in a way she never got to wear while roaming the Americas with her Pack. The sage green looked good against her pale skin and red hair, or so Lucy had told her.

Her cousin-in-law had been extremely helpful in picking out new clothes when they'd gone shopping for some maternity things for the Bobcat Shifter. Lucy was pregnant and getting bigger by the minute. Sheila snorted and stopped in her tracks.

Holy shit.

She could be pregnant, too.

Not yet, her she-Wolf spoke inside of her, and she wasn't sure if she felt relief or sadness. That alone was a wonder.

"Sheila?" Leo inquired with a raised eyebrow.

"Nothing," she said and just looked at him as his cousin George rushed to meet them.

Aunt Patricia had shown her a picture of the man on her phone, and she recognized him immediately. Like most Lions, he had tawny-colored hair, and he was big and tall, though not as massive as her mate. He had a pleasant face and green eyes she found unique. So far, all the Lions she'd met had some combination of brownish-gold eyes.

"Leo," he greeted her mate, and nodded at her respectfully.

"George."

"Sorry, I have not had the pleasure," George replied and smiled.

He might have looked at her a second too long because Leo smacked him in the back of the head.

"Ouch! She's hot. No disrespect," he said quickly, and averted his gaze to the floor.

"The name is Sheila, and you will have to forgive him, George. We are newly mated, after all," she explained with a smile in her voice.

Sheila felt that smile down to her toes. Happiness was new, but it was good, and she was really looking forward to getting used to feeling this way.

Pleasure rang through her at being able to say those words aloud with no trepidation. This might have started as a ruse to help Leo work out what was happening within his Pride, but it was real now. She'd been so caught up in her personal emotional conflicts that she'd almost forgotten about why they were there to begin with.

"Shit, you claimed the Wolf? The elders are gonna be more pissed now than ever," George whispered.

Leo smacked his cousin on the head again, this time it was followed by a similar slap from Sheila.

"Ow! I'm sorry," George mumbled his apology.

"Good job, Sheila," Leo said, and damn, but he sure looked proud of her.

"Crap, cousin, you know I think she's perfect for you," he said, rubbing his head as he walked with them and explained the day's agenda.

"Did you find the healer?" Leo asked.

"That's what I wanted to talk to you about. The schedule says the healer is supposed to check with your father once a week, but when he called me back yesterday, he was surprised."

"Oh?"

"Yeah, he said his last six appointments had been canceled. Leo, he hasn't been here in over a month and neither has the other staff. Just Montgomery."

"What? Why?" Leo asked.

"He didn't know. Just said your father canceled the appointments."

"My father has not been himself for months now. The last few weeks he's been practically incoherent. How could he cancel his appointments?"

"I don't know, Leo," George replied.

Sheila took a step closer, breathing in his scent to determine if he was telling the truth. Oddly enough, he was. Leo's amber eyes flashed with his Lion.

"Is he coming here now?" her mate asked.

"Yes. I told him to meet us at ten, it's 9:45 now."

Sheila listened to the byplay curiously. Leo was right, there was something rotten within the Pride. It was her Pride now too, and the fact that someone was fucking with it really pissed her off.

"Did you tell anyone else we were going to see the King?" he asked.

"No," replied George. "I didn't have time. It was all I could do to get dressed in time to meet you."

"Leo, I think we should hurry," she said and the hairs on the back of Sheila's neck were standing up.

She raced beside her mate, the younger Lion trailing them, and together they entered the King's rooms. Lying on the large bed was an older version of Leo and the sight brought Sheila to a hard stop. Donovan Crowley looked pained and confused, but not as much as the man hovering over him trying to force feed him from what looked like a child's medicine dropper.

"Car, Car," the King moaned, and pushed at the man's hand, but he was too weak to do much.

"Montgomery?" Leo's shocked voice seemed to spur the man into action.

"You aren't supposed to be here!" he snarled.

"Montgomery, these are my father's quarters. I have every right to be here. What are you doing to him?"

"You were supposed to choose a Lioness," he said between clenched teeth.

The man looked crazed, and he stank of fear and madness. The smell was so thick, Sheila almost choked on it.

"For what, Montgomery?" Leo asked.

"As a mate, you were supposed to choose from your own kind," he sneered.

"I see," Leo said and moved in front of Sheila, placing himself in harm's way. "But Sheila here is my fated mate," he continued, naming her so as to make her more real in the madman's eyes.

Fat chance, Sheila thought, but applauded his effort. She knew Leo was trying to get the man to put down whatever that was in his hand. She admired his tactics. Came with being a cop, she guessed.

That was so hot.

She blushed at the turn of her thoughts. Ooh, she could just picture him in his dress blues, doing a little striptease that ended with one of them bound to the bed and the other in charge.

Grrr.

"Stay back!" Montgomery waved the vial and growled.

Sheila refocused. Yikes. Here they were with a madman waving around some sort of poison, and she was thinking naughty thoughts of Leo and a pair of handcuffs.

Okay, so she was proud of him. Proud of her Prince and his chosen career. Of the bravery it took to face criminals such as this, every single day. He could've simply stayed home and lived the life of pampered royalty, but he didn't. He'd worked hard and put his life on the line to protect Shifters and normals alike.

Her she-Wolf growled low and deep inside her. Sheila never minded bending the rules before, but now that she had her own personal police officer, she vowed to be more mindful just as soon as they stopped this traitor.

"How can you rule with that Dog at your side?" Montgomery snorted and pointed at her wildly.

"She is my fated mate, surely you know what that means," Leo tried again.

"So what? Your father said he couldn't live without his fated mate, but when I got rid of your whore mother, he hung on. I had to fix his mistake, but he wouldn't die! Then I decided to get rid of him for good, so you could takeover under my and the elder's guidance but look at you! You ruined everything! I'll kill you and your slut, too!" Montgomery shouted and spittle ran down his chin.

The snarling valet turned on the three of them with his Lion bursting forth. His animal was wiry and lean, strong despite his age, but Sheila wasn't worried. She'd seen her mate's beast, and this man was no match for him. Her only worry was for the King who'd slumped onto his side, remnants of whatever that was oozing from his mouth. He must've imbibed some before they'd gotten there.

"Get back!" Leo shouted.

George dove to tackle the shifted Montgomery while still in human form, but the Lion swatted him away like a fly. Poor George crashed into the dresser. Hitting his temple on the sharp corner, he crumpled to the floor.

The big Cat roared and hissed, leaping over the bed, he crouched in front of Sheila. Before she could blink, Leo was on him. Her mate had half-Shifted. Holy hell, that was rare and spoke to his power.

His arms and legs tore through his clothes, building in bulk and muscle. His hands shifted into his beast's claws while maintaining most of his human face and biped appearance.

This sort of half-change was not something many Shifters could pull off. It required great reserves of strength, discipline, and that special supernatural power that made them what they were. Sheila watched in awe as Leo squeezed and squeezed, keeping his stance tight as he crushed the Lion's throat between his powerful arms.

His eyes locked on hers, glowing gold with his beast, and Sheila nodded for him to go ahead. This was about more than revenge for his mother's death, and for the attack on his father. It was about more than his threat against his mate. This was about a Lion King fixing a very real wrong within his Pride.

"It has to be done," she said, and with her words Leo struck, snapping the neck of the mad Lion, and tossing his carcass to the floor.

Sheila jolted across the room and gripped him in a fierce hug, ignoring the sounds of footsteps headed their way. She had her mate in her arms and reveled in the fierce way he clung to her.

"Are you alright?" he asked, and she nodded.

"Yes, you?" she returned.

Her heart was pounding, and shivers raced through her body. It was the adrenaline, but it was more too. Their *matebond* wrapped around her strongly. Through it, she felt all his love for her, as well as his anxiety over the present situation.

"Car, Car," mumbled the King, and they both rushed to his side.

"Easy, father," Leo said and checked his father over for signs of physical harm. The older Lion coughed and retched over the side of the bed, a sour stench came from the poison he vomited, and Leo wiped his face with a cloth. Sheila went to check on George.

"He'll be fine," she said, and returned to where her mate stood next to his father.

Sheila crouched down and gingerly lifted the medicine dropper.

She sniffed the tube and her she-Wolf growled. Whatever it was, it was clearly poisonous.

"What is going on in here?" Aunt Patricia's voice rang through the room as she and Ariella, along with another older man, burst through the doors. She leaped to her son's side with her daughter in tow.

"George? Donovan? Leo? What's been happening here?" the Lioness spoke a mile a minute and Sheila answered her, trying to calm her.

"Yes, George is okay, just a bump on the noggin'. Montgomery there was poisoning the King with this," she held up the dropper.

"That's a pretty big noggin', little bro," Ariella snorted at her little brother, who was moaning and groaning for all he was worth.

"*Shyaddap*, daughter. Now come on, cupcake, open your eyes," Patricia said, rocking her son in her arms.

"What is wrong with the King?" the stranger asked.

"You're the Pride healer? I'm Sheila," she began.

"Sorry," Leo said, "this is my mate, Sheila Rand. Sheila, this is Tom Royce, the Pride healer."

"Pleasure," he said and began taking the King's temperature. "So, why have you canceled my appointments with the King these last few weeks?"

"What? I haven't canceled anything," Leo growled, and Sheila placed a hand on his arm.

"I see. Well, someone has, using your seal. Now here, help me turn him over."

The healer and Leo worked together to turn the King onto his side so the man could begin an examination of his spine.

"Excuse me, gentlemen," Sheila interrupted. "Boys!" she yelled when they didn't answer.

Every pair of feline eyes locked on her, and she straightened her shoulders. Bunch of pussies! It seemed Cats really didn't like to listen, no matter how big or small they were.

"The King has been poisoned with this, I figured you might need it," Sheila said and held up the discarded medicine dropper.

"Give me that, carefully," Tom held out his hand.

"Sorry, mate," Leo mumbled.

He took her hand in his and kissed it. She could see he was riddled with worry, and she could not blame him.

"No need," she assured her mate.

Really, there wasn't any call for him to apologize. The last few minutes had been quite a lot for anyone to go through. Even Princes had their limits, she supposed.

"Thank you," Leo said once more as the healer investigated the contents.

"This is Carbofuran. It's a pesticide with the greatest acute toxicity known to man or beast, cats especially," he told them. The healer's outrage was echoed by everyone in the room.

"Farmers in Africa use that on wild lions to stop them after they've killed one of their Cattle. They lace the carcass with it and sometimes poison entire prides with the stuff," Ariella snarled, and her outrage was damn near contagious.

"In a Shifter, with our fast metabolic structure, only large doses would be lethal. If Montgomery were dosing your father daily with this amount, it would cause confusion, loss of control physically, diminished motor skills, memory loss, and eventually paralysis. Ultimately, the loss of all normal neurological function followed by death, but that would only occur after months of this torture," he explained angrily and grabbed his medical bag.

"What can you do for him?" Leo asked.

"I am going to start by hooking him up to an IV and flushing this junk out of his system. Here, hang this bag of fluids from that post," he gestured to one of the grand columns that surrounded the King's bed.

"Okay, you two got this."

Sheila squeezed Leo's hand and turned to the women who were helping George to stand.

"Can you three get some bodies in here to clean this mess? I want only the most trusted Lions," she instructed.

"Yes, *Princess*," Aunt Patricia replied with a wink and pointed to her neck.

Sheila felt her cheeks warm. Holy crap! She was blushing, and fuck it all, yes, she was now officially a Princess.

"You got it," Ariella agreed.

"Yes, ma'am," George replied.

"Sheila," Leo called her name, and she returned to his side, certain now that things would get done.

"Mate," she walked into his open arms and nuzzled his neck, thoroughly enjoying the pressure of his arms as they squeezed her to him.

"Tom says my father will be okay," he told her, and she felt his joy at the news reverberate through her as he kissed her temple.

It fucking amazed her they had gotten to this place, but here they were. Together. And she knew now, she was never letting him go. Sheila's place was right there beside her mate. She wanted to share every woe and triumph, every battle and victory—even the defeats, with him.

Equals. Lovers. Soul mates. Friends.

"Thank you so much. Gods, I love you."

"Of course. That's what mates do, pussycat," she said, and ran her hands over the remnants of his ripped shirt. "Come on, let's get your father settled."

"Are you gonna call me that all the time now?" he asked with mock anger.

"Maybe," she replied and winked saucily.

Sexy man. My very own Prince.

They spent the next few hours re-calling in the King's guard. All of them had been sent away over the last few weeks by the now dead traitor. After they disposed of Montgomery and cleaned the King's chambers, Aunt Patricia entered the bedroom and insisted she was going to stay by the King's side until the man could send her away himself.

"I might not be your aunt by blood, Leo Crowley, but I was your mother's best friend. My children are your honorary cousins and I absolutely insist you march off to your room and take care of your mate. Look at her, poor thing, she's dead on her feet!"

"What?" Sheila gasped, outraged by the notion, but then she caught the twinkle in the older woman's eye and played along.

"Yes, uh, I could use some food, a shower, maybe a rubdown," she suggested and shrugged.

Leo's protective male instincts flared, and he swept her off her feet before she could blink. His chest rumbled with his Lion. The beast within him purred as he carried her to their room, and Sheila swallowed her moan. She never knew a purr could be so sexy.

"Mate," she nipped the sensitive skin at the base of his neck and loved the tremor that ran through him.

What a lucky Dog I am!

T*hree weeks later...*

Leo entered the King's interview room with Sheila on his arm resplendent in hip-hugging denim and a soft white blouse that emphasized her womanly curves. The leather cut she wore over it sporting the DWMC patch had him drooling with the desire to strip off all her clothing, save for that one particular article.

He caught her wide-eyed stare and shrugged. Not like he could help it. The female aroused him every second of the day. The feisty Dire Wolf snickered, and he couldn't help but pinch her right on that spectacular ass of hers. She yelped and glared back at him despite his innocent expression.

He'd spent each day going over every move Montgomery had made since before his mother's death. They'd had experts pour over his computer and found hidden emails and documents that pointed to not one, but two accomplices. Oddly enough, Montgomery's sister, a member of the elder's circle, Maribel Clover, was found innocent of any wrong doings.

Except one, of course. Sheila had been pretty pissed when she'd found out the Lioness had been pitching her daughter as a mate for Leo. A night of sweaty, panting sexy fun times and a re-claiming bite had eased his little Wolf's worries and made his Cat super fucking happy.

Montgomery's emails had named Margaret Donner as a co-conspirator against the crown, and the Pride had had her arrested. Leo had alerted the Council of Shifters, the one governing force that all Shifter groups obeyed, to come and take her away after they'd presented them with all the evidence. She did not even try to defend herself.

Apparently, she had been a childhood playmate of Donovan Crowley and had always assumed he would take her as his mate. When he'd come back from an expedition abroad with a human woman in tow, jealousy had driven her to commit the heinous actions of conspiracy to commit murder against the Queen, Caroline Crowley, and poisoning the King.

He had spent the past three weeks putting the Pride back to rights. His bosses at the police station were happy to see him take his accumulated vacation time with the promise he would return to the job soon. Something his mate was also fiercely happy about. She didn't mind being called a Princess now and then, but he could tell she longed for a little space from the dozens of Lions who once again roamed the Palace halls.

"Son!"

Leo's head shot up at the sound of the familiar bass, and he vaulted towards the throne where he'd failed to notice his father, the King was waiting for them. This was the first time Leo had seen his father resplendent in his own navy suit bearing the medals of his station since he'd come home.

Donovan Crowley looked better than ever. His father's mane of silver streaked dark blonde hair was thick and healthy once more, as was his face which had filled out over the past few days. Leo watched as his father's amber eyes glowed gold as his beast rose to meet him. He stilled and waited for the challenge, the animosity that they had both always feared would rise as a result of their dominant natures, but nothing. Nothing happened. He had to remember that those rumors were pushed onto the Pride by Montgomery and his cohorts. None of it was real.

"Son, I am so proud of you. Come here," he opened his arms and Leo went to his father and embraced him in a fierce hug with his mate beside him, tears shining in her bright blue eyes.

"I am so sorry I listened to them and let them keep us apart. Sorry I couldn't save your mother, I didn't know," the King confessed.

"That's not your fault. You trusted them. They were your Pride. I'm sorry about Mom, Dad. And I am sorry I stayed away so long," Leo wiped his face and reached for Sheila.

"Thank you, son. Ah, you've brought my new daughter to see me, welcome Sheila," the King opened his arms and embraced Sheila warmly.

"Thank you, *er*, your majesty?" she squinted, and the King laughed jovially.

"Nonsense, you must know by now we aren't that kind of Kingdom," he said and winked. "A Lion Pride is like any other Shifter group. King is our word for Alpha, that is all."

"Well, what do you know?" Sheila nodded at Leo. "I knew this guy was just an uptight butt-sniffer, and he tried to tell me he was Prince."

The King blinked slowly, then he grinned. Soon that grin turned into a full-blown belly laugh. Leo appreciated that his mate amused his dad, but an uptight butt-sniffer? Someone was getting spanked later. And he couldn't wait. In the meantime, he'd just have to remind her who she was mated to.

"Oooh! Leo," she crowed when he scooped her up and spun her around.

"What was that again, mate?"

"Okay, okay, I give," she said when he started tickling her.

"Alright, children sit down while we discuss the future," the King said and waved them towards a pair of chairs and they sat and listened.

"So, as you can see," his father said after a while. "I am quite fit to continue my rule now that we've weeded out the bad seeds. You are my heir, Leo. You and your children are destined to lead, no one and nothing can change that, but perhaps, it won't be as soon as you thought."

"I see," Leo returned.

"What are your feelings on this, son?"

"Actually," Leo turned and glanced at the current and only owner of his Lion's heart.

Sheila's lovely face was carefully blank, but she could do nothing to stem the scent of confusion from reaching his nostrils. That confusion soon turned to hope as he spoke. He knew then and there that he was about to deliver the correct answer for them both, and his chest swelled with pride.

"I am actually really glad to hear that, Dad. My mate and I won't mind having a closer relationship with you, the Pride, and *Eat Well Live Proud*, but I have a few more years left on the job, and Sheila is building a business with her Pack mates."

"So, what are you saying?" asked the King.

"I am saying that I think this arrangement works very well for all of us. What do you think, mate?"

"Yes," she answered without hesitation, "oh, yes."

"What is going on here? Donovan, you said fifteen minutes, and I've been waiting twenty!" Aunt Patricia walked into the room holding one gold-painted helmet under one arm and waving the other with her hand.

"Hiya, kiddies," she said and winked. "Tell Phoenix I am going to need some more *oomph* added to my engine," the older woman said to Sheila.

"Ah. Yes. I'm coming, dear," the King replied, and growled at the Lioness as he stood up.

George rushed over and handed him a leather vest, which he exchanged for his suit jacket. Leo looked from one to the other, his confusion growing.

"Wait, aren't you related?" Sheila asked.

"Honey, I was your mate's mom's best friend, and I am his godmother, but me and your daddy-in-law don't share any DNA, otherwise this would be too kinky even for me," Aunt Patricia replied and tossed the helmet at Leo's dad before she slapped him on the ass.

"Later, son," the King said, and the two older Shifters headed outdoors.

"Wow, I was not expecting that!" Sheila's look of astonishment matched his own, before the two of them fell into a fit of laughter. Leo growled and tossed his mate back over his shoulder.

"What are you doing?"

"I'm taking my mate down the hall to our room, where we are going to pack our suitcases and break out of this place."

"Then?"

"Then I am going to take you home and claim you on my bed."

"A bed? Now, that's kinky," she growled and swatted his ass.

Fuck, if he didn't get hard at the sharp contact. Maybe they should stay for a little? No. If they didn't leave, they'd never get out. He loved the Pride, but he was years away from taking over and he wanted to have his mate all to himself for a while yet. Just then, the scent of his mate's arousal reached his nostrils and his resolve wavered.

"Behave or else," he threatened.

"Or else what?" she teased.

"I'll just have to show you," he promised.

He entered the bedroom and stalked towards the unmade bed. Flipping her onto the soft mattress, Leo didn't hesitate to slice through her jeans and blouse, leaving her in her leather vest and lace thong.

Sheila sat up and took off the cut, tossing it onto the chair beside the headboard, her eyes never leaving him. He stroked his length beneath his pants and licked his lips. Fuck, she was so hot, her Wolf's musk and the spicy sweetness of her cream tempted him like no other.

"Mine," he growled, but he didn't move to touch. He simply watched as she wiggled and writhed on the bed.

"Yours?" she asked, and he nodded.

"Show me," she demanded.

He squeezed his hard length through his pants, liked the flash of her eyes as she watched him slowly take off his clothes. Once nude, he took his cock in his hand once more, spreading the pearl of precum over the broad head, and cupping his balls with the other hand. She was a goddess bathed in fire and light, and he loved looking at her.

She moaned as he touched himself and moved her hands down to cup her breasts and tug her nipples. She kneaded the flesh under his rapt gaze and bit her lip while her right hand snaked down her luscious body. Pulling her knees up to reveal her glistening pink lips, Sheila skimmed her fingers over her clit.

"Fuck baby, do that again," he growled, watching as she parted her slick lips and dipped her finger inside her honeypot.

Sheila moaned and slid that long, wet digit free, gliding it along her plump little nub. She circled the tiny button of her desire, faster and faster, panting as Leo stroked his cock.

"Hey, little Wolf?"

"What?" she grinned.

"You touchin' my pussy?"

"Mine," she teased and moaned, speeding up those tiny little circles as she rubbed her clit.

"I don't think so, baby, that's my pussy," he growled and let go of his dick.

Leo crawled across the mattress and kneeled at her splayed legs. He nuzzled her hand out of the way, bringing it to his mouth and licking her digits clean. Sheila mewled in response.

He knew what he wanted. Had known since he first laid eyes on his sweet and sassy little Wolf. He rubbed his thick length along her slit, torturing them both to near madness before finally he filled her with one perfectly aimed thrust.

"Leo?" she murmured.

"What, mate?" he growled, trying hard to pace himself, to make sure she came first.

"You know how you said this is your pussy?"

"Mine," he growled and pumped harder.

"Well, I think you're wrong," she said, and that got his Cat snarling and stopped his movements long enough for her to flip them both over.

Astride him and proud as any warrior, Sheila grinned wider like the wicked little Wolf she was. Her breasts thrust forward, and Leo growled as her molten heat squeezed him tightly.

"Fact is," she said, her blue eyes glittered at him even as he tried to catch his breath.

"You," she rocked her hips.

"Are," grind and slide.

"My," she lifted up.

"Pussy!" and she slammed back down.

"Fuck me," he grunted.

"I am, *pussycat*, and I will. Always. Mine."

Me-ow.

EPILOGUE

DIRE WOLF MATES

"Whoa, wait a second," Lucy said and looked from Leo to Sheila and back again. "So, you're a Prince and you mated Sheila?"

"Yes," Leo nodded.

"Yes," Sheila echoed, and rolled her eyes.

Leo was a Prince. She explained it ten times already. So, what was the big deal, anyway? He was also a detective, a Lion Shifter, and wonder of wonders, he was her one true and fated mate.

Phoenix scoffed.

Thor looked carefully blasé about the whole thing.

Brock was noticeably absent.

Cole pinned Leo with his silvery stare for all on two seconds before giving her the thumbs up.

"Oh my gods! You're a fucking Princess," Weylin snorted, and Phoenix grinned too.

"Idiots." Lucy rolled her eyes and popped another French fry into her mouth and chewed, then her pregnant cousin-in-law reached for her iced tea.

The rest of the guys just sat there quietly once they'd stopped making rude noises. Most of them with a beer in hand. Only her cousin was missing. Derrick had gone back to make sure the alarm had been activated at *Serious Moonlight* since everyone came running when she'd come to the Pack House to share her news.

"I just can't believe you mated, Sheila." Weylin faux gagged, and Sheila smacked him upside the head.

"That's my mate you're talking about," Leo growled.

"Shit on a shingle, can't you boys control yourselves? Sheila is a woman now and Leo is her mate," Lucy growled and closed her eyes. Then she yelled for her mate.

"Derrick!"

Her mate hauled ass not one second later through the back door, claws out he looked around and tried to control his breathing. Holy cow. Remind Sheila to never scream for her mate like that unless she was in actual trouble.

"Dammit, woman, are you okay?" Derrick growled and walked to her side.

"Yes, I'm fine. Derrick, it's gotta happen," she said, and her purple eyes flashed at her mate. Everyone in the room felt the intense bond between the Alpha pair.

"Now?" he questioned, but he should have known better than that, in Sheila's opinion. Not that she had any idea what the fuck Lucy was on about.

"Yes," the feisty Bobcat insisted. "Right now."

"The cubs?"

"They're fine. Thor, get the box," she called out, and pushed herself up out of the chair.

"What's going on?" Leo asked.

"Uh, I think Lucy is going to get her tattoo," Sheila said with wonder in her tone.

"Tattoo?" Leo asked.

"Yes, it's a sacred Dire Wolf ritual," she whispered. For some reason, it felt disrespectful not to.

"Like a tradition?"

"Yes, but deeper, much deeper than that. Thor, our Enforcer, is more than just muscle. He's got *the touch,* the graybeards called him *favored by the gods.*"

"Really?" Leo's eyebrows raised, but she could tell he was taking it all in stride.

Modern times or not, all Shifters believed in magic. How could they not when they shared their souls and switched bodies between human and other? Magic existed. They were living proof.

"When Thor channels the Fates, they answer. They work through his skilled fingers to depict a Shifter's true heart through ink and blood, until he connects with that person's *matebond* and shows them their path," Sheila explained.

She watched as Leo's eyes dilated, then flashed gold. It was clear his Lion was interested in her story. Then, without pause, he surprised her with his next request.

"I want one," he said.

"Are you sure?" she didn't dare give in to the hope that threatened to spill over in the form of tears yet. Not until he answered her.

"About you?" her Lion asked and grinned wickedly. "Sheila, you are about the only damned thing in this world I am sure of," he said and claimed her mouth with his even as he stood and led her into the living room.

"It hurts, you know, getting ink," she said and laughed when Leo looked affronted.

"Little Wolf, I'd crawl through glass, walk through fire, go to Hell and back for you, a little ink is nothing, my love. It means a lot, but the pain is worth it. As are you."

He touched her face and kissed her quickly.

"You sure?" she asked one more time.

"*Absofuckinglutely,*" Mr. Law and Order answered, and Sheila laughed aloud, wondering what horrified expressions the guys would make if they heard him talk like that.

He stood up and turned around, leaving her to follow him into the huge living room of the Pack house. It was no Palace, but it was the first home she'd ever known.

As of about an hour ago, however, Sheila and her mate were the proud owners of a three story colonial just down the road. Leo agreed that they couldn't live in the Pack house, or in the rented place he occupied in town. They needed privacy. Of course, proximity to Serious Moonlight and his Pride had been a priority.

The recently abandoned house fit all their needs. Yes, it needed a shit ton of work, but surprisingly, she looked forward to building a home for the two of them. Leo seemed keen, too. Sheila inhaled slowly as she took in the scene and her Pack surrounding her. The Dire Wolf MC was a group of rare Shifters who understood what it meant to be part of something. She was so proud of them all, and she was proud to be among them with her mate.

Lucy was sitting on a chair with Thor kneeling by her leg. He'd taken ink and bamboo needles from the metal box with the original Dire Wolf Pack glyphs etched on the outside. It was a sacred relic of theirs, as was the magicked ink he used to complete the mating ritual according to Pack law.

The large bald Wolf had dozens of tattoos across his enormous body. The most prominent being the wrath of flames circling his neck. His eyes were glazed over as he continued to repeat the same phrase in an ancient language that few knew or recognized as a special dialect of the Dire Wolves of old.

In his trance-like state, Thor etched a scene onto the pregnant Bobcat Shifter's calf. It showed her, her mate, and their cubs all in their animal forms. It was a tinier version of Derrick's tattoo, although in hers she was feeding their cubs, and he was watching over them tenderly.

Everyone was silent in the circle they'd formed around the pregnant Alpha fem, only Derrick approached, cradling her in his arms and claiming her lips with a soul-searing kiss that had even the men teary-eyed.

Normally, Thor was wiped out after one tattoo, but he held out one muscled arm and pointed a finger in Sheila's and Leo's direction. She looked at her mate and saw he was already removing his shirt, revealing his tanned, muscled perfection.

Dear gods, she loved his body. He was so handsome, big, strong, and powerfully built. Perfect for her in every way. Sheila wasn't exactly all sunshine and roses to deal with, but he managed her just fine. The past month had proved that.

He looked at her with his large golden eyes sparkling, and he winked before he made his way to the center of the circle. Thor turned him around so that his back was facing the big man and Sheila sucked in a breath.

Nerves made her tremble as the sheer overwhelming thought that this was actually happening occurred to her. This was more than just a big deal. It was bigger than kissing, biting, and even fucking. This was the real claiming as far as Dire Wolf tradition went.

This was their true mating night. She bit her lip as Thor lifted the ink and poured some into a clean bowl. He took a new bamboo needle and dipped it into the magickal substance before he began carving the path of Leo's destiny across his broad back. Her Lion didn't make one single move.

His face remained still and impassive as the huge Dire Wolf behind him cut through his skin and marked him permanently. Unprecedented in her time and never in her memory, Thor raised his left arm, and he pointed a finger at Sheila. She looked at Derrick, who nodded at her to step forward.

The Enforcer tugged her arm and tore the sleeve, causing a slight rumble from Leo, who quickly ceased the sound when she touched his hand. As Thor continued to draw with ink across Leo's shoulders, he began marking her using the same long arches with the sharpened bamboo. Prick after prick with the wooden blade, Thor worked. His pace was furious and sweat soaked through his shirt before he was finished. The Pack remained present, witnesses to the ritual, until finally the big man laid down his tool.

He breathed heavily, collapsing onto the floor as sweat dripped from his brow. Leo and Sheila looked at each other, awestruck and completely in sync. She felt their *matebond* pulsing around them, a living thing it warmed and protected, sheltering her in his love as she sheltered him in turn.

He was her clarity, her focus, her one true and fated mate, and she would do her best to make him happy. It was all she could promise, and it was enough. It was everything.

"I love you," she whispered as he reached for her.

"Love you, mate." He cleared his throat, and she gasped.

"Sorry, I didn't mean to touch it," she said and turned him around to look at the scene Thor had created with guidance from the Fates themselves.

A mighty Lion stood in a mossy field with a Dire Wolf at his side. They were standing together, equals in all and everything. The Wolf's head was turned towards him, her gaze looking at her future, and the Lion was focused solely on her as well. Sheila's heart pounded as she turned her right arm to see what it was she'd been tattooed with, to her consternation the scene went up her shoulder.

"What is it?" she asked, and she almost howled when no one answered.

Leo pressed a kiss to her skin before he spoke. She heard the awe in his tone, and it filled her with love and joy.

"Oh, baby, it's a Wolf's paw, a Dire Wolf's paw, and it's right over a heart that's surrounded in a mane of flames. I've seen that before, it's a depiction of a Lion's heart. My heart. Your claw isn't a threat, it's not piercing the heart, it's uh, it's carrying me. You're lifting me up, little Wolf. Just like you do, every single minute you're with me," his voice tightened, and she trembled, near to bursting with emotion, but he wasn't done.

"Sheila, baby, there are glyphs too. A circle with two wavy lines intertwined—"

"That's the symbol for fated mates," she said with a ridiculously happy bark of laughter.

"And another one, this one I recognize. It's the ring of circles, like on my bedroom door at the palace. The symbol for greatness," he whispered, and she felt the grin in his voice as he kissed her shoulder.

"Well, I am pretty great," she said, and he turned her around and claimed her lips. Breaking her sass with three little words she hadn't heard him say since the night they'd mated under the full moon.

"I love you, little Wolf."

"I love you too," she returned. And she did. With all her heart.

The end.

Liked this story? Want more Dire Wolf Mates?
Grab the next book, Pinch of Sass, at https://www.cdgorri.com/books/pinch-of-sass.
Or
Follow the whole series at https://www.cdgorri.com/seres/dire-wolf-mates.

Thank you and happy reading!

PINCH OF SASS

DIRE WOLF MATES

BLURB

DIRE WOLF MATES

Will this stoic Dire Wolf admit the sassy feline is his fated mate and stake his claim?

Ariella Golden needs to persuade sexy Dire Wolf Beta, and the amazingly talented chef at Serious Moonlight, Brock Laurent to use her Pride's corporation, Eat Well Live Proud, for all the roadhouse's needs in order to win her company's coveted quarterly prize.

But that's not the only reason this Golden girl is chasing this grumpy Wolf!

EWLP offers the best organic, non-GMO, and responsibly harvested fish and meat—going with them is a no brainer. The problem is the stubborn lil' doggy happens to be her fated mate, but he's in denial! Can the Lioness break down his barriers or will she get hurt in the process?

Brock is perfectly content to cook good food, listen to classic rock, and hang out with his Pack at their new place in Blue Valley, New Jersey. Settling down is hard on his animal, but so far so good—except for the fact he's being hunted by a pesky she-Cat.

Can't this female take a hint? He is better off alone, but this curvy, curly-headed goddess is all he thinks about lately.

Trying to ignore the pull of his mate is a losing battle. Desperate, Brock develops a plan to test whether the virginal hellcat can handle all of him. It's time to confront his fears.

Here, kitty kitty.

Stunned when Brock propositions her, but with the encouragement of her family, Ariella agrees to a single night in the sexy Dire Wolf's arms to seal the deal that will put her in the running for EWLP's quarterly prize, but that's not all. One night is all she has to get the big dumb chef to realize Ariella is exactly who the Fates designed for him.

One mate custom made with curves galore and a pinch of sass.

Will she prove she can take anything the Wolf man dishes out?

PROLOGUE

DIRE WOLF MATES

The evening breeze was cool and sweet as Brock stood surveying the lot behind the busy commercial kitchen he now oversaw. He'd spent years cooking and mastering the finer of the culinary arts, but he rarely had a chance to practice his skill on the road.

Being part owner of the Dire Wolf MC's new roadhouse meant he was also head chef. It was a dream come true. But as with most dreams, it had its drawbacks. Like his loud as fuck Pack mate, who was right about to intrude on what was a rare moment of silence before Brock finished his shift for the night.

"Yo, Brock," Phoenix called as he walked around back.

Serious Moonlight was large for New Jersey roadhouse. One of a kind, really. The Dire Wolf MC had recently purchased, renovated, and now the restaurant/bar that sat on the outskirts of Blue Valley. Life was different now. They'd all parked their motorcycles for good and were trying their hand at making this their real home.

Each member of the Pack had something he or she handled and excelled at. Derreck was the Alpha and ran just about everything, including money stuffs, paperwork, and permits. Phoenix was their resident mechanic. Brock the head chef. But they all pitched in at the bar.

Between that and the occasional weekend road trip, Brock could safely say he was pretty fond of life right now. Or he would be if everyone could remember he was the Pack Beta, second to the Alpha, and deserving of some damn privacy.

"Brock? Where are you, man? Moody fucker," Phoenix mumbled, and Brock bit back his snarl.

He might be a genius when it came to cooking, but he had zero tolerance for interruptions of any kind, especially when he was working. Phoenix's caterwauling was a motherfuckin' interruption.

"Dammit, Brock," Phoenix continued to yell. "I appreciate that sometimes a man needs a bit of quiet, and I hated to intrude," said with more than a little snark, "but I need your signature in this EWLP purchase order, for fuck's sake!"

Brock frowned. He knew when Sheila had insisted, they start ordering meat from the local Lion Pride's corporation, *Eat Well Live Proud,* that shit was going to get fucked up. Just because she was mated to one of those big, fussy-haired pussies didn't mean Brock had to jump when they snapped.

That was not saying he was not glad for the change. Brock would be the first to admit that *EWLP* offered the best organically fed and environmentally conscious raised beef, pork, lamb, and fowl he'd ever tasted. He hardly minded singing their praises, even if it meant giving props to the feline run firm. Word was their fish was decent, too. He just hadn't gotten around to ordering some.

Time really flew when you were busy making a home. Even now, he could hardly believe it was almost ten o'clock at night. Where had the day gone?

Brock scratched his head, heaved out a sigh. He was still ignoring his Pack mate, fucking Phoenix was totally cold, checking for Brock near the woods that bordered their land.

He wondered if time was going to keep moving this quickly since they'd parked their bikes for good. Life was different now. Derrick and Sheila had both found mates, but that kind of thing was not in his future.

"Brock? The fuck, man!" Phoenix yelled, still looking for him, and it was actually kind of embarrassing at this point.

Couldn't the man scent him? Even without using that sense, couldn't he see the enormous blond Dire Wolf Shifter that Brock was standing not four yards away from him? He just had to look around the empty crates stacked neatly against the back wall. He'd have to tell Derrick the Pack needed to spend some time re-training their senses.

Yep, shit was weird now. Brock hardly recognized them anymore, and that wasn't necessarily a bad thing. The Dire Wolf MC he grew up in simply didn't exist. Each of his Pack mates had willingly turned their backs on their nomadic heritage when they bought this land and opened up shop.

Even the Alpha's dam, who rode with her own MC of widowed and single she-Wolves, could hardly imagine them running a road-house bar and grill. She'd visited just last month to meet her son's mate and to congratulate them on the coming birth of their first cub. Derrick had picked good when he found Lucy.

Brock admired the spunky little feline and did his damndest to stay on her good side. Hell, even if he pissed her off, he could always bribe her with the double chocolate caramel brownies she could not get enough of in her fertile state. Sometimes, it really paid to be a chef.

Business was good. Everyone was happy. Well, *sort of*. Even Phoenix seemed to appreciate having time to devote to exploring ways to renovate and improve the custom modifications he made to cars and motorcycles for Shifters and other supernaturals. Human machinery just couldn't handle the wear and tear of lugging around a man who harbored an eight hundred pound monster inside of him. He'd even started selling them.

Good for Phoenix.

But honestly, Brock was content. Thanks to their Alpha's business savvy and his mate's grit, Sheila's badass attitude and marketing skills, they had a good thing going here.

He ran a hand through his dark blond hair and shook it out before he re-tied the plain black headband he wore to keep it out of the way while he cooked. Normally, Brock hated shit in his hair, but when he was in the kitchen, safety and health precautions took precedence over personal style preferences.

His Dire Wolf pressed against his skin, the beast agitated. That was nothing new. He'd felt that way for months now. He rubbed his chest and closed his eyes, wrestling with his inner animal until the Wolf was calm once more.

Shit.

That was close. He would have to go for a run later. Brock was just so unfocused lately. Hardly his fault, he thought, narrowing his eyes. Ever since Sheila had come back home with her very own Lion Prince mate, the roadhouse had been crawling with the pesky felines.

Fucking furballs were everywhere. Of course, Brock didn't usually get riled up because of one Shifter group or other. He wasn't a speciesist. He just wanted to be alone sometimes. Was that too much to ask for?

As a rare and prehistoric species of Shifter, Dire Wolves were often more dominant and growly than most. Very few Shifters could match their inherent size and strength, which was why his kind typically roamed. Challenges were a Shifter's way of life, but not theirs. Dire Wolves were basically pacifists, separating them from other, more instinct-run Shifters.

His objections to the feline furballs were really reserved for one spectacularly sassy feline in particular. And the reason behind that was so shameful, so twisted, so damned embarrassing, he could hardly admit it to himself.

But what else could Brock do? Ariella Golden haunted his every waking—and sleeping—hour. She was temptation personified. A woman custom built to suit his tastes by the gods themselves.

Fucking hell.

The woman had him waxing poetic over something that had everything to do with hormones and nothing at all to do with deities.

It was just a fluke of nature. A Biological imperative created to ensure the propagation of the species. Nothing else. Nothing special.

Keep telling yourself that, bro.

So, what if her skin reminded him of freshly rendered cream? And if her hair was deep and rich like his favorite espresso beans? That didn't mean shit. Who cared if her full lips and golden eyes made him wish for things he hadn't dared long for since he was a pup?

She was nothing to him. Nothing at all.

Even as he thought it, he felt the lie burn his soul. His Dire Wolf pressed once more, the beast letting him feel his rage with a snarling snap of his jaws that made Brock's own head ache like hell.

Fuck.

He might as well admit it, if only in his head.

Ariella Golden was his fated mate.

CHAPTER ONE

DIRE WOLF MATES

Knowing you had a fated mate, and claiming said mate, were two entirely different things. Especially for him. Brock was not built for a mate.

Period.

Sure, Ariella Golden was the one woman the universe had destined to be his. Unfortunately, the universe had fucked up. He had no plans to take her, claim her, fuck her until his mind went blank and his body was finally sated.

Grrrr. What a visual!

Whatever. He couldn't do a thing about it. So Brock had been avoiding her like the plague. Ever since the first time he'd taken the curvy female for a ride on the back of his Harley, Brock had been trying to fight it. Even now, memories of that ride had his dick growing hard in his pants.

He could almost feel her as she'd been that day. The woman had squeezed him so tight, she damn near busted a rib. But it would have been worth it. The feel of her tits smashed against his back, her hot womanly core snuggled up to his hips, had made him feel ten times a man.

He suspected her Lioness had scented what they were to each other. Brock had seen the shocked glee sparkling in her golden gaze as she'd looked up at him in the smoky, dim light of the bar later that very same night.

But like a fucking idiot and worse, a coward, he'd turned around and walked out. Ever since, he'd been pretending not to notice her. Hell. Ignoring Ariella was the hardest fucking thing he'd ever done, but he'd been pulling it off for months now.

Brock had choked big time, and now he didn't know what to do. It was stupid, really. A bad memory from the past was killing his future, but the truth was he didn't know if he could handle another rejection. That's why he decided to stay away.

Like a fucking coward.

His Wolf growled, and he rubbed his chest to quiet the beast. He didn't like being called a coward, but what else was it when you ran from the woman the fates decided was yours? Not like she took the hint anyway, he thought with a shake of his head.

Ariella Golden had made it her business to visit *Serious Moonlight* with increased frequency. Which, of course, only made things harder on him.

Literally.

She had him so out of his mind Brock was snapping at everyone lately. Cursed more, too. And he'd been walking around with a fucking bat in his jeans, trying to run the kitchen staff as if no one could tell. He was fighting with his Pack mates, and himself. His Wolf wanted to kick his own ass.

Derrick had called him into his office three times this week. Lucy, his pregnant mate, had developed a nose for romantic schemes and Brock wanted no part of it. She'd even threatened him with some magical matchmaking nonsense.

Slick one, that Lucy. When she wasn't trying to fix up members of the Pack, she was making them move the heavy, wood furniture she'd had them refinish, from room to room for no specific reason at all.

Just whenever she got the notion. Which seemed to be constantly, the last few weeks.

Derrick had simply smiled at his mate like the lovesick fool he was and called it her nesting period, which to a Dire Wolf made no fucking sense, whatsoever. They weren't birds, for fuck's sake. True, Lucy was a feline, but as far as Brock knew, they didn't have nests either.

Then again, who was he to judge? Brock was outside in the dark because—*let's face it*—he was hiding. Him. A badass Dire Wolf Shifter. Beta to the Pack. And head chef at *Serious Moonlight*. Hiding.

The shame!

He'd known the moment Ariella had walked into the roadhouse that night. He had felt it in the air. The woman caused the very electricity in the atmosphere to alter whenever she appeared.

It was the same damn thing every single time the female entered any room near his immediate vicinity. And yet, he was still too weak to do a thing about it.

Echoes of past wounds still hurt, despite his denials. Brock wasn't sure he could take a chance on being spurned again. Not with Ariella. He couldn't risk it. Something inside told him he would never survive if that golden-eyed beauty rejected him. Admitting that one solitary fear made his entire body tremble with emotion.

Shameful. Weak. Alone. Always alone.

He growled and cursed himself ten times a fool. Brock froze when, at that moment, the sounds of her laughter reached him as the bar's side door swung open. He closed his eyes, gritting his teeth at the tidal wave of lust that damn near bowled him over.

He still wasn't prepared for the fierce punch of desire that slammed into him, hitting him right in the gut whenever he caught sight, sound, or scent of her. His Wolf growled, pulse raced, and fuck, he was sweating.

Yes, it was all because a certain sexy siren had walked into the bar looking like heaven and smelling like sin. Brock's Wolf had been growling nonstop ever since. He'd just cooked her meal and sent it out with their best server. Then, he hightailed it out the back door. He just had to escape, get away from her moans and groans as she enjoyed her dinner.

Ariella was very vocal when it came to her enjoyment. Satisfaction flashed through him as he pictured her eating the food, he had made just for her. Of course, that was followed by another pang of carnal lust so strong he doubled over and had to readjust his cock inside his chef's pants.

He'd never worn the things until she started coming to the bar to eat every other day, but jeans were simply too constrictive. At least, this way, he wouldn't punch a hole through the baggy material with his stone hard dick.

And wasn't that the source of all his issues?

Most guys would be giddy as all hell with a cock that size, but Brock knew better. Being big wasn't all it was cracked up to be. Sometimes, it was downright fucking tough. Females were not as fond of size as they implied. Especially inexperienced females.

Brock couldn't stomach the idea she might be afraid of him in bed. And it was not something he relished finding out.

The door swung shut again, and with it went the sound of her voice. Thank fuck. He was glad she was enjoying the food, but for fuck's sake, the sound of her moans was almost unbearable.

Mine, growled his Dire Wolf, his animal scratching hard against his skin.

It was difficult to wrestle for control, but he managed it, promising the monster a good long run later that night. It was all he could do to stop himself from hunting her down and rutting her like a beast.

We are a beast, the animal returned, and not as if it were a bad thing.

Brock growled deep in his throat as he wrestled for calm. He wasn't a self-hating Shifter. Not exactly. He just happened to have a past. Didn't everyone? It would be better for them both if she simply moved on.

Vexing female. Stubborn beauty.

He should just leave when she came in. But he didn't. His Wolf would not let him.

Possessive monster.

In fact, he was the only one who handled her food when she came into the bar. No one else touched Ariella's plate. Not ever. It was an unwritten rule in the kitchen and the entire staff understood and steered clear.

Well, duh.

His Wolf growled, the animal seeming to roll his eyes from inside that plane of existence where he waited for Brock to call on his furry form. His staff wasn't stupid. Almost all of them were Shifters, and they knew what was up.

Especially after he'd tossed the former sous chef out the back door, head over teakettle, for adjusting the amount of sauce on Ariella's grilled *mahi-mahi* a few weeks ago. No one had made that mistake again.

Mine, growled his Wolf, and Brock rubbed his chest harder this time.

His keen ears picked up the sound of Phoenix. The fucker was finally rounding the right corner to find Brock's little hiding spot. He braced himself for the intrusion.

"Hey, bro, I've been looking for you," his Pack mate said and grinned. In his hand, he held a tablet and a stylus. The prick didn't even look pissed he'd been walking around ten minutes trying to find Brock. Lucky fucker, having no worries.

"You gotta sign this, bro."

"Thanks," Brock grumbled and scribbled his signature on the order.

They'd been slowly transitioning all their needs from various butchers and fishmongers to *Eat Well Live Proud*. It wasn't for any other reason than the fact the Lions delivered a superior product—*organic, non-GMO, and sustainably harvested.*

Win-win.

Truth was, Shifters had refined palates. Some of the other supernatural species as well. They really appreciated the finer quality of the meat, game, and fish EWLP offered. Derrick left the kitchen up to him, so it was completely his choice, and yet he'd delayed in switching their entire line of produce, meat, and fish to the feline run corp.

Some would say it was because he was still undecided about what to do with his unclaimed mate. Of course, should those people voice this opinion out loud, they would find themselves following his former sous chef out the back door, ass over teakettle, as it were.

"So, Ariella's inside," Phoenix idiotically pointed out.

"Yes," Brock answered while he read over the order.

"And you're out here?"

"Your point exactly?" Brock growled.

"Nothin' bro. Just sayin' because, you know, her mom's in there, and if I didn't know any better, I would say Aunt Patty's got a vial of catnip up her sleeve," Phoenix muttered.

The casual reference was to the only herbal supplement that had the power to act like a drug in the systems of feline Shifters. Brock's head shot up. Patricia Golden was the most shockingly carefree, potentially dangerous, feline over sixty Brock had ever met. The woman was a party animal. And she was not above involving her daughters in whatever hairbrained scheme she thought of next. Lucky for her son, he was too much of a stuffed shirt to become entangled in her wild affairs.

On the other hand, Ariella—*sweet, beautiful, innocent, and probably frustrated as hell if she felt anything like he did*—Ariella was just ripe for the picking. Brock closed his eyes and tried to rein in his beast. Patricia Golden was inside *Serious Moonlight* right now, possibly dosing her daughter with the one substance as close to a narcotic as it got for cat Shifters.

Oh, for fuck's sake.

"Well, you know the mess she caused after the last time that ol' Lioness pulled a stunt like this," Phoenix continued, rubbing his hand on the back of his neck.

Brock immediately thought of the incident a few weeks ago when that cunning older Lioness had spiked all the kegs under the bar with *Magibrew* enhancer, a special potion made by Witches that could slow Shifter metabolism when applied to alcohol, getting them just as knackered as normals.

"Anyway, bro, I thought I'd give you a heads up," Phoenix ended his muddled up explanation and wisely took a step back.

This was not good. If Brock remembered correctly—and he did, while under the effects of the *Magibrew* every Shifter in the bar had gotten drunk as hell. Drunk Shifters meant fistfights, and that meant they'd had broken bottles, barstools, a few tables, and one window to replace afterwards. Not to mention having to turn the hose on their customers because of all the outdoor fucking that had gone on.

Lucy had even made them sanitize the entire outdoor parking lot with a pressure washer and outdoor bleach, the commercial kind. It had been a total shitshow, and he was not looking forward to a repeat.

Of course, he'd also learned something interesting during that night. When drunk, naïve little Ariella was not only extremely agreeable, but she was also somewhat prone to falling asleep. Which is how he'd found her, passed out with a smile on her lips in the bed of a pickup truck with two Bear Shifters who'd been about to cart her off to their hometown to mate her.

Brock had nearly Wolfed out and killed both those fuckers. Luckily, Derrick had saved him from manslaughter and talked the drunk Bears out of it. Offering them a case of honey mead to take home in exchange for the Lioness. Brock had carried her to the Pack House, where she'd slept it off in his room.

He'd had to stay in Wolf form, outside his bedroom window where she slept it off for the duration of the night, otherwise he might have claimed her himself.

"How did she get it inside past Thor?" Brock asked his Pack mate.

"Don't know. Maybe she hid it?"

Fuck.

Patricia was always trying to get their Enforcer to search her. Crazy flirtatious woman. She needed a mate to settle her, but Brock didn't think any of the Dire Wolves were it for the Golden matriarch. Hell, the woman needed a keeper. Putting her daughter in harm's way, she should be ashamed of herself! And Brock should have his head examined.

What did he care? He was not taking the younger Golden as his mate, so what did it matter if one Bear or two took her home?

Fuck that. Of course, it mattered. His Wolf almost ripped out of his skin at the mere thought. How did he ever get entangled in this mess, anyway?

"You know, this is all Sheila's fault. Ever since she mated Leo, this place has been crawling with crazy felines," Phoenix muttered, and Brock had to agree.

And he liked Leo! But why did Sheila have to adopt his totally inappropriate and possibly insane extended family and bring them here?

Fuck. Fuck. FUCK.

"I'm gonna ban that woman," Brock growled, grabbing his cell phone.

He started texting the rest of the DWMC, alerting them of Patricia's shenanigans. It was all fun and games till someone got kidnapped and forced into a mating with two Bears! Brock growled even louder at the thought.

"I mean, Patricia Golden is one spunky Lioness, but I don't think she means any harm," Phoenix said.

Phoenix was right to a point, Brock conceded. The Golden matriarch simply had a penchant for trouble. Sure, they all lovingly referred to her as Aunt Patricia, but Brock strongly felt the woman had a responsibility to Ariella she was negating.

At the very least, she had some very unusual ideas about what constituted proper mother-daughter outings. Like the strip show she'd taken Ariella, Sheila, and Lucy to last week. She'd claimed it was a ballet, but when Derrick had thought to surprise his mate, he'd found her waving dollar bills and laughing her ass off while a group of men danced on poles in nothing but banana hammocks.

"I mean, Derrick is still pissed about the strip show," Phoenix added.

"As our Alpha has every right to be, Phoenix, and you know it."

"Come on. I mean, did he really have to scoop Lucy up and carry her out to his new Suburban? They argued loudly and made up even more loudly. The moans and rocking of that big ass SUV about scarred me for life! Do you know I had to stand guard and listen to that? Gross, bro! Like hearing your parents fuck," Phoenix mumbled, his cheeks turning beet red.

Brock shuddered at the imagery. Gross. He'd been desperately trying to forget that whole incident for days now. Phoenix was right about one thing. That little anecdote had all the charm of hearing your parents having sex, and Brock was dutifully grossed out by it.

He'd been there too and had quietly convinced the other ladies to let him drive them home. They'd agreed, but only after "Aunt" Patricia stuck a hundred-dollar bill into the g-string of one extremely oiled up dancer. She'd insisted on tucking it right between his cheeks.

Ouch.

Even his Wolf cringed at the recollection. Dammit. If she was here and had a vial of catnip, it could only spell trouble. The question was, for who?

His cell phone buzzed, and Brock answered it curtly. It was Sheila confirming what Phoenix had just said. Ariella was at the mercy of her crazy mother and a damn vial of catnip. If he didn't move his ass, who knew what would happen?

Grrr.

CHAPTER TWO

DIRE WOLF MATES

M*eanwhile...*

"OH MY GAWD!"

Ariella Golden moaned loudly and slammed her hands on the uncovered wood table of her favorite new Blue Valley haunt. She was in the throes of culinary ecstasy.

"Yes. Yes. YES!" she cried out like Meg Ryan in that famous movie scene.

The salmon sashimi appetizer with slices of fresh avocado, wasabi ginger sauce, and little fried wontons on the side—necessary bits of deliciousness used to scoop up the plump pieces of fish—was possibly the best damn thing she had ever eaten.

If the place wasn't already famous for the generous drink menu, featuring locally brewed IPAs and artisan liquors, kickass live music, and the over-the-top gorgeous owners, *Serious Moonlight* would be a hit for the food alone.

The establishment was still fairly new to town and, as far as the normals new, it was owned and operated by an ex-motorcycle club. She knew better, of course. Being a Shifter and all. The Dire Wolf Motorcycle Club might be retired, but the badass prehistoric Shifters still liked to ride. She'd even been on the back of one of their bike's once—the memory replaying in her head like a favorite reel on social media.

The DWMC had only recently moved to Blue Valley, New Jersey, buying this property and settling down for the first time in their history. But that wasn't the reason she dined there three times a week, minimum. The truth was, Ariella just couldn't stay away.

Despite the constant disregard he'd shown her, her Lioness was stuck on the Pack Beta. Silly kitty insisted Brock Laurent, head chef and sexy as fuck Dire Wolf, was her fated mate.

Prrrr.

Oh, she had it bad. Feeding her lonely heart on the mere fact he was near to her whenever she ate at the rustically charming road-house had been her only recourse. Ever since that one fateful ride where she'd scented his masculine musk and fur, she'd known he was hers. But he didn't feel the same, as evidenced by his hasty withdrawal and ghost act.

Sigh.

So, eating out became her go to. Maybe she could catch him off guard, wear him down or something. Then maybe his beast would choose her as surely as hers had chosen him—*if only.*

Hell, she would go every single day if she thought it might help. But then he might catch on to her plan. Not that she had a plan, but she was working up to one. Ariella didn't want the man to assume the worst about her. Like the fact she was little better than a stalker.

Double sigh.

But what was she supposed to do? Ariella tried to forget about him by throwing herself into work, but every night when she lay alone in her bed, there he was, big and blond and larger than life, playing inside her brain like her own personal home movie.

Unfortunately, every attempt she'd made to discuss their possible fated mate status, or any relationship at all, had ended with a curt glare and him walking away. Sure, she hated to see him leave, but she loved watching him go. That boy filled out a pair of jeans better than she did.

It was getting old, though. The whole thing where she tried to talk, and he gave her dirty looks and ran away. Ariella hardly ever got a word out past his name. He was always growling and angry at her no matter what she did—and he never, ever listened!

Ugh.

Bad qualities for a mate. Really. And yet, he was everything she ever wanted. Ariella had even started doubting whether her Lioness was right about the whole fated mate thing. Maybe it was just a stupid crush. She had been guilty of that a time or two, but she never thought any of them were her one and only. Maybe it was just a stupid myth, like some Shifters believed.

Rrrrrawr.

Her she-Cat roared as she always did whenever Ariella doubted herself. Her feisty feline was spunky and honest in ways her human side still feared. Ariella readily embraced that side of herself, knowing full well the big kitty was a big ol' toughie on the outside and had a heart softer than a kitten's fur on the inside.

"How is everything tonight?" a passing server asked.

Her dinner date—*her baby brother George*—nodded politely, his brown eyes wide as he stared at the pretty young waitress. He was even worse than Ariella when it came to dating. Poor guy. But he was just so much fun to razz!

"Tell the chef it would be even better if he used higher quality fish," Ariella responded and smirked at the sudden paleness of her face.

No one wanted to confront Brock with a comment like that.

"She's kidding. It was great," George said, covering Ariella's mouth and nodding at the poor girl.

"Oh, that's funny. Ha ha," the server mumbled, walking away.

"What is wrong with you? You wanna get her fired?" George scolded.

"I was only teasing, but George, you know EWLP has better stock," she shrugged.

"I swear you are getting nuttier by the day, Ariella," her brother replied, heaving a sigh as he went back to his smart phone.

As the King's new personal assistant, George Golden had his hands full. What a stuffed shirt her brother was! Couldn't even relax for an evening meal. He was alright, for a boy, but she wished one of her sisters had been free this evening. Toni was busy with some spreadsheets, and Annabeth was busy spreading beneath the sheets with her new mate.

Hmmm. Maybe she should have gone the matchmaker route too? Oh well. Too late now. She already knew who her fated mate was. He just wasn't into her.

Sad prrrr.

"So, give me some Pride gossip, *Georgie Porgie,*" Ariella said, using the nickname he hated.

"You live in the Pride community, Ariella," he grumbled.

"Yeah, but I'm not inside the Palace, like you. What's going on with King Donovan and Mom, anyway?"

Donovan Crowley was King of the Blue Valley Pride. He'd been poisoned by his trusted valet for months before his son, the prince, Detective Leo Crowley, and his mate, Dire Wolf Shifter, Sheila Rand, discovered the matter and solved it promptly.

Ariella's mother, Patricia, was the king's late wife's best friend. She'd stayed inside the Palace after those horrible events to nurse King Donovan back to health. But something had happened, and she'd hightailed it out of there like her tail was on fire. Always up for a party, something was off with their mom lately, and that rat George knew about it, she was sure. Patricia was behaving wilder than usual.

"I am not privy to the King's private affairs, and even if I were, I would not discuss them with you," George replied, ignoring her.

Ariella snarled and pinched him beneath the table. Satisfied she hurt him enough after George yelped like a cub, Ariella's thoughts drifted back to Brock.

Again.

She was usually shy with men but being ignored had turned her into the aggressor. That was a new experience, for sure. Furthermore, it was not something she particularly liked.

Frowning, she thought about the past few months. Work was always a good outlet for amped up nerves, and she'd been killing it at *EWLP*. Ever since Brock Laurent had all but rejected her, she'd thrown herself into work.

Ariella had gone after every unclaimed account in the region to add to their client list. Her boss had even announced she had single-handedly made *Eat Well Live Proud* the biggest sustainably harvested seafood distributor in the area. It made sense since most of the other reps seemed to concentrate on their meat products to boost numbers. Fish was a tougher sell, but Ariella had grit and determination on her side.

She achieved her goals by securing entire bulk orders for many of the smaller, top quality, but lesser known high end food stores, restaurants, and catering businesses across Blue Valley, and the neighboring towns of Maccon City, Barvale, Northern, East Cove, Daniels' Bay, Maverick Point, and the little known town of Castor's Corner. Signing several small accounts at once was the same as landing any big hotel chain, and she was on the track to hunt down the regional manager of Stein Luxury Resorts—if she could only find out who he or she was!

Serious Moonlight was another hold out. Yes, they ordered most of their meat and had sampled fish from *EWLP*, but they'd yet to go exclusively with the feline firm. And that was what she was after—exclusivity.

Ariella still firmly believed small business was where she would get the most for her efforts. It was her unique one-on-one approach that had gotten her this far. Where most of the others in her department had four or five large clients, Ariella now had a hundred and seventy accounts up and down the East Coast, most in New Jersey.

She worked harder than anyone she knew, but that was okay. Ariella enjoyed the challenge and the claim that she now had the most accounts accrued in a single quarter. If she were lucky, she would also boast the most revenue earned out of all her Pride mates at the corporation once the quarter ended.

That particular contest was something of a big deal since the winner got an all-expense-paid-two-week-vacation to Moongate Island. The exclusive resorts located there had special suites catering to the supernatural crowd. Ariella had always wanted to go. In fact, their website had been bookmarked repeatedly. It was the one destination where she placed all her romantic fantasies.

Sigh.

The honeymoon of her dreams existed somewhere on that island. She'd been picturing it since she was a cub. Images of a big strong man who could handle her Lioness' curves and less than gracious exuberance with ease and diplomacy. A man who wanted and loved her. She used to imagine herself mated to a big Lion male, but lately it was a Dire Wolf haunting her dreams.

A tall, blond, sexy Dire Wolf Shifter, with a wicked grin and a body she couldn't wait to explore. A man who wanted her, appreciated her, and was willing to be equal partners in a mating that mattered. Someone who knew his way around the kitchen, who would hand feed her delicious island delicacies in between bouts of erotic lovemaking.

Yowza. Was it getting hot in here?

Ariella bit back her moan as naughty images of her and Brock sunbathing in the nude in a tropical paradise flashed through her brain. Okay, so it wasn't a G-rated fantasy, but it was hers, and she would not apologize for it.

Sigh.

Ariella had always imagined what would happen the day she found her mate. They'd meet, they'd kiss, and they'd live happily ever after. Okay, there was some stuff in between—like super sticky smexy fun times she was glossing over because a virgin could only imagine so much—still, that was generally how it was *supposed* to happen.

Only, it hadn't gone down like that. Not at all. Brock just didn't have the same *boom-you-are-mine* reaction she did when they met. And now, her Lioness was stuck on a male who did not want her.

Sad sad prrrrrr.

Not everyone believed in destiny, but Ari was a dreamer. She'd spent years waiting to lavish the never ending supply of love and affection she'd been saving up since forever on some lucky male. Her fated mate. Her one and only. And yep, that wasn't all she'd been saving.

Ariella was still technically untouched—as in virginal. She'd been waiting for her special someone to come along to initiate her into the carnal arts. Oh, Ari enjoyed sexy fun times as much as the next girl, but most boys were so fragile they could hardly take getting to third base with her. Lionesses were strong as fuck. So here she was, almost thirty-years old, and she'd never done the deed with an actual male.

All the vibrators and sexy toys in the world couldn't make up for how it would feel to be claimed by her one true mate. But the stuck-up, goody-two shoes, all about himself, Chef and Beta Wolf, Brock Laurent, didn't want her.

Pfbbbbtttt.

Joking aside, it hurt like hell that he didn't feel anything for her at all. Pain at the reminder shot through her, replacing the euphoric haze she'd been in after consuming every last bite of her appetizer.

Dang it.

She hated when that happened. Maybe Mom was right. Maybe all she needed was a one-way ticket to boinktown. Then she could forget the slap of Brock's rejection. But how was that going to happen when he was the only man who made her hot and bothered?

Mate, her inner kitty growled.

Ari rolled her eyes at her inner Lioness. The traitor. All the big she-Cat wanted to do was rub herself all over the six-and-a-half foot Wolf whom she idiotically worshipped and couldn't wait to sink her teeth into. It wasn't like she hadn't given him the opportunity to give her a good, long sniff or anything during that crazy bike ride. The man had taken off with her clinging to his back like a bat out of hell down the highway on his Harley Davidson FXSTB Night Train.

Yes, she had the name of his ride memorized after he'd nearly gone apeshit when she'd referred to it as merely a bike. Okay. She was exaggerating—something Ariella did often. Brock hadn't exactly gone nuts, he'd just growled, and sniffed like she'd passed something decidedly unladylike on his precious Harley.

Whatevah.

He could just take his snobbish, standoffish behavior and stick it where the sun never shined! She couldn't abide folks who thought they were better than everyone else and judging from his attitude, that was Brock Laurent to a T.

But what did he have that she didn't besides the obvious? And wasn't that what they were supposed to have to, *er*, get a move on with things?

"Hey, what happened to your highlights?" George interrupted her train of thought.

"My hair?" she asked, bunching up her dark curls.

"Yeah. I thought you were bleaching and straightening these days," he muttered, taking a sip of his club soda.

Pussy.

"I only did that to try to blend in with Cousin Margaret for her wedding party. Those haughty beyotches always give me shit cause my hair is dark, but I decided to go back to my natural brown. Why, does it look bad?"

"No. It looks fine," George replied noncommittally. "But are you sure you aren't trying to tempt a certain Dire Wolf Shifter to glance your way? I heard Brock mention disliking fake things last time we were here," he murmured, still looking at his phone.

Ariella growled deep in her throat. George was such a fucker. He always pretended not to notice shit and then he spilled things like that. Whatever the reason she'd stopped dying her hair, it didn't matter. Ariella and Brock Laurent were at a stalemate.

"I'm over him," Ariella told her brother with feigned nonchalance.

"Are you? I thought you said he was your fated mate?"

"Yeah. I mean, I might have been wrong about that."

Like dead wrong. Her heart squeezed painfully in her chest, but that didn't change facts. Ari had to stop wasting her life and stressing over the man.

"So, what now?"

"Well, mom always says a good backscratching could solve a lot. Maybe I need a date!"

"Ariella, what are you on about?"

"Of course, that's just another euphemism for sex, George. I mean, I don't want to be an old maid. Is that still a saying?"

"What?!"

"Sex, George. I'm talking about getting laid. I need D-I-C-K."

"What the hell, Ari?! Oh my God! I do not want to have this conversation with my sister and especially not in public," George hissed, looking around like someone overheard us.

"Come on, George. Don't you have friends? Call some of them up to meet us here. Be my wingman!"

"You have lost your mind," he muttered, shaking his head.

"Mom says I have fantastic assets, which she attributes to herself, of course, but she said I could have my pick of men if I just get out there. Come on, help a girl out," she begged.

"I can't believe this. Ariella Golden, you are ruining my dinner," he grumbled.

Ari snorted with laughter. She was only half-kidding, but it was worth it just to see Georgie Porgie sweat a little. And for the record, she wasn't conceited, but she was pretty, even if she had curves on her curves.

Along with plenty of T and A, she had long legs and flawless skin, sparkling amber-colored eyes that glowed gold with her Lioness, and an awesome sense of humor, if she did say so herself. She had plenty to offer the right male.

"Want dessert after we get our entrees?" George asked, frowning at the menu.

Her brother was always hungry, and he often ate like a damn pig, but he never gained an ounce. Lucky fucker. He straightened his tie as he glared at the dance floor. There was some kind of ruckus going on, and Ariella smirked. Prim and proper was her baby bro.

Total dork.

And yet she was the last virgin standing in their family. Sometimes, life was just utterly unfair.

Grrrr.

CHAPTER THREE

DIRE WOLF MATES

"Seriously, Ari, you gonna split the tomahawk steak with me?" he asked.

"No, you ate almost all of it last time, and I was starving."

"You don't look like you're starving," he muttered, and she kicked him under the table.

The band was on break, and someone put a loud dance song on. Ariella didn't mind, but she knew George hated just about anything other than rock music. She grinned and shook her head, bopping to the beat.

"Get your own dinner, dork face," she replied.

"Fine."

The server returned for their entrée orders, and Ariella tried to appear nonchalant about the whole thing. She wondered if Brock was even in the kitchen tonight. So far, she hadn't seen hide nor hair of the blond giant. George was rambling on about something, but she was too busy wallowing in self misery to pay any attention.

Stop it.

"Hello? Earth to Ari. I am talking to you. Why are we here?"

"You're the one who followed me, *Georgie Porgie,*" she swallowed down another mouthful of the sumptuous white wine she'd ordered with her appetizer.

"I told you I had to drop off some legal forms to Leo, and Sheila is always my best chance of pinning that man down. You know how he is."

"Yes, Georgie, I know," she replied and bit back her laughter at her brother's annoyed expression.

It was always fun teasing her baby bro. Ari sighed and pushed her now empty plate towards the center of the table. The appetizer had been sublime. She might be pissed at Brock, but he was one hell of a chef. She continued to think so as the next course was served.

"Gimme a bite," George whined, sticking his fork in her swordfish steak.

"There's three pounds of Argentinian beef on your plate, George, hands off my fish," she snapped at him.

Seafood was her weakness, and nothing was better than a perfectly fried Atlantic cod. The dish was almost perfect. Only one thing could make it better. Some of that good quality sustainably harvested seafood that only Eat Well Live Proud could deliver.

If only she could convince him to switch all his fish to their new eco-friendly seafood line. It was of a much better grade than what he was serving now, and this was good stuff. But she was certain she could do better for Brock, *er*, that was, for the restaurant. Not the man. He was not hers to do anything for. Or to.

Gulp.

What?

"I bet this place could take number one in *Blue Valley Monthly's* Top Ten Eateries," George said, and he wasn't wrong.

The list was posted every month like clockwork in print and on the monthly magazine's website. Who didn't want that kind of free advertising? She shook her head and took another sip of wine, emptying the glass as she contemplated the problem.

Her own palate was highly developed and where she appreciated the seasoning and superb technique Brock used to create his dishes, the fact was this was not the best seafood available, and really, why shouldn't it be?

Taste buds still tingling with delight, Ari eyed her brother's food and, just because she could, she reached over and snagged George's still untouched side dish. She scooted it a bit closer to her side of the table, scooping the delicious creamed spinach into her mouth and moaning triumphantly at the wonderful texture and flavors.

George simply rolled his eyes and pushed it all the way in front of her.

"Go ahead, Ari. I told you, I didn't want the creamed spinach when you ordered it," he grumbled.

Ariella didn't want to overdo it, but one more bite wouldn't hurt. The creamy goodness had a hint of lemon zest on top. So good, it actually made her forget it was an actual vegetable dish.

"Well, thanks for inviting me, sis. But next time, maybe we do lunch instead," George frowned as the band came back on stage. They were tuning their instruments, and the lead singer started getting the audience hyped up with some banter.

Ariella looked on and grinned. Things were gonna be fun tonight. She could already feel it sizzling in the air, like magic.

"I mean, Brock is a talented chef, but this place is so, so—"

"Fun?" she supplied and giggled at her stick-in-the-mud sibling's expense. "Georgie, you need to let your hair down."

He wasn't the only one. Her inner Lioness purred happily, and she patted her now full tummy with a smile on her lips. It was a fact, her would-be mate was a genius.

"Oh crap! Ari, we should go now. Mom is here," George was half turned in his chair and squinting at where a loud ruckus sounded out from across the bar.

Sure enough, Patricia Golden, their own mother, with her silver streaked hair and a pair of pleather pants that should be deemed illegal painted on her butt, was the cause of it.

It was eight o'clock on a Saturday night, and the band was just right, playing the kind of rock and roll music that made you want to dance and fuck and fight maybe all at the same time to the already hyped up crowd. New Jersey was a wonderful melting pot of human and supernatural cultures, and *Serious Moonlight* attracted them all.

Of course. It made perfect sense. Why wouldn't their mother be in the middle of all this? Ariella grinned in her mother's direction.

"I know," she answered George. "I invited her."

Ariella laughed when her brother groaned and held his head as if it was the worst thing in the world to happen. She had three older sisters, and one baby bro, but out of all of them, Ariella was the only one who thought of their mother as her BFF.

Their mom could be quite the handful. Of course, her recent flirtation with the Lion King of their Pride had started several rumors that the two were about to get hitched. But far as Ariella knew, the older, but still hot, Lioness was decidedly ringless.

Good thing, or not? The jury was still out on that one.

Hence, the reason she'd joined her daughter and son for a couple of rounds of tequila shots, and some good old fashioned hell raising, like only those of the Big Cat persuasion could really appreciate. Ari was just depressed enough to want that kind of trouble. After all, things were going nowhere and fast with Brock.

She stood up and looked at her brother with narrowed eyes. It was the kind of look she'd given him as a cub just before she'd pinned his ass to the floor.

"What?" he asked.

Increasing the power of her stare, she almost gave the game away by grinning when he squeaked. Georgie never could best her in that game. Getting the message, he reached for his wallet and dropped two bills on the table.

Having practically licked her plate clean, she purposely left half of George's on the plain white ceramic dish. Brock might be able to ignore her, but if there was one thing that really miffed the big buff doggy, it was when someone didn't finish their food.

Well, tough furballs!

She walked away from the table and left her baby bro to follow, joining their mother with a quick hug and kiss.

"Hey kids! Mama's on a roll," she hooted and pointed to the row of lovely golden shots waiting for them.

The fabulously redheaded Sheila Rand-Crowley smirked as she set a shaker of salt and some sliced limes next to the little shot glasses all lined up like soldiers going off to battle. Ariella supposed they were in a way.

"Hello ladies, and George," Sheila greeted them with a wink.

Ari nodded back. She liked their new princess. A lot. Sheila might be a Dire Wolf Shifter, but she'd married the crowned prince of the Lion Pride and was now officially one of her kin seeing as how Ari was Leo's honorary cousin and all.

"Um, Mom, I don't think—"

"Don't think, Georgie, just have a shot," Patricia Golden said and pressed the small glass against her youngest cub's lips until he had no choice but to swallow the fiery liquid.

Typically, alcohol had little to no effect on Shifters unless—and that was a big UNLESS—it was taken in rapid succession or mixed with one of the handful of herbs whose chemical makeup would render the Shifter's naturally enhanced metabolism nil.

Like *Magibrew*—which was recently banned from this establishment. There were other things that could behave in a similar fashion. Highly concentrated catnip drops could produce the same effect. They were sometimes used to help Lionesses and other feline Shifters during labor, to ease the birthing of one or several cubs. She'd made her mother promise never to trick her into taking that stuff again, so she was not worried.

A mistake, Ariella realized after she swallowed down her first shot, and noted a very familiar and very distinct bitter flavor. Dang it all to heck, it was catnip!

Having been dosed a time or two by her mother and sisters over the years, Ariella knew her stuff. Never George, though. Her baby bro was too much of a stick in the mud for those kinds of shenanigans.

Fucking hell.

The herb was fast-acting when concentrated like this, and her mother would have gotten some very hard to find, medical grade stuff. Her inner Lioness' eyes dilated, and Ariella felt as if her blood was boiling. Confound it, that woman did it again! Her mother had played her.

And here of all the places! She had only minutes before she could become completely uninhibited. And who knew what would happen then? Ariella closed her eyes and turned to confront the woman who'd given birth to her.

"Mom! Did you put catnip in my shot?"

Ariella stomped her foot for affect but her mother waved a manicured hand in her face and made shushing noises.

"Shush up, baby, the band is playing!"

She should have suspected when she'd told her mother the trouble she'd been having with Brock that the woman would resort to some sort of wild extremes to help Ari get his attention.

Prrrr. Good Mama.

Shut up!

She shook her head, trying to ignore her feline and tried to think back to what she'd said to make Patricia lose her dang mind. Ugh. It must have been when she'd confessed to her mother, she suspected Brock was her fated mate. But in her defense, she only expected the woman to just give her some motherly advice or bake cookies or something. She should've known better.

Sigh.

Her mom used to pull stunts like this all the time, but after months of dating King Donovan, Ari thought she'd settled down. Something must've happened between them. Rumors of weddings aside, there must be a reason her mother was acting this way. Ariella's eyes flashed at the woman, who was gyrating like mad in her pleather pants.

My eyes!

"I am not done talkin' to you, Mom. And for fuck's sake, stop doing that before you bust a seam again!"

"I don't mind givin' them a show, baby girl. If they can't stand the heat, they know what to do!"

Patricia winked and sashayed away, leaving Ariella to follow. A wave of dizziness hit her, and Ari closed her eyes as the effects of the catnip dosed alcohol made themselves known. Not that she was normally a tight ass. Well, not exactly, but Ariella had been working harder than ever lately. Probably had something to do with the fact her mate didn't want her. Just thinking about it made her sad beyond measure, and sad was not how she wanted to feel.

Dance, purred her she-Cat.

The suggestion sounded good to her. She'd often envied normals their ability to have a drink and simply unwind. The problem with her was her pesky supernatural ability to metabolize alcohol. Heck, she'd need a few bottles to even get a buzz.

Catnip laced booze fixed that. Ariella grinned. She had some liquid courage in her now. Heck yeah, she should dance. Sure, her mom's way of bonding with her cubs was unorthodox, but it was fun, and mostly harmless.

Ariella's limbs felt loose as she brought her hands to her face. She let her cool fingers brush the warm skin of her cheeks and neck, tying back her mane of curly dark hair. She was feeling warmer by the second.

Ari searched the room with half-lidded eyes, head bobbing to the music. Maybe she should embrace this new, uninhibited feeling as a gift from her mother. Yeah. She could do that. Have a little harmless fun, right? After all, she was an unattached female, and she was not getting any younger.

"You feeling alright, Ari?" Sheila interrupted her thoughts.

Ari turned to her cousin-in-law, noting the red eyebrows that seemed to disappear into her hairline as Ariella wobbled a little on her feet.

Oopsies.

CHAPTER FOUR

DIRE WOLF MATES

The bass was thumping, and the guitar sounded amazing. Serious Moonlight always had the best bands, she thought and shimmied where she stood. Ariella really liked this song. Not usually a dancer, she could hardly keep her hips from moving.

"Ari, did your mother put something in your drink?" Sheila whisper-screamed, leaning over the bar.

"Ow, Sheila my ears! Don't worry about it. My mom is always putting something' in my drink," Ari replied, and giggled.

Wow. She never giggled. Mom must have gotten a higher concentration than she'd had the last time she'd dosed Ari. That was on her spring break eight years ago in Florida.

Ariella had been dumped by her boyfriend the second they'd gotten to their hotel for a skinny Fox Shifter in a two-piece. Miserable and embarrassed, she'd called home and her mom was there within three hours. She'd crashed Ari's vacay, but in a good way.

The week-long festivities had ended with only a couple of tickets and a fine for indecent exposure after she and her mother had been caught lounging naked in the fountain outside of the Miami Grand Hotel.

"Should I call someone for you?" Sheila asked.

"Nah! I'll be *fiiiiiine*."

Ari nodded her heavy head and stretched her arms wide, spinning in a circle. The only way to get the catnip out of her system was to sweat it out. Simply nothing else to be done, so she might as well enjoy it.

The effects would wear off soon—about twelve hours, judging from last time. And like the last time, hopefully, Ariella's clothes wouldn't be staying on tonight either. Staying a virgin was just not appealing at the moment.

"I got it!" Ari said aloud with a wicked grin plastered on her face.

"You got what, honey?" Sheila asked.

"The solution to all my problems!"

"Oh, fuck" the she-Wolf grumbled.

But Ari was not going to let her bring her down. She knew what she had to do to get out of this rut she seemed stuck in. Ari was going to lose her virginity to some lucky guy, and afterward, she would use her newly acquired seductive wiles and smexy time skills to find a mate despite Brock Laurent!

"Ariella, please tell me what is going on in that head of yours," Sheila said, taking hold of Ari's hand.

"I got it all figured out, cuz. No more rejected mate blues for me. I know what I'm gonna do," Ariella told her.

She squeezed the woman's hand and smiled like the cat who ate the canary. Her plan was a little foggy, but Ari blamed that on her catnip and tequila soaked brain. It would all come together. It had to.

Her mother, who upon closer observation turned out to be wearing a pair of practically painted-on leopard-spotted pleather pants—a sort of irony if you will, being everyone knew Lionesses were better than Leopards any day—was currently shaking and grinding between two enormously buff strangers.

"Mom!" she yelled, but Patricia waved her away.

For an older woman, Patricia Golden sure knew how to get her groove on. She was her hero and Ariella knew she was lucky to have Patty as a mom. The older feline would know just how to help Ariella lose her maidenhead.

Then maybe she could forget all about men who didn't want their mates.

"Earth to Ariella. Hey, talk to me, honey. What are you talking about?"

Sheila seemed to be speaking rather slowly, but Ari just winked at her. Silly she-Wolf. So lucky to have her mate. She just did not understand Ariella's predicament. Grabbing the bottle of tequila from the bar, Ari chugged the last of it.

"You are sweet to worry about me, Sheila, but I got a plan. I'm gonna lose my virginity tonight," she said.

"What did you say?" Sheila shook her head and pointed to her ears.

Dang it. Her friend couldn't hear her above the noise.

"I said," Ariella yelled loudly—*and wouldn't you know it, the band stopped playing that exact moment.* "I'm going to lose my virginity tonight!"

She looked around and laughed loudly as the rowdy group of bar goers applauded and cheered her on. Giggling at their encouragement, she took off to join her mother on the dance floor.

"You go, girl!"

"I can help with that."

"Virginity is overrated!"

"I'd tap that!"

"Hey, knock it off!" Sheila yelled at the customers still waiting for their drinks.

"I can fix your problem, baby," one of the strangers said, and Ariella giggled.

He wasn't even unpleasant looking. Maybe finding a sex partner wouldn't be as difficult as she thought.

"Back off, buddy, or you are out of here! Shit. Ariella, don't you move," Sheila ordered and grabbed her cell phone from behind the bar, but Ari was already walking away.

She felt too good and loose for any yelling and nonsense. Ari didn't want to do anything but have a good time. What was so wrong with that?

The music was loud and sounded like a carnival ride. Between the band and the lights, and the catnip of course, Ariella felt young and pretty and alive for the first time in a long while. The crowd was bouncing up and down joyously and she joined them, clapping her hands and shaking her booty for all she was worth.

"Hey, baby girl. You look great," her mother yelled.

"Thanks, Mom. I feel pretty great," she yelled back.

"That's good, honey. I got that *'nip* from a new guy. It's supposed to be extra potent," her mother informed her with a winked.

"Mama, I think I want to lose my virginity tonight," Ariella yelled into her mother's ear while keeping up with the bopping and swaying.

"Okay, honey, but be careful," her mother said.

Patricia Golden pinched her daughter's cheek, then turned around to dance with a very tall and thin older man with an Aussie accent. One sniff and Ari was sure he had to be an Ostrich Shifter. Again, thoughts of their Pride leader plagued her, but that was her mom's affair, not hers. She'd learned early to stay out of her mother's love life.

Ariella hated to admit it, but this was the best she had felt in weeks. Not something she expected after meeting her fated mate. But then again, nothing had gone as planned since she laid eyes on Brock Laurent. All her childhood fantasies of happy-ever-after's had been tossed to the wind the second he walked away from her.

Bastard never even looked back.

That was it. She was done. She'd tried everything she knew to get him to acknowledge what they were to each other, short of tattooing the words *claim me already* on her forehead—or as her brother George insisted, Ariella was rocking a solid a fivehead—five fingers fit on her forehead. Gods, she hated her brother sometimes.

Jerk.

Sniff.

Whatever. If her forehead was big, it was because she was a smarty pants. That's what Mom always said in her defense. Anyway, back to that dang dog boy. NO matter what she did, Brock still stubbornly refused to accept she was made for him. It was both insulting and infuriating.

What was so bad about her, anyway? What was so horrible that he didn't want her?

Ariella wasn't ugly. Heck, she was downright cute, even if she wasn't blonde, regardless of what her snooty cousins said. She'd spent the last few months alternating between lust and anger for the hunky Dire Wolf. But no more. She decided tonight was her night and it was time to check out her options.

Like the big, *sniff* , Bison Shifter, who'd sided up to her during the band's lively cover of *Paradise City*. Ariella always was a *Guns N' Roses* fan. If she squinted hard, the stranger kinda looked like Slash.

They jumped and swayed, clapped, and sang along until the stranger felt secure enough to lean down and whisper in her ear. He smelled a little like hay, but that was alright, she supposed.

"Hey, baby, how about we get out of here?" he grunted against her ear, and his beard kind of tickled her skin.

"Well, I was planning on losing my virginity tonight. I'm interviewing for the position, you interested?"

"Hell yeah. I can help with that, baby," he returned, and she smiled at him through a haze of tequila and catnip.

His hair was curlier than hers, she thought giddily and nodded her head. Sounded like a plan. She could finally have sex, just to see what the fuss was about, then she could walk away.

Isn't that what men did? No strings sex?

Yep, that was a damn fine idea. She looked at the big man and frowned. He seemed even bigger than before.

"Hey," she said, swaying slightly. "Are you getting taller or am I shrinking?"

"Aghhh!" the Bison Shifter yelped.

Before Ariella could utter a response, she noticed a pair of big hands gripping the Bison by his wide shoulders. Suddenly, the man was flying through the air.

"Hey! We didn't even get busy yet?" she growled, disappointed.

Next thing she knew, Ari was staring into the steely blue eyes of the one man she'd just given up on. Her heart pounded, and she felt both bitterly disappointed and confused when she looked at the outrageously handsome Dire Wolf.

"Ariella," he growled her name, and she seemed to sober up for a split second as every inch of her went on high alert—*like it always did around him.*

Brock was the only man in the whole world who could make her Lioness purr like a kitten. Damn him.

"Geez, Brock," she shouted and stomped her booted feet. "I was gonna have sex with him!"

"The hell you were," he growled, and she wanted to roar her outrage.

Stupid pussy-blocking, butt-sniffing, asshat!

"Ooh, you make me so mad," she stomped her foot one more time and narrowed her eyes at the snooty Wolf.

"Ariella, I am warning you—"

"Oh, are *you* warning *me*? You know what? You can just *eat my fur*!"

Even as she yelled the old childhood taunt, the same one she and her siblings used to taunt each other, her inner, perverted she-Cat had another type of eating in mind instantaneously.

Traitor, she scolded her feline, but it was no good.

Brock crowded her personal space, and before she knew it, his face was directly in front of hers. She breathed in his forest fresh scent, and damn if she didn't feel even more intoxicated from that one good whiff of him.

"Why do you always smell so good?" she asked, but did he answer?

Of course not. Ariella huffed out a breath and turned to walk away when he stopped her with a hand on her arm.

"Mine," Brock growled so softly she almost missed it.

Ariella blinked up at him in sheer surprise at the possessive one-syllable word. Next, he scooped her up in his big, strong arms and walked out of the bar with her. Where he was going, she didn't know, but oh, could she hope.

Yes, please. Prrrrrr.

CHAPTER FIVE

DIRE WOLF MATES

"I *was gonna have sex with him—"*

That damn sentence was on repeat inside his head. Anger, rage, and a certain green-eyed monster sat on his shoulder, egging him on as Brock carried the squirming female outside, through the woods, and to the small stream that ran across the property in back of the Dire Wolf Pack house.

Ever since he'd met the woman, he hadn't been able to think straight. Right then, he could hardly see two feet in front of him. His Wolf was snarling and snapping at the image of that fucking asshole. Fucking Bison Shifter. He obviously wanted to go home missing a hoof or two for touching his Ariella.

My Ariella? No. She's not mine.

Yes, she is, his beast argued.

Fuck. Brock was shaking with emotion. No, he hadn't claimed her, but that didn't make his Wolf any less possessive about the little wildcat.

Okay, fine. He was an asshole. He'd freely admit it, but there was a reason he hadn't rushed into things with the woman. But yeah, he was a prick for keeping that reason to himself.

Maybe it was time they had a serious discussion. Of course, not now. Not when she was three sheets to the wind and probably wouldn't remember half of what they said. Brock would have laughed if there was any chance she wouldn't get even more pissed off at him.

As it was, the normally sweet and shy Ariella was busy punching, kicking, and cursing him out. She wasn't hurting him, but damn, the woman had some wiggle to her. Brock was trying his damndest not to drop her on her fine ass.

Grrrrr.

He hadn't needed Sheila's text to tell him there was trouble. Between Phoenix and his own senses, he'd anticipated it before it happened. Of course, he did not know she would proclaim her virginity so spectacularly.

Saturday night and the place had been crowded as all get out when she'd made her announcement. His head snapped to the side, and he thought he heard something in the woods. This part of their property was private, but that didn't mean the odd patron didn't try sneaking around back there despite their security measures.

A virgin. Fuck.

He'd known it, but that wasn't the same as having her shout it. It seemed tattooed inside his brain. Maybe not tattooed. Maybe more like a neon sign flashing on and off with the word virgin in bold letters.

Ariella was a virgin.

Mine. Claim. Now.

Fucking hell.

A part of him felt even more ferociously possessive of her now. Unfortunately, so did half the fucking bar. If there was one thing Shifter males coveted, it was claiming a virgin bride. Don't ask why. Fucking Neanderthals, the lot of them. Apparently, he was no different. Once he'd thought those words, they got stuck in his brain.

Virgin bride. My virgin mate.

A picture of Ariella decked out in a white gown made of silk and lace flashed through his mind and his Wolf growled appreciatively. She'd be a beautiful bride. His beautiful bride.

No.

Grrr.

"Stop squirming or we are both gonna wind up on the ground," he chided as he stepped over a mound of fallen leaves.

"Brock! You put me down right now," she yelled and wiggled, but he only held her tighter.

Having his arms full of the voluptuous, sweet smelling, tempting as hell she-Cat might have been hell on his nerves, but damn, it was sweet to hold her. It was all he could do not to turn his head and give her a love bite on her plump cheek.

Her musky scent invaded his nostrils, and Brock was drowning in it. He would give anything to taste her. To memorize every nuance of her unique flavor. Putting one foot in front of the other was a chore. She made him lose all focus and reason.

Finally, he got them to the grassy shore of the creek. Brock hoisted her princess style into his arms, and Ariella's large amber eyes appeared confused. She yelped and clutched at his shoulders.

"You'll drop me," she hissed, and he raised one eyebrow and growled his reply.

Silly she-Cat, he could more than handle her weight. The thing that was driving him crazy was her scent, and the fact her chest was heaving. Even through the loose sweater she wore, he could make out the swell of what he knew were perfect breasts.

Sexy sexy woman.

She was full and round as a woman should be. More than enough to make his mouth water. It might be poor timing, but fuck it. Brock dropped a hard kiss on her open mouth and watched her eyes flash with heat just before they opened wide as she realized his intentions.

"Hold your nose, kitten," he growled and tossed her into the icy water before she could reply.

Little hellcat needed to sober up before he told her what he had in mind for the two of them. Of course, he had no idea if a dunk in the creek could freeze the catnip out of her. He was going to have to chat with her mother, and soon. Having been told of the older Lioness' hijinks by both Phoenix and Sheila, the latter of whom had called him minutes ago with the news that his would-be-mate had just announced her intention to lose her virginity to the entire bar. Thank fuck Brock had already been on his way inside.

He'd almost swallowed his tongue when he'd heard that little blip of information. That she was pristine and untouched in this day and age somehow resonated with his primordial beast.

Caveman much?

Fuck yes.

His Dire Wolf was prehistoric in more ways than one. He wouldn't apologize for it. Brock never claimed to be anything other than what he was. Imperfect and wholly unrepentant. It was just another reason for his whole *hands off* approach to Ariella.

He'd seen the half-eaten plate of food she'd left on her table. The waitress had almost peed herself at having to tell him what she said. Little minx. Brock wasn't conceited, but he knew there were two things in life he did very well. One was ride. The other was cook. If Ariella didn't finish a meal he'd prepared, it was a message. One he would ponder another time. He was currently busy making sure she was staying afloat in the creek.

"You sober yet?" he asked.

"Dammit!" she sputtered and struggled to keep her head above the surface.

Ariella could typically swim like a fish—*yes, he knew that from spying on her.* But she was having a hard time now. He frowned. She must've been more affected by the catnip than he'd previously thought.

"Ariella, you, okay?" he asked as she spit out some of the water she'd swallowed back into the stream.

"No! I'm freezing and I'm all tangled in my skirt. Brock, get me out of here," she wailed.

"You can do it. Come on, swim to the side. Well, put a little effort into it," he chided, uncertain whether the little minx was angling for a way to splash him.

"My clothes are dragging me down," she gasped and went back under.

Hell, he should've considered that seeing as how it was early Spring and she'd been wearing a long flowy skirt with leather boots and a creamy white sweater that left one shoulder deliciously bare.

Fine. Yes, he paid attention to her. Any detail he could take in, study, agonize over late at night. His Wolf was snarling at him to hurry up and dive in, but he hesitated. She was a Shifter and should have had no problem staying afloat.

"Stop playing around, Ariella," he frowned and waited a beat.

Shit.

This wasn't good. When she didn't come immediately back up, Brock panicked. His Wolf snarled and snapped, and he cursed soundly before jumping in clothes and all.

"Ari?" he yelled and dove beneath the chilly water, searching for her among the tall grass and rocks.

It was dark and murky, and he couldn't see shit, never mind the fact his sense of smell did not work in water. His Wolf was agitated, furious at him, and he was more than happy to let the beast chew him out, but not yet. Not till after he found her. He breached the surface to suck in more air before preparing to dive back under.

Of course, he should've known better than to panic. The sassy little minx was waiting for him behind one of the larger boulders that sat at the bottom of the creek. She must have great lungs, he mused after Ariella snagged his foot and pulled him down.

"Yip," he squeaked—*to his Wolf's unending shame,* Going under and swallowing a mouthful of creek water.

She was a Lioness, so he should have known she was strong. But damn, Ariella was really *really* strong. More than he'd imagined she would be. She held him under easily, causing his chest to burn, but in a good way.

The game was officially on.

They wrestled under the water playfully. She got him good a few times, but Brock soon got the advantage and made it to the surface with her in tow. He sucked in the cool, fresh air greedily, watching Ariella's pretty pink-cheeked face as she did the same.

"Have you had enough?" he asked.

"Not on your life," she growled, just before tackling him once more.

Brock barked out a laugh as he caught the wily and surprisingly sporty woman. He was stunned at the vigorous rough play and the fact that she was so at ease with him after months of her shyly watching him with those killer amber eyes and deliciously pouty mouth.

Ariella was using her Shifter's natural agility and strength against him. Shocked and full of admiration, he damn near had his ass handed to him in this unexpected bout of underwater wrestling. He could hardly believe it.

What Shifter male could resist a bit of frolicking with a sexy female? This luscious little tidbit had been haunting his dreams ever since he'd met her.

"I thought you were afraid of me," he growled when she landed on his back and tried to pull him under.

"Afraid of a big ol' puppy dog? Never! I eat dogs for breakfast," she snarled and snapped her impressive teeth.

So, she thought she could get the best of him, did she? After vying for dominance, he finally overwhelmed her with a tickle pinch combination that had her yowling and calling mercy.

"You give?" he asked, wrapping his arms around her waist, and pulling her tempting body as close as he dared.

She was so small compared to him. Positively tiny. Fragile even.

Brock worried for a moment that he'd been too rough, but there she was, smiling up at him like a naughty little siren. He never would have guessed she would hide in the cool water, dragging him under for some aquatic rough housing.

He was surprised and, for the first time in a while, Brock had fun.

It had been a long time since he could say that for real. She looked beautiful with her hair all wet, floating around her shoulders.

Of course, if he could ignore the throbbing boner in his soaked chef's pants, that was all this would be—*harmless fun.*

But it was more than that. Everything about her was enticing from the rivulets of water that rolled down her cheek, to her neck, and down her chest to disappear somewhere in her generous cleavage.

Damn, that drop of water had the life!

He wanted to follow its path with his mouth and tongue. Brock wanted her. The strength of his desire gave him pause, but she didn't seem to mind it. Not even when she brushed up against that part of him, he was certain would terrify the sweet little innocent.

Surely, if she was afraid of someone his size, she would've jumped or distanced herself, but not Ariella. She kept her hands on his shoulders and her body close to his even as he treaded water with her in his arms. Thank goodness they were in the shallower end of the stream.

"Okay, I give," she said and laughed. "But just for a minute. I need to catch my breath."

Her eyes sparkled with mischief, and she laid her head down on Brock's shoulder, allowing him to hug her even closer. The contact was shocking, as it was novel. Her body was warm despite the water. This was as close as he'd ever been to Ariella except for when she'd ridden on his Harley. They played under the cold water until his lungs felt like they were going to burst, and he frowned. She must be tired. That and the catnip were why she snuggled closer.

Tell yourself that, his Wolf grunted.

Fuck.

She was going to be the death of him. He exhaled slowly, and Ariella simply sighed in contentment. During their games, she had flung off her sweater and had been tormenting him with hints of her lacy bra and pale skin as she played in and out of the water. She sat up, and he accommodated her with both his hands cupping her sweet ass. Ariella wrapped her legs around his waist, and her lace-covered breasts were pressed against his unfortunately still-covered chest.

"I got you good, didn't I?" she said breathlessly, laughing as her dark hair clung to her scalp.

Her cheeks were pink from either the cold or the exertion. Or maybe from the effects of the catnip and booze. Either way, between that and the way her mascara was slightly smudged, making her thick lashes stick together, the feline looked positively adorable.

Pretty pussy cat. Tempting. Perfect. Ours.

In truth, he had never seen a woman look more beautiful. He felt his Wolf peek through his eyes and knew what the animal wanted, but Brock forced the beast down. He had to resist her, even though she was clinging sweetly to his shoulders so closely that her warm breath tickled his earlobe.

"I haven't had this much fun since the fourth of July when Mom put magicked sparklers in everyone's drinks at the Pride's annual barbecue."

"What happened?" he asked, curious about her, wanting to know more.

Fuck, he was pathetic. Brock should know better. He should stay away. But he was greedy for any snippet of information he could glean about her life.

"Well, Mama has always been a joker. So, at one o'clock in the morning, every single sparkler she'd given out went off—and with a bang, at that! There were tiny fires everywhere. Half the Lion Shifters who came to the event, especially the ones who were stupid enough to wear too much hairspray, went home soaking wet after their fires had been put out, with hats and scarves wrapped around their heads, and scowls on their faces. My cousin Layla's beauty salon was booked solid for a month, and she had to special order hair extensions from overseas after buying out every supply store in the states," Ariella told him, laughing out loud the entire time she told the story.

The sound of her joy was intoxicating, contagious even. But it was more than that. Her voice, her enthusiasm, and her general openness were just plain refreshing. Like a pinch of bright lemon zest, the kind he sometimes added to brighten up recipes.

That was his Ariella to a T. She was his own personal *pinch of sass.* Changing his point of view, shaking things up, and making him stop and smell the roses.

How many years had he spent alone? Always riding on the open road with his Pack with no end in sight. How many lonely miles sat between him and a conversation such as this one?

Fuck. Be honest, his Wolf snapped.

He'd never had a conversation like this one. She blinked up at him, mouth slightly open in a half smile as she waited for some reaction from him. That was his cue and, to his surprise, he found himself wanting to talk with her.

"Interesting party," he answered and almost moaned aloud when her spicy, musky scent filled his nostrils and his lungs.

She smelled divine and if he was a wagering Wolf, he'd bet on her tasting even better. As a chef, Brock knew when he was choosing ingredients which were best by scent alone, and Ariella was the best of everything he'd ever come across.

There was nothing false or overly sweet about her. No cloying perfume or globs of face paint hiding her from him. Ariella was natural and unblemished, superb in her raw beauty, and he wanted more of it. More of her. Like the finest spices and top shelf herbs, she was rare and unique.

Mine.

He'd been fighting a losing battle. Insects chirping, the sounds of flowing water, and the steady night breeze made a symphony around them, but all he could hear was his and Ariella's hearts beating in time. His Dire Wolf pushed him for more, but he held steady.

Once upon a time, young Brock had thought himself in love and the rejection was still sharp in his mind. But was he doomed to live in the past forever? Brock shook his head, and grabbing his nerve, he leaned down and brushed her lips with his.

He might be unsure of Ariella's reaction to him in bed, to the reception he would get from a virgin, but he was downright cocky about his ability to kiss her mindless. So he did.

Ariella moaned gently and opened for his invasion while he kicked his feet to keep them afloat.

"Oh, Brock," she moaned as his lips traveled from her mouth to her cheek and her neck.

"Ariella," he ground out against her skin and held her tighter.

This was it. His big moment.

Brock was going to tell her, to confront her—no, to confess to her that *yes*, he was aware of what they were to each other. A knot formed in his stomach, and his heart threatened to beat him to death. He had to tell her why he'd been denying them and delaying the inevitable.

Do it now.

"Ariella, I need to talk to you," he began and tried to fight the gnawing fear that had built up to incredible proportions suddenly. "Ari?"

Turned out Brock had zero reason to worry. Expelling a deep, calming breath, he narrowed his eyes as his burden grew unexpectedly limp in the cool water.

Since when was his hellcat a plaint, submissive female? One look down told him all he needed to know about her unusual complacency.

His golden goddess, his little hellcat, his sweet, lovely, and virginal Ariella had passed out on him.

Grrrrrrrr.

CHAPTER SIX

DIRE WOLF MATES

"I never want to drink again!" Patricia Golden groaned and held on to the wall as she stumbled forward.

Her short velvet robe and oversized bunny slippers were horrifying, but Ariella was grateful for them. Last time her mother had crashed her apartment, she had walked around the next day in the nude on account of losing her clothes somewhere between the bar and home.

Yikes.

She was still having nightmares. She shivered at the memory and watched her mother slink all the way to the coffeepot. It was her favorite appliance in the world. The stainless steel goddess inspired machine sat on the counter and filled the kitchen with the strong fragrance of freshly brewed, aromatic, revitalizing, lifesaving coffee.

"This is the nectar of the gods, baby girl!"

"Shhhh!"

Ariella hushed her mom. Her head was still buzzing like she had a hive of bees floating inside. She would never forgive the woman for this. Crazy she-Cat had dosed Ariella—her youngest baby daughter—

with a high potency herbal supplement meant for she-Cats in labor, for fuck's sake. And at *Serious Moonlight* of all places.

Prrrrrrrrrr.

Her kitty was still acting as if the night had been some kind of success, but she did not know why. The level of embarrassment Ariella felt was something she didn't think she'd ever get over. And now she had to rush into work for an emergency meeting.

Crap. Crap. CRAP.

She growled and grabbed her cell. The stupid thing had been going off all weekend. Ariella looked down and opened the text from anonymous and found a giant dancing eggplant gif.

Perfect. Just perfect.

"Not another one!"

"Shhhh, baby girl, please. I carried you for nine months, and I think the least you can do is give me some quiet," her mother moaned.

"This is your fault, Mom. When are you going to stop, already?"

"Stop what? I was only trying to get you to loosen up, baby girl."

"Ugh. Well, I got loose alright," she mumbled, unable to stay angry with her mother for any real amount of time.

Besides, worse things had happened after going on one of her mother's adventures. So, what if Ariella announced her virginity to the entire bar? Big deal, right?

Well, she'd been getting spam calls and PMs on all her social media accounts from dozens of men, and a few women, ever since. Even operating at less than a hundred percent, she'd managed to identify a few fake accounts belonging to her sisters and her awful cousins, offering lewd suggestions.

Those perverse pussies. Ugh.

They were always big on the texts, but never to her face. Still, she admitted as she sipped her coffee and scrolled through her messages, there were some halfway decent *indecent proposals* in there.

Many of whom were offering to relive her of her little problem in the most imaginative of ways. What exactly was an Eiffel tower? And did she need to not shave her armpits to do it?

Hmmm.

“Oh, gawd! Eat my fur,” she muttered and blocked another pervert, who’d stupidly sent her a video of his limp and unimpressive member.

Like that was gonna seal the deal, pal! Whatevah.

Ariella rolled her eyes. She might be green as spring grass when it came to actually having sex, but she knew it took a little more than a Tootsie Roll, for Pete’s sake!

“Oh, even my eyes hurt,” Patricia moaned into her steaming mug of coffee.

Of course, she’d used the one shaped like an enormous purple wang, drinking from the tip deeply. Her mother had the most obscene tastes, but Ariella adored the woman.

“Serves you right,” she mumbled and glared at her mother. “What is going on with you, Mom? Are you moving back in? Did something happen with you and King Donovan?”

“I am not discussing that right now, child. Hey, it’s a full moon this week. Did you know that? Oh, look at the time! Get going. You have work, right?”

“I’m going, I’m going, sheesh,” Ariella mumbled, shaking her head.

That woman could have a full discussion and never let another person make a sound! She grabbed her purse, slipping on her lowest pair of heels before taking off for another fun filled workday.

Snark snark snark.

The cutesy little smart car was adorable when driving in her little hometown of Blue Valley, but she would never take it on the highway. The tiny lime green two-seater would be little more than a coffin if it came up against an eighteen-wheeler. She only used it to go to and from work and the condo she sometimes shared with her mother.

Patricia had been spending so much time at the palace lately, Ari wondered if she’d be living alone soon. She secretly believed the rumors that the now hearty and healthy King had fallen for her mom, but maybe, like some men she knew but would not name, Donovan Crowley just couldn’t come around to actually making a commitment.

Poor Mom.

Ariella frowned thoughtfully as she pulled into a free parking space outside her office. The *Eat Well Live Proud* building was not as big as some international corporations, but it suited the Pride just fine.

Keeping the supernatural world secret was tantamount to every organization run by Shifters regardless of personal agenda. The Pride had done well, developing the land bought and paid for by the royal family into a gated community complete with business section. It was like the Lions had their own little world, and Ariella grew up pampered and protected compared to some.

Nerves filled her stomach as she thought about her workday. Competition was fierce and she was still feeling hungover from the catnip, and other things. She could have sworn she'd been skinny dipping with Brock, but that couldn't be right. Could it?

Gulp. Game face, girl.

She could not let her guard down here. Maybe later she would shift to her Lioness and go for a quick run. There was a gorgeous patch of forest running parallel to the Pride lands. Some of it was owned by them, some owned by the Dire Wolves on the other side of the creek she'd bathed in last night.

Shit. There went her mind again, traveling forbidden paths. She could not afford to slip up today, or everything she'd been working for the past six months would have been for nothing.

Back to her thoughts of romping through woods. Yes, they did lead to private property owned by the DWMC. But it was easy to avoid their land. If that was what she wanted to do. Of course, Ari's beast knew a shortcut through the trees that led to the parking lot behind *Serious Moonlight* and the Dire Wolf Pack House. Not that she ever took that route. Well, not lately, anyway.

Or had she?

Just how did Ari make it home last night? She recalled waking up at five o'clock in the morning, glaring at the neon green numbers on her old-fashioned alarm clock. She had several of the things around the house, otherwise she might never wake up. Cats loved to sleep. Even Shifter Cats.

Hmmm.

She grabbed her bag, exiting the vehicle and tried to recall her steps last night. She could have sworn she had been swimming, and yet, Ariella had woken up in dry clothes in her own bed. Last thing she remembered was dancing and getting propositioned by a stranger. Her attempt at flirting back had been cut short by Brock.

Actually, the angry Dire Wolf had tossed her would-be-deflowerer, aka the Slash lookalike, across the bar. He then picked her up, curvy ass and all, and carried her out of the bar.

Shivers racked her body at the remembered touches, and Ariella didn't know whether to laugh or cry. He had seen her at her absolute worst. True, it was the longest she'd ever spent alone in his company. And even if, from what she recalled, it had been thrilling for her, Brock would probably avoid her more than ever now.

She'd been thoroughly under the influence of catnip infused tequila, but Ari still had a wonderful time. OMG! Had Brock really kissed her? She racked her brain for proof or some sign she was making that part up—call it wishful thinking, but no, even her she-Cat seemed certain.

Okay. So they kissed. Ohmyfuckinggawd!

Her heart was pounding her to death as she worried about what had happened. Kissing Brock was like the culmination of all her daydreams over the past few months. Ariella had had boyfriends, but she never really liked kissing them. What if she sucked at it?

Crap.

That was it. She totally sucked at it. After all, she had woken up alone. If she'd been good at kissing, she highly doubted a healthy male would have left it at that. How much more embarrassing were her memories going to get? Ugh. Ari tripped over a crooked slap of the sidewalk as the dreaded thought entered her brain.

Okay, she needed to remain calm. Ari had kissed boys before. They just never seemed able to handle her exuberance. Sure, boys had wanted to have sex with her, just no one she was interested in that way. After all, Ari couldn't give herself to someone who needed to take frequent breaks from just making out.

But that was what she typically attracted—skinny mama's boys with no idea how to handle her. She needed an apex predator. A strong one. None of the males in her Pride were interested in any of the Golden sisters.

Especially not after Adrianna had damn near castrated her high school boyfriend for cheating on her. It had been slim pickings from then on for all four of them, truth be told. Speak of the devil, Ariella damn near jumped out of her skin when her sister grabbed her arm.

"Ari, you coming inside or what?" Adrianna asked.

"Eeek! Holy fuck, Adrianna! Make some damn noise next time you sneak up on a bitch," she growled.

"Ha! I heard someone got in the catnip last night," she replied in an annoying sing-song voice.

Ariella just grunted. Annabeth and Antonette were waiting inside, and she cringed at the thought of what her three siblings had in store for her. Pranksters, all of them. Best to just get it over with.

Ari heaved a sigh and readjusted her purse on her shoulder. The great kissing question would just have to wait. Newly mated Annabeth was trying unsuccessfully to hide a smirk as Ari walked by. That she-Cat never could hold in a giggle.

Brats. All of them. They were definitely pulling something Ari. As the baby of the four, Ariella was used to it. Generally, she was a good sport about things like that, but her nerves were positively frayed at the moment. She only hoped they didn't go overboard.

The Golden sisters were not typically meanspirited. But shit had been known to go too far sometimes. Like when Ad put hair removal cream in Toni's leave-in conditioner before prom senior year. That one was particularly memorable since the cat fight that broke out between them had destroyed their grandmother's last remaining tea set. Good thing Nana hadn't cared a fig for tea. She'd been too busy shouting instructions at her fighting granddaughters.

Ariella supposed it was her turn to take some heat. After all, they had all ganged up on Annabeth when she'd come home with a mate a few months back. Of course, the sexified gift basket they left was bird themed for her new Falcon Shifter mate. If you asked Ariella, it was downright thoughtful of them. Especially, the sun butter part. That had been her idea.

The time before that, Toni had been in the hot seat. It was her own fault though. She was the one who woke up stark naked on the Palace lawn with Gavin Green, a Rabbit Shifter from town, with a half-eaten bowl of banana pudding and one green flip-flop between them. Adrianna and Ariella took photos—how could they not?

They even sent the images to a couple of producers of pornographic magazines and Toni had received no less than twelve offers. Rumor had it she was to be featured in the *Naughty or Nice Christmas Charity Calendar* which was rumored to be Shifter run non-profit that selected a different cause every year as beneficiary.

Ariella couldn't blame her if she posed for them. Toni was simply gorgeous and had a rockin' bod. Besides, it was for charity.

"So, how are you?" Annabeth asked, interrupting her musings.

"Fine."

Ariella squinted. She was sure Annabeth would crack, but the brat turned her head with a squeak. Being mated must have given her some backbone. Lucky beyotch.

"I see," Adrianna said, coming between the two of them. "Nothing you'd like to discuss, honey?"

"Like what?"

"Well, if you ever need advice on, *you know*, anything," Toni said, tucking one hand in the crook of Ari's elbow and waving the other one in the air.

"What is wrong with you three?" Ariella asked. She did not trust them at all. Not one little bitty bit.

"Nothing!"

"Sheesh."

"Can't sisters just be nice?"

"Wait a second. It can't be true! Didn't you bang *Hairy Henry* on prom weekend?" Annabeth asked in a stage whisper.

"*Oh my gawd*! Shut up, Annabeth. And no, I didn't bang *Hairy Henry*," she whisper screamed back at her nosy sibling, painfully aware of the questioning eyes of her coworkers and Pride mates surrounding them.

What the heck was going on? Fucking hell. This was going to be awful. She just knew it. Practically felt it in her gut.

"Well, I mean, Mom said you found your mate, so we were just shocked when the tweets went out about you still being a virgin and all," Annabeth said and shrugged.

"Tweets? I saw it in a TikTok," Adrianna added.

Ariella groaned.

"Oh no. Please tell me she didn't," she moaned, covering her face with her eyes.

"Wish we could, cupcake," Adrianna added.

"Mommy dearest sent out a Pride wide alert asking for help in *devirginizing* her youngest daughter," Annabeth informed her.

"I will put hair remover in every single bottle of shampoo in all of your apartments, I swear on my firstborn," Ariella growled, and tried to stop the tide of embarrassment that was currently threatening to drown her.

"Well, we're in luck then, sister. Cause if you ain't getting' any, you ain't havin' any cubs," Toni snarked, a wicked grin splitting her pretty face.

Beyotches. All of them.

Ariella could not believe it. Her own mother had outed her. Again. That was it. She was so going to show everyone the pictures of her mother, *pre-bikini wax*, she'd been holding over the female's head.

"Alright, I get Mom's lunacy, but you three are behaving very suspiciously. What did you do?"

Ariella quirked an eyebrow and followed them down the hall, noting the snickers and giggles from her co-workers as she walked to her desk.

"Now, don't get mad," Adrianna began seriously, but ruined it by snorting.

That was when Ariella saw it. The mother of all pranks. Right on her desk inside the offices of *Eat Well Live Proud,* her place of business, where she had a reputation to uphold, was an enormous gift basket.

"You had it coming," Annabeth said in a singsong voice, and she was not wrong.

After all, Ari had gleefully taken part in a similar such thing for Annabeth. Only, this was her place of work, and this basket was not fruit and stale crackers with awful nuts and cheese that no one liked.

Nope. This was filled with other things. Scandalous, gossip producing, funny if it was happening to someone else, horrifyingly embarrassing things.

Sigh.

Her coworkers, which included three sisters, eighteen cousins, and various other Pride members, stood around smirking and giggling as Ariella's eyes grew wide with horror. Naturally, the most prominent object inside the oversized basket that was topped for some reason with a big pink glitter ribbon was a stuffed poodle.

The dayglo purple pooch was about four feet high and sporting a strap-on which happened to have the biggest, pink glow-in-the-dark dildo Ariella had ever seen. Not to mention the pink leather ball-gag tied around the pornographic puppy's neck.

Next to the dildo dog was an assortment of vibrators, nipple clamps, whips, chains, and—*oh shit*—a straight up gallon of strawberry flavored lube. There was also a thick, hardcover copy of a fully illustrated Kama Sutra, translated by a Harvard scholar, apparently. Beside it were more instructional books on *how to train your puppy.*

Dog collars, leashes, a box of *wee wee* pads, and an assortment of rawhide and chew toys were scattered throughout. Not to mention, a giant box of peanut butter flavored dog treats, and a giant jar of peanut butter. The creamy kind.

"We just thought we could help you snag that dog you're after," announced Adrianna to a round of laughter and applause.

"What the hell is going on here?" her boss, Maggie Pierce, one of the King's new circle, yelled from the doorway and everyone snapped to attention.

"Um, nothing," Ariella answered.

She clapped a hand over her mouth, trying to stand in front of the giant dildo basket, but to no avail. Her boss did not like smarty pants. Especially anyone who was dumb enough to answer what was clearly a rhetorical question.

Shit.

This was not good.

"Well, if you are all finished with what I am going to assume is a basket of dog training supplies, maybe we can get on with the meeting and our workday. Oh, and Ariella, while I appreciate your virtue is the gossip of the hour, let's keep it down until after work, shall we?" Ms. Pierce snarled.

"Yes, ma'am," she replied in a low voice.

"Good. Get that basket out of here. Now."

"Yes, ma'am," Ariella whispered again.

She lugged the tremendous thing down to her tiny car where it took up all of her trunk, even spilling over to the passenger seat, which she had to lay down. Ariella bit her lip and wondered if the strap-on was visible from the outside now that she had a ball gag wearing purple poodle as a passenger.

FML.

She groaned and ran back inside. Ariella was only fifteen minutes late to the meeting. Mrs. Pierce waited until the end of her long drawn out speech over new import laws and procedures at the docks to announce the top contenders for this quarter's leaders.

Ariella held her breath when the top three were announced. The entire room did, as a matter of fact. Call it a predator's need to win, whatever it was, this quarterly contest was very motivational.

Ariella had never won. Not once. She'd been very determined this time around. Had worked her butt off too. What else did she have going for her at the moment?

Besides Fluffy, her new BFF that was waiting in her car. Sigh.

"Well, ladies and gents, this has never happened before, but it seems there is a tie for the lead between Cornelia Higgins and Ariella Golden," Ms. Pierce announced,

"You have a few more days till we close out the contest. Good luck, you two."

"Ari, that's great!" Adrianna whispered.

Her sisters accompanied her, while her work friends offered congratulations, as she walked back out to her desk. She was both happy and bummed. Ari just couldn't believe after all her hard work, she was still tied with Cornelia Higgins. How did that woman do it?

Well, it was her own fault for pussyfooting around the *Serious Moonlight* account, and not going in for the kill. She'd already hit up every other small business in the area.

She needed that Wolf run bar, and not just half of what she offered. Ari needed to get *all* their business, darn it. Freaking Brock was standing in her way. The only reason he'd ever offered even a portion of their business to Ariella was because of her connection to Leo, Sheila's mate.

Rawrrr.

Her Lioness objected loudly to the insinuation that their mate wouldn't do it out of devotion to her alone. Silly kitty didn't understand that while Brock smelled like her mate, and looked like her mate, the guy simply was not interested in being her mate.

RAWRR!

Ariella winced. Angry kitty was loud kitty, and she was still recovering from the whole catnip thing. Her she-Cat needed to tone down her sass.

Sigh.

She could not think about Brock right now. Ariella had other things to worry about. Like the blond mantrap headed her way.

Cornelia Higgins was technically Ariella's second cousin, but their families were not close. Bad blood over one slight or other over the years had led to a little feud between the Higgins and Golden families.

As a result, Cornelia had always been a real bitch to Ari and her sisters.

None of them liked her. Still, Ariella had to admit Cornelia was good at her job. Even if she only landed her clients by sleeping with them. Rumors could be nasty things, but these were more like what people called *open secrets*.

"She gives us all a bad name," Toni mumbled as they exited the conference room.

"Why? Because she'd rather gain clients on her knees than with her brains?" Adrianna snarled loudly, and Ari pinched her arm.

Talk like that would only bring Cornelia herself over their way to flaunt her achievements in their faces. The woman loved to brag, and unscrupulous or not, she had the numbers to back it up.

"Well, well, well, if it isn't the *Golden girls*," she said and gave an unfriendly smirk. "Say that show was about a group of old women with no men in their lives, right? Like you four?"

"No, I don't think that's right. After all, one was rather promiscuous," Toni said.

"That means she was a slut, Corny. Kinda like some females we know," Annabeth hissed.

"Oh, so one of them was getting some," replied Cornelia with her perfect upturned nose in the air, making Ari want to gag. "I guess those girls weren't like you four, after all? Seeing as how none of you can get a man, unless you count a canary."

"Watch it," snarled Annabeth, but Toni held her back.

"Anyway, Ariella, I wanted to congratulate you on your attempt to win the quarterly contest. It is too bad, though."

"What's too bad?" Ari asked.

"Well, let's see, this will be my fifth win in a row, and you never even won once, have you? In fact, none of you have, right?"

"Yeah, we know how you won, Corny," murmured Annabeth, but Toni elbowed her to shush up.

"You know, I have to say so far, the new laptop was my favorite prize. Of course, the deluxe premium smart phone package was great too. The year-long spa treatments went very well. I mean, we all know those are amazing," she said, and looked at the four sisters scathingly.

"Then again, maybe *we* don't do we, ladies? Anyway, I am really going to enjoy winning this year. The week-long vacation for two sounds divine," Cornelia finished and tossed her perfectly flat-ironed blond locks over one slender shoulder.

Skinny beyotch.

"You haven't won it yet," Ariella responded, eyes narrowed and rising to the bait like a freaking amateur.

"Haven't I?" she crinkled her nose and Ari wondered for a moment how she would look with blood gushing out of it.

Rawrrrr.

"You know, I was going to stop by that little Wolf motorcycle bar for dinner tonight," she taunted.

"I wonder what, or should I say *who,* I might find there. Maybe someone looking for a woman with a little experience under her belt. Maybe my next client," Cornelia said, pursing her lips and winking at Ari before she walked away.

Of course, she didn't get far before Annabeth reached out with her exceptionally long legs and tripped her. Ariella bit her lip to stop her laughter from exploding out of her mouth.

"Hey!"

"Oops, my bad," Annabeth said, fake smile just innocent enough to not raise suspicion.

Ari knew that one was for her, and she was grateful to Annabeth. Shit. She was positively dying on the inside. She couldn't compete against Cornelia's sexual prowess. After all, what if the woman was right?

What if her virginity was just another, even bigger, obstacle between her and Brock? Cornelia had just poked at an open wound, and Ariella did not know if she would recover. Anger, fear, determination warred within her. Should Ariella just give up now? Hand over the prize to Cornelia and slink away with her tail between her legs.

Fuck. No. Rawrrrr.

CHAPTER SEVEN

DIRE WOLF MATES

"Four porterhouses up," Brock yelled over the dull roar of activity that seemed constant in the busy kitchen.

He'd outfitted the space with the best equipment, though the design was simplistic/ Fitting, seeing as how the menu was mainly grilled meat and fish. He kept things orderly, neat, clean, and his staff knew what their jobs entailed. Anyone caught cutting corners, was fired. No second chances.

Some might call him a cruel boss, but he wasn't. Brock simply needed the best from his team. It was what he gave, and what he demanded in return. Being head chef was a dream come true, but it was hard work.

Cooking was the fun part. Menu creation a close second. He changed it up every few weeks or so, with different side dishes based on availability and what was in season. The core was the same—steaks, chops, filets, fowl, and whole fish. The ingredients were all top quality. But it was the cooking technique that mattered most, in his opinion.

Brock grunted as his assistants sprinted to get food on plates and out to the servers. Having everything run smoothly and efficiently was of the utmost importance, and as such he believed in quick delivery from flame to plate to customer.

No fuss, no delays.

Shifters had extremely sensitive tastes and food left to sit for any amount of time had already started to spoil. No one wanted to prolong that. True, he wasn't classically trained in a culinary school, but he had wandered the world for many years and had a natural eye and a nose for tastes.

In his travels, Brock had picked up a lot from various master chefs and above average kitchen Witches over the years. Dire Wolves aged even slower than most Shifters and supes, though he was nearing seventy, he still had the appearance of a thirty-year-old.

Shit.

He'd begun to feel his age just lately. Watching Derrick and Lucy make a home for the cub they were expecting over the past few months had been intense, welcomed, and exciting for sure, but Brock had also started to feel envious of his Alpha.

It was not a good feeling. He was a loyal Wolf, and he loved Derrick like a brother. But yeah, he was jealous, he admitted, even if only to himself. Brock wanted that, too. A family. A mate. His mate.

Ariella.

Her name echoed through his mind. The mere thought of her sent his Dire Wolf to growling. The big, almost white Wolf was completely besotted with the feline. That single kiss they'd shared in the cool creek had not been nearly enough. But he would never take advantage of a woman under the influence, and certainly not one who'd fallen unconscious in his arms. No. he was too much a gentleman for that.

He had simply seen her home, safe and sound. Brock wondered if it wasn't kismet that she had passed out before things could progress any further. They weren't there yet. Maybe they wouldn't ever be.

Fuck. He wasn't cut out for a mate. Frolicking in the moonlight was one thing. A stolen kiss, another. But having to subject her to his enormous size when she was untried and innocent, well, that was something else entirely.

What if she panicked and ran from him like Jacqueline had all those years ago?

That one experience was the root of all his anxiety. And yet, Brock wondered, how could the Fates be wrong? Warring arguments sounded loudly in his brain until he was practically vibrating with frustration.

Hell, even their resident Pack spitfire had found a mate. Sheila and Leo were like water and oil, but they made it work. Why couldn't he and Ariella?

He could've gone on being lonely forever, but then Derrick mated Lucy and Sheila mated Leo. He had to admit the Lion was a pretty cool guy for a hard ass cop who was also a Prince. Leo was the reason Brock had met Ariella, who was an honorary cousin of the male.

So, he could say Leo was the cause of all his angst, worry, and the ever-growing feeling that something was missing from his life. The fucker. Brock ran a hand over his face. It didn't matter if Leo was to blame or Sheila, or whoever the fuck. Ariella was fucking worth it.

He recalled the way her soft lips had parted so readily for his. The woman had a mouth made for sin with a sightly plumper upper lip that he wanted to nibble on for days. Her wild curly hair was glorious, a dark halo circling her head. She was beautiful. Perfect.

Mate, his Wolf growled.

Well, fuck.

His dick hardened in his chef pants and Brock was practically vibrating, he was growling so much. He couldn't concentrate. Not like this.

"No more than three minutes to a side on those four inch steaks, Carlo. That meat goes out rare," he grunted and handed his tongs to his new sous chef, a half-Fae kid of about three-hundred years old, who'd decided he wanted to be a chef.

The man looked even younger than Brock, but he worked hard and was never late. Carlo nodded and took over the grill with all the seriousness required for the job. The last thing Brock needed was for some Shifter customer to freak the fuck out over a badly cooked steak.

But he had no reason to worry. He had already worked on the sauces for the rest of the dishes, and his staff knew what they were doing. Brock barked out a few more orders, checking one last time to make sure the fish and veggies were all prepped before he walked out of the kitchen.

He trusted his crew. Knew they could handle the Monday dinner rush with efficiency and professionalism. They were a great team and Cole, one of his Pack, was always there to step in if they got in trouble. Brock simply needed some time to think.

"Chef?" Tim, a new server, and Fox Shifter, came rushing into the small locker room they kept for staff. Brock was sitting there with his eyes closed, trying to calm his inner beast. "There's a woman here to see you."

Brock opened his eyes and his Wolf stilled inside of him, like the predator he admittedly was who had his prey backed into a corner. Ariella, he thought, and took off his apron. He could hardly contain himself as he stalked through the full tables and weaved between folks just standing by the bar.

He'd been waiting ever since Saturday night for her to call him. Where was she? Brock ran a hand over his head and encountered his tied kerchief. He ripped the thing off and tossed it on an empty stool. It didn't matter. He had dozens of the things. It would not matter if he lost one. Whatever. He'd just wanted to look better when he saw her again.

There was nothing he could do about the checked chef pants and black chef coat he still wore, but hey, she knew what he did for a living. She wouldn't have come there expecting anything more. Curiosity got the best of him as he retraced his steps through the dining room and back to the bar once more.

Was she playing some sort of game? He looked over the head of a busty blond who smelled like a flower shop and made his nose itch.

The ridiculous woman looked as if she was going to fall over, trying to get his attention.

"Hello there," she said, offering him with what she must have thought was a seductive smile. Brock was not interested. He nodded and continued to look around for Ariella.

"Excuse me, you are the chef, right? Brock Laurent? I'm Cornelia Higgins," she said in a husky voice, and offered a freshly manicured hand. Brock looked down at it, making no move to touch the female.

"Yes, I'm the chef. Did you have a question? I don't have much time, I'm sorry, I am waiting for someone," he replied, gingerly shaking her offered appendage.

He tried to extract himself, but the woman was cloying. She refused to let go.

"Yes, that would be me," she replied to his utter confusion, using his momentary lapse as an excuse to push her slender body against his.

What the hell was going on? Where was Ariella? Brock looked through the sparse crowd, but she was nowhere to be found.

"Excuse me, I don't think so," he returned, putting space between them, and tugging his hand free of hers none too gently.

He knew she was a Shifter, having scented her fur, which was why he thought it strange she would be so forward. Shifters, especially powerful ones like Dire Wolves, did not like to be touched unless it was invited. Brock was definitely not interested in her hands anywhere near him.

"I asked the server to go get you."

"What? Why?"

"Well, it is your lucky day, Mr. Laurent," she started and grinned again, not put off in the slightest that he was less than welcoming. "I'm here to meet the famous chef of the newest Blue Valley hotspot, and to give you the deal of your dreams."

"Yeah, look, there has been a mistake. I'm busy," he said and turned to walk away, but the woman grabbed his arm, and it was all he could do to keep still.

His Wolf was snarling. The beast did not want this female to touch him. He hated it.

"Maybe I was not being clear enough. I'm Cornelia Higgins and I represent *Eat Well Live Proud,* Mr. Laurent. I am completely at your service," she said and emphasized the service part by tracing every line of his body with her eyes.

Brock stiffened, repulsed by her overly suggestive comments and too intimate glances. He stepped back, away from her grasp. He wasn't a fan of this Lioness and could tell from the start she meant trouble. He quirked an eyebrow and turned to see Weylin wander over. He was bartending tonight.

"Need something, bro?" Weylin asked.

"Miss Higgins?" he questioned out of courtesy only.

"I will have a white wine," she replied and seemed quite pleased with herself.

"I'll have a mineral water," he told Weylin.

"I have been dying to meet the genius behind Serious Moonlight's innovative menu, and now that I have," she began, her eyes roaming over him again, making him squirm uncomfortably. "I can tell this deal is going to be my pleasure entirely. I don't normally offer our exclusive meat line to just anyone, you know."

Brock was feeling like a piece of meat himself. He even backed up, putting a stool between them, pointing towards the glass of wine Weylin set down on the bar before she could stand and follow him.

Sheesh, get a hint, lady.

Cornelia's offer was basic. She wanted to move their account to *her* management and give him the *personal attention* he was presumably missing. But Brock had already stopped listening. A familiar, delicious musk seemed to float across the room and wrap around him. He recognized the scent. It belonged to the only person he was interested in handling his accounts.

Clearly, Miss Higgins was used to conducting business in a certain manner—*like on her back.* Something he would never pursue, especially not with her. Not even in the slightest. There was only one feline he was interested in.

As if on cue, Ariella Golden chose that moment to walk in. Cornelia droned on, clearly delusional. Her badly veiled innuendos were obvious, and cliché. Her intent to seal the deal with a night in the sack was distasteful to both him and his Wolf.

As if he would ever be interested in her. But the idea did get him thinking. He turned his head and met Ariella's large amber eyes. They glowed gold with her Lioness for a moment as she seemed to take in the situation before she turned and left.

Oh, that wouldn't do. Not at all.

"Excuse me, Miss Higgins, you seem to be operating under the misinformation that we don't have an account handler with Eat Well Live Proud, which I am sure if you looked, you would see we do, with Ariella Golden. Secondly, you seem to think I would be interested in you sexually, and you are using that imagined sexual interest to misguide you. If you came here thinking I would take you up on your offer to sleep with you in exchange for our business, well, you are grossly mistaken. The answer is no," he said and moved to leave.

Unfortunately, what Cornelia Higgins lacked in scruples, she made up for in speed. The wily feline stood in front of him and placed a hand over the semi-hard erection in his pants.

"I think you look and feel plenty interested. This is really quite the package you have here, Mr. Laurent. Better to go with a woman who knows how to handle it then some virgin who might faint on sight," Cornelia said, biting her lip and blinking up at him with the same practiced look she must have given dozens of men.

Of course, his semi-hard state was pretty much the norm for whenever Ariella was in the same zip code as him. It had nothing whatsoever to do with this aggressive female. She grinned again, gave his cock another squeeze, angering both him and his Wolf.

Brock growled and removed her hand with perhaps a tad bit more force than necessary. She was a Shifter, and quite strong. The fact she had attacked his one area of weakness aside, Brock could see Cornelia had issues of her own. Unfortunately for her, he didn't care one whit for them. His concern was for Ariella alone.

"I am not interested in you or your offer, Miss Higgins. I can't say it any plainer than that. You see, I've found my fated mate. Now, I will say this once and only once—Do. Not. Touch. Me. Ever. Again."

Cornelia gasped at whatever she saw in his gaze and backed up rubbing her hands Together. He would have felt guilty, but she was too damn pushy and needed the reality check.

"B-but what about the deal? There's a quarterly contest and the prize is an island vacation. I intend to win it. If you help me, you can be my plus one, Mr. Laurent."

"A contest? You would spread your legs for a man who clearly is not interested, for a contest? No deal, Ms. Higgins, and I suggest you get some help."

"How dare you! Look, I will overlook your lack of taste, but if I have your account then— "

"I already said we have a rep. If you want to win something, I suggest you work harder. Now, I suggest you leave and don't come back, Ms. Higgins."

Brock turned around and chased the enticing trail of musk and spice that Ariella had left in her wake. Shit, that encounter took too long. Was he too late?

He jogged, then ran out the side door. Fuck. Where was she? The sun had already set for the evening, and it was dark and chilly in the Spring breeze. The sound of leaves rustling caught his attention, and he rounded the back, searching behind the small outdoor storage closet. Another rustle of leaves and branches sounded, and he stepped into the woods where Brock's eyes zeroed in on the most beautiful thing he'd ever seen.

Ariella Golden stood in her skin and nothing else. Her eyes flashed at him, and she hissed angrily before changing into her fierce and magnificent Lioness. Her shift was fast, though not as fast as his. The sound of bones cracking and muscles reknitting themselves was loud in the back of the restaurant, but he understood. She was upset and it was his fault.

The she-Cat roared before sprinting off into the woods and Brock grinned. He wasn't leaving well enough alone. Not tonight. If a chase was what she wanted, she was about to get one. He ran towards the stand of trees where the glorious golden feline had just disappeared. Without a thought for his clothing, he called his Dire Wolf forward.

After decades of shifting, his change was instantaneous. His animal was enormous, far larger than the average Wolf Shifter, and he had light, buff-colored fur that was almost white on his chest and face and darkest on his back. In his Wolf form, all of his senses seemed to increase tenfold. Including, his sense of smell.

The intoxicating fragrance coming from his mate was almost overwhelming. He didn't need to see or hear her to find her, he just had to follow his nose.

He loosed a howl and sprinted after her. All his earlier fears about their mating forgotten when he was in his fur. The beast had no such qualms, knowing in his heart that he was the perfect mate for his sweet kitten.

Brock's Wolf growled with the knowledge that he was the only male in the entire universe who could give her everything she could ever need or want. It was why he was born, after all, to be Ariella's mate.

Mating fever.

The thought crashed into him as his stomach tightened and he pumped his legs faster, straining his muscles to catch up to her. The pull of the near full moon was making his desire even stronger.

Hell, he felt it in his very soul. The strength of his need for her was undeniable. Brock tossed his lupine head back and sniffed good and long.

This way.

The sound of leaves and twigs snapping under his massive paws only fed his predatory instincts. He had to reach her. His Wolf knew she was upset, that she had misinterpreted what she'd seen, and he was pissed as hell at Brock for not pushing the other woman off immediately. But that was to be expected, mates were often very possessive of one another, and his animal's nature didn't always follow or approve of his human side's need to act with a certain degree of civility.

Things like manners and decorum were not important to a Dire Wolf. He had to make it right, to prove that she was his one and only. The sound of a splash caught his attention, and he turned right.

Was she headed back to their stream?

Seemed like his kitty wanted to go for a swim. Brock's Wolf howled once more into the night air before he took off in that direction. His sassy little mate had no idea what was coming for her.

Game on.

CHAPTER EIGHT

Dire Wolf Mates

Ariella couldn't believe her Lioness right now! She wanted to hightail it out of the parking lot, but her beast decided she needed her fur now.

Ugh.

As if that was not bad enough—Miss Kitty ran right back to the scene of Ari's abject humiliation. As if she hadn't had enough of that.

Ugh.

The little creek behind the Dire Wolf Pack House was just as clear and chilly as her fuzzy memory recollected. She chuffed as she vaulted into the invigorating water. Her feline side figured it was worth a try. Maybe she could forget about her sorrows with an energizing swim. But Cornelia Higgins? Did it have to be her?

She just could not believe her own eyes. Seeing that female with her hands on him sent Ari on a downward spiral that had her shedding her clothes in the woods not twenty feet from the crowded roadhouse.

Rawrr.

Sure, he had walked outside and caught her. But he was not there for Ari. No way would she even entertain that line of thought. Brock had probably been getting his bike ready, so he could follow Cornelia to her den of carnal delights.

That Wolf didn't want a virginal mate any more than she wanted to be a virgin. Good for him, getting his rocks off with a born seductress. Ariella couldn't seduce her way out of a traffic ticket.

Sigh.

Wasn't that the embarrassing truth? Her unfortunately timed announcement that she was untouched, *and therefore unwanted,* ruined any chance she could have had at playing the siren. She should just give up and move far away from Blue Valley and the Pride already.

If only she had beaten Cornelia to the roadhouse. If only she had beaten Cornelia, period. Then she could have stopped that woman's come ons before they'd happened. Darn it.

Rawrrrr.

Winning the contest was important to Ariella, but it was nothing when she compared it to claiming her mate. But Brock was simply unattainable. And Ari never flirted with clients. She would never sleep her way to the top. It just was not her style. Rumors about Cornelia's unsavory ways had been circulating for months. But Ari was naïve, she supposed. She simply could not fathom it. She had worked hard for every single one of her accounts.

It wasn't slut-shaming or woman-hating that made her lip curl at the thought of Cornelia coming on to Brock. Having a hearty appetite for sex was all fine and good, but why did the woman have to go after him? The fact she was using her body to land accounts was none of Ariella's business.

Though, it was probably against company policy. She really had no shame about it, either. The woman flaunted it to everyone at EWLP. There was a code of ethics they were all supposed to follow, but Ari did not have them memorized or anything.

Still, she doubted Cornelia's activities were kosher. And the way the female bragged and made fun of the women and men who refused to conduct business in that manner was just horrid. Cornelia was like a walking, talking throwback to some shady businesswoman stereotype, and Ariella would never use her methods to build her client list like that, nor did she want that kind of reputation.

To Ari, intimacy was supposed to be *intimate.* As in personal, between two people who had mutual respect and feelings for one another. Probably why she was still a virgin.

Sad rawr.

The leaves stirred, and her leonine eyes took in the beauty of the forest. She was lucky to live in this place. New Jersey was known, and ridiculed, for its highways, but it had some of the prettiest woods she'd ever seen. From beaches, to mountains, farmland, and cities. It had a little bit of everything. Or, as her mom said, something for everyone—though the Lioness might have been talking about the food court at the new mall down on Route 35 at the time.

Anyway, it was obvious to her Brock didn't care for her shy and private nature. Maybe he wanted someone who was more an exhibitionist. Like Cornelia. He sure looked fine and cozy chatting with her at the bar.

Sad sad rawr.

Ariella exited the stream and laid her big furry body out on a large bolder on the bank. The enormous rock was still warm from the afternoon sun. She was soaked but felt better now, calmer, and relaxed after her swim. She closed her eyes for a catnap but was startled by a huge splash.

The cold water shocked her into standing up. She turned her head to see an enormous white Wolf swimming across the stream to where she lay. Ariella hissed loudly at the male invading her space. She just wanted to be alone, dammit.

Taking a deep breath, she caught the Wolf's scent and recognized it immediately. Heart pounding, her hiss turned into a purr as the Wolf neared her.

Brock.

Her *would-be-mate,* who, according to her calculations, should be at second base with Cornelia by now, was headed straight for her.

Before she could talk herself out of it, she switched fur for skin without bothering to care about her nudity.

Most Shifters had grown up around that kind of thing, and she was too amped up to be properly embarrassed by her fleshy thighs and soft belly. Why was he here? She just had to know, and supernatural or not, she could not talk in her fur.

"What are you doing here?" she asked as he climbed to shore and shook out his fur, shifting back to his skin at the same time.

"I came to talk to you," he said and continued to shake his head in a manner that reminded her of his animal.

She couldn't help but smile as her eyes followed the movement. Ari bit her lip, her gaze wandering over him in a manner that was decidedly against Shifter protocol.

Fuck it.

Ariella felt entitled. She'd spent so much time imagining the moment the two of them were naked together, she might as well take advantage. If pressed, she could always argue she was helpless in his presence. It was not a lie.

Gulp. Beautiful, sexy, muscly man.

Her eyes devoured every inch of him from the top of his damp blond hair to his wide shoulders, amazing pecs, rippling abs, and lower still. Mouth open, she flat out stared in shock as she reached that large, unfamiliar part of him that seemed to grow, jutting out proudly from its bed of damp blond curls.

"Ariella, if you don't stop looking at me like that, this conversation is going to be a short one," he growled softly, and she noted his eyes glowing blue with his Wolf.

If Ariella didn't know any better, she would think he was desperately trying to keep control. Imagine that? The big, gorgeous hunk of man was having a hard time keeping a lid on his Wolf because of her. That knowledge was incredibly empowering, and she tucked it away like a secret she would keep with her always.

If Ari was staring, then so was he. His bold gaze roamed up and down her curves, and she felt damp heat pool between her legs. Need and desire rose like the tide, and she swayed on her feet. Throwing caution to the wind, Ariella stepped over to where he stood, encroaching on his personal space. She noted with delight the way his eyes dropped to her swaying breasts and lower to the carefully cropped curls that shielded her sex from his piercing gaze.

So, he isn't as immune as he pretended to be. Good to know.

"So, you wanted to talk?" she asked, stopping inches shy from touching his body. She gestured for him to get on with it.

"Is it true that there is an employee contest at *Eat Well Live Proud?*"

"What?"

Ariella was confused. What kind of question was that? It had nothing to do with anything. Here she was tingling with want and he was asking about work.

What. The. Actual. Fuck.

"Is it true?" he reiterated.

"Yes," she replied cautiously.

"Where are you in the running?"

"Why do you want to know?" she asked.

"Because," he returned vaguely. "Just tell me."

"Okay, yes, there is a contest, and right now I am tied for first with your new friend," she emphasized the word and crossed her arms.

"That woman is not my friend. I just met her tonight. She wants my business," he began, a cocky grin splitting his face. "And that wasn't all she wanted."

"I bet," she huffed.

A burning jealousy built inside of her, the same feeling that had Ariella running out of the bar earlier and shifting into her she-Cat. She couldn't stop the hiss that escaped her throat at the mention of Cornelia. Lucky for that beyotch, Ariella had some sense of decorum, otherwise she'd have ripped her hair out.

"I turned her down," he added, watching her closely.

"Why?"

"Because I wanted to offer it to you. The same deal she offered me."

"What do you mean?"

"I mean you will have *all* of Serious Moonlight's business, if—"

"Really? You will go all in for our beef, lamb, wild game, poultry, and ALL of our seafood products?" she asked and bounced on the balls of her feet in her excitement.

She stopped the second she heard his growl, his eyes glued to her swaying breasts. Ariella cleared her throat, fighting the burning blush she felt creeping up her face. It was gratifying he was finally noticing her as a woman. Maybe they could spend time together and get to know each other. That would be amazing.

If Brock got to know her, maybe he would like her and eventually, they could come to some kind of an understanding. So lost in her fantasy, Ariella could not believe his next few words. Maybe she did not hear him correctly.

"I'm sorry, what did you say?" she asked, blinking up at him.

"I said, you can have all our business, Ariella, if you agree to stay on as our rep with Eat Well Live Proud, and if you agree to spend the night with me."

Ariella's mouth hung open. Could he mean what she thought he meant? His proposition echoed in her head. His offer filtering through her lust-addled brain. Brock Laurent was finally admitting he wanted her, but only for a night.

Yessss, hissed her she-Cat.

No, replied her brain.

How could she live with herself if she gave him her body to use for the night? Well, at least she could say she had him, right? This was an impossible choice.

Fuck.

She was frozen solid. Ariella could hardly breathe as her entire world came crashing down around her head. This was too big, too important to decide right now. Her heart constricted in her chest and her lungs threatened to seize up as breathing suddenly became difficult.

"Um, *er,* I'll call you later with my decision," she said and turned away from him, unwilling to have him witness the myriad of emotions racing through her.

Did he think all the women from EWLP were for sale, like Cornelia? Did he simply have no respect for her? She wished she could be outraged, but mostly she was confused. And if she were being honest, she was intrigued as well.

"Ariella?" he called, but she didn't turn around, just raised her hand as she walked towards Pride lands.

"I need to think, Brock. Call me later, and you'll have your answer."

"Fine. But I will call, Ariella."

She nodded, uncertain whether that was a good thing. Swallowing down her shock, she made plans to call her sisters. It was time for a Golden girls meeting.

Rawrrr.

CHAPTER NINE

DIRE WOLF MATES

"You're a fucking idiot," Derrick, his Alpha and best friend, said and tossed back a shot of Mason Lane's newest artisan distilled whiskey, *Peanut Butter Bite*.

The dark-haired Alpha nodded at Phoenix, who then added a few cases of the liquor to their regular order. It was bound to be a hit with canid Shifters and Pachyderms who frequented the place.

How normals never caught on to Shifters was a mystery to Brock, but whatever. He supposed most people only saw what they wanted to see.

"You know, if you chase that with this *Jersey Devil's Brewery Sour Raspberry* ale, it's like eating a PB&J," Phoenix remarked and wagged his eyebrows.

"Great. Put it on the cocktail specials for this month," Derrick said to him, then turned to nod at Brock.

"Phoenix, what do you think of this idiot over here?"

"Oh, he's fucked," Phoenix said.

The Wolf grinned, ducked and reached a hand upward, plucking the shot glass Brock threw at his head from out of the air. Weylin and

Thor were busy picking up supplies in town, and Cole had left a few days ago for a ride.

Out of all of them, he'd been having the hardest time adjusting to life off the road, so they all understood when he needed to get gone.

"Fuck you," Brock retorted, then dropped his head in his hands.

He didn't know where he'd gotten the brilliant idea to proposition his mate, but it was all he could think of to save them both from the horrifying possibility that he was simply too much for her to handle.

Like Jacqueline.

His Wolf snarled at the hated memory.

"Shit, Derrick. What am I gonna do? She must think I'm a fucking asshole, man," he growled.

"Yes, and she would be right."

His Alpha smirked annoyingly. Fucking asshole. But that was not true. Brock knew Derrick for a long time, and the man was as good as they came. He cared about their Pack and was a great leader.

"Look," Derrick said, taking pity on him, thank fuck. "Do you love her?"

"Love? I don't know," Brock replied, cocking his head to the side as if he'd never considered the possibility. Fuck. Did he love her?

"Well, how do you feel about her, man?"

"I want her like crazy. I mean, Ariella is all I think about. She's my fated mate, Derrick. There is no doubt. I can feel it in my blood. My Wolf knows it, The beast wants her. But what does that have to do with love?"

"Have you learned nothing from me and Lucy? It has everything to do with it. I mean, look, the pull to mate was so strong, I nearly claimed her in the first ten minutes of meeting her. But love followed immediately after, too. I swear, every minute I spend with my mate, I love her even more."

"Ew, man, cut that shit out," Phoenix grunted and made a face at the two men. "Sappy motherfucking shit might be contagious."

"Hell, you'd be lucky! Besides, you're going to have a long wait for someone to take on your sorry ass," Derrick rumbled and tossed a rag in his Pack mate's face.

They continued their ribbing as their Alpha moved on to the next shot. He passed a second glass to Brock. He sniffed the Vanilla Bourbon liquor they'd just received from a Gator Shifter family down in Kentucky.

It was good stuff, Brock acknowledged as he took in the smoky depths of the bronze-colored liquid and sniffed it for hints of oak and sugar. The color reminded him of Ariella's eyes. That haunted expression she wore as she had left the woods last night, had almost been his undoing.

Fuck.

Was everything going to remind him about her from now on? He had yet to call her. Truth was, he'd chickened out. Again.

"Look, bro, I know you have some hang ups, but she's a Shifter man. Not some human who isn't prepared for the ferocity of your ardor. She is not Jacqueline. Ariella can more than handle anything you got," Derrick said point blank.

He spoke in a low voice out of respect for the sensitivity of the discussion, and Brock's Wolf appreciated the consideration. He wanted to believe him. Really, he did.

"Call her or I will fucking order you to," Derrick said before turning back to his task.

"Alright," Brock replied.

There was no holding back now. He had to do it before he lost his chance and she walked away from him for good. He stood up and walked a few feet away, trying to find his balls. Grabbing his cell phone, he dialed her number and waited while it rang.

"Hello."

"Hey," he answered.

Relief filled him so quickly it was dizzying. Brock realized he hadn't been sure she would even deem him worthy enough to answer his call.

"Brock?" she asked when he said nothing for more than a beat, and he snapped himself out of his stupor.

"Yeah. It's me."

"I know. I have caller id."

"Ariella, I wanted to talk about what I said last night—"

"My answer is yes."

"What? You're saying yes? Are you sure—"

He could hardly believe what she was saying.

"Yes, Brock, I will spend one night with you, and in return you'll sign the contract for Eat Well Live Proud to be the sole supplier of meat and fish for Serious Moonlight."

"Ariella, are you certain?"

"Yes, I am sure. See you at eight tonight, alright?"

"Eight o'clock. Alright."

"Alright, then."

He waited for her to end the call, then turned around and slid the phone back into his pocket. Now he was the one who was confused. Ariella had agreed to spend the night with him. He knew she was a virgin. Knew what he'd asked was stupid and cruel.

Why would she agree to it, though?

"She said yes?" Derrick's voice raised an octave as if he was just as baffled as his Beta.

Brock nodded. He was lost for words. Of course, his Dire Wolf was completely on board with getting Ariella to bed him any way he could. Maybe it would work out, maybe it wouldn't. But one thing he knew, he couldn't fuck this up again.

He had to come clean and tell her the truth. He'd been running from her because of a bad experience from his past, punishing her for the sins of another. It was petty and stupid.

But one night? Was she serious? He had to hope and pray she'd commit to more than a night. Fuck, once he had her, his Dire Wolf would never let her go. He knew that with a certainty he wasn't altogether familiar with. It was more than the beast, though. Brock couldn't picture walking away from her.

Could Derrick be right? Was he in love with the lovely Lioness after all?

"Chest hurt?"

Derrick interrupted his thoughts and Brock looked down to see he was rubbing the center of his chest with his palm. He nodded at his Alpha.

"Yeah," he said, and tilted his head to the side, waiting for an explanation.

He felt like a fucking cub. Completely at sea in the vast ocean that was the complexity of his feelings for the woman. Derrick motioned for him to sit and continued.

"Find yourself confused a lot lately? Anxious when she isn't near?"

Again Brock nodded. How did Derrick know about that?

"Capable of hammering through a concrete wall with your cock whenever she is close?"

"Yes," Brock growled unhappily.

The Alpha chuckled. This was not the shit he wanted to talk about with another man. But Derrick was more than that. He was their chosen leader. Trust and loyalty were only two of the emotions he felt for the male.

Derrick was a good man and an awesome leader. Their bond as Beta and Alpha made their relationship a strong one. If he couldn't talk to him, who could he?

"Then the answer is simple. You are royally fucked, son, because yes, she is your fated mate, and yes, even if you did not realize it, you're already halfway in love with her."

"Why half?"

"Have you kissed her properly yet?"

Brock shook his head, and ignored the fact that his cheeks were burning, and were probably bright red. He felt like a fucking idiot. He had kissed her once, but it was not nearly thorough enough to suit his feelings for her.

"The second you do, your Wolf will want to gut you from the inside out if you don't stake your claim and mark that woman for the rest of your lives. The desire you feel now is nothing to how you will feel after you give her your bite."

"It gets worse?" Brock scowled.

What the fuck? Was he doomed to walk around a slave to this woman for all time?

Yesss, the Wolf inside him growled. *And it will be the best fucking thing we could ever hope for.*

"Son, you don't know the half of it, but if you're lucky, she'll let you claim her and then she'll claim your sorry ass right back. Best fucking time of my life, having Lucy bite the shit out of me. I'd die for that woman, Brock. Even scarier, I'd kill for her. Do terrible things to keep her safe and happy. She knows it too, and her love for me is a bottomless well. I can feel it in our bond. I am a lucky bastard," Derrick rumbled.

They clinked glasses and took the next shot, this one was a new brand of tequila that went down smoothly. Brock turned his shot glass upside down and sat looking at his hands with Derrick by his side, enjoying the silence. Of course, it did not last long.

Both men turned as the side door to the bar came swinging open and a very pregnant Lucy came strolling through with bags on each arm and a rosy, pink glow to her cheeks. Her belly seemed to enter the roadhouse a step before the rest of her body, and he felt Derrick tense in his seat next to him. The Alpha stood already on his way to her side, but Phoenix beat him there, taking her burdens from her hands and leaving her free to greet her mate.

"Hey boys, come help me," she said when she entered, and Phoenix nodded, already heading out to the car to unload her goodies.

Derrick was already across the floor and lifting her up in his arms for their usual hello kiss and embrace. Normally, the others turned away out of respect, but this time Brock watched and what he saw fascinated him.

The couple nuzzled each other softly, whispering words he couldn't quite make out before kissing one another. When they connected, it was like their entire bodies glowed with the soft ethereal light of their matebond. The two of them fucking oozed love, and for the first time ever, Brock admitted he wanted that for himself.

Not with Lucy, or Derrick, for that matter—but with Ariella.

He wanted her to accept his claim. To share her life with him. To have a strong matebond. To make a family.

Now, he just had to convince her.

At eight PM, he pulled up to her apartment, noting the large lion statues on either side of the lobby's main entrance. Brock rolled his eyes in exasperation. Leave it to a bunch of cat Shifters to emulate themselves in stone for all to see.

SMH.

His Wolf growled inside his mind's eye. But Brock simply smirked and walked up the stairs. Ariella's apartment was on the second floor. She had offered to meet him outside, but he wanted to treat this like the real date it was, especially after having fucked up so royally.

A dozen long-stemmed red roses in hand, Brock walked down the hall to her door, and pulled on the jacket of his custom tux. It was his, not rented, as he needed it tailored for his extra-large frame. He'd combed back his longish blond hair, scrubbed himself from head to toe in the shower, and even shaved his facial hair for the occasion. He'd wanted to look his best for what he had planned.

Brock rang the bell and waited with bated breath for her to answer. Even then, he was unprepared for the sight that met his eyes. Holy hell. She was drop dead gorgeous. The personification of every dream, *wet and otherwise,* he'd ever had.

He swallowed loudly as Ariella stood at the door. Her golden eyes, while contemplative at first, filled with delight as he held out his meager offering. Meager compared to her. She wore a deep red gown, hugging her generous curves, embracing, and caressing them like a lover's hands, and he had half a mind to tear the thing off.

Was it possible to be jealous of clothes? Well, he was. He managed not to rip it from her skin—barely. The confection ended mid-calf, but his gaze traveled lower, paying attention to the slit revealing her smooth thigh, supple calf, slender ankle, and down to the pair of strappy red high-heeled shoes completing the ensemble. Damn outfit should've been illegal. Probably was in some places.

Brock had always been a sucker for women in heels, and the ones she had on were spiked and sexy and made him want to drop to his knees and worship at her feet. Her dark curls floated around her shoulders like a velvet cloud and he was tempted to run his fingers through it, but he knew better than to touch a woman's hair without invitation.

Later, he told himself, and handed her the roses.

A deep breath told him she had company, but he wasn't worried about it. They were her family. Still, it nagged at him. They probably thought he'd propositioned her for an evening. Soon enough, the record would be set straight.

"Thank you," she said shyly, placing the vase of flowers on the table.

"You said to dress up," she spoke in a breathless whisper of a voice that shot sparks of electricity right to his cock. "Is this okay?"

"Yes. It's perfect," he said with pure honesty.

His Wolf made his voice gravelly, and he cleared his throat before he continued, feeling much like a pup on his first date. In effect, he was.

"Shall we?" Brock offered Ariella his arm and felt ten feet tall when she placed her small hand in the crook of his elbow so trustingly.

He'd put her in a bad position, yet still, she trusted him. The thought was humbling, and he thanked the gods for the blessing she truly was in his life. Emotion filled him to the brink. Thunder roared in his ears and his chest was damn near to exploding. He knew then Derrick had been right.

I love her.

Fuck, yes, he did. He was head over heels for Ariella Golden. The acknowledgement burst a dam inside of him. Brock felt better than he had in weeks. She smiled up at him shyly, and fuck, he felt it down to his toes. She was more important than anything else had ever been in his whole life.

Loving her was easy, he realized. If he was lucky, Brock would get to do it for a very long time.

Mine.

CHAPTER TEN

DIRE WOLF MATES

Earlier that evening...

Ariella's pulse raced, and her heart was hammering inside her chest. She couldn't believe her own mother and sisters had talked her into accepting Brock's insane proposal.

If only it was a proposal, her Lioness lamented.

Sad rawr.

The head over heels she-Cat wanted to use the upcoming night as an excuse to claim her mate, but Ariella had absolutely shut that plan down. Either Brock didn't know she was his mate, or he didn't care. Either way, she was not biting him.

Besides, wouldn't her fated mate know who she was and want her above all others? She felt a pang of sadness at the thought he could simply leave her after a night. It was almost worth her calling off the whole thing.

But her she-Cat couldn't stand the idea of any other male getting near her, and this might be her only chance to experience carnal bliss. Winning the contest with *Serious Moonlight's* contract might provide a balm of sorts for the future, she reasoned, even though the prospect of trading sex for his signature left a bad taste in her mouth.

Ariella didn't want to die a spinster. Not like her poor Aunt Alicia, who had died only last year. Poor woman had never found a man to look beyond her ample ass, or so her mother said whenever her unfortunate sister's name was brought up.

Maybe this was her shot to change his mind?

"Easy girl," Patricia Golden grunted as she'd zipped up the scarlet red gown Ariella had bought on impulse months ago, but never had the nerve to wear.

"That puppy doggy of yours is gonna flip his lid when he sees you in this!"

"Hell, yeah, you look all juicy and red like a strawberry ice pop!" Adrianna giggled.

Ariella looked down at herself and groaned. The ensemble was super tight and so over the top she couldn't imagine why she had bought it in the first place.

Ugh.

But it was love at first sight and she'd put it on her credit card and kept it tucked away in her closet. Even the months she'd spent paying off the ridiculous thing would prove worth it if Brock fell head over heels for her after tonight.

"Are you sure I should wear this one?"

"Am I sure? This little number practically screams *gimme your eggplant emoji*. You just listen to your mother, and you will bag yourself a puppy tonight! Just remember honey, we she-Cats mark in two ways, with teeth and claw. You just scratch him, and that doggy is all yours. Get 'em!" Her mother slapped her on her butt and spun her around to face the mirror.

"Mom! Ohmygawd! Is that me?"

"Mom's wight, Awi," Annabeth said with a mouthful of snacks. *"You wook gweat! Hank agwees, I sent him a pwic."*

Her sister's exuberance for her outfit was followed by some serious *nom nom noming*. Good thing Ariella spoke fluent *Lioness-with-mouth-full*. She rolled her eyes and covered her face with her hands.

This whole thing was borderline insane. Ariella's shock when

Brock had made his indecent, and yet exciting, proposal had basically caused her brain to shut down. Her hormones were going into overdrive.

Panicked and shocked, she had to leave the woods, and him, just to clear her mind. On the verge of fucking up her life, she did the only thing she could think of. She'd run home to her mother and found her and all of her sisters having a good old time with her last bottle of tequila and the new bag of chips and jar of mango jalapeno salsa she'd brought home the night before.

"Those chips were mine," she whined.

"Come on, sugar," her mother said.

She'd dragged her up in a big mom style hug, and Ari had poured out the whole sob story. Her sisters commiserated and made Ari a plate and a mango margarita on the rocks with a sugared rim—her favorite cocktail—while they hatched a plan.

"Are the drinks laced?" Ariella had wisely asked.

"Nope," Annabeth said, and shook her head, dislodging some crumbs from her otherwise lovely face.

She was staying the night since her mate was out taking his favorite client on a cross-country ride. Hank, Annabeth's mate, owned a limo service company. He was a decent guy, even if his Shifter animal was an overrated parakeet—a constant point of contention between Annabeth and her Lioness family. Of course, they were only kidding. Mostly.

Whatever. Everyone knows Cats rule.

"You sure about this, sis?" Adrianna asked, handing her a shot glass full of liquid courage.

"I am," she sighed, and turned to look at three pairs of similar golden eyes.

"I love him. He's my mate, and this is my only chance to show him that. Now, what about this drink? Was Mom anywhere near it?"

"Oh, sweetie," Adrianna said, ignoring her question. Her sister sniffed and blew air kisses at her. "I can't believe you found your mate!"

"Oh, he hasn't agreed to let me claim him, but maybe after tonight," she said and bit her lip, her uncertainty growing by the second.

"Look, we confiscated Mom's catnip yesterday. But if you need some?" Toni inquired and narrowed her eyes, but Ari shook her head.

"I will be okay without it."

"Good, because you look amazing. Now for some dirt, after we got here last night, King Donovan called and Mom went a little nutso," Toni whispered while their Mom went to the other room to grab Ariella's wrap.

"I swear, I don't know what he did, but she was seriously pissed."

"Yeah, lucky we were here to cheer her up with 'ritas," Annabeth replied and smiled widely, looking more like the Cheshire cat than the Lioness she was.

"Oh no, I wonder what's going on between those two?"

"Beats me, but the rumor is he isn't ready to move on—"

"Here it is!" Patricia announced, waving the shimmery wrap around.

"What is going on? You know, I can smell gossip a mile away, and I will not have it about me or the leader of our Pride."

"But Mom, maybe we can help?" Ariella asked.

"You can't. It's over between me and the King, but we will still respect him and not give in to petty gossip. Now, Ari, drink that shot, and then put this on, and fix your lipstick," she instructed.

"Yeah, then explain this whole thing from the top," Toni said.

So Ariella did as she was told. Mostly. She placed the wrap on the back of the chair. Took the shot. Fixed her lipstick. Then, she told her family Brock's proposal one last time.

"Lucky dog!"

"Good for you, sweetie."

"About time you get laid."

Varying degrees of acceptance and teasing followed. After offering her comfort and support, the kind only mothers and sisters could give, they all agreed she should accept and then bag the Wolf!

Ariella still didn't know if it was the right thing or not, but here she was dressed and ready.

Ding dong.

"He's here!" squealed Patricia Golden, and with that, she grabbed Ari's sisters by the hems of their shirts and dragged them out of the room.

"Have a good time, honey! Be adventurous," she whisper-screamed.

Ariella knew they could hear and probably see everything from their spots on the floor behind the kitchen island, but she needed them there. They were her support system, no matter how nutty and unconventional.

Opening the door and seeing him standing there, like some tall, gorgeous Prince Charming to her, very unlikely, and a little bit chubby Cinderella, made her smile like a loon.

But this is no fairy tale.

Ariella had to repeat that several times as he led her to a gorgeous, low slung, luxury sports car that she hadn't even realized he owned.

"This is beautiful," she said as he helped her get inside.

"Yes. Very beautiful," his gravelly voice seemed to strike a chord deep within her and she looked up to see his eyes were on her, and not the car at all.

"Where are we going?" she asked after they had been driving for a few minutes and he hadn't given her a single hint.

"Oh, uh, we're going to the cabin," he returned, and she frowned.

A cabin? Why was she so dressed up then? Ariella quirked an eyebrow as they flew past the sign that read *Exiting Blue Valley*. Wherever they were going, she sure hoped she was ready for what was coming.

"Do you like music?"

"Who me?" she asked and noted the playful curl of his lip as he waited for her response. "Sure. I mean, yes, of course."

"This is a demo from one of the bands who recently auditioned for the bar. I think they're good," he murmured and tapped the display screen to play songs across blue tooth from his smart phone to the car.

The music wasn't exactly rock, but it wasn't country either. It was something in between and had a great chorus and melody that made the listener want to move with the beat. The singer's voice was deep and clear, and Ariella liked it right away.

"Is it okay?"

He seemed to care about her answer, so she nodded and smiled. They chatted a little, about the weather, the car, nothing important, but it helped her nerves. When she shivered slightly at the brush of his hand against her thigh as he switched gears, he reacted by turning the heat on for her. It was sweet and thoughtful. Two words she would've never associated with the typically hotheaded chef.

"We're here," he said, and she was surprised to see they had been driving for an hour.

But wherever *here* was, it didn't seem like they'd arrived. She looked out the window at the dark woods rounding them, which only seemed to be lit by the glowing, nearly full moon.

"Where?" she asked as Brock turned down a narrow lane that had suddenly appeared and seemed hidden off the regular traffic route.

That tiny road suddenly gave way to a much larger two-way intersection and an enormous parking lot. Beyond that was a large building that would in no way cause Ariella to think the word *cabin*, and yet, there it was in large blue letters over the enormous entrance.

This was not a rustic shack in the woods—thank fuck. It was a resort of some kind, snug in the woods off the parkway past Blue Valley. *The Cabin,* she read the sign again. Ariella wondered how she had never heard of this, *judging from the number of cars,* obvious hot spot.

"What is this place?"

"Well, have you ever heard of Stein Luxury Hotel & Resorts?"

"Yes, I mean that's a Shifter run hotel chain. Some of their smaller locations have started ordering products through EWLP."

"Yes, but they are not strictly Shifter. Frank employs all supernatural creatures in his global hotels and resorts, catering to our kind while keeping under the radar. This one is pretty new. Opened for just a month."

"Wow. They built this in a month?"

"Yes, well, like I said, Mr. Stein is not averse to hiring any supernatural beings, and it's been said he dabbles in magical arts," he shrugged.

"You mean like Witchcraft?"

"You can turn into a Lioness, love, and you doubt the existence of Witches?"

His smile made her feel like an idiot, but she supposed she had been quite sheltered. Lions stuck close to their Pride. Power in numbers and all that. Plus, her mother was quite hands on.

"I guess I just never thought about them to this extent. I mean, Mom buys all kids of herbs and concoctions from kitchen Witches, but I never thought about the rest of it."

"There is a lot of magic in this world, Ariella. Some of it is right in front of us," he murmured and pulled to a stop in front of a harried looking valet attendant. Brock took her hand in his before she could exit the vehicle.

"Look, I want you to know I am glad you came with me."

"I am too," she responded, knowing he could hear a lie.

It was the truth. Even if she both feared and anticipated the end of the evening with equal parts excitement and anxiety.

Brock walked around the vehicle with the confident gait of a man used to being in charge and tossed his keys to the eager valet. Ariella understood the sentiment all too well. The butterflies in her stomach were doing a mambo as it was.

"Come on."

He took her hand in his big warm one, and those butterflies all seemed to swoon at once. From the second they entered the elegant hotel's entryway, Brock was greeted like an old friend, and she was treated with the utmost respect and courtesy. They surpassed the line and were immediately shown to a snug little booth in the back of the jam packed hotel restaurant.

"How come we didn't have to wait?"

"Oh, well, actually the MC has an interest in this establishment," he said, and she noted his cheeks turn a dusky shade.

Was he embarrassed? She grinned, and he shrugged, trying to play it off. This was a side of him she had never seen. Curiosity got the better of her, so she leaned forward, wanting more from the surprisingly shy, secretive male.

"An interest?"

"Yeah, we have a longstanding friendship with Mr. Stein, and the executive chef as well. In fact, we are expected."

Brock appeared nervous as he sipped his water and looked around, and Ariella wondered why.

"Really? Why would he be expecting us?" she asked, eyebrows raised.

"*She* is always available whenever Brock Laurent drops by," a feminine voice coming from right behind her had Ariella almost falling off the booth.

The woman managed to startle a Lioness. How embarrassing! Ariella swallowed her yowl and took in the tall, thin female. The stranger wore a pristine white chef's coat and a small hat to help hold back the wealth of blond hair that hung in a braid down her back. Her beautiful face was positively perfect.

She was gorgeous, and it seemed she knew Brock. Intimately if her smile was anything to go by. Ariella swallowed the pang of hurt. Why would he take her to meet an old conquest?

"Hello, *mon cher*," she said warmly, and Brock stood up and embraced the stranger with more familiarity than Ariella had been prepared for.

"Susan, you look wonderful," he said, and his smile was genuine as he stepped back to look at her with mischievous blue eyes.

Ariella's stomach dropped. What the hell was this? She looked down, trying to weigh her options, as they continued their familiar greeting ritual.

"As do you, but then you always look well, darling," she touched his face with affection before letting her hand fall back to her side, and once more Ariella's heart twisted.

The woman was clearly in love with him, but Brock seemed to not notice. Was that a thing with him? She wondered unkindly. Did he just collect women's hearts and break them casually without thought or care?

Well, that was it. She had had enough. Before she could stand, Brock's warm hand clamped down on her shoulder and he made small circles with his thumb that immediately soothed her beast.

"I want you to meet someone," Brock said quietly. He looked down at Ariella and his eyes were warm and kind, almost apologetic as he continued. "This is Ariella Golden. Ariella, this is Susan Stoker, the head chef here at *The Cabin*."

"Ah, this is the representative from *Eat Well Live Proud*, the little Lion Pride's corporation you told me about," the woman said.

She was all business now as she sat down with a wide smile. Probably relieved because Brock had placed Ariella in perspective for his lovely friend. Confusion clouded her mind, but Ariella managed to fight through it. She answered Susan's questions with aplomb and courtesy. She was a Lioness after all, majesty was in her blood.

"Brock here has been after me for weeks now to sign over our entire meat and seafood departments to your tiny hands," the chef said and looked Ariella up and down like she was scat.

It was not the first time a female had underestimated Ariella, but she refused to be cowered by the woman. No need for aggression. She was a Lioness, and as such, Ari did not need to announce it.

"Excuse me, ladies. I will leave you to chat while I get us some drinks," Brock murmured.

He stood up and left them alone. Ariella wanted to scream at him for doing so. This was so not the dream date she'd imagined. The skinny blonde eyed her coolly and crossed her legs in the slim black pants she wore under her chef's coat.

"So, what is it that makes you so special that Brock Laurent would not only mention you, but sing your praises and bring you to me in *my* new restaurant?"

"He is a man who knows quality when he sees it," Ariella replied.

She smiled widely, allowing a bit of her inner predator to show through. The moment the woman figured out that she was more than just a harmless female, Ariella felt slightly better. She couldn't put her nose on what Ms. Stoker actually was, but she was not a normal, and not a Shifter either.

"Indeed. So, tell me, are you lovers?"

"I don't see what that has to do with this," Ariella stated. "The fact, Chef Susan, is I work for the finest organically raised meat, fowl, and sustainably harvested seafood distributor in the area. We cater specifically to those businesses frequented and run by people like us. Creatures with a finer palate and heightened appreciation for freshness and quality. Our clients' success is of the utmost importance at *Eat Well Live Proud*, and all of my accounts are handled with care and seen to personally."

"But you deal with small restaurants, yes? Not establishments of this caliber and size."

"I often work with local business, but our corporation is large and internationally known. I more than confident in my ability to meet your needs."

"I see," Susan said and looked up as Brock returned with a bottle of wine in hand. "Ah, 1993 was a wonderful year, wasn't it, Brock?"

Her knowing smile made Ariella cringe internally, but she hid it well as he poured three glasses.

"Ariella is a fan of white wine, aren't you?" he replied and smiled at her in a way that made her heart thump inside her chest.

Bum bum bum.

Her inner Lioness practically swooned at his smile and Ariella grabbed a piece of focaccia from the breadbasket in self-defense. She chewed a bite slowly, trying to calm her nerves. Why did he have such power over her?

With something akin to panic rising inside of her, she swallowed down the lovely dry white wine and winced as it went down the wrong way. Maybe she was just hungry.

"Do you recall the time we hunted for truffles?"

"Of course."

Ariella blocked out their conversation and took another bite of the delicate rosemary infused focaccia. Brock was busy rehashing old times with Chef Susan, and she was entirely out of her depth with their conversation. Talking business was one thing, but with this woman, every word uttered held a memory or innuendo Ariella was not privy to and it was rather annoying.

Ignoring it became something she had to actively work at, and even though the meeting was all of twenty minutes, it felt much, much longer. Ariella had already decided to leave by then, but she would wait for the Chef to go away first, then she would request an Uber.

Finally, and to her utmost delight, a small, dark-haired man wearing a similar chef's coat approached the table and whispered to the woman. Her eyes widened, and she nodded.

"I am sorry to cut this short, but I am needed in the kitchen—"

"No worries, Susan, I understand," Brock said, smiling warmly. He stood up and extended a hand.

Ariella was surprised by his suddenly curt and rushed manner, it seemed he had enjoyed the lady's company, but whatever was going on between them he was happier to see her go. She'd been demanding of his attention and had repeatedly cut Ariella out of their conversation.

But, if she was being fair and diplomatic, Brock had always found a way to bring the topic back to include her. Susan nodded in Ari's direction before addressing the tall, almost too handsome Dire Wolf Shifter once more.

"Well, Brock, it has been too long, and I admit I was surprised when you called me back after weeks of ignoring my messages. But I am angry at you, you didn't tell me it was quite this important."

"I wanted to, Susan, please forgive me," he replied.

"I see, and that is why you did not mention this creature here. She is quite lovely, your little huntress," Susan said, and Ariella sniffed loudly.

She did not like being spoken about as if she was invisible, but for some reason the predator in her understood something about the woman the human did not. She inhaled again, silently, and found it quite odd that she could not detect a scent other than the herbs and spices that clung to her chef's coat.

"Well, I see no reason to delay. You have convinced me, dear boy. Miss Golden, I would like you to add *The Cabin* to your weekly routes of deliveries as soon as possible. Here is my card," she said and nodded.

The man who had come to fetch her presented Ariella with a plain white card with bold black font that read Susan Stoker, Executive Chef, and had her contact information beneath.

"Oh, yes, of course, I will email you an order form," Ariella said, stunned, but finally recalled how to speak. "You can select what you will require at the end of each week for the following one. We require notice roughly twenty-four hours before you'd like the delivery."

"Perfect. I will look for your email. Ciao, Brock, and goodbye."

"Susan," he nodded.

"*Goodbye*," she reiterated, and winked at Ariella.

If the Lioness inside of her thought the tension had been unbearable when the strange woman had been there, she was in no way prepared for it to worsen after she'd gone. But Ari had given up on playing games.

"What is this all about, Brock? Why did you invite me here?"

"I'm sorry, it must seem odd," he said, exhaling deeply.

"Yes, it is. You have ignored me for a long time. I'm not sophisticated enough to play this way. In fact, I think I should leave. I'm going to call an Uber," Ariella murmured, placing her napkin on the table.

"Wait," he hissed, closing his eyes. Brock reached out and placed it on hers, and she stilled.

Sadness filled her and disappointment. She was confused and her emotions were a wreck. Didn't he know how hard this was for her? Was he using his indecent proposal to make the other woman jealous? What was Chef Susan to him, anyway? So many questions. They battered at her until she thought she would scream her frustration.

"No, Brock, I can't—"

"Please, Ariella, please," he begged, weakening her defenses. "I promise, I am not playing with you, and it will all make sense, I swear. Just don't go. Stay. Eat with me," he whispered.

Brock nodded his head to someone over her left shoulder, and suddenly a myriad of tasty little plates was set before them. She'd never seen him beg or look so vulnerable. As each dish was placed on the table, he seemed to hold his breath. Like he cared if she liked the selections he'd made.

"I thought you might be hungry by now, so I ordered when I went to get the wine."

Brock motioned towards the dishes, and to her utter embarrassment, Ariella's stomach grumbled. She was starved, but she wasn't a fool. There was something very odd about all this. Something she didn't understand going on behind the scenes with him and with their so-called date turned business meeting.

Give him a chance, her Lioness urged.

Ariella wanted to. She really did. It was incredibly uncharacteristic of her to agree to his indecent proposal, but to have it turn into some kind of farce in her face was almost too much to bear.

"Will you stay?"

His big blue eyes were so clear and dark, like a moonlit pool. There was something about Brock that made her reckless. Something that, if she wasn't very careful, was going to cost her more than her virginity.

Yes, please, her Lioness purred.

Ariella crossed her legs and shook out her napkin before dropping it back on her lap.

"Alright. I'm hungry anyway. Surprise surprise," she added sarcastically.

Ariella huffed out a breath and avoided making eye contact with him. She picked up her fork only to have him take it from her.

"Let me. Here, try this," he whispered and held a tiny little confection with slivers of smoked salmon and caviar to her lips.

She leaned forward, feeling a little silly that he was hand-feeding her in public, but that thought vanished and Ariella moaned aloud the second she nibbled the delectable morsel.

"That is amazing, but it's impossible. The salmon tastes like yours," she said and tilted her head to the side. She couldn't believe her eyes when he seemed to blush.

"I studied under Chef Susan for a time. Many years ago, Ariella," he confessed.

"Oh," she said and wiped her mouth.

"No, love, it was not like that," he explained. "She has been a friend of the DWMC for many years and was my mother's maid of honor, in fact," he added.

"Wait, I know some Shifters age slowly, but she isn't a Dire Wolf. What is she?" Ariella asked.

"I told you this place was not just Shifter run. Susan is a Vampire and though she may have given the wrong impression, she is more like my aunt. I swear she was never a girlfriend," he said and made a face like the idea would be borderline gross. Ariella laughed aloud, relief filling her.

"I believe you," Ariella said, knowing full well her Lioness would have smelled a lie.

He seemed to relax a bit after that, and they sampled half a dozen more appetizers before a server came out pushing a cart with what looked like an entire rack of lamb.

"*Monsieur*?" the server asked.

"I will carve, thank you," Brock said and stood.

With the utmost concentration, he selected the choicest cuts of rare lamb for Ariella. She bit her lip in amazement. He was catering to her needs, like she was special to him, and the idea was breathtaking.

He filled her plate with expertly roasted meat, adding some of the unique sides and a hint of cucumber mint relish to her plate before he bothered fixing one for himself. Ariella felt cared for in a way no man had ever accomplished. She waited for him to sit before trying the food.

"Don't you like it?" he asked, brow furrowed.

"It is very good," she said and watched as relief and pride seemed to pass across his handsome face.

He really was undeniably good looking. She wondered why he wasn't more like his Pack Mates. Weylin, Phoenix, and Cole all seemed to have a different girl every night. But not Brock. He never dated.

Even before they had met, if Sheila was to be believed, and the woman had no reason to lie. Not that Shifters did to begin with. Too tricky trying to maintain a lie when the people around you could so easily detect it.

"I'm glad you like it," his deep voice had the most delicious rumble, and she turned her attention to him.

"It's wonderful."

"Good. For dessert, I have something else in mind," he said, and his voice held a hint of promise in it that made her knees weak, even though she was already sitting down.

Whatever the Wolf had in mind, Ariella was sure to be game.

Purrrr.

CHAPTER ELEVEN

DIRE WOLF MATES

Mate. Mate. Mate.

Brock's Dire Wolf had kept up the mantra throughout the entire evening. He couldn't help it. Everything about her, from the surprising way she handled herself with Susan to the way she seemed to accept him on his terms, was remarkable. Perfect even.

After they'd eaten, he took her hand and led her out of the restaurant for the private suite he'd rented for the night. No obligations. No pretenses.

That was what he'd told himself, and now it was his turn to tell her. He could scent her desire and her nervousness. Both were tempting beyond his experience. He could've killed Susan for sitting with them for so long and purposely giving the wrong impression to Ariella.

His honorary aunt, the woman who had taught him almost everything he knew about cooking, was as far from a lover as one could get. No, he hadn't answered her messages because the confounded Vampire would've questioned him about his love life the first chance she had. Furthermore, she would've known immediately that he was hiding something.

As it was, he'd braced himself for a barrage of emails and phone calls he was bound to get after tonight from Susan and his own mother, who had started riding with the Dire Wolf Widows MC after her mate and his father had passed away. Brock wasn't ready for them to get involved just yet.

First, he had to square things with Ariella, and who knew how easy that was going to be given the mixed signals he'd been sending? Fuck and damn, he could've lost her for all his stupidity. That thought alone had his Dire Wolf howling in outrage.

"Wow," Ariella's softly spoken gasp of surprise reached his ears once the suite doors were opened.

Romantic music was playing low in the background, the fire was lit, a table was laid with champagne, and a cart with fresh berries and ingredients for his special zabaglione was set up. Red roses filled every nook and cranny and since they were on the top floor, a skylight above gave them a perfect view of the moon and the stars in the navy velvet sky.

"This is really something," Ariella murmured.

She walked to the far window, her bright gold eyes on the view. Brock was equally ensnared by a vision of beauty, only for him, that vision was her. Hell, he almost swallowed his tongue at the sway of her hips in that killer dress.

Twinkle lights decorated the trees in the courtyard and the lake sparkled with light from the moon. It was a lovely view, and he imagined the hotel would do very well. But he wasn't all that interested in the success of another Stein Luxury Hotel. He was only interested in whether he could make a go of this thing with Ariella. Either way, he owed it to them both to try.

"Brock?"

Ariella turned and startled when she realized he'd stepped right behind her. How could he resist? Her sweet and spicy musk filled his senses, leaving him on edge and needy for just a small taste of the sweet Lioness.

“Yes?”

From this close, he could see the spark of fire in her gold eyes. Fuck, she was so beautiful. Her Lioness so regal and powerful. He was a lucky Wolf, truly and well beyond what he deserved.

“Why did you bring me here with you? To act as a buffer between you and your family friend?”

“No,” he said immediately. “I wanted to finally spend some time with you, Ariella. I know it must be confusing for you.”

“Why now? You’ve been avoiding me like the plague, then you proposition me and idiot that I am I ran at the chance. You must think I’m desperate or foolish, to tell you the truth, I wouldn’t even blame you,” she said, shrugging and causing the straps of her dress to fall from her smooth shoulders.

“I don’t think that at all,” he said, voice rough with his beast.

Before she could move to fix the straps of her dress, he replaced the tiny pieces of fabric with his hands. Touching her was like holding a livewire. He couldn’t contain his growl as little bites of electric pleasure zapped through him from the mostly platonic contact.

“Fuck, Ari, I have been torturing myself by staying away from you,” he growled.

“Why? I don’t want you away from me,” she moaned, swaying closer and closer until her soft belly came into contact with the hardness he couldn’t hide.

Breathing heavily, Brock stilled, waiting for her to react, to move away, but she didn’t. She simply rested against him and waited for him to speak.

“Because,” he growled in frustration.

"I’m trying to understand, Brock. Help me,” she begged.

“I can’t be around you and not want to touch you! Fuck, every time I see you, I think about kissing you. I want you, Ariella. My Wolf wants you. Mine,” he growled.

His touch on her shoulders grew rough as he pulled her closer. One hand clamped around her neck, the other at the small of her back. She was trembling against him, spiking his protective instincts. Fuck, he wanted her so damn badly. Brock lowered his head slowly, giving her all the time in the world to move back.

That she didn't gave him all the more reason to take what he wanted. And all he wanted was her. Ariella boldly wrapped her arms around his neck, pulling him closer. She lifted her beautiful face to his, opened her lips, and crashed her mouth against Brock's own hard, unrepentant one.

He growled, greedily giving in to the passionate tempest that seemed to overwhelm him. Their kiss was explosive, complete, and the best fucking thing he had ever experienced in his long life.

"Mine," he growled again, grinding against her mouth and dragging her body against his.

He wanted her with a desperation that almost blinded him to anything else, and yet Brock found himself keenly aware of her at all times. Every whimpering mewl and shaky breath, every wiggle of her body and press of her tongue meant something else.

He read her like a book. Every movement a signal, a clue that he could follow to give her all the pleasure she craved. Everything she wanted and yearned for, he vowed to deliver. That was his sacred vow to her as man, as Wolf, as mate.

"I want you too," she moaned, and it was like music to his ears.

He wanted her alright, but not for one night, as he'd led her to believe. No, Brock wanted her for much more than that. Lifting her in his arms, he carried her to the bed and placed her gently on the silky comforter.

The hotel's design was of the finest quality and expense, which meant muted colors and sublime textures. Everything he looked for in accommodations, which, given he'd spent so much time on the road, might seem unusual, but Brock knew what he liked.

But all the surrounding luxury was nothing compared to the softness of her skin, or the sweet pleasure he took in her kiss. Shrugging off his jacket, he felt her hands tremble as she tugged on his tie and buttons. He wasn't prepared to be quite so gentle, and in one move he tore the fine shirt off his torso and growled aloud as she leaned forward and kissed her way from his navel to his neck.

"Ari, that feels so good. My turn," he growled, and reached for her zipper, noting the way she froze.

"I will stop if you want me to whenever you want me to. All you have to do, Ariella, is just say the word," he said despite his Wolf's warning growl.

"I, I don't want you to stop. It's just, I've never done this. I have never even undressed for a man," she confessed shyly, and her honesty and innocence humbled him.

"I see, maybe we should talk first."

"Oh, I didn't mean for you to stop," she said quickly and bit her lip.

Her cheeks turned pink, and fuck, she was so beautiful. He adored her.

"I plan on giving you everything I have, Ari, but I have something to tell you," he said as she kissed the corner of his mouth, his lips, and then his chin.

"Brock, please," she said, and ran her short nails over his pecs and abs, stopping just shy of his throbbing cock.

"Don't stop. I'll go mad if you do."

"Ariella," he growled her name,

Her shy touches grew bolder with every swipe and her golden eyes locked onto his. The next time she ran them down his body, she continued down his hips until his shy little virgin mate cupped his balls in one hand and traced him from root to tip with the other.

Brock froze. This was the moment Brock had feared the most. The one when this virginal little hellcat got a glimpse of his size and girth for the first time. Echoes of his past horror came pummeling through his brain, the sounds of the girl who in his youth he'd foolishly believed was meant for him.

"Get away from me with that thing!"

The embarrassment was nothing compared to the deep psychological scars the experience had given him. From that day on he'd never dated a normal, or a virgin, in fact, he never dated at all. He hadn't lived like a monk.

Brock had engaged in sex, but it was infrequent and mostly with other Shifters who knew the deal. He'd chosen professionals who were well experienced so as not to be afraid of his extraordinary size. Using sex as a means to relieve him of the tension he'd felt every few years or so was all he could do to sate his beast. Those encounters were as impersonal as a handshake, and he never felt good afterwards.

This was something else entirely. No comparison. At all.

"Brock? Where did you go?"

"You, uh, you're touching me," he said as her hands still gently explored him through his pants.

"Yeah, I am," she replied, and grinned shyly. "Is that alright?"

"Yessss."

"Can I see you, too? I want to see you. Take these off," she begged.

"Ariella, I don't want to frighten you," he mumbled and stilled her hand, trying hard not to hate himself at the look of hurt on her face.

"Am I doing something wrong?" she asked.

"No! God, not at all."

"Well, isn't this why you brought me here? A night with you for the roadhouse's business?"

He closed his eyes. Fuck. He knew that had been stupid.

"Actually," he confessed. "That was a ruse to get you here."

The scent of her disappointment crashed into him, and he opened his eyes. Seeing her misery was too much to bear.

"So, you don't want to spend the night with me, and I don't get *Serious Moonlight* as a client?"

"No! I mean, *yes*. Wait—"

"I think you better explain what the hell you're doing, Brock. I mean, you are hot, then cold, then hot again, and I have had about all I can take."

"Okay, look, I brought you here to meet with Susan to get her to sign on with you. This hotel does a huge business, and you'll most likely win your contest and knock your competition out of the park—"

"And is that all you think I care about? I wasn't going to sleep with you because of work, Brock! You're my mate, you idiot! My Lioness knew the second I met you," she yelled and pushed away from him.

The hurt on her face hit him right in the gut. Fuck, he was losing her. He was messing this up. And the hurt was unbearable.

"No. Of course, I didn't think that. Ari, you have to believe me!" Brock scrambled to explain.

"You know what, Brock, this whole thing is a mistake. I was wrong. You can't be my mate."

She struggled to get off the bed in her tight dress, and he used it to his advantage to pin her down beneath him. He couldn't give up now. Not without making her listen.

"Wait, dammit, Ari, I need you to listen. Please," he growled as she struggled beneath him. "I want you so fucking bad right now, if you don't stop squirming Ariella, this is going to go in another direction sooner than either of us is ready for," he growled, and pressed his hips down until she felt the proof of what he was saying.

"Oh!"

"Now, will you listen or not?"

She stilled beneath him. Her chest heaved in her dress as she tried to catch her breath, but he could tell she was still spitting mad. And damn, she was even more beautiful when she was angry.

Shit.

He was a sick fuck. Whatever. The woman was driving him mad.

"I'm fucking this all up, Ari. I have been from the beginning, but maybe I can try to explain."

"You better," she huffed.

"Alright," he eased off of her and they sat face to face while he told her the truth behind his actions.

"I had a girlfriend a long time ago. She was a normal, and we were kids. She was my first kiss. My first date. And I was the first guy she'd ever seen naked. We tried to, *you know*, have sex, but when things got close, she pushed me off and ran away. She was screaming, saying I was killing her because I was *too big* to fit. She said I was not normal, and a girl would have to be crazy to sleep with me," he growled.

Fuck, he hated this. Brock hated having to reveal all his insecurities and past embarrassments, but he owed it to her.

"I am so sorry, Brock, that must've been awful," Ariella whispered and placed her hand on his shoulder.

She met his eyes with nothing but concern in hers. Why should he have been shocked when she was everything kind and sweet and caring in the world? He exhaled the breath he'd been holding in, hope filling him to near bursting.

"Um, are we here just to see if you could have sex with a virgin? To overcome some fear? I know you don't really want me—"

"Not want you? Fuck, I really am an asshole, aren't I?" Brock groaned and covered his face with his hands. He laughed self-deprecatingly and turned to stand.

"The first time I saw you, I wanted you so damn much. You struck me dumb with your pretty face and gorgeous, guileless eyes. Then, you shocked the shit out of me, climbing on the back of my bike, and wrapping your hands around my waist. I damn near claimed you right there. Your Lioness had it right from the start, Ariella. So did my Dire Wolf. We are fated mates. You belong to me. And I belong to you."

"So you knew? You knew what we are to each other and yet you denied us," she said, and the pain in her voice brought tears to his eyes.

She shook her head and covered her mouth with her hands. The soft gasping noises she made were worse than if she would've balled her hand and punched him in the face. He sure as fuck deserved it. Instead, she sat back on the bed, eyes brimming with tears, the hurt on her face plain as day as she waited for him to continue.

"Finish it," she demanded.

Grrrrr.

His Dire Wolf snarled and snapped, the beast had been angry with him for stopping and talking when he should've been showing her his feelings, and now he was even more angry because he put that sad look on her face. Brock turned and dropped to his knees in front of her. If he was going to confess, he might as well assume the position.

"Ariella," he breathed her name and closed his eyes. "I was a coward. I was scared. I know this might not be enough, but you have haunted my every moment since that very first day. Your golden eyes, that dark curly hair, your incredible body, and that musky scent that invades my senses and completely overpowers me whenever you're near. I want you so much, I don't know what to do. I love you so much. I need you. But I am so afraid I will scare you or hurt you—"

"Wait, that's why you stayed away?" she asked and furrowed her eyebrows. Brock wanted to reach out and smooth the crease, and he did, but she slapped his hand away.

"You're afraid to hurt me," she stated with wonder in her voice.

"Yes. Why do you think I told you that story?"

"I thought you were confessing that you still loved some childhood sweetheart, you jerk!" she yowled and pushed him right off the bed, landing on top of him with a thud.

"Are you alright?" he said, his voice muffled under the fierce hug she was currently giving him.

"Am I alright?" she looked up at him, her eyes wide with wonder, but she didn't appear angry and for that Brock was grateful.

"You said you loved me. I am more than alright, but I want to know one thing."

"What? I'll tell you anything you want to know," he vowed, and meant it.

"Are you going to claim me or what?"

He stilled beneath her. Then, rucking up her dress to her waist so he could move them to a seated position, Brock's hands cupped her ass as he struggled with his Wolf. He didn't know whether to feel relief or like a fucking idiot for wasting so much time.

"I have every intention of claiming you, but first I need to apologize. My ultimate failing and why I am so unworthy of you, is that I knew you were my fated mate, and I still made up this stupid proposition to give you our account for a night with you in the hopes to seduce you into accepting my claim—"

"So, are you saying you don't want to spend the night with me?" she asked, her amber eyes glowing with mischief.

"Of course, I do. But I don't want it as payment. That's why I brought you here, to *The Cabin*. I'd mentioned *Eat Well Live Proud* a million times and Susan had already agreed to try your products. This account will take you over the top and even though you have Serious Moonlight's business, I don't ever want you to feel obligated to be with me because of that."

"Brock, you are the dumbest Wolf in the world. Now, shut up and kiss me," she growled and leaned forward, crashing her mouth to his.

He couldn't believe it. She was kissing him. Even after every stupid idiot move he'd made. That was probably why he wasn't prepared when she shoved on his chest and pushing them back onto the carpeted floor with a heavy thud.

"You ambulance chasing jerk!"

His arms were still full of his sassy Lioness, but this time she was cursing and wailing on him. The next punch she threw was caught gently with his fist.

"What? What's wrong? I told you everything—"

"That is what's wrong. You bone-burying, hydrant-pissing, butt-sniffing furball! You've told me everything. All these months, you made me think you didn't want me, that you found me lacking, and here you are telling me everything and I, I just don't know what to say to you," she growled and sat up, still straddling his hips. Her tight dress was still bunched around her waist, revealing long, smooth legs, and sexy lace panties he wanted to rip off with his teeth. His beast surged forward once more.

"I know. You're right, Ariella, let me make it up to you? Let me show you how much I want you. I will do whatever you say. You are in control here. I'm yours, Ari. All yours. If you still want me."

His heart pounded like a steel drum inside of his chest, and he could hardly breathe waiting for her answer. He needed this chance, this opportunity to show her what they could have, what it would mean to be mated to him. Brock had waited almost too long time to stake his claim. He'd fucked up, he freely admitted that. But the heat in her golden gaze told him he still had a chance. He just couldn't fuck it up again.

"How do I know you won't hurt me again?"

"Because it would be like hurting myself. My Wolf would gut me if I even tried. Even I'm not that dumb. Now, come here, hellcat, let me have you," he growled.

Mine.

CHAPTER TWELVE

DIRE WOLF MATES

Ariella didn't know whether to scream or cry after Brock finished his confession. Mostly, she felt confused. The big, gorgeous dummy was scared from some teenage incident she'd rather not think about, and that was why he'd been avoiding her.

"So, when I announced my virginity the other night. It probably didn't help with your insecurities, huh?" she asked, and worried her lower lip.

"Actually, that might've pushed my Dire Wolf over the edge. My animal is chomping at the bit, dying to claim you before anyone else gets any ideas. Knowing I will be your only lover is driving him insane."

"I see. Possessive much?" she asked as he slowly sat up with her, his hands caressing her bare hips.

Dang it.

She hadn't noticed their positions until now. Her dress was up around her waist, revealing more of her than she'd have liked. Heat flamed her face, but before she could wiggle away, Brock was there kissing her shoulder, then her neck, her cheeks next, and her mouth last.

The slow invasion of his tongue was seductive and hypnotic, rousing as all hell, too. She was quite aware of what was happening, but in that precise moment she would've done anything he wanted. Striptease, rip her clothes off, parade around stark naked, as long as he didn't stop kissing her.

"I want you on the bed," he whispered, and she felt herself nodding.

Before she could slide off him, her powerful mate was already lifting her up from their position on the carpet. He stood with her in his arms as if she weighed nothing at all, and crazy as it seemed, she felt cherished and cared for in that position.

The scent of his Dire Wolf beneath his skin was making her Lioness go crazy. So, hell yes, Ariella thought the bed sounded like a great idea. What better place to get him naked? Then she could rub herself all over his body, mark him with her scent, then stake her claim with her fangs and claws, too.

Rawrrr.

Her pulse raced as she recognized the signs of mating fever taking hold. Whatever Brock was afraid of happening between them, he probably hadn't considered the fact she was an apex predator herself and more than capable of handling anything he could dish out.

The question was, could he handle her?

So far, so good.

"I got you. This okay?" he asked permission even as he gently sat her down on the bed and unzipped her dress.

Ariella couldn't nod her head fast enough. Her skin was boiling. She needed the dress off now. Moisture pooled in her panties, readying her body for his invasion. Seeing him in his pants made her feel seriously anxious and impatient. Her mate had too many clothes on.

"Not yet," he growled and smirked as he caught her staring. Her own growl reverberated in her throat.

"Don't worry, my little hellcat, I promise you will have as much of me as you want. No more, no less."

She believed him, and yet somehow, she knew he was going to take some convincing. Ariella wanted all of him. Every last inch.

He was her fated mate. Ari was built just for him, and she was going to stake her claim and lay to rest every one of his fears. Tonight, they would begin their lives together.

"I want it all, Brock," she whispered, purring her contentment as he petted her skin, removing her dress.

Brock leaned back on his heels, a deep rumble reverberated in his chest as he stared at her body in the tiny lace panties she had on. The dress had a built-in bra, making it possible for her to wear anything else beneath the silky, hip hugging fabric. She felt empowered and beautiful under his stare.

Going up on her knees, she leaned down, facing him on all fours. Her large breasts swayed, and her sex grew even wetter, desire building inside until she was panting with it. She crawled forward until her face was right in front of that part of him she wanted most. What a shame he'd kept his beautiful cock under lock and key because of some bad memory.

"Ariella," he growled her name.

Brock ran his big hands over her shoulders, down her back to the curve of her ass, tracing the little heart tattoo she'd gotten just over her right cheek when she'd been in college.

"Who put this there?" he grumbled the question.

"Toni," she answered and grinned at his snarled response before she added, "my sister."

"Naughty hellcat," he grunted and pinched her on that same cheek.

Her nipples pebbled under his rapt attention and moisture dripped down her thighs, but she was too curious to give up her position on her knees. Hands reached for his waistband, and his growl grew louder.

"Brock, let me see you," she begged.

"Ari," he grunted, but she was already unzipping the exquisite black fabric and sliding it down his muscular thighs.

He stood still as she undressed him, allowing her to explore with her eyes and hands. Beneath his pants he wore tight black navy blue briefs, and as lovely as they were, Ari knew they had to go. Looking up at him, she raised one finger on her right hand, and popping a single sharp claw, she cocked her head to the side and waited.

"I'm all yours, hellcat. But, uh, be careful with that thing," he tried to joke, but she knew he was tense.

Not for long, her Lioness promised.

She was eager for him. The wild forest scent that clung to him was doing all kinds of marvelous things to her insides, spurring her on, making her wild with desire. She couldn't wait until her skin was covered in his scent, marked with his bite, and filled with his delicious sex.

"Mine," she growled and sliced through the fabric.

"Oh, wow, s'beautiful," she hissed.

His scent was stronger now. He smelled like mature pine trees and clean earth to her sensitive nose. She couldn't wait for a taste.

Prrrrrr.

She inhaled and this time his scent was pure and strong like his Wolf after a good hard run. Then it was like promises and laughter. And pure, hot sex. Ariella was running on instinct now, and she couldn't seem to help herself. Brock licked his lips and watched her, his blue eyes glowing with curiosity and his Dire Wolf.

She reached up and kissed his face, tangling her tongue with his until he was moaning and growling into her mouth. He was so fucking hot, and all her thoughts were on him. Brock was her mate, her one and only, and she wanted him to know just how she felt about that fact.

It was time.

Ariella kissed his lips one last time, licking and nibbling her way down his neck and chest. She swirled her tongue around each flat male nipple and loving the hiss that escaped his mouth as she took one between her teeth and gave it a good tug.

"Ari," he moaned her name, and she felt him swell against her belly as she made her way down to that part of him, she so desperately wanted.

His hard abs contracted as she leaned forward and stroked his thick, long cock with her hand. Fuck, he really was so big and thick. She needed both hands to wrap around all of him. She had seen naked men before.

Duh.

Ariella was a Lioness. Nudity was part and parcel of the whole Shifter gig. But she had never seen anything quite as superb as her mate, naked and fully aroused. Brock's legs were thick and heavily muscled, much like the rest of his six-foot five-inch frame. His dark blond hair hung down over his forehead and his blue eyes glowed as he focused on her every move. But she wasn't quite done looking just yet.

He had a smattering of darker blond hair on his chest and upper thighs. And a nest of soft curls that crowned his gloriously thick dick. She leaned down, pressing her face close to him, and felt him throb involuntarily.

Ariella couldn't have stopped herself even if she wanted to. She opened her plump lips, watching him from underneath her thick eyelashes, and licked her way from root to tip, swallowing down the pearl-sized drop of precum that seemed to swell at the slit just for her.

He growled loudly, nostrils flaring and fists at his sides as she swiped him once, twice more with the flat of her tongue. Damn, he tasted delicious. His cock was gorgeous, magnificently formed with a perfect mushroomed head and a thick, even girth from stem to tip. He had a slight curve that was making her legs tremble in anticipation.

This was a perfect cock.

And though she was a virgin, this was something she and her sisters had discussed at length during one of their many slumber parties. Ariella had hit the jackpot, *er*, make that the *cockpot*! She couldn't wait for him to fill her.

"Brock," she moaned as she bent down to continue her new favorite pastime.

Loving on her man with the flat of her tongue. He was incredible and she wanted to show him just how much she appreciated his size. Silly man, thinking he could scare her with what she was guessing was thirteen and a half inches of rock hard gorgeousness.

"Fuck, Ari, I'm gonna come if you don't stop," he growled with his hands fisted at his sides.

"I want you to come," she growled back, taking hold of him with one hand. Ariella pumped his shaft even as she swallowed down as much of him as she could.

Even the ridiculous dildos her sisters had stuffed inside her gift basket couldn't have prepared her for the sheer size and raw beauty of Brock's incredible sex. He was so thick and hard, but his skin was soft like velvet, and he tasted incredible. She just couldn't stop sucking on him.

She swirled her tongue up and down around his wide girth, and soon he was moving with her, flexing his hips, and gripping her head with his hands. Good, she wasn't a delicate flower. Ariella was a powerful Lioness, a strong as fuck she-Cat and a hunter in her own right. She could and would give her mate pleasure.

"Fuck, Ari," he growled louder, and she moved faster.

Licking, sucking, and pumping, finally, Ariella lifted her mouth and pressed his cock between her large breasts. Her own pussy throbbed in need, but this was about him, about his learning that she could take him any which way, and what was more, she wanted to.

Brock growled aloud as his orgasm rushed over him, and her Lioness echoed the sound. Her inner feline loved the way his hot cum felt across her chest, marking her in his scent and claiming her in this small way was the best fucking feeling in the world.

It was raw and primal, but in the best possible sense. Her mate had finally marked her, and she hoped it was the first of many times to come for them both. Brock's chest still reverberated with his growl, and his nostrils flared as his eyes zeroed in on Ariella's breasts.

"Let me clean you, hellcat," his voice was gravelly as he moved.

Moving quickly to the bathroom, he returned with a wet washcloth and gently wiped her clean with it. What had started as perfunctory soon became seductive, and she could hardly keep quiet as he smoothed his skillful hands over her pebbled nipples. Brock pressed her breasts together, adding his tongue to the mix as he suckled her until she was writhing beneath him.

"You're so beautiful," he growled, coveting her with his body.

"Mine. Tell me you're mine, Ariella," he groaned, and she loved the possessive edge to his voice.

"I am yours," she answered.

Of course she was. Always had been, and wasn't that the truth?

"There's no going back now. You are it for me, Ari. I love you," he declared, and his eyes met hers before his lips crashed against hers.

Ariella wrapped her legs around his waist, bringing him into stark contact with her needy sex. This was everything and the only thing she had wanted since meeting him. The physical expression of her commitment, her feeling for him, was vital to her very being. Shifters ran on instinct, and there was nothing more natural than wanting to be claimed by her mate.

"I only want to move forward, Brock. With you. Only you."

"Good mate," he growled. "Now it's my turn," Brock hissed as he slid down her body.

Her Lioness wanted to snarl and order him to come back. She wanted to feel more of that wonderful cock of his pressing deep, so deep inside, she'd be blind to everything but it. But it seemed her soon-to-be mate had other ideas.

"You're not the only one who likes to lick, my sassy little hellcat," he said gruffly, as if he'd heard her beast's whine, and maybe he had.

Fated mates could sometimes get inklings of each other's feelings even before the matebond was fully formed. It only spoke of how perfect they were for each other. And Brock was perfect for her. And he proved it by driving her out of her mind.

Brock's sexy growl vibrated through her body as he dropped hot, biting kisses down her body. She moaned aloud as his hot breath came into contact with her throbbing sex. Then she couldn't think anymore.

He pressed his nose against her soaked folds and inhaled a deep breath. He sucked in a deep breath, seeming to savor the scent of her heat if his growl was anything to go by. Tiny little electrical currents rocketed through her body, turning into lightning bolts as the pressure of Brock's tongue increased. He swiped a path from her asshole to her clit in a move so singularly perfect she almost came right then and there.

Her body tensed and the Lioness inside of her purred loudly as he pressed her knees farther apart with his hands, granting him better access. Brock's growling reverberated from his mouth through her core, the rapt attention making her more and more susceptible to every nuance of that fine-tuned appendage.

"Brock," she moaned his name, and pulled on his hair.

"That's it, my little hellcat. Sexy little purr, sweeter than my Harley. Gimme more," he growled and slid a finger into her slick heat as his tongue flicked back and forth over her swollen clit.

Fuck yeah. She purred. Louder. Stronger. Harder, so hard. She damn near fell off the bed from the vibrations alone.

"Close," she growled, and tugged tighter on his thick hair until he was right where she wanted him.

"Come for me, Ari," he commanded, and his tongue and finger worked in time to push her right over the edge.

There it was. So close. Right in front of her. She could almost taste it. Harder. Faster. Bliss waited at the end of the road. All she had to do was grab it. And suddenly, Ari bucked her hips, grinding her pussy into Brock's mouth until it was right there.

There, there, there, oh fuck! RIGHT THERE!

Ariella roared as her first ever orgasm with a man raced through her. She hardly noticed Brock slide up her body until he was pressing his thick cock slowly and surely inside of her tight, slick sheath. Pressure filled her, stretching, burning so damn good.

Fuck.

She had no experience with anything like this, and while his mere size was shockingly bigger than expected, everything about him was perfect. He was beyond anything she could've ever imagined. And in the best possible way. She felt him everywhere. Aftershocks of her first orgasm kept zipping through her with every slip and grind of his thick sex. Her mate truly was fantastic.

"You okay? Am I hurting you?" he asked, concern shining in his Wolfishly blue eyes.

"S'perfect, Brock. So good."

She meant that. Literally. Everything about him was good. And together, they were perfect. Brock leaned down, nuzzling her mouth, kissing her deeply, and driving her mad. He held himself still, giving her time to adjust, but Ariella didn't want that kind of treatment. She nipped his lip and almost laughed when he pulled his head back in shock.

"What was that for?"

"That was just a taste of what's gonna happen to you if you don't stop fucking around, Brock Laurent. Claim. Me. Now," she growled and watched as his eyes went from confused to focused.

"Hellcat," he growled.

"Damn straight."

"Mine," he replied and pulled out inch by delicious inch, only to slam back in all the way to the hilt.

"Yes. And you are mine," she growled, tugging him closer and mashing her mouth to his.

Mine. Mine. MINE. RAWRRRR!

CHAPTER THIRTEEN

DIRE WOLF MATES

Mine. All mine. My Ariella. Mate.

His Wolf could not stop celebrating the fact his mate was well and truly claimed. Their first time together had been incredible. Life altering. And Brock was still reeling from it.

He separated half a dozen eggs and grabbed the large wire whisk, keeping the flame on the copper pot low as he prepared Ariella's favorite dessert. He'd gleaned that little tidbit after a brief conversation with her mother, who'd called him up to tear him a new asshole the night he'd propositioned her daughter.

His opinion of Patricia Golden had changed dramatically after that conversation. His little hellcat had a lot of her mother's spunk, and he admired the clever way Patty had described, in detail, what she was going to do to him if he did not change his ways. He'd promised her he meant only the best for her daughter, and afterward, the Lioness was thrilled.

"My girl always wanted a puppy. Be sure to behave or I'll have you fixed," were her exact words.

The imagery still made him shake his head. Patty, as she insisted he call her, was certifiable in some ways. Damn entertaining in others.

Of course, Ariella hadn't been aware of that little conversation before they'd spent the last couple of hours claiming each other all over the luxury suite he'd rented. They had no secrets between them now. Like none.

Brock had never felt happier. There were no words to describe the heaven he experienced sliding into her sweet body and knowing he was the only one who would ever get to have her. She was his now. And he was hers. In every sense of the word.

Brock Laurent and Ariella Golden were well and truly mated.

Fuck, just thinking about it made him grin like an idiot, but he didn't care. He'd never felt better. Her body was a wonderland made just for him. Every supple curve and valley, a place for him to worship and explore. He'd memorized every nuance as best he could by sight, touch, scent, and taste, and he looked forward to experiencing every change the future had in store for the both of them.

She was sublime. Designed by the fates as if specifically ordered. She suited every one of his preferences, and gods be blessed, he filled hers. Her spicy musk scent was ecstasy inducing, and now it was ingrained inside of him.

He lived for her responsiveness. Fuck, her sighs, moans, shivers, and shakes drove him insane. The feel of her pussy rippling around his cock as he'd brought her to orgasm again and again, got better each and every time they made love. Brock was one lucky sonovabitch. Ariella had taken to his size and appetite with gusto.

He worried at first, because he was insatiable. Brock wanted her again, right now, and it had only been a few minutes since they'd last made love. Yes, it was love. He loved her. Everything about her. She was multi-faceted, shy, and sweet even with her sailor potty mouth, Maybe even because of it.

She was cute as hell when she was pissed. Aggressive as she was disarming, brilliant and confident, while at the same time humble and unassuming. Fuck, he loved every inch of her, inside and out.

"Favorite color?" she asked from her place on the bed while he got the food ready.

They'd been playing twenty questions on and off for hours, and while they knew most things about each other, he liked the game.

"Amber," he said, and she laughed at him. Her eyes were stunning and were the exact shade he preferred.

"Mine's blue," she returned pertly.

"Favorite book?" he asked.

"Hmm. I have to think about that. I am a whore for indie romance books," she said, and while she pondered titles, he whisked.

Mated Dire Wolves were said to become so enamored of their mates that they became the sole purpose of their existence. He'd been troubled by that description in his youth, but he was just fucking fine with that now. No more doubts or misgivings. The sassy little hellcat was all his. Belonging to her in return was his new favorite thing.

Brock would spend every moment of his life making sure Ariella knew just how wholly and completely she was wanted and loved by him. They'd both professed their feelings a dozen times over the night, and being Shifters, they knew they spoke the truth about it. The strength of their love was evident in their matebond. Powerful and strong, even now he could feel it pulsing softly around them.

"Mmm, that smells divine," Ariella moaned.

Damn, he loved her vocalizations. She rolled over onto her side, and he got a view that was so fucking amazing he almost burned the sugar. Brock grunted and refocused, whipping the delicate Italian cream dessert into little fluffy peaks in no time.

He scooped it into the little ceramic bowls the staff had left them and added slices of strawberries and plump raspberries. Grinning, he walked over to the bed with the fragrant confection in his hands.

"Is that for me?" she asked, biting her lip, and wagging her eyebrows.

Ari sat up, reaching for the bowl, but Brock shook his head. He pushed her gently back onto a mound of pillows behind her.

"Sort of. See, this one is for you," he growled and fed her a raspberry.

"Mmm."

"And this part is for me," he grunted, lifting a slice of strawberry dripping zabaglione.

Ari gasped as he dropped the warm cream and fruit onto one of her own little ripe berries. The confection landed perfectly on one pert nipple, and he did the same to the other. She giggled. The sound soon turned into a long, drawn out moan, as he licked the sweet dessert off, suckling her breasts until they were clean.

"I'm still hungry," he grumbled, and she gasped again as he added another dollop to her navel.

"Are you going to share?" she asked, but he held the bowl just out of reach.

"Maybe, but only if you moan like you did the last time you were at *Serious Moonlight* eating the dish I made for your brother," he grinned and held a plump raspberry dipped in cream between his lips.

"You heard that, did you?"

Brock nodded and wagged his eyebrows. Ariella leaned forward and claimed her prize, chewing the berry with a deep, throaty moan that went straight to his cock before claiming his lips once more.

"I love the noises you make when you eat," he growled and licked cream from her inner thigh.

"You do, huh?"

"Uh huh."

Brock focused his attentions to her luscious curves. Bite for bite, he fed her dessert from interesting body parts until they were both a sticky, sweaty mess.

"Time for a bath," he growled and lifted her up like the cherished treasure she was.

He carried her to the large bathroom where he'd already started filling the enormous tub with warm water.

"Brock?"

"What is it, hellcat? Do you need something?"

"Yes," she said, pulling his head down for one of her soul-searing kisses. "You. I need you."

That soft plea was Brock's undoing as he followed her into the tub.

Sitting with his legs straight out on the bottom, he lifted her over him, loving the way she thrust her chest out and opened her legs, sliding down and taking his thick cock inside of her with one sublime roll of her hips.

"Fuck, Ari, you bring me to my knees. Do you know that?"

"Good," she moaned and rocked again.

That was just like her, he thought, and squeezed the perfectly round globes of her ass, lifting her higher and slamming her back down as hard as the water allowed. She fit him perfectly. Like a vise, gripping and caressing his cock with every subtle flex and roll.

Strong. Supple, Sumptuous female.

Much to his delight, she appeared just as enamored of him as he was with her. Her appetite matched his, and fuck, he had to admit he liked every little thing she did.

His Wolf howled inside of him, the beast so fucking elated after finally having claimed his mate. In fact, claiming her again was a top priority at the moment. He just had to wait for that moment when her sweet pussy would clench and ripple with the start of orgasm.

So, why not help it along? His sly Wolf growled, and Brock liked the suggestion.

He claimed her mouth with his, kissing her deeply, thrusting his tongue in and out of her mouth, mimicking the invasion of his dick inside her hot channel. He increased speed and strength, taking control by lifting her and bringing her back down, faster, harder until her walls began to contract, and she dropped her head back.

Then he struck, his canines sliced through her skin just above her breast and he swallowed down her life's force even as her sex squeezed and milked him. Pleasure like he'd never experienced built up inside of him as her sharp Lioness' claws raked the skin of his shoulders.

She had already bitten him, but he'd heard tales of Big Cats who twice-marked their mates. Feeling it, of course, was something else entirely. His shoulders were on fire, but that paled compared to the raw pleasure that was coursing through his veins.

"Love you, mate," Ariella whispered as she clung to him in the aftermaths of their shared orgasm.

He felt her love wrap around him, pulsing through their mate-bond, and wanted to howl it to the entire world. Ariella loved him, and Brock was the luckiest fucker on the planet.

After a good long nap, he ordered them both some clothes from the boutique in the hotel lobby. With breakfast finished and another shower behind them, Brock and Ariella headed back to her condo in Blue Valley. It was, after all, a workday, and although she'd be a tad bit late, it was important she went in.

"I could call out," she said, but he shook his head.

"Nope. Come on, get your things. Today is the day, and you worked too hard to miss it. I'll wait for you, love," he encouraged, smiling at her like she hung the moon.

"Okay, I'll just be a minute," she said and stepped over the remnants of chips, salsa, and tequila.

He quirked his eyebrow before shrugging. Brock knew her sisters and mother had been there last night. The females must've continued with their little party, and of course, they hadn't bothered cleaning up. He shook his head as he cleared away the debris and started the dishwasher.

"What are you doing here?"

Patricia Golden came tumbling out of one of the closed bedroom doors, wearing a large silk caftan with her hair sticking up in all directions. He cleared his throat and poured his mate's mother a mug of the coffee he'd just brewed.

"Good morning, Patty. Ariella is just changing for work, and I thought I would clean up a bit for her," he said.

"Shhh! Do you have to be so loud?"

"Oh—" Brock tried not to laugh, but it was difficult. "I apologize, ma'am."

"Don't you ma'am me," she sniffed and drank deeply from her mug. "So, did you claim her yet?"

"Uh, yes, Ariella and I are mated," he smiled as he said it, but when the woman didn't respond, he looked up to find her squinting at him, arms crossed defensively over her chest.

"*Hmph*. Well, you better do right by her, or I swear to the gods you'll find yourself neutered and tagged for the pound, you hear me?"

"Uh, yes, of course, I would never hurt her in any way."

"I don't want to hear it. You just give her space and let her be herself. Mating isn't about taking over someone's life, you know," she mumbled, but stopped as Ariella strolled back in.

She was wearing a dark brown pencil skirt and a buff colored silk blouse that was almost sheer. His mouth went dry. Damn, she was beautiful, but she looked nervous.

"Hey," he said and walked up to her, handing her the cup of coffee. "Did you email Susan, yet?"

"Yes, last night when you said, but Brock—"

"Drink this," he instructed and rubbed her shoulders while she took a hearty sip of the coffee he'd prepared just the way she liked it—strong with a drop of cream and one sugar.

His Wolf liked the idea of providing for her, of giving her sustenance from now until eternity. Of course, he wanted to hunt and drop dead animals on her doorstep, but for now, he figured this was better.

"You are walking in there today with both *The Cabin* and *Serious Moonlight* under your belt," he began. "You are going to knock them dead, my little hellcat."

"After the whole basket incident, I don't know if I could take another day of pranks and Cornelia's snootiness," she mumbled.

"What basket?" he asked curiously.

Grrrrr.

CHAPTER FOURTEEN

DIRE WOLF MATES

"What basket?"

Shit.

Had she said that out loud? Ariella groaned at her faux pas having neglected mentioning the dildo basket and chew toys, for obvious reasons.

"Show him, honey!" Patricia laughed from her perch on one of the stools surrounding the kitchen counter, and Ariella's eyes landed on her nosy matriarch.

How had she missed the fact her own mother was sitting there listening to them?

"Mom," she moaned and closed her eyes.

Just then Brock leaned over and nuzzled her neck, the little gesture of affection did more for her than any number of cups of coffee. And the fact he did it in front of her mother?

Sigh. Huge bonus points for her little Pookie.

She'd dubbed him that after a bout of tickling last night where she'd tried to make him heel using the names Fido and Spot. Of course, by the time she'd gotten to Pookie, she had his balls in her hand, literally, and smart man that he was, he gave in. The nickname was going to stick, but only in the bedroom she'd promised.

Public displays of affection only meant one thing in the Shifter world, he was seriously in love with his mate. It was one thing to bring a girl to orgasm dozens of times behind the closed doors of a hotel suite where no one could hear or see them, and quite another to drop a tender kiss on her neck in front of her mom.

While she thoroughly enjoyed the hotel escapades, Ariella admitted to being a little nervous about how he would react back on their home turf. As it was, this was her place, not his. The jury was still out on that one, but she had to give him credit. Brock had been nothing but supportive and encouraging all morning.

"What? It's over there," Patricia said and pointed—unhelpfully—in the direction of the horrible thing.

"Mom, *ixnay* on the *asketbay*!" Ariella hissed at the woman.

"I admit, I'm curious."

Brock smirked and walked over to where her mother and sisters had been hanging out the night before, obviously pawing through their gag gift. She closed her eyes as Brock sifted through the goods, listening for the slam of the door as he walked out on her, but surprisingly, it didn't come.

In fact, her amazing Dire Wolf mate just chuckled out loud. She blinked up to see him holding the gallon of lube in one hand and the elephant-simulated-cock dildo in the other.

"Is this supposed to be for you or me? Never mind, I don't want to know," he mumbled and shook his head.

"It was a stupid gag because of the night *mommy dearest* dosed me. You know, when I announced I was a virgin in the bar," she whispered, knowing full well her mother could hear her perfectly.

"I see," he said and dropped the small-compared-to-his—*lucky her* —elephant cock dildo and picked up the bag of peanut butter puppy treats.

"And who is this for?"

"Oh, dang it," she moaned and covered her face with her hands.

Ariella ignored his deep chuckle as he walked back over to her. She felt his large hands cover her hips as he pulled her up against his big, tall body and wrapped her up in his steely arms. She loved being close to him, loved how he made her feel small, despite being a curvy woman.

"Uncover your eyes, Ariella. Come on, you can tell me," his tone soothed her frayed nerves, and she knew it was his Dire Wolf reaching out to the Lioness through their matebond. Still, she did as he asked.

"I knew you were my mate the first time I met you, and I kinda sorta confided in my sisters," she said.

"And they thought puppy treats and chew toys would win me over, huh?"

He furrowed his dark blond brows and Ariella bit her lip.

Shit.

He was gonna think they were freaks! This was it. The moment he walked out on her. Ariella huffed an exasperated breath. If he couldn't take a joke, he could just keep on walking. Her sisters were natural pranksters and if he was her true mate, he would just have to deal with it. But inside, she was shaking like a leaf on a tree.

"Wait till they get their Christmas presents," he promised and bit her gently on her ear.

"You really are perfect," she moaned and squeezed him to her.

"Enough with the PDAs. I'm your mom, and this is gross."

Brock laughed, and Ariella sighed in relief. Her mom was a lot, but she was still her mother. She loved that he could just take it all in with a chuckle and a hug.

Ariella felt like laughing and crying and yelling all at the same time. Her hormones were completely out of control. She wanted to rub herself all over him *again*, and yet, she wanted to yowl at him for making her nuts.

"Hey, you better leave, your sister just texted me. The quarterly meeting is starting early. Apparently, Corny has some announcement," her mother interrupted and Ari was back to wanting to scream in frustration.

"Come on, my car is faster," Brock winked.

He was right. In no time at all, he was pulling up to her office building. She grabbed the handle of the car door and looked at him. Reluctant to leave him so soon after their mating, she leaned over and kissed him quickly. There was so much still unsaid, but she needed to get in there.

"I'll come get you when you're finished, yes?"

"Yes," she smiled nervously.

"Ariella, I love you. We're mated now, and it's all gonna be okay. Now, go show them what you're made of, my little hellcat."

She nodded again and hurried to the door. The office was dead quiet, which was not all that odd, since everyone was inside the conference room. Ms. Pierce was sitting and listening to Cornelia, who had the floor, when Ariella slipped inside.

"It has come to my attention that one of our own has been using her body to get clients! Bargaining sex for a leg up to win this quarterly competition. I have a folder here with images of the person in question, and I think, Ms. Pierce, that you will want to act accordingly," Cornelia said, grinning triumphantly as she walked forward.

"Oh my!" Maggie Pierce's eyes bulged out of her head as she quickly peeked inside the envelope.

Whispers ran rampant around the room. Mainly because no one could figure out how Cornelia had the balls to out someone else for using sex as a trading tool for work. It was well-known she slept around with her clients to secure their accounts. The cheap cheating hussy!

"I am telling the truth about Ariella Golden," Cornelia said loudly and nodded at Ariella, who up until that time did not know what was going on.

"Wait? What?" Ari gasped, eyes wide.

"I have pictures of you naked with one of your clients and we can only imagine what you were doing to get that account," she said haughtily, and Ariella wondered if the she-Cat believed her own bullshit.

"Well, I admit I am truly shocked, Ms. Golden, you see, before you finished updating your portfolio this morning, you were behind Cornelia here in the quarterly contest—"

"Yes, and it isn't fair. She shouldn't win with *Serious Moonlight's* account after banging the head chef to get it! Admit it. You're not a virgin anymore, you had sex with that dog!" Cornelia screeched.

Ariella was shaking in her shoes, but not with fear. It was rage. Pure and unfiltered, and she was doing her best not to let her she-Cat out, but hearing that woman speak ill of her mate was so not a good thing.

"Ariella? Are you in a relationship with Chef Laurent?" Maggie asked.

There was no way around it. She had to answer, but this was wholly unfair. Stilling herself against the fury of her inner feline, Ariella took a steadying breath before she answered.

"He is my mate."

"You see! Mates can't stay away from each other. I bet she still reeks of his scent, don't you? Imagine coming in here smelling like dog—"

"Cornelia, one more word out of you," Ariella threatened, but Ms. Pierce held up a hand to silence the women.

"And yet, Cornelia," Ms. Pierce continued. "Ms. Golden hasn't updated the Dire Wolves' account, have you Ariella?"

"No, I haven't," she smirked and listened to the gasps from everyone in the room.

It was common knowledge she'd been after that account for months. But unbeknownst to all but her, she'd already switched the account to her sister Antonette's profile. Ever grateful for the support of her siblings, she felt their combined strength as they stood behind her.

The Golden girls indeed.

She smirked at a baffled-looking Cornelia. The Goldens were known for being pranksters, but they always had each other's backs. Unnecessary as it was, since no one really liked Cornelia, and this latest display was more than the pot calling the kettle black. It was indescribably juvenile and petty.

"But she's been lusting after their head chef for months now and this proves he only gave her the account after she performed sexual favors on that stuck up, conceited Wolf," Cornelia grumbled and stomped her foot as she spoke.

"What did you call my mate?" she hissed, her inner she-Cat had been pacing ever since she'd heard the woman talk about her Pookie.

"This isn't fair!" Cornelia gasped as Ariella leaped over the table and had the woman by the throat.

"My mate is none of your business," Ariella growled into Cornelia's suddenly very pale face.

So, her Lioness was a little territorial. Could you blame her? Her mating mark was barely scarred over, and this chick was challenging her position as a mated feline.

Hell. No.

The whispers in the room grew louder after that and it was all Ariella could do to control her beast and stop her from snapping the woman's neck like a twig.

"Oh snap."

"Damn."

"Corny is about to get her ass whupped."

"Ariella," Ms. Pierce interrupted. "That is enough, I think."

Ariella let go of Cornelia and blinked down at her boss. After all her hard work, was she really going to lose this quarter because of this? She was about to speak when Ms. Pierce held up her hand.

"Cornelia, head over to HR and sign up for our classes on sexual harassment and bullying, or else pack up your desk and get gone," Mrs. Pierce commanded.

She waited as the other woman hurriedly grabbed her belongings and headed out the door.

"As for everyone here, I suppose it's only fair that I announce the winner of this month's quarterly contest. By landing the most small business accounts in this state, and the next two to the north of us, and securing a brand new major hotel, which is part of a much larger chain and has enormous potential for growth, Ariella Golden, you have won yourself a paid vacation for two to *Moongate Island*! I suggest you bring your new mate," Ms. Pierce announced and smiled as she extended a hand for Ariella to shake.

The room broke out into applause, and congratulations were shouted. Ariella could hardly believe it. Then again, she had totally worked her butt off and Cornelia was really just a big jerk. Whatever that woman's malfunction, Ari hoped she figured it out—albeit very far away from Ariella and her mate.

She laughed and smiled with everyone as they sliced cakes and passed around other munchies, as Lion Shifters were wont to do. After she had outlined the details of her new client, *The Cabin*, and secured their upcoming order courtesy of Chef Susan—which was admittedly bigger than any of her other clients—Ariella sat back down and listened as the others gave their own reports with barely concealed impatience. The urgency to leave to be with her mate was growing with every passing minute.

Her Lioness was pacing in the metaphysical plane where the creature waited till called. The large feline rubbing against her skin. She wanted out. She wanted her mate. The minutes ticked by, and Ariella did her best to soothe the animal. Not an easy feat with a kitty who was actively experiencing mate withdrawal.

"These are for you," Ms. Pierce said and handed Ariella the manilla envelope Cornelia had given her and whispered in her ear. "You go on and get out of here, Ms. Golden. Start your vacation right now. You deserve it. Oh, and Ariella? My congratulations on your *very impressive* mate."

The older woman winked, and Ariella blushed furiously. Whatever was inside that envelope would have to wait. She wasn't opening it with her snooping sisters peeking over her shoulder.

Her thoughts traveled back to Brock, and she felt her whole body glow. She couldn't wait to see him. The fact she got to share her news with him, that he was right then, waiting for her to come back to him, was so amazing. Gods, she loved him.

It was crazy how quickly he had become the most important thing in her world. But then again, maybe not. They were fated mates. It was destiny. But even without that, she loved Brock more than she had ever loved anyone or anything in her entire life.

It was all really that straightforward. After all the misunderstandings and miscommunications, finally admitting they loved each other and consummating that love made everything else seem trivial.

Ariella was pleased that she won, but she actually felt sorry for her workplace nemesis. She hoped Cornelia would find her own mate someday and stop living so maliciously.

Dang, she really wanted Brock. Like now. Wanted to discuss what had happened with him, but he would probably be at work now.

Sad rawr.

"Hey Ari, someone's here for you," Toni shouted from her own desk as Ari's head shot up.

She guessed she didn't have to wait at all. Striding down the hall was her sexy as sin Dire Wolf, his laser like focus narrowed on her. Ariella felt a purr build inside her chest as the pine fresh scent of her one and only invaded her senses.

Putting a lid on her little kitty, she hurried across the room and met him halfway. He uncrossed his arms, a knowing grin on his handsome face.

"Hey, there," she said.

"Hi yourself, hellcat. Did you win?" he asked excitedly.

He grabbed her hands loosely in his. The hold was casual, but she noted the flare of his nostrils and the heat in his gaze. His Wolf was pushing him just as fiercely as her she-Cat. She bit her lip and nodded as he grabbed her bag and tugged her out the door.

"Yes! I knew it. Congrats, minx," he growled, giving her a back-breaking hug, and she loved every second of it.

"Thank you. Come on. The boss said I could leave now," she said, thrilled he was there and seemed so proud of her.

"Good," he growled. "Sorry, I just couldn't wait to see you," he said and pulled her outside and tossed her things into the saddlebag on the side of his Harley.

He backed her up against the bike, making her swoon with one of his patented kisses designed to make her fall to her knees in worship of the man's skill alone.

Would it always be this good, she wondered? Not at all surprised when he nodded. Their matebond was warm and bright, pulsing all around them like a living, breathing connection. It was quite possible he heard her thoughts.

"Always," he growled, confirming her suspicions.

"Mmm, I love you," she moaned and whimpered when he pulled away.

"Love you too, mate. Let's get out of here before we give everyone a show," he grunted and reached out, giving her ass a little pinch that had her yelping and jumping to get into her seat behind him.

It wasn't easy in her skirt, but she managed just fine. Anything to get closer to him.

"You know, that hurt," she whined as he fastened the helmet on her pretty little head.

"Don't worry, minx. I'll kiss it better, I promise."

"You better," she said and squeezed his middle with her arms snug around his waist.

It was his turn to yelp when her hands moved a little lower, stroking his impressive length. Brock growled playfully before pulling them back up and over his belt.

"I'd like to get there in one piece, hellcat," he grunted and revved the engine loudly.

"So, who's running the kitchen?"

"I left everything in Cole's capable hands. He can answer any questions the cooks have, besides Carlo is almost ready to be head chef on his own. I needed some time off with my mate."

"Yeah? How about two weeks," she said and couldn't hide the pride in her voice.

"For real? That's the prize? Yes!!"

"I won fair and square. Run away with me to an island?" She yelled her question over the roar of his Harley as he zoomed down the highway towards Blue Valley.

His low-slung sports car was a dream of a ride, but Ariella loved being on the back of his motorcycle even more. It was big and loud, but like everything else he did, Brock was positively fluid and thorough in his handling of the finely tuned machinery.

He revved the engine and sped up, stopping when they got to the Pack house. The fact was, Ari would go anywhere the big man led, but she was a tad disappointed at the idea of sharing him just then.

"Don't worry," he said, seeming to read her mind again. "You get me all to yourself later, but after your announcement, this couldn't wait. I want to do things in order."

"What things, Brock?"

She followed him inside the Pack house, confused and amazed at the same time. It was early in the evening, her workday had flown by, and the Spring air was crisp and cool. Thor sat in the living room with a thick book in his hands. The bald, tattooed giant grunted as he closed the book and looked from Brock to her, then back again.

"You sure, bro?"

"Yes," Brock said, and the context went right over her head.

"I'll get the box. You call the others."

"Brock? What's going on?"

"Ariella, I know I've said it before, but I love you," he whispered against her lips. "More than I ever thought possible. We have already claimed each other, but for my people, there is more."

"More?"

"Yes. You see, when a Dire Wolf finds his fated mate, there is a ritual that needs to happen to make things permanent."

"A ritual?" she said with wonder, touching his face with cautious fingers, unwilling to break the spell he was weaving around them.

He was so damn beautiful her breath got stuck in her chest. Ariella did not know what he meant, but she was all for it. Whatever she needed to do to be his forever, she was game. She'd assumed things were permanent, after all, they'd claimed one another, but who really knew in this day and age what permanent meant.

"It means forever, hellcat. I'll never let you go. I love you. You are a part of me, and my testament to that and to us is this," he said.

Brock nodded towards where Thor was now kneeling on the floor of the living room with a strange wooden box in his hands. It was the answer to every single one of her spoken and unspoken prayers. She loved Brock Laurent with every last piece of her heart and soul, to have him confess his feelings to her was like a dream.

"Are you sure?"

"Ariella Golden, I have never been surer about anything in all my life."

Pride and love beat through her veins like blood, a mad temp that made her breathless. Ariella reached up and kissed her mate, loving the gentleness she found there. He was so hard and focused when he was working or concentrating, but she got this part of him. His softness was only for her, and she adored it all the more for that reason.

"I love you," she said.

"I love you too, mate."

CHAPTER FIFTEEN

DIRE WOLF MATES

Brock gave his beautiful little hellcat a reassuring kiss, then tilted his head back and loosed a howl that each member of his Pack in the vicinity was sure to hear. Thor was almost finished with preparations for the marking ritual, and he needed Derrick with him.

"You see, love," Brock explained. "Thor is what we Dire Wolves call *favored by the gods*. He will see our path and engrave it on my skin."

He'd caught Ariella eying him curiously as Brock unbuttoned the thick flannel shirt he'd been wearing. He pulled that off, and the tank top he had on underneath next. Tugging it up and over his head from the back.

He'd been thinking about this moment ever since he'd met Ariella. It was an honor he had never expected to experience and the fact that she accepted and welcomed him into her life, body, heart, and soul, made him the luckiest fucker on the planet.

"yeah, what he means is Thor's a bit touched," explained Phoenix with a wicked wink. The big man came in and untied his apron, tossing it on the couch, before high-fiving Ari.

"Shut up, you idiot," Sheila said, following behind him. She smacked her Pack mate upside the head to Brock's unending amusement and Ari's sweet giggle.

Fuck, he loved it when she was happy and made a vow to always try to make her laugh. As their Beta, Brock had some authority over his Pack, but why would he want to stop some good old fashioned sassing? Especially when his own mate added that little pinch of sass in his life, he'd never known he needed.

It was quite an event, bringing a mate into the fold, but he had never been surer of anything in all the world. His little feline was all he had ever wanted and, now that he had her, he wasn't letting go.

"Hey, y'all tried to start without me!" Lucy accused as she padded into the room on slippered feet with a bowl of popcorn in one hand and a large, frosty milkshake in the other.

"Dammit, woman, wait a second and I'll carry all that for you," Derrick growled from the other room.

He followed behind her with a roll of paper towels, and the ever present glass of iced water she'd been keeping on hand the last week or so. For some reason, the expectant mama couldn't get enough fluids in her diet.

"Now, Ari, Brock is gonna go over there and kneel in front of Thor. Thor is going to channel the fates and mumble some such shit we won't understand, then he will get a vision. That vision is Brock's true heart and his path now that he's found you. He's gonna ink that shit on your hunk a burnin' Wolf. Ain't it great?" Lucy grinned and sucked some thick chocolate milkshake through her straw.

"Really? I didn't know," Ari whispered, and it seemed right that she had.

Pride filled him at her knowing intuition. She was one hell of a woman, and he would do everything it took to keep her safe and protected, cherished, and loved for the rest of their entire lives.

Thor lifted the first bamboo needle and dipped it in the jar of magicked ink and Brock felt his eyes glowing with his Wolf as the ritual began. His Pack mates closed in around him, including Ari, who stood just in front. Locking eyes with her, he saw her love shining out like a beacon, calling him home, and he knew he was home wherever he was with her.

She was the central part of his circle now and as tears welled in her eyes, he knew those tears were full of love and pride. He remained focused on her, on their bond as Thor worked. Brock knew his eyes would be overcast with the trance-like state he was in, channeling the Fates and bringing that vision from his mind and onto his Pack mate's skin.

The image was in the center of Brock's wide back and though he had the odd tattoo, this was the first major piece the Wolf had ever sat for. It took over an hour, but he was strong and steadfast. The rags soaked with his blood that Thor had mopped up as he etched into his skin with the sharp needles sat in a pile.

When he lifted his hand and dropped the needle, Weylin and Phoenix rushed to Thor's side. The huge Dire Wolf Shifter sometimes got drained after a long process, such as this had been. Brock was exhausted, too. The inking process was not a matter of merely getting tattooed during this ritual, it was like having someone wriggling around inside your very soul and pulling out what he saw there, scratching it onto his skin for everyone to see.

The very idea was astounding. A fantasy brought to life. Thor was a legend among his kind, and Brock sucked in a breath and whispered his gratitude. His beautiful mate came forward, kneeling before him and placing his hands on her shoulders to steady him.

"Are you okay?" she asked anxiously.

"Yes, now that I have you, hellcat," he replied easily. Brock grinned and kissed the hand she'd brought up to caress his face.

"Damn."

"Wow," Sheila gasped.

"That is, really, I am just," the Alpha fem stuttered, and then Lucy started bawling.

"Come here, kitten," Derrick scooped up his wife and held her while she cried.

"I am so proud of you two, Brock," she said through tears, and he nodded at his Alpha fem, then looked back at Ariella.

"What is it?" he asked and turned around.

Her gasp made him nervous, but he waited for her to speak.

"Oh wow, Pookie. I mean, I knew you loved me, but wow," she said, and he heard her grin in her voice.

"Pookie?" Phoenix asked to the stifled snickers and snorts of the rest of them.

"Stuff it, asshat," Brock growled at him, then asked his mate to describe the tattoo.

"There's a circle of like hieroglyphs or runes, a heart, a stone, a star, a moon, and at the center is a White Wolf lying near a stream, beside him is a Lioness. They're side by side, looking out to the future, together. Oh Brock, it's beautiful," she said, and this time it was tears thickening her beloved whisper.

Turning, he took her hands and pulled her into the circle of his arms. His skin was tender, but as a Shifter he had already begun to heal. He wasn't worried about it, not when Ariella wrapped her arms around him and hugged him close to her heart. It was the only place in the world he ever wanted to be.

Afterwards, they invited her sisters and mother over to the restaurant, where they held a celebratory meal over their mating. It was like the Shifter equivalent of an engagement party. Fitting, since at the end of dinner Brock surprised his mate with a solitary sapphire in a band of yellow gold and a marriage proposal that had every female in the place teary eyed.

"I got a question for you, Ariella," he said and kneeled down to her wide, golden-eyed stare. The entire room had gone still, and Brock took the ring out of his pocket and held it up to her. A small token of his love and esteem.

"I know I fucked this up in the beginning, but I promise to spend every second of every day from now until the end of time making it up to you. I don't care what we do, where we go, as long as I am with you, I have everything I will ever need. I love you. We are paired in the

Shifter world, but I want you everywhere I can get you, hellcat. So, it would make me the happiest man on the planet if you agreed to be my wife. Will you marry me?" he asked.

"Get up," Ari whispered.

She sniffed, and Brock stood slowly. Had he gotten this wrong? He wondered that for all of two seconds before she vaulted into his arms and yelled the word yes like a banshee ringing in his ears.

It was the best fucking sound he'd ever heard. Except for Ariella's moans whenever she was eating. And he vowed to be there for every meal from then on.

Mine. Mate. Wife.

EPILOGUE

DIRE WOLF MATES

"Greetings and Welcome to Moongate Island, Mr. and Mrs. Laurent. I am Mr. Gordon, the manager here at Stein Luxury Resorts, please allow me to show you to your rooms," the smiling hotel manager said.

Ariella grinned up at her new husband and mate while a bellhop wrangled their luggage. Brock returned her smile with an affectionate kiss on her brow and took her hand as they followed him to their honeymoon suite.

Eat Well Live Proud, having heard of her sudden nuptials, had upgraded her prize and sent them on the two-week honeymoon she'd been dreaming about since she was a cub.

Of course, Ms. Pierce was hoping she would land them more of the international hotel's business—but this was not a working holiday.

After they found themselves alone, Ariella walked over to where her husband was standing near one of the floor-to-ceiling, one-way windows. She licked her lips nervously.

Being seductive was not something that came naturally to her, and yet there was nothing more instinctive than wanting to please her mate. The flowy white dress she'd worn on the private jet he'd rented them felt too constricting on her skin and her Lioness pressed against her, egging her on.

"Brock?"

"Yeah, love?"

He turned, but stilled instantly when he noticed her heavy-lidded stare. She knew he could sense her mood, scent her need, and Ariella reached for the straps to her dress and tipped them off her shoulders, tugging the elastic material down until it pooled at her feet. Brock's soft growl was audible in the otherwise empty room as he stared at her in the skimpy little lace thong and bra she wore, just for the occasion.

"Mine," he growled as his legs ate the distance between them.

There was nothing better than kissing Brock, except maybe making love to Brock. Her mate was just as hungry for her as she was for him. He ripped off his clothing and lifted her in his arms. The bed was too far away, it seemed, but they did manage to make it to the thick rug that sat on the warm wooden floor.

"Oh Brock," she moaned as his tongue found her heated center.

Ariella draped her legs over his shoulder while her mate suckled her sex with expert flicks of his tongue. When he growled, she practically went cross-eyed with pleasure. Who needed a vibrator when her mate could rumble against her clit with the best of them?

In minutes she was coming, and her greedy Wolf insisted on sucking down every last drop of her juices before he slid up her body. Good thing she was already ready for round two.

"It gets better every time," she moaned as he positioned his heavy cock against her swollen lips.

"That's cause you're perfect, hellcat," he growled and mashed his lips to hers as he invaded her slick flesh.

The perfect pressure of his girthy length stroking her had Ariella spiraling out of control in mere moments. Her body belonged to him. It was as if it recognized the pleasure he could bring instinctively. She scratched him with her claws, loving the fact that each time she claimed him, she felt their bond grow and strengthen.

"Love you, mate," he groaned as he flexed his hips, swirling against her pubis until they were both drowning in ecstasy.

Hours later, after they were both sated, Ariella and Brock headed down to the beach for an evening swim. He'd ordered them a secluded meal to be served on the shore in a special private cabana he'd rented.

"This is gorgeous," she sighed the sentiment, so happy she could damn near burst.

"It is," he replied and kissed her head, wrapping his arm around her as they lounged in the two-person chaise and watched the waves through the open section of the sheer curtains that hung around their private cabana.

Everything was perfect. Ariella finally had her mate. She was thoroughly claimed and mated, and so happy she could hardly believe this was her life. Even better, she got him all to herself for two whole weeks of loving.

"What are you thinking, hellcat?"

"Mmmm. Just thinking how wonderful it is to be here with you, in paradise, alone," she murmured, raising her lips for one of his toe-curling kisses.

Ariella spoke too soon, she thought as the curtains to the left of their chaise suddenly burst open and Patricia Golden ran right into their private little honeymoon.

"There you two are," the Lioness said, ducking behind their lounge chair.

"Mom?! What are you doing here?'

"Look, honey, you gotta hide me. He followed me here!"

"I don't believe this," Ariella moaned, and Brock blinked from mother to daughter.

"Is that any way to talk to your mother? After all I did to get you two together? Dosing you and setting this big puppy up to fall for you. You would think I'd get a little bit of help when I ask for it," she growled, and turned in shock when a billowing roar sounded just outside the cabana followed by a massive, silver streaked male Lion.

"Now, Donovan," she said and ran behind Ariella.

"King Donovan? Mom, what the hell is going on?" she asked her mother, but the woman was too busy trying to back away from the obviously angry male, who just shifted back to his very naked, very human skin.

"*Ohmygawdmyeyes*," Ariella yowled.

Brock tossed the man a towel, to which King Donovan Crowley nodded his thanks.

"I will tell you what is going on, stepdaughter. My *mate* keeps running out on me!" the King of the Blue Valley Pride roared loudly and Ariella and Brock both busted out laughing.

"You two are mates?" Brock asked.

"Yes, we exchanged bites two weeks ago and ever since I haven't seen hide nor hair of her," he pointed accusingly.

"Mom! Is that why you've been so upset?" Ariella asked and crouched next to her mother, who was wringing her hands in her lap.

"I just didn't want to lose myself to some dominant pussy! Look, I'm not going to change, Donovan, even if you are the king!"

To that, the king kneeled in front of his mate and Brock and Ariella stood up and slowly backed away.

"I don't want you to change. I love you, Pat, always have," he said and smiled, and Ariella's mother smiled back. Then they were kissing, and it was time for Ari and her mate to haul ass out of there.

"Ari, um, I think, maybe we should—" Brock began.

"I hear you, loud and clear," she said and grabbed his hand.

She loved her mother, but this was *her* honeymoon. After a few phone calls, Ariella and Brock moved to a private cottage on the beach, away from other hotel guests, and they transferred the other suite to her mother's name.

"You good with this," she asked Brock as they lay in a tangle of arms and legs in the hammock outside their private hut.

"Hellcat, I am perfect as long as I have you."

"Yeah?"

"Yes. I love you, mate."

"Love you, too."

With that said, Ariella reached around his superb body, and she pinched him right on his gloriously muscled ass. With a loud shriek, she jumped up and ran, her own naked ass jiggling the whole way down their private section of the beach, hoping her mate would follow.

Brock let out a playful Dire Wolf howl, then follow her, he did.

The end.

Liked this story? Want more Dire Wolf Mates?
Grab the next book, Kickin' Sass, at https://www.cdgorri.com/books/kickin-sass.
Or
Follow the whole series at https://www.cdgorri.com/seres/dire-wolf-mates.

Thank you and happy reading!

READING ON A BUDGET?

Hello Readers!

I am so excited to be able to offer you exclusive bundles available only on CDGORRI.COM for readers using my BUY DIRECT option.

Right now, I have several bundles available at a whopping 30% off the listed prices and there are several series bundles to choose from.

Orders will be delivered via BookFunnel email. Just download to your favorite app and READ!

Thank you for buying direct. Have an awesome day!

xoxo,

C.D. Gorri

JOIN THE PACK!

Looking for a Paranormal Romance series that is loads of growly fun?

Welcome to the Macconwood Pack!

These stories are split into two series, the Macconwood Pack Novels Series, and the Macconwood Pack Tales.
Each story features one or more Pack members their journey to their one true and fated mate. They can be read alone, though they are better read in order, as characters may show up in each other's stories.

Pack is family for the Macconwood wolves, and when you read their tales, you become family too. What are you waiting for?

Join the Pack today!

https://www.cdgorri.com/series/the-macconwood-pack-novel-series/

No cliffhangers. Steamy PNR fun.
Go and read your next happily ever after today!

OTHER TITLES BY C.D. GORRI

Contemporary Romance Books:

Cherry On Top Tales

Her Yule His Log

His Carrot Her Muffin

Her Chocolate His Bar

Wild Billionaire Romance

His Wild Obsession

Jersey Bad Boys

Merciful Lies

***

Paranormal Romance Books:

Macconwood Pack Novel Series:

Charley's Christmas Wolf: A Macconwood Pack Novel 1

Cat's Howl: A Macconwood Pack Novel 2

Code Wolf: A Macconwood Pack Novel 3

The Witch and The Werewolf: A Macconwood Pack Novel 4

To Claim a Wolf: A Macconwood Pack Novel 5
Conall's Mate: A Macconwood Pack Novel 6
Her Solstice Wolf: A Macconwood Pack Novel 7
Werewolf Fever: A Macconwood Pack Novel 8

**Also available in 2 ebook boxed sets*
**Look for discreet editor paperback and hardcovers*

Macconwood Pack Tales Series:
Wolf Bride: The Story of Ailis and Eoghan A Macconwood Pack Tale 1
Summer Bite: A Macconwood Pack Tale 2
His Winter Mate: A Macconwood Pack Tale 3
Snow Angel: A Macconwood Pack Tale 4
Charley's Baby Surprise: A Macconwood Pack Tale 5
Home for the Howlidays: A Macconwood Pack Tale 6
A Silver Wedding: A Macconwood Pack Tale 7
Mine Furever: A Macconwood Pack Tale 8
A Furry Little Christmas: A Macconwood Pack Tale 9
The Wolf's Winter Wish: A Macconwood Pack Tale 10
Mated to the Werewolf Next Door: A Macconwood Pack Tale 11
Wolf's Scottish Geek: A Macconwood Pack Tale 12
No Otter Lover: A Macconwood Pack Tale 13

**Also available in boxed sets:*
The Macconwood Pack Tales Volume 1
Shifters Furever: The Macconwood Pack Tales Volume 2
Shifters Furbidden: The Macconwood Pack Tales Volume 3
Shifters Fur Keeps: The Macconwood Pack Tales Volume 4

The Falk Clan Tales:
The Dragon's Valentine: A Falk Clan Novel 1
The Dragon's Christmas Gift: A Falk Clan Novel 2
The Dragon's Heart: A Falk Clan Novel 3

The Dragon's Secret: A Falk Clan Novel 4
The Dragon's Treasure: A Falk Clan Novel 5
The Dragon's Surprise: A Falk Clan Novel 6
The Dragon's Dream: A Falk Clan Novel 7
Dragon Mates: The Falk Clan Series Boxed Set Books 1-4
Dragon Mates 2: The Falk Clan Series Boxed Set Books 5-7

The Bear Claw Tales:
Bearly Breathing: A Bear Claw Tale 1
Bearly There: A Bear Claw Tale 2
Bearly Tamed: A Bear Claw Tale 3
Bearly Mated: A Bear Claw Tale 4
Also available in a boxed set:
The Complete Bear Claw Tales (Books 1-4)

The Barvale Clan Tales:
Polar Opposites: The Barvale Clan Tales 1
Polar Outbreak: The Barvale Clan Tales 2
Polar Compound: A Barvale Clan Tale 3
Polar Curve: A Barvale Clan Tale 4
Also available in a boxed set:
The Barvale Clan Tales (Books 1-4)

Barvale Holiday Tales:
A Bear For Christmas
Hers To Bear
Thank You Beary Much
Bearing Gifts
Bearly Friends
Also available in a boxed set:
The Barvale Holiday Tales (Books 1-3)

Purely Paranormal Romance Books:
Marked by the Devil: Purely Paranormal Romance Books

Mated to the Dragon King: Purely Paranormal Romance Books
Claimed by the Demon: Purely Paranormal Romance Books
Christmas with a Devil, a Dragon King, & a Demon: Purely Paranormal Romance Books
Vampire Lover: Purely Paranormal Romance Books
Grizzly Lover: Purely Paranormal Romance Books
Christmas With Her Chupacabra: Purely Paranormal Romance Books
**Purely Paranormal Romance Books Anthology Volume 1*

The Wardens of Terra:
Bound by Air: The Wardens of Terra Book 1
Star Kissed: A Wardens of Terra Short
Waterlocked: The Wardens of Terra Book 2
Moon Kissed: A Wardens of Terra Short
*Now in a boxed set and in audio!

The Maverick Pride Tales:
Purrfectly Mated
Purrfectly Kissed
Purrfectly Trapped
Purrfectly Caught
Purrfectly Naughty
Purrfectly Bound
Purrfectly Paired
Purrfectly Timed
Purrfectly F*cked

Dire Wolf Mates:
Shake That Sass
Breaking Sass
Pinch of Sass
Kickin' Sass
Love That Sass
Kiss My Sass

Wyvern Protection Unit:
Gift Wrapped Protector: WPU 1
Tempted By Her Protector: WPU 2
Alien Protector: WPU 3
Unexpected Protector: WPU4
Thrilled By Her Protector: WPU5

Jersey Sure Shifters/EveL Worlds:
Chinchilla and the Devil: A FUCN'A Book
Sammi and the Jersey Bull: A FUCN'A Book
Mouse and the Ball: A FUCN'A Book
Chicken and the Paparazzi: A FUCN'A Book
**Jersey Sure Shifters Books 1-3 anthology*

The Guardians of Chaos:
Wolf Shield: Guardians of Chaos Book1
Dragon Shield: Guardians of Chaos Book 2
Stallion Shield: Guardians of Chaos Book 3
Panther Shield: Guardians of Chaos 4
Witch Shield: Guardians of Chaos 5
Vampire Shield: Guardians of Chaos 6
**Guardians of Chaos Volume 1 Books 1-3*
**Guardians of Chaos Volume 2 Books 4-6*

Twice Mated Tales
Doubly Claimed
Doubly Bound
Doubly Tied
**Twice Mated Tales Omnibus*

Hearts of Stone Series
Shifter Mountain: Hearts of Stone 1
Shifter City: Hearts of Stone 2
Shifter Village: Hearts of Stone 3

Shifter Scrooge: Hearts of Stone 4

Moongate Island Tales

Moongate Island Mate

Moongate Island Christmas Claim

Accidentally Undead on Moongate Island

Mated in Hope Falls

Mated By Moonlight

Speed Dating with the Denizens of the Underworld

Ash: Speed Dating with the Denizens of Underworld

Arachne: Speed Dating with the Denizens of Underworld

Asterion: Speed Dating with the Denizens of Underworld

Hungry Fur Love

Hungry Like Her Wolf: Magic and Mayhem Universe

Hungry For Her Bear: Magic and Mayhem Universe

Hungry As Her Python: Magic and Mayhem Universe

Island Stripe Pride

The Tiger King's Christmas Bride

Claiming His Virgin Mate

Tiger Claimed

Tiger Denied

Tiger Rejected

*Tiger Tales Anthology Books 1-3

NYC Shifter Tales

Cuff Linked

Sealed Fate

Virtue Saved

A Howlin' Good Fairytale Retelling

Sweet As Candy

Standalones:
The Enforcer
Blood Song: A Sanguinem Council Book
Spring Fling (co-written with P. Mattern)

Witch Shifter Clan
The Hybrid Assassin

###

Coming Soon:
Fire Wolf: Witch Shifter Clan 1
Snow Fox: Witch Shifter Clan 2
River Dragon: Witch Shifter Clan 3
If The Shoe Fits: A Howlin' Good Fairytale Retelling

###

Young Adult/Urban Fantasy Books

The Grazi Kelly Novel Series
Wolf Moon: A Grazi Kelly Novel Book 1
Hunter Moon: A Grazi Kelly Novel Book 2
Rebel Moon: A Grazi Kelly Novel Book 3
Winter Moon: A Grazi Kelly Novel Book 4
Chasing The Moon: A Grazi Kelly Short 5
Blood Moon: A Grazi Kelly Novel 6
*Get all 6 books NOW AVAILABLE IN A BOXED SET:
The Complete Grazi Kelly Novel Series

The Angela Tanner Files
Casting Magic: The Angela Tanner Files 1

Keeping Magic: The Angela Tanner Files 2
**The Angela Tanner Files Paperback 2 Book omnibus*

G'Witches Magical Mysteries Series
Co-written with P. Mattern
G'Witches
G'Witches 2: The Harpy Harbinger
G'Witches 3: Summoning Secrets

Witches of Westwood Academy
with Gina Kincade
Water Witch
Air Witch
Fire Witch
Earth Witch
Blood Witch
Spirit Witch

**Be sure to check out my BUY DIRECT BUNDLES and get 30% off when you buy available only my website.*

BEWARE... HERE BE DRAGONS!

The Falk Clan Tales began as my stories surrounding four dragon Brothers and how they find their one true mates, but when a long lost brother arrives on the scene, followed by a few more Shifters...what can I say? The more the merrier!

Each Dragon's chest is marked with his rose, the magical link to his heart and his magic. They each have a matching gemstone to go with it.

She's given up on love. But he's just begun.

In The Dragon's Valentine we meet the eldest Falk brother, Callius. He is on a mission to find a Castle and his one true mate, one he can trust with his diamond rose....

His heart is frozen. Can she change his mind about love?

In The Dragon's Christmas Gift our attention shifts to Alexsander, the youngest brother of the four. He has resigned himself to a life alone, until he meets *her*.

Some wounds run deep. Can a Dragon's heart be unbroken?

The Dragon's Heart is the story of Edric Falk who has vowed never to love again, but that changes when he meets his feisty mate, Joselyn Curacao.

She just wants a little fun. He's looking for a lifetime.

We finally meet Nikolai Falk and his sexy Shifter mate in The Dragon's Secret.

She doesn't believe in fairytales, until a Dragon comes knocking on her door.

Meet Castor Falk, the long lost brother of our original four Dragons, and his sassy mate Josette. The Dragon's Treasure is full of adventure and laughs.

Nothing can surprise this six hundred-year-old Dragon, except maybe her.

Devine Graystone meets his match in Sunny Daye, an irrepressible Wolf Shifter with a heart of gold. Read their story in The Dragon's Surprise.

He's a hardcore realist until she dares him to dream.

Nicholas Gravestone doesn't know what to think when he spies Minerva Lykos on the property his Dragon covets. Can this unlikely pair come to a truce? Find out in The Dragon's Dream.

Thanks for reading.

xoxo,

C.D. Gorri

*Dragon Mates & Dragon Mates 2 boxed sets are now available in hardcover, paperback, and ebook.

EXCERPT FROM SEALED FATE

It was snowing, but that wasn't new. Konstantin huddled beneath the broken concrete and waited for the big men to leave. He'd heard the shouting from all the way down the street when he'd gone to pick up his little sister, Alina, from her ballet lessons.

Though his family was poor, Papa and Mama sacrificed much so she could learn to dance. Konstantin was proud of his sister's already budding talent at just six years old. She'd been a surprise to the older couple whose son was already a teenager, but they all doted on her.

Konstantin was almost old enough to work the docks with his father, but Mama insisted he finish school. At nearly seven feet tall and still growing, it was proving difficult to remain unnoticed by the local bratva. That was something his mother feared more than anything.

"Be a good boy, Konstantin. Stay away from the gangs, and criminals," she'd told often him.

After all, it was his dealings with the local crime bosses that had left his Papa with a permanent limp and physical disabilities from the multiple toes and fingers that were missing from his feet and hands.

Shifters could recover from many wounds and injuries, but not amputations. That was something even their enhanced healing abilities could not overcome.

The screams got louder, and Konstantin picked up Alina who'd just started to cry. The sounds were coming from the building where his family rented an apartment from Ivanovich. The head of the local bratva had many slums on the city where he took advantage of the many poor Shifter families.

His inner beast scratched and roared, but he was no match for the many members of the bratva waiting for their boss outside. Instead of facing them and risking Alina's life, he covered her mouth with his hands and hid them both in the cellar of the neighboring building.

The old man was yelling about missing rents and late payments. He was going to use Konstantin's father as an example, or worse, take it out on his mother. That was something, he could not allow.

"Alina, will you stay here? Hidden for me, yes?" he asked his baby sister.

Blue eyes clear as the sky looked up at him, swimming with tears. She nodded her head, already older than her six years and he nodded, cursing roughly under his breath. He prayed he was not too late.

By the time he reached the apartment the men were gone, and his mother was wailing over the prone body of his father. Papa was gone. Killed by the bastards who ruled over all of them.

"Konstantin!" she cried, standing up and going to him, still covered in her mate's blood. "You must run. Go to your Uncle. Je will put you on a ship---"

"What about you? Alina?"

"Where is she?"

"In the basement next door. Let me get her," he said, frantic with worry.

"Yes, get her. I will pack."

When he once again returned to the apartment, he found the neighbors gathered. They shook their heads and turned their backs on him and his family, shunning them even as his father's body grew cold on their kitchen floor. Anger surged, but his mother was there, stopping it before he could blow like a steam engine.

"Come. Now. There is no time," she said, handing him a suitcase and taking the whimpering child from his arms.

They ran through the street, ducking in alleys, and moving faster then the humans around them. Tiger Shifters had night vision and traversing through the ice slicked alleys was quick work for them. They reached his Uncle's house in no time at all.

"You've come," Uncle Petyr said, grabbing his sister in a quick hug.

The man took his niece and handed her off to his wife who cuddled the child close. All the adults were trying not to cry, but Konstantin could feel their grief. Shared it with them.

"Can you get him out of here?" Mama begged.

"Only the boy. I am sorry," Uncle Petyr said.

"It is good. he will make a good life and we will come later," she said, nodding. "Okay Konstantin? Yes?"

"I want to stay with you," he said, a boy's dream.

"No, I won't let them have you too," Mama cred, holding him tight to her breast. "I love you son, but I need you to live. Here, there is only death waiting for you. Now go. Be strong. Be the man I know you can be. We will be together one day."

"We go now," Uncle Petyr said, grabbing the suitcase and taking Konstantin's hand.

"Mama? Mama!"

"Come now, boy. Be quiet or you will bring those monsters here."

That fact shut him up faster than if his Uncle had slapped him. Konstantin looked one last time at his mother and sister, who'd returned to her side. He waved and nodded, biting back his own tears, then he left his Uncle's apartment. And Russia.

And he never looked back.

Grab the rest of the story here: https://www.cdgorri.com/books/sealed-fate

ABOUT THE AUTHOR

C.D. Gorri is a USA Today Bestselling author of steamy paranormal romance and urban fantasy. She is the creator of the Grazi Kelly Universe.

Join her mailing list here: https://www.cdgorri.com/newsletter

An avid reader with a profound love for books and literature, when she is not writing or taking care of her family, she can usually be found with a book or tablet in hand. C.D. lives in her home state of New Jersey where many of her characters or stories are based. Her tales are fast paced yet detailed with satisfying conclusions.

If you enjoy powerful heroines and loyal heroes who face relatable problems in supernatural settings, journey into the Grazi Kelly Universe today. You will find sassy, curvy heroines and sexy, love-driven heroes who find their HEAs between the pages. Werewolves, Bears, Dragons, Tigers, Witches, Romani, Lynxes, Foxes, Thunderbirds, Vampires, and many more Shifters and supernatural creatures dwell within her worlds. The most important thing is every mate in this universe is fated, loyal, and true lovers always get their happily ever afters.

Want to know how it all began? Enter the Grazi Kelly Universe with Wolf Moon: A Grazi Kelly Novel or pick up Charley's Christmas Wolf and dive into the Macconwood Pack Novel Series today.

For a complete list of C.D. Gorri's books visit her website here:

https://www.cdgorri.com/complete-book-list/

Thank you and happy reading!

del mare alla stella,
C.D. Gorri

Follow C.D. Gorri here:

http://www.cdgorri.com
https://www.facebook.com/Cdgorribooks
https://www.bookbub.com/authors/c-d-gorri
https://twitter.com/cgor22
https://instagram.com/cdgorri/
https://www.goodreads.com/cdgorri
https://www.tiktok.com/@cdgorriauthor

www.ingramcontent.com/pod-product-compliance
Lightning Source LLC
Chambersburg PA
CBHW020352310726
48979CB00015B/2562/J

* 9 7 8 1 9 6 0 2 9 4 3 3 3 *